Liz Heron grew up in Scotland and, after post-student years in Paris, Madrid and Venice, she settled in London. She edited and contributed to *Truth, Dare or Promise: Girls Growing up in the 50s* (Virago 1985, 1993) and is the author of *Changes of Heart: Reflections on Women's Independence* (Pandora 1986). Her translations include fiction, film criticism and philosophy, and books by Nanni Balestrini, Hervé Guibert, the French Decadent, Rachilde, and, as co-translator, the recent anthology of Italian stories, *The Quality of Light*. She has written for many publications in Britain and abroad as a literary and photographic critic.

D1100958

STREETS OF DESIRE

Women's Fictions of the
Twentieth-Century City

*edited and introduced
by Liz Heron*

Published by VIRAGO PRESS Limited September 1993
20–23 Mandela Street, Camden Town, London NW1 0HQ

This collection, notes and introductory material
copyright © Liz Heron 1993
Copyright © in each contribution held by the author

The right of Liz Heron to be identified as editor of this work
has been asserted by her in accordance with the Copyright,
Designs and Patents Act 1988.

A CIP catalogue record for this book is available
from the British Library

Printed in Great Britain by
Cox & Wyman Ltd, Reading, Berkshire

CONTENTS

Contents

ACKNOWLEDGEMENTS

A number of people have been generous with help in my pursuit of material and copyright holders, or in giving a variety of practical assistance. I am grateful to Philippa Brewster, Margaret Busby, Ann Caesar, Michael Caesar, Martin Chalmers, Liliane Landor and Marsha Rowe; to Ruthie Petrie, my editor at Virago, and Lynn Knight for their editorial support; to Gil McNeil and Ann McGonigle for advice on clearing permissions; to Sonia Lane who typed part of the manuscript; and to the staff of the Reading Rooms at the British Museum for the patience and good humour which help to keep the place such a haven of democratic reading.

Special thanks are due to Alison Fell, Malcolm Imrie, Pat Harper and Maggie Millman.

Permission to reproduce the following stories and extracts is gratefully acknowledged:
extract from Honeycourt, Vol. 1 of *Pilgrimage* by Dorothy Richardson, published by Virago Press 1979, © Rose Odle 1967, reprinted by permission of Virago Press and University of Illinois Press, Urbana, other extracts reprinted by permission of Virago Press;
extracts from *Alberta and Freedom*, trans. © Elizabeth Rokkan, published by Peter Owen Ltd, 1963, © Cora Sandel 1931, reprinted by permission of Peter Owen Publishers, London;

extracts from *Mrs Dalloway* by Virginia Woolf, published by Hogarth Press 1925;

'Night Out 1925' by Jean Rhys, from *Sleep It Off Lady* published by André Deutsch 1976 and Penguin Books 1979, © The Estate of Jean Rhys 1976, reprinted by permission of Penguin Books Ltd, London, and Wallace Literary Agency, New York;

extracts from 'Vagabond's Song' by Hayashi Fumiko, from *To Live and To Write: selections by Japanese women writers 1913–1938*, edited by Yukiko Tanaka, published by Seal Press 1987, © Seal Press 1987, reprinted by permission of Seal Press;

extract from 'Self-Mockery' by Hirabayashi Taiko, from *To Live and to Write: selections by Japanese women writers 1913–1938*, edited by Yukiko Tanaka © Yukiko Tanaka, reprinted by permission of Seal Press;

extract from *Early Spring* by Tove Ditlevsen, translation © Tiinna Nunnally, published by Seal Press 1985, © Tove Ditlevsen 1967, reprinted by permission of Seal Press;

'The Standard of Living' by Dorothy Parker © Dorothy Parker 1941, renewed © 1969 by Lillian Hellman, from *The Portable Dorothy Parker*, by Dorothy Parker, Introduced by Brendan Gill, reprinted by permission of Viking Penguin, a division of Penguin Books USA Inc, and by permission of Gerald Duckworth & Co. Ltd;

'Paris qui rêve' by Elsa Triolet, from *Bonsoir Thérèse*, published by Editions Denöel 1938 and Editions Gallimard 1978, translated © Liz Heron 1993 as 'Paris Dreaming';

extracts from *The Beauties and Furies* by Christina Stead, published by Peter Davies Ltd 1936 and Virago Press 1982, © Christina Stead 1936, reprinted by permission of Virago Press;

extracts from *After Midnight* by Irmgard Keun, published by Victor Gollancz 1985, © Econ-Verlag GmbH, Dusseldorf 1980, translation © Victor Gollancz Ltd 1985, reprinted by permission of Victor Gollancz Ltd;

'A Moving Picture of Shanghai' by Agnes Smedley, from

Acknowledgements

Chinese Destinies, published by Hurst and Blackett, London 1934 and Vanguard Press, Inc. © The Estate of Agnes Smedley, reprinted by permission of Laurence Pollinger Ltd, Literary Agents;

extract from 'The Siege of Leningrad' by Lidia Ginzburg, from *Soviet Women Writing*, published by Abbeville Press 1990, compilation © Lidia Ginzburg and Abbeville Press, Inc, 1990, translation © Abbeville Press, Inc, New York, reprinted by permission of Abbeville Press;

extracts from *Journey from the North* by Storm Jameson, published by Collins Harvill Press 1970 © Storm Jameson 1970, reprinted by permission of the Peters Fraser and Dunlop Group Ltd;

extract from *The Street* by Ann Petry, published by Houghton Mifflin, © Ann Petry 1946 renewed 1974, reprinted by permission of Houghton Mifflin Company, all rights reserved;

'Pillar of Salt' by Shirley Jackson, published in *Mademoiselle* 1948 and in *The Lottery and Other Stories* © Shirley Jackson 1948, 1949, renewed © 1976, 1977 by Lawrence Hyman, Barry Hyman, Mrs Sarah Webster, and Mrs Joanne Schnuser, reprinted by permission of Farrar, Straus & Giroux, and by permission of Brandt & Brandt Literary Agents Inc;

extracts from *Nada* by Carmen Laforet, © Carmen Laforet 1945, published by Wiedenfeld, translation © Carmen Laforet 1958, reprinted by permission of Agencia Literaria Carmen Balcells, S.A.;

extract from *The Doves of Venus* by Olivia Manning, published by William Heinemann Ltd 1955 and Virago Press 1984, © Olivia Manning 1955, reprinted by permission of William Heinemann Ltd;

extract from *The Bay is not Naples* by Anna Maria Ortese, published by Collins 1955, © 1955 Anna Maria Ortese, reprinted by permission of Anna Maria Ortese;

extract from *Beyond All Pity* by Carolina María de Jesús, translated by David St Clair, translation © 1962 E. P. Dutton & Co. Inc., New York as *Child of the Dark*, and Souvenir

Press, London, reprinted by permission of Dutton, an imprint of New American Library, a division of Penguin Books USA Inc., and by permission of Souvenir Press Ltd;

'A Place for Coincidences' by Ingeborg Bachmann, from *New Writing and Writers 14*, published by John Calder (Publishers) Ltd., London, © Klaus Wagenbach 1978, © English translation John Calder (Publishers) Ltd., 1978, translated by Agnes Rook, reprinted by permission of Calder Publications Ltd., London, and Riverrun Press Inc., New York;

extracts from *L'Astragale* by Albertine Sarrazin, © 1965 Jean-Jacques Pauvert and © 1979 Société Nouvelle des Editions Pauvert, translation © Liz Heron 1993, by permission of Société Nouvelle des Editions Pauvert;

extracts from *The Microcosm* by Maureen Duffy, published by Hutchinson & Co., 1966 and Virago Press 1989, © Maureen Duffy 1966, reprinted by permission of Virago Press;

'This is Lagos' by Flora Nwapa, from *This is Lagos and Other Stories*, published by Nwamife Publishers Ltd, Nigeria 1971, © Flora Nwapa 1971, reprinted by permission of Nwamife Publishers Ltd;

'Tokyo Pastoral' by Angela Carter, from *Nothing Sacred*, published by Virago Press 1982, © Angela Carter 1982, reprinted by permission of Rogers, Coleridge & White Ltd;

extract from *Mothers and Shadows* by Marta Traba, published by Readers International 1986, © Siglo XXI Editores, S.A. 1981 and © Gustavo Zalamea (estate of the late Marta Traba) 1985, English translation © Readers International, Inc., 1986, reprinted by permission of Readers International;

extract from *Tar Baby* by Toni Morrison, published by Chatto & Windus 1981, © Toni Morrison 1981, reprinted by permission of Chatto & Windus, London;

extract from *On The Stroll* by Alix Kates Shulman, published by Alfred Knopf 1981 and Virago Press , © Alix Kates Shulman 1981, reprinted by permission of Virago Press, London;

extract from *The Colorist* by Susan Daitch, published by

Virago Press, London, 1989 and Vintage Books, New York, © Susan Daitch 1989, reprinted by permission of Susan Daitch;

extract from *Cassandra* by Christa Wolf, published by Hermann Luchterhand Verlag 1983, © Hermann Luchterhand Verlag 1983, translation © 1984 Farrar, Straus & Giroux, published by Virago Press 1984, reprinted by permission of Virago Press;

extracts from *Angelo a Berlino*, by Giuliana Morandini, published by Edizioni Bompiani 1987, © 1987 Gruppo Editoriale Fabbri, Bompiani, translation © Liz Heron 1993, by permission of Gruppo Editoriale Fabbri, Bompiani;

extract from *The Morning Gift* by Dea Trier Mørch, published by Forlaget Vindrose 1984, © Dea Trier Mørch 1984, translation © Christine English 1987, published by Norvik Press in *No Man's Land* 1987, reprinted by permission of Norvik Press Ltd, Norwich;

extract from *The Piano Teacher* by Elfriede Jelinek, published by Rowohlt Verlag 1983, © Rowohlt Verlag, published in English by Grove Press, New York 1988 and by Serpent's Tail, London 1989, translation © 1988 Wheatland Corporation, reprinted by permission of Grove Press, Inc., New York, and Serpent's Tail, London;

extract from 'A Too-Richly-Flavoured Neapolitan Sweet' by Ida Faré, from *Racconta*, published by La Tartaruga Edizioni, © La Tartaruga Edizioni 1989, translation © Liz Heron 1993, by permission of La Tartaruga Edizioni.

'Summer in Sydney' by Barbara Brooks, from *Leaving Queensland*, published by Sea Cruise Books, 1983, © Barbara Brooks 1983, reprinted by permission of Barbara Brooks.

INTRODUCTION:
WOMEN WRITING
THE CITY

BECAUSE IT teems with strangers and with difference, the great city is unknowable. Because of its plurality, it offers infinite possibilities for freedoms untasted, for aspirations unfulfilled. It holds secrets, 'the lovely, strange, unconscious life of London' that Miriam Henderson, the protagonist of Dorothy Richardson's *Pilgrimage*, refers to; or, some five decades later, in Sylvia Plath's *The Bell Jar*, 'the mystery and magnificence' that Esther Greenwood hopes might rub off onto her '. . . if, I walked the streets of New York by myself all night'.

It is the city's world of the unknown that intimates its infinite possibilities, and when is the city more unknowable than at night; and yet more promising of freedom and transformation. In Miriam Henderson's passion for walking the night-time city streets lies the desire to take possession of London, to make it hers within the space of solitude and darkness.

The nineteenth century denied such freedoms to unaccompanied women, 'respectable' women that is, and Miriam is one of twentieth-century fiction's first woman characters to claim the urban landscape with such confidence. Miriam, a middle-class white-collar worker on a pound a week, emerges from the ranks of the 'New Women', those daring early feminists who challenged sexual hypocrisy and the sacred values of hearth and home, who

1

smoked and bicycled wearing plus-fours and who entered
fiction around the turn of the century. But this literature of
bold and sometimes sexually frank feminist protest tended
to be bounded by the terrain of moral argument, its
characters typifying female dilemmas and conflicts. Miriam
is a New Woman, but no representative figure. She differs
from the protagonists of New Woman fictions in her
relationship to the city, fulcrum of the modernist perspective
on the world, whose excitements derive from the
dynamically accelerating pace of urban life as the century
enters an age of motorised transport and ever faster
communications. Simultaneously, the strictures on women
that compelled George Sand to adopt male disguise as a
passport to the streets of nineteenth-century Paris by night
(like Rachilde's decadent fictional heroine, in her novel
Monsieur Venus,[1] the libertine Raoule de Vénérande)
became looser as twentieth-century dress and appearance
turned into a more ambiguous index of respectability. By the
early 1920s it was harder to distinguish between 'good'
women and 'bad' as they walked the streets.

Like Virginia Woolf's early novels, *Pilgrimage* is a
landmark of modernist fiction, whose fractured narratives
and interior monologues are shaped by the new urban
consciousness. It is with modernism that women's fiction
truly enters and lays claim to the city, thereby claiming new
possibilities for women's autonomy. This anthology looks to
the city as the site of women's most transgressive and
subversive fictions throughout the century, as a place where
family constraints can be cast off and new freedoms explored,
as a place where the knowledge acquired through urban
experience not only brings changed perceptions of identity,
but inescapably situates the individual within the social order.

NARRATIVES OF SELF-DISCOVERY

City fictions are often narratives of self-discovery, and, by
removing women from the family unit, these female

Bildungsromans (*Pilgrimage* among them), whose complications are various, seem to insist on the autonomous status of female experience, something otherwise robbed by the projections of men's needs, desires, fears or idealisations.

Rootlessness and displacement are at the heart of the city novel. The classic narrative of the city as a new beginning, a stage embarked upon in early adult life, has specific features for women in that the very notion of female self-invention defies the nature-culture divide; women being traditionally the stable, fixed point in a universe whose spaces wait to be explored by men, so that woman endures while man transcends. In some of Toni Morrison's novels (notably *Tar Baby* and *Jazz*), besides being all these things, the city is also a historical stage in the story of black Americans, the place where rural migrants converge and where women come into their own: the voice that articulates historical experience as urban.

It is in fictions of the city that collectivities of race and class assume a subjective viewpoint. Claire Etcherelli's *Elise or the Real Life* brings these together at a crucial point in French history, the Algerian War; 'real life' begins as Elise boards the train that will take her to Paris, where, like Etcherelli herself, she will work on a car assembly line. She begins a love affair with an Algerian worker in the same factory, and comes to know the contradictions of black-white class solidarity, and painfully to feel the city's racist hatred in the abuse and brutal policing of Arab workers. Yet the city's streets, though hazardous for such a couple, are also a refuge – 'Paris was an enormous ambush through which we moved with ludicrous precautions . . . our happiness transformed Paris' – a lover's city for all that. Through the tragedies of love and politics, Paris teaches Elise what real life is really about.

In Elise the progress of self-knowledge is synonymous with claiming the city. The novel ends with a drive through Paris – 'Here's Paris', where Elise's commentary on the streets traversed is also a commentary on everyday life and everyday oppression, conveying a sense of her own new-learned knowledge of the city. Likewise, in Carmen Laforet's *Nada*, the streets of Barcelona become a territory whose step-by-step mapping in the course of one year corresponds to Andrea's coming of age and passage into a sense of self. 'My dear, a big town is a sink of iniquity, and of all the cities in Spain Barcelona is the most wicked', her aunt warns her on arrival, and the warning serves to tantalise. Andrea's wanderings allow her escape from a fraught and claustrophobic house whose family tensions could well be seen as allegorical in this post-civil war Spain.

There's a similar sense of movement from hopeful ignorance to a state of knowing self-possession in a very different novel, Olivia Manning's *The Doves of Venus*. The eighteen-year-old Ellie Parsons has arrived in London as an escapee from Eastsea. At the novel's start Ellie is entranced by the city at night and tries to imagine what its mysteries might have in store for her, who she might become: 'Would she ever rap on doorknockers with the urgency of important emotions? And run round a corner wearing a fur coat? And lifting a hand to an approaching taxi, impress some other girl named Ellie and fill her with envy and ambition?' It ends as she boards a bus 'journeying westwards into the transformed city where Ellie has her home'.

Manning wrote very much within the mainstream of English fiction, whose distinguishing feature is a very middle-class, character-based realism, and many of whose women writers rarely escape the confines of the domestic. Manning's adventurousness as a writer lay in her relation to the life of elsewhere. In *The Balkan Trilogy* and *The Levant Trilogy* she described wartime Bucharest, Athens and Cairo with the vivid rapture of discovery, but London was her own first city and here it communicates a special kind of rapture, that of the young girl who has just embarked upon womanhood – with a job and a bedsit of her own. Ellie's elated first step is to fall in love and discard her virginity.

The city, and the economic independence it affords her are prerequisites for this sexual freedom.

Rapture is the state that most characterises Miriam Henderson's experience of the city. *Pilgrimage*, written entirely as a stream-of-consciousness narrative of Miriam's perceptions, thoughts and feelings, situates most of its thirteen-book cycle in London. Miriam's extravagantly-voiced consciousness merges oceanically with the city as she loses herself in 'her beloved London night-streets', surrendering to the reverie and intoxication they inspire ('I am always drunk in the West End'). To her the city offers scope for consciousness to be in a perpetual movement of discovery, continually to be plunged into life's plenitude. Because of 'the vast spread of London' it can contain the world's mysteries, and therefore their potential revelation: '. . . She saw upon the end wall the subdued reflection of London light, signalling the vast quiet movement of light about the world. It held a secret for whose full revelation she could wait for ever, knowing that it would come.'

Miriam, the New Woman perpetually in rebellion against the 'addlepated masculine complacency' that fails to allow women the authority of their own experience, finds a transcendence of identity in the city: 'She would be again, soon . . . not a woman . . . a Londoner.' If her wanderings through London's streets arouse incomprehension and sometimes disapproval, the city itself is benign in its indifference.

The idea of death transcended through the city as a continuing organism made up of living beings is also present in *Pilgrimage*, as it is in Virginia Woolf's *Mrs Dalloway*: '. . . Did it matter that she must inevitably cease completely; all this must go on without her; did she resent it; or did it not become consoling to believe that death ended absolutely? But that somehow in the streets of London, on the ebb and flow of things, here, there, she survived . . .'

In both novels the city transforms the individual self into the social self through a sense of urban empathy – kinship with other quite different human beings. In both, the ease or difficulty with which the spaces of the city are negotiated plays out the symbolic drama of women's visibility or invisibility. In this plotting of mobility, women's cultural and social status is explored.

THE *FLÂNEUSE*

Miriam Henderson's ability to wander, observe and lose herself in the streets of a beckoning London makes her an unmistakable descendant of a nineteenth-century literary figure most usually thought of as male: the *flâneur*, the stroller with time on his hands to idle in the streets and public places of the city and to contemplate the passing urban spectacle. The *flâneur*, representing both the estrangement from and proximity to others that is the productive ambiguity at the heart of metropolitan life, is a key figure in modernity, his marginal and superficially purposeless relation to the urban panorama endowing him with the faculty of pure experience, and with access to the city's minutiae, to the infinite city beneath the city which Walter Benjamin envisioned as a source of living history.

Benjamin's writings on the *flâneur* take up Charles Baudelaire's poetic legacy of the Parisian phantasmagoria. The *flâneur* – the all-seeing eye – is the origin of the urban detective; the *flâneur* is the man in the crowd and the writer in the making ('the *flâneur* who goes botanising on the asphalt').[2] Through the *flâneur*, who both merges with and stands back from the urban scene, the boundaries of public and private space in the perpetually altering modern city can be revealed.

The gender of the *flâneur* has become an issue for feminist critics. Elizabeth Wilson notes that '. . . the *flâneur* as a man of pleasure, as a man who takes visual possession of the city . . . has emerged in post modern feminist discourse as the embodiment of the "male gaze". He represents men's visual and voyeuristic mastery over women. According to this view, the *flâneur*'s freedom to wander at will through the city is essentially a masculine freedom.'[3]

Wilson argues that as the nineteenth century ended, and with the growth of female white collar occupations, women were emerging more and more into public spaces, becoming more visible in the increasing number of eating establishments which by now as a matter of course numbered women among their customers – like the ABC tearooms so familiar to Miriam Henderson. (Miriam even has a midnight haunt, a friendly café on the Euston Road.) The development of the department store – both a landscape and a room, in Benjamin's words, also enlarged the public area in which a solitary woman might loiter, and on her way to and from these places, become a part of the urban crowd.

As the twentieth century draws to a close, public space remains in question as far as women are concerned. Walking alone through late-night streets or entering pubs and restaurants unaccompanied can still be seen as inappropriate for a woman. While the emphasis now is on safety rather than on respectability, the two are stubbornly linked in the language of policing or judicial judgements. Yet, throughout the century, fictions of the city suggest that, whatever the social restrictions imposed on women's mobility, the city itself offers invitation enough to women to ignore these and to follow their own inclinations. The very danger that conformity warns against may thereby be a lure.

Women do have to contend with the possessing male gaze, but this can be less a feature of city life than of a narrower social environment like that of the provincial town. In Maureen Duffy's novel *The Microcosm* (1966), Cathy has newly arrived in London from the north of England: 'It would take her a long time to get over this feeling of freedom, Cathy thought, walking the streets of the city at night without the continual fear of being emotionally molested, set upon by catcalls, shouted invitations . . .' There are echoes of this in a much earlier novel, Cora Sandel's *Alberta and Freedom*, set in Paris before World

War I: 'Alberta was never afraid in the street here, as she
had been at Rivermouth and in the alleys at home in the
small Arctic town.'

Nonetheless, Verena Stefan's account of a woman's
harassment on the Berlin streets suggests that the more
informal dress and demeanour current among young women
by the early seventies, and coding the period's emphasis on
informality and sexual liberation, made her particularly
vulnerable to unwanted attention on the streets. Perceptions
of how 'decent' women ought to dress and comport
themselves in public have radically altered since the sixties.
Dress, indeed, has come less and less to conform to any
expected messages about sexual availability or even about
class, blurring the once clear distinction between the 'lady',
deemed especially worthy of male respect, whether gallant
or obsequious, and the working-class woman.

Whereas Virginia Woolf's *Mrs Dalloway* speaks from and
inscribes the position of the middle-class woman with an
assured place in society (the sense of displacement Clarissa
Dalloway registers being internal, while an aspect of
gender), the female protagonist of city fictions is more often
a socially marginal figure, making her way in the world
somewhat precariously. Woolf's securely middle-class
creations are anomalous by comparison with the vagabonds
and transients, the cosmopolitan outsiders and sexual
deviants, the hard-pressed working women who populate
the fictional world of the metropolis throughout the century.

Elizabeth Wilson notes how much marginalisation, be it
social or economic, is implicit in the stance of the *flâneur*, a
stance that heightens the ambivalence bred by the city's
contradictory experiences – intimacy and estrangement,
curiosity and indifference, poverty and abundance. The
flâneur, Wilson concludes, is more an androgynous figure
than a potent voyeur. It can be argued that the fictional
flâneuse shares in this androgyny (an androgyny affirmed by
Miriam's 'not a woman . . . a Londoner') and that her
conscious, often chosen marginality within the very

boundarylessness of the metropolis gives her a paradoxically enlarged territory of the self, and crucially, in keeping with the trope of the *flâneur* as writer-to-be, an impulse to see beyond the limits of the self, to occupy imaginative positions other than her own. Miriam Henderson's interior dialogue shows a mind and sensibility full of contradictions; she can be snobbish and insufferably high-minded, but what her intellectual immaturity and moral confusions reveal are the workings of a youthful consciousness trying to make sense of the world and achieve its own integrity. This consciousness is in a ceaseless agitation of questions, some of whose answers, a more transcending inner voice intimates, might lie waiting in the city.

A similar process of interrogating the city for answers to the uncertainties of identity can be found in Cora Sandel, the Scandinavian writer who is virtually Richardson's contemporary. Sandel lived in Paris from 1905–1921, and in *Alberta and Freedom*, the middle volume of her autobiographical Alberta trilogy, she gives a picture of the city before World War I. This is also a picture of a youthful life aware of its rootlessness and persistently interrogating the city in its search for purpose and self-knowledge. Alberta scrapes a living as an artist's model, pawning her possessions when she has no work, and alone, on restless afternoons and evenings, she drifts on the flow of the city, wandering idly through its streets and squares, or venturing into a twilit park. At night when anxieties and doubts disturb her sleep she eases the wakefulness by 'feverishly writing on scraps of paper that were thrown unread into the trunk'. Scraps of paper on which the unknown future writer begins to shape the identity that she seeks in the fragmented cityscape. As with Richardson's Miriam Henderson, whom Regent Street's marvels prompt to write a letter, the intoxication of walking and looking urges words on the imagination.

THE PROSTITUTE AND THE BAG LADY

As the woman without a family, or at any rate without a husband, and bent on independence, the protagonist of many urban fictions becomes an outsider, a woman whose marginality makes her a deviant of sorts. It is not surprising that in so many of these fictions the most marginal and deviant of all female figures, the prostitute, should have a part to play.

If men in these fictions see prostitutes only as the exotic or contemptible other, the impure fusion of desirable commodity and seller, women do not. The city spawns an unsentimental awareness of the prostitute's kinship with the 'respectable' woman, for the prostitute represents the marginal woman who survives through the economy of her sexuality in a more stark and open surrender to the economic relations of sexual inequality than do other women. Emotional commitment is no answer for the woman who knows she must depend for her keep on a man who sees her as a lesser being, however beloved. 'There is no freedom for me, a middle-class woman without a profession. They should give me a streetwalker's card,' declares Elvira in Christina Stead's *The Beauties and Furies*, facing the brutal truth of her situation, a truth taught her by her stay in Paris as a runaway wife caught between husband and lover.

Economic antagonism between the sexes inflames Stead's writing with much of its angry and eloquent passion. In Jean Rhys's fiction, relations between men and women repeatedly founder in a mire of money-entangled emotional dependency. Whether in London or Paris, her heroines are too passive and reliant on their femininity to see any way out of their impoverishment other than to have a protector, a man who will take care of them. 'Night Out 1925', in which a woman exercises proxy male generosity towards women who sell their sex shows a little turn of the worm.

In 1920s Tokyo the impoverished aspiring writer in Hayashi Fumiko's 'Vagabond's Song' fails to get a factory job, shrugs that there is no point in asking for an advance in a house in the red light district and gets herself taken on as a bar-girl instead. There's a matter of factness about this just as there is in Rhys. Just as there is in the abrupt verdict of Tove Ditlevsen's childhood narrator in the Copenhagen of the twenties: 'A whore is a woman who does it for money, which seems to me much more understandable than to do it for free', or in her parents' conflicting views on the eviction of the young neighbour who also does it for money: 'Stop comparing yourself to a whore' the father protests to his wife.

The young white Russians who entered prostitution en masse in the Shanghai of the 1930s described by Agnes Smedley are there by historical circumstance, finding themselves drastically exiled from the class and privilege birth had seemed to allot them. Fallen women are usually pushed, like the needy teenage Boots in Alix Kates Shulman's *On the Stroll*. Ann Petry's Lutie Johnson in *The Street* fights tooth and nail against the predatory hands poised to force her down as poverty defeats her hopes of a better life, but poverty need not be knocking hard at the door for women to imagine selling sex as an option. Having rejected bourgeois marriage for the sake of an independent career as a journalist, and struggling to make middle-class ends meet in the Italy of the 1950s, Irene in Alba de Céspedes' *Between Then and Now* confesses to her friend Adriana: 'I sometimes envy whores. Not the ones who . . . but those who can laugh, as you say, and go to bed with a man for the sake of a mink coat.' It is the sense of struggle the two friends share, their recognition that life might be a lot easier without the desire for equality on one's own terms and with a husband to pay the bills, that makes this joking admission of weakness highly logical. Men have more money. With the one-off luxury compromise, day-to-day integrity might be easier to maintain.

Albertine Sarrazin's Anne in *L'Astragale* is a rare example of the fictional prostitute as a triumphant heroine who keeps her own integrity. Anne's choice, like that of Sarrazin in life, is an existential one, the defiant election of deviancy in which prostitution involves a willed control at every moment – one that demands total alertness and the ability to outsmart the customer. Not an occupation for a victim.

When Miriam Henderson describes herself as a '*batteur de pavé*' the sexual connotation inherent in the phrase's literal meaning is given no resonance. For her, walking the streets of London is an act of claiming and belonging to the city. Importunate male approaches on the streets are merely an intrusion. But the consequences of urban marginalisation repeatedly haunt those women conscious of how their independent choices jeopardise future security and leave them exposed to the status of the total outcast. There comes a night when Miriam is confronted with the price she might some day have to pay for her freedom: '. . . the figure of an old woman bent over the gutter . . . the last, hidden truth of London . . . she met the expected sidelong glance; naked recognition, leering from the awful face above the outstretched bare arm. It was herself, set in her path and waiting through all the years.'

Whatever autonomy the prostitute can achieve in the face of social degradation depends initially on her market value, usually the selling power of her relative youth. By comparison, through the loss of any such assets, the old woman reduced to the streets represents a final and irredeemable rejection, the sentence of invisibility that cancels out the prostitute's flagrant visibility. Male eyes drawn to the streetwalker (an appellation that seems in itself to indict any woman who would claim the city's pavements) are averted with distaste for the bag lady; female eyes may linger with ambivalent dread.

In *On the Stroll* Shulman twins the two aspects of outcast female status: the vulnerable, easily exploited young Boots, and Owl, the bag lady with her crazy visionary wisdom and her stubborn, albeit unsteady hold on the memory of a life rich in experiences. Out of the populous promiscuity of the Times Square area, whose multiple parallel existences go on without meeting, she aligns their stories in an eventful symmetry. Another eighties novel, Susan Daitch's *The Colorist*, establishes a more direct narrative connection between the woman whose body is commodified and the woman reduced to the worth of human detritus. *The Colorist* employs a number of narrative levels, both as actuality – the story we are reading, whose main character is Julie, the artwork colorist living precariously from job to job – and as fantasy and simulacrum. Julie is an outsider, witness to the city's decay and social dissolution; Electra is a comic-book character in outer space, whom Julie reworks by having her arrive on Earth with no understanding of terrestrial monetary exchange values; dollar bills are discarded as indecipherable paper signs. Pursuing futile attempts to make sense of the city's fragmentation, she ends up living on the street, becoming dirty and 'constructing her possessions from what other people threw away', blotting out her 'memory of a life of privilege, extravagant intelligence . . .' One day Electra's underlying youth and beauty are perceived by a predatory photographer who imprisons her and compels her to pose for the nude photographs from which he makes a living.

Daitch's New York is Baudelaire's and Benjamin's nineteenth-century city of growing commodification taken to its post-modern conclusion, where consumption is surpassed by an ever-inflated production of merchandise, where in order to resist the mirroring of this process in human identity – the obliteration of any hold on the self through the tyranny of mask and simulacrum – women need to keep their wits about them. Self-possession, which Electra loses, is the key to retaining productive meaning in this urban universe of signs.

TALES OF THREE CITIES: NEW YORK, LONDON, PARIS

The New York of *The Colorist* is also, like Baudelaire's and Benjamin's emerging modern metropolis, the city where paths

13

cross wildly and strangers hold secrets, where, in scanning
the faces in the crowds your eyes brush against one you
might have loved but will never see again (like Baudelaire's
passante)[4] or glimpse what could be the face of a long lost
sibling or parent, or a childhood friend now inhabiting a
world unknown to you. Fate has more scope for coincidence
in the great city, the laws of chance get shaken up repeatedly.

This random potential in city life is what sets things
spinning in *The Golden Spur* (1962), Dawn Powell's boozy,
brittle, Manhattan fairytale of the fifties. Powell mocks the
search of her hero from the sticks for the father he never
knew, and for 'real life' in bohemia; indeed in satirising the
fauna of Greenwich Village, she mocks all her characters'
pretensions to serious art or serious sentiment, showing
them to be fickle and mutable. The city itself is the most
reliable of her characters, still fond of its own threadbare
myths, its characters willing dupes of them, sacrificing all to
the promise of New York, which in Powell, besides being
the perennial promise of success, is the promise of salvation
from the wholesome hell of domesticity. New York is what
despised normality is not: the option of bohemia, or at least
life lived in a shabby hotel, at a suitably ironic distance from
experience – 'You ought to read and find out what life is all
about' the cocktail-swilling Mrs Vane tells her daughter in
Powell's *Angels on Toast* (1940). This is city life as style; the
ultimate meaning of urbanity.

Can New York be disputed as world capital of urbanity?
In the USA, whose literary culture is not renowned for irony,
New York is where ironists grow. Dawn Powell was a
quintessential New York writer in the Dorothy Parker
mould; her world of smart hats and highballs, where
characters exist, movie-style, in their throwaway dialogue,
and where women disdain feminine virtues or homemaking
impulses, is a bracing comic antidote not only to the
repressive family morality of the Eisenhower years, but to a
sentimental family tendency in much contemporary US
fiction. New York's urban alienation is such that not

belonging, or rather, not feeling 'at home' is an implicit aspect of the urbanite's *modus vivendi* – in the sense that any easy domestic affinities are banished from human discourse. In a witty Jean Stafford story, 'Children are Bored on Sunday' (1948),[5] the acquisition of such a resolutely guarded and unsentimental sensibility becomes daunting to Emma, who is intimidated by the sophistication and stylisation of the intellectual milieu she has entered on her arrival in the city, yet craves its acceptance.

To be a part of the city the New Yorker has to accept her outsider status, squandering her illusions of an easy welcome and instead taking on the city as a battleground, alluring partly through its intimations of danger, its powerful sense of individuals routinely estranged from one another, and slugging it out. For Jadine in Toni Morrison's *Tar Baby*, New York – 'that barfly with the busted teeth and armpit breath' – represents the sexiest and most exhilarating of cities, the ultimate challenge to the would-be city dweller, and therefore the ultimate place to be for non-takers-of-shit '. . . if ever there was a black woman's town, New York was it'. The very abrasions of New York life make it an energy vector, breeding elation as well as apprehension, exaltation as well as paranoia. In taking on New York the hazards may be great, but the stakes are high. It is where winning and losing become fateful occupations.

Nowhere is the savagery of this more breathtakingly demonstrated than in Christina Stead's *A Little Tea, A Little Chat* (1948). Here, the city is a hell of parasitism and wartime profiteering, whose denizens, if not out-and-out dupes, are so many sharks and jackals. Between the monstrous Robbie Grant and Barbara Kent, chief protagonists of this novel, there is played out a frenetic game of pursuit and evasion, bluff and counter-bluff, whose sex/money stakes are continually being measured and revised in terms of profit, loss, dividend and bonuses, while everywhere diabolical scams are set in motion to gull and cheat for the sake of even the tiniest gain. This city is driven by a knowledge that everything and everyone has a price. Barbara Kent, who ruthlessly defines her relations with men in terms of whose payroll she is on, has a head start in the game compared with those women whose instincts are blunter and whose assets are less marketable. (The narrator in another Stead novel, *Letty Fox: Her Luck* (1946), observes of women's progress: '. . . the ability to sell ourselves in any way we like is a step towards freedom.')

Ambition is the commonest New York story. The earliest of this century's notable New York fictions by a woman writer, Edith Wharton's *The House of Mirth* (1905), is a story of ambition pursued – and thwarted. The loser, Lily Bart, is a woman whose hopes of finding a place in society through a marriage go awry, and Lily's uneasy passage through the streets seems to mirror her lost, outcast fate. *The House of Mirth* is really a nineteenth-century novel in terms of its social themes. Its New York of old money and time-worn oppressions is a long way from the modern city that begins with the transit of millions from Europe via Ellis Island, bringing the likes of Emma Goldman and other radicals who would find their home in the Greenwich Village Djuna Barnes describes, and the Jewish immigrant masses whose representatives populate the Lower East Side tenements and sweatshops of Anzia Yezierska's stories at the start of the century – a New York that has echoes in Grace Paley's stories of daily life, kinship and locality several generations of immigration later.

For all its violence and poverty, Paley's New York world displays heartening levels of resilience and human empathy. These are an everyday survival response to what in other fictional scenarios can easily be defeating or panic-inducing, especially to the outsider or the woman alone and losing her footing. Of all the great cities in the industralized west, New York can be the most phantasmagoric and persecutory, as it is in Shirley Jackson's 'Pillar of Salt' or the Julie Hayden story 'Day-Old Baby Rats' (1972)[6]; the most existentially indifferent, as in Hortense Calisher's 'The Scream on 57th

Street', or another story of hers, 'The Woman who was Everybody' (1953), which narrates a young woman's hopes and gradual disillusionment with New York working life as she comes to identify with the city's straitjacket of normality, its work-ethic-imprisoned subway commuters. New York's promise and disappointment remain a theme of women's fiction into the nineties, and as ever, a commentary on the pitfalls of the American dream, invoked, with astringent subtlety, as malaise in a recent Deborah Eisenberg story 'A Cautionary Tale'.[7] Eisenberg's characters are rarely recipients of enlightenment, even though everything in her narratives works through them. They can arrive at only a sense of unease. The journey the *Bildungsroman* takes is surely a European one, after all.

It was 'the vivacity, the incredible energy, of ordinary New Yorkers', the city's profligacy, its casual waste and excess that most struck Storm Jameson in 1948, as she later recorded in *Journey from the North*. Though that profligate and now messy spectacle has acquired nightmare proportions by the nineties, the city still thrills and charms the cisatlantic visitor. In *In the Eye of the Sun* (1992) Ahdaf Soueif's central character compares New York to her native Cairo, with its human muddle and chaos, its beat-up taxis, its loud rudeness and friendliness. New York, unlike Cairo, is a city where she can drink in a bar alone, and, like Esther Greenwood before her, imagine with yearning how it might be 'to wander the mean streets in the night'.

Yet it is not in New York, but in London, a city of ever-stretching boundaries, that these yearnings to scorn nocturnal dangers have their most recurrent fictional enactment. In novelists as different as Dorothy Richardson, Doris Lessing, Olivia Manning and Maureen Duffy, the image of a woman walking alone at night – in search of understanding, identity, a future – is hauntingly present.

New York, London and Paris are the world's most fictionalised cities. Besides being great literary centres, all three have been a major destination for immigrants and exiles. Although it was as a nineteenth-century capital that London gave its most enthusiastic welcome to refugees fleeing persecution, World War II renewed its role as a haven from tyranny. The reputation lingers, perhaps even helped by the perennial dinginess so often remarked upon by writers from elsewhere, and by the possibilities the city's vast surface may seem to promise. The revolutionary's widow, Nadezhda Krupskaya, wrote in her *Memories of Lenin*: 'We were astounded at the tremendous size of London. Although it was exceedingly dismal weather on the day of our arrival, Vladimir Ilyich's face immediately brightened up, and he began casting curious glances at this stronghold of capitalism, forgetting for the while Plekhamov and the editorial conflicts.'

This was in 1902. Subsequent fictional first impressions often stress the dismalness. A grey chill predominates in Jean Rhys's *Voyage in the Dark* (1934), whose heroine, Anna, warms herself with memories of the Caribbean. Colonials, travelling in inverse direction from the route their forebears took to spacious, land-conquerable zones, shrivel inside London's claustrophobic denseness. Doris Lessing, off the boat from what was then Rhodesia, was dispirited by 'the interminable streets of tall, grey, narrow houses', and by the post-war 'atmosphere of stale weariness'. This encounter with working-class London, recorded documentary-style in *In Pursuit of the English* (1960), is where Lessing's novel *The Four-Gated City* (1969) begins. Nothing could be more slovenly and greasy, cracked and stained and smeared than the fish and chip café where the reader first encounters Martha Quest at the book's start. Yet these opening pages also establish this as a place of safety, its warm-hearted owners having given Martha lodging. The city's dinginess is also cosiness, and bomb-scarred London is Martha's landfall to freedom, its as yet untidied wartime mess a paradoxically edenic setting for '. . . nights spent walking with men and women as enjoyably vagrant and as footloose as she . . .'

The drawbacks of Dickens's city are undeniably fair game for caricature. In Margaret Atwood's *Lady Oracle* (1976) Joan's first stop is 'a damp bedsitter' and London consists of 'a lot of traffic and a large number of squat people with bad teeth'. Bedsits and their attendant miseries, along with small-minded landlords and landladies, feature largely in London fictions of new beginnings, equally for London writers like Maureen Duffy and Shena McKay, in whose *Music Upstairs* (1965) the whole city has a giddily-noted shabbiness as its decor.

Yet London has a glamour, a 'gloomy charm' (Jean Rhys) that derives from its very citiness, its importance as a great metropolis. London exists in fictional monochrome, its promise perpetually fogged, but nonetheless there. By the 1980s, however, the West End streets display both the sheeny brightness of plastic-enhanced consumerism and the signs of collapse and decay, of a polity gone to pot. In *The Radiant Way* (1987), Margaret Drabble's novel of post-war reckoning for a trio of old friends, this is despairingly perceived by Alix, at the moment of the 1984–85 miners' strike: 'Alix, sitting on the bus on the way home, stared blankly through the streaming panes at the wet shoppers of Oxford Street. Despite terrorists, despite unemployment, despite the horror of Oxford Street itself, still they throng. Perhaps anywhere, thought Alix, would be better than London.'

London can stand for the state of the nation – far more than New York, in relation to which the rest of the USA is somewhat alien and remote (although it is in New York that the American Dream potentially acquires its apotheosis of success). For newcomers, like Lessing's Martha Quest, London can verify notions of Englishness or propose a reality that contradicts myths either fixed in the colonial mind or fabricated daily by the newspapers. Martha observes the city's class rigidities and stark inequalities, and also their somnambulant denial: '. . . this was a country absorbed in myth, doped and dozing and dreaming, because if there was

one common fact or factor underlying everything else, it was
that nothing was as it was described . . .'

Paris is more a writer's city than London has ever been,
loved for its harmonious architectural beauty, its more
manageable human scale, the freedom of its cafés that
Simone de Beauvoir inhabited with such exemplary ease,
and for its sense of truly public spaces, so important to
women. Where London, by its spidery quasi-suburban
breadth, is traditionally a comfy metropolis that lacks a
cosmopolitan heart, and is therefore enclosing in its
Englishness, Paris is the most cosmopolitan of cities. It is
also a city alive with history, a living archaeology, its streets
and squares, its half-hidden arcades secreting convergences
of past and present; its literary echoes amplified.

Ezra Pound proclaimed it 'the paradise of artists,
irrespective of their merit or demerit'. Gertrude Stein
pronounced it 'the capital of the twentieth century', in other
words the foremost capital of modernism, the magnet of the
European avant garde, a Utopia of the creative spirit.

It is not from the British, but the enamoured North
Americans that we derive the Anglo-Saxon vision of
romantic Paris, where a great cultural past meets modernity.
Among the expatriots of the avant garde in the early years of
the century were a significant number of women, a literary
community that included Djuna Barnes and Gertrude Stein,
Sylvia Beach (who, in 1922, published Joyce's *Ulysses*, and
whose lover Adrienne Monnier opened France's first lending
library)[8] and Nancy Cunard, Caresse Crosby, Nathalie
Barney and Janet Flanner – whose regular 'Letter from Paris'
in the *New Yorker* from 1925 onwards detailed social,
literary and political life in the city. Cosmopolitans all, they
were translators – important cultural go-betweens – as well
as poets and novelists, publishers and essayists.

This group is the focus of Shari Benstock's invaluable
study, *Women of the Left Bank*.[9] Stressing the support, both
financial and otherwise, that these women gave to one

another, she argues that they and other women writers around them represent a more progressive, liberal and optimistic strain in modernism than does the largely better-known work of their male contemporaries.

The physical experience of Paris is not the substance of the fictional experimentation that issued from this milieu. But the experimentation flourished as a product of the city's intellectual vigour, and the openness that made it a refuge for thousands escaping Prohibition and US-style Puritanism, and in the case of black intellectuals like the Harlem Renaissance writer Jessie Fauset, US-style racism.

On the margins of the avant garde itself are fictions by women writers that convey the permissive and ample public space which the city offered to those entering the quasi-bohemian undercurrent of expatriot life: Sandel's *Alberta and Freedom*, the novels and stories of Jean Rhys, whose heroines, however badly down on their luck, could find in Paris a consolation London would withhold. In *Quartet*, the impoverished Maya Zelli is trapped in an emotional triangle that gives her only dependent, victim status. Her sole compensation for loneliness and the powerlessness of her situation is the city; its streets, where Maya wanders alone, the cafés where she drinks solitary cups of coffee, and the cheap restaurants where she eats are the novel's glimpses of light and air, its release from claustrophobia. On one of her walks through Montparnasse, she meets another foreigner, the painter Esther de Solla: 'There are hundreds of women round here painting away and all that,' she tells Maya. Such a congregation is hard to imagine anywhere but Paris. Paris, historic city of light (*ville de lumières*, both as Enlightenment and literal illumination) and of revolution – for the Surrealists, a spatial and architectural configuration of revolt, one that Elsa Triolet evokes in 'Paris Dreaming'. Paris, city of night, of a dark and deviant sexual literature with which Albertine Sarrazin's fiction could ally itself.

But Paris as Paradise is also a place of the imagination. The Paris of the Jazz Age and the Lost Generation, 'the place where good Americans go when they die', as Oscar Wilde had put it earlier, has become legendary to the point of synthetic cliché. The experience of Americans in Paris would in the end reach Hollywood and influence everybody, by way of Hemingway and Fitzgerald, Gershwin and Cole Porter – adding to the city's already mythic components.

The myths interested Christina Stead. *The Beauties and Furies*, which is the better-known of her two Paris novels,[10] can be read from start to finish as a commentary on Paris and the glamour of its myths, as well as being a scathing critique of the status of women.

The Beauties and Furies spans the year from November 1933–34 and is set against the backdrop of a notorious financial and political scandal, the 'Stavisky affair'. It begins as Elvira, a London doctor's wife, leaves her solidly bourgeois husband to join the younger Oliver in Paris and become his lover. Oliver, also English, is engaged in writing a study of French working-class movements. He makes insistent comparisons between Paris and London, in which the latter city is damned for its bourgeois dullness and the deference of its working class – a city in which history moves too slowly, if it moves at all.

Just as class relations are more nakedly antagonistic in this Paris than in London, so are sexual politics. Elvira, like Maya in *Quartet*, finds interiors stifling and oppressive, and what she learns she learns through café talk with women whom social barriers would have distanced her from in London. It is women who have the truest perceptions in the novel, all of them aware of what one character, the young Frenchwoman Coromandel, describes as 'the insufficiency of men': men's refusal to see women in terms of their own individual human selves, rather than as dependent, or if independent, as overbearing; as aesthetic or erotic objects, or merely as objects of scorn. In other words as either beauties or furies.

Paris itself is sardonically viewed in the light of the characters' subjectivities, in particular that of Oliver. He is at first intoxicated by the city's historical glamour, its archaeology of revolutions, and he idealises the Paris proletariat. As he is gradually discovered by Elvira to be a 'sham-socialist', at heart a would-be bourgeois, a man of decaying principles, his intoxication becomes literal. He succumbs to wild drinking bouts and to a decadent eroticisation of the Paris streets, an eroto-feminisation that is an all too familiar male construct: the city as a plenitude of female sexuality there for the taking by men.

Stead writes against the grain of male fabulations in which women are the city's whores and corrupting angels. Even in the choice of her characters' names she recasts the quasi-medievalism of the decadent/symbolist project. Oliver and Marpurgo are not the prey but the predators in their relation to Elvira, Blanche and Coromandel, none of them dark ladies. All of them, though, active sexual subjects, independent of male projections.

Stead fills the novel with more and more Baudelairean echoes: Oliver encounters prostitutes who recite Baudelaire, as street-corner bait for passing trade; 'Baudelaire loved us, girls like us . . .' one of the street-girls explains to Oliver in exchange for a meal. As he is drawn more and more into this transgressive city of the night he finally undergoes a hallucinatory collapse in which women appear to him as the monstrous *femmes fatales* of the overheated *fin-de-siècle* male imagination. Paris itself becomes a sinister and fearsome woman, a scapegoat for failed moral energy and irresponsibility.

Against the Paris of Oliver's corruption is balanced the Paris of Elvira's bitter getting of wisdom. 'I used to sneer at women with their cheap truisms. Travel and learn,' she says, as the novel runs to its close.

EXCESS AND THE CITY

In the giving of genders to cities, Paris has always been regarded as feminine. But besides being the feminine of the male imagination, it can also be regarded as a woman's city,

Introduction

so much has it been claimed by women, through its
multiplicity, its space for the heterogeneous. Different,
darker histories have made of the divided Berlin, and
Vienna, also split between East and West in the aftermath of
World War II, significant cities of exploration for the
fictional female psyche. In the work of writers like Elfriede
Jelinek, Ingeborg Bachmann and Giuliana Morandini, the
cultural intersections of old Empire, the devastation of war
and the instability of Cold War power plays have created the
fissures and cracks whereby women can inhabit
subterranean levels of the city's life.

Jelinek's Vienna in *The Piano Teacher* (1983) is a sexual
inferno into which a woman voluntarily descends.
Bachmann's only novel, *Malina* (1971),[11] is a complex and
fragmented work rich in literary, philosophical and
psychoanalytic references, a condensation of myth, history
and desire, where Vienna's topography is marked out as a
series of shifting boundaries and memory zones. Poetic
repetitions and images from the unconscious rise out of the
restless stream-of-consciousness narrative. This city is a
crossroads of many different languages, a convergence of
personal and public traumas. This city, in which
psychoanalysis has its own history, is both the scene of
events and the onlooker, the site of the fabled 'Once upon a
time . . .' and the utopian 'A day will come, when . . .',
linking past, present and future in a desperate struggle to
affirm a passionate and autonomous female subjectivity.
Images of fire run through the novel, both as emblems of
destruction and of female desire.

Bachmann, it would seem, was an inspiration to Jelinek.
She is an avowed influence on Morandini, whose
melancholic and enigmatic *Angelo a Berlino* (*Berlin Angel*),
the third novel in what could be seen as a middle-European
trilogy, has a female protagonist alert to the Berlin of the
eighties while quizzing the city's unconscious in the manner
of a detective faced with solved but not wholly explained
crimes. This Berlin, like Morandini's digressive narrative,

24

her allusive, cryptic characters, is labyrinthine, and in probing its repressed and forgotten history, its protagonist, Erika, also interrogates the female unconscious, through the sexual history of her mother and sister. Against the rigid, containing presence of the Wall, Morandini sets the idea of boundarylessness – in polyglot language and in a vocabulary of polymorphous female sexuality.

It is implicit in the work of these three writers that, for women, occupying the social-historical space of the city entails a refusal to be invisible, a refusal to be silent, a refusal to be merely the desired; desire being unequivocally active. The voice that articulates these refusals is the voice of excess, the insistent, circling voice of rapture (like that of *Pilgrimage*'s Miriam Henderson); the ardent, soaring voice of transgressive passion; the voice that pushes language into the realm of music. It is a supremely operatic voice, echoing the desperate arias of those operatic heroines whose burden it is to carry the world's emotion as well as their own unendurable suffering; what Catherine Clément calls the voice of 'delirious reason',[12] the voice maddened by a truth denied. Christina Stead too is an operatic writer, though it is towards the Brechtian that her characters' hectic talk and furious monologues tend (it is easy to imagine the New York of *A Little Tea, A Little Chat* as Mahagonny).

The modern city not only urges different rhythms on language but pushes it towards forms that can express its underlying shifts and energies, the pulse of the present in the making, the past's vibrating notes, the varying tempo of forward movement. Modernism's liberating break with the past meant not only seeing, but hearing the world differently through the inner ear that the interior monologue depended upon, with language embodying a simultaneity of tenses. The musical analogies are not hard to find – in Gertrude Stein's fugue-like repetitions or the texturing of Joyce's linguistic invention. With its Wagnerian effects, the first novel ever to employ the technique of interior monologue, Edouard Dujardin's *The Bays are Sere* (1887), to which

Joyce acknowledged his debt, quite explicitly establishes the musical affinities of non-linear, stream-of-consciousness writing. In Dujardin Paris itself surges out of this music. Language as consciousness is modulated by the city's rhythms. The break with the realist flow opens up possibilities for women's different relation to language (no longer as the other, the secondary subject of it). This is also evident in Toni Morrison's prose, where the urban syncopations of jazz and the echoes of the blues heighten the force of her narration. The city that so extravagantly exerts the primacy of the visual, with its abundant passing spectacle, its stream of unknown faces, can also be a stage for polyphonous sound – a sensory arena less bounded by gender.

Does their excess, their intense connecting of language with the body, place writers like Bachmann, Morandini and Jelinek in the theoretical category of *écriture féminine*? It could be so argued, but this conclusion risks an undeserved narrowing of their territory. This is 'women's writing' only in the sense of 'a violent, direct literature' that Marguerite Duras speaks of, which will 'reverse everything, including analysis and criticism . . . and make women the point of departure in judging . . .'[13]

To this end, such a literature compels a perception of women as women, not merely in relation to a normative male universe, but as the subject of their own experience, speaking not from one but from many different places, to elude the hasty definitions of unseeing eyes.

Liz Heron,
London, 1993

NOTES

1. Rachilde, *Monsieur Venus*, translated by Liz Heron, Dedalus (1992). This first novel written by Rachilde (the pseudonym of Marguerite Eymeri) who was the solitary female figure of the French Decadent movement in literature, was banned for indecency on its first publication in 1884.
2. 'The Flâneur', in Walter Benjamin, *Charles Baudelaire – A Lyric Poet in the Era of High Capitalism*, translated by Harry Zohn, Verso (1983).
3. Elizabeth Wilson, 'The Invisible Flâneur', in *New Left Review* 191, Jan/Feb 1992.
4. The sonnet 'A une passante' ('To a woman passing by') is one of the most famous poems in *Les Fleurs du Mal*, and speaks of the possibility of love with a stranger whose eyes meet the poet's, as the two pass in the busy street, never to meet again.
5. In the collection *Children are Bored on Sunday* (1953), and reprinted in the *Penguin Book of International Short Stories 1945–1985* (1989).
6. In her collection *The Lists of the Past*, published by Viking Penguin USA.
7. In Eisenberg's collection *Under the 82nd Airborne*, Farrar, Straus & Giroux and Faber & Faber (1992).
8. It is a small but significant item of feminist genealogy that in *The Prime of Life* Simone de Beauvoir records how Adrienne Monnier's library was the source of much of her reading in the twenties, particularly world literature – books which were often passed on to Jean-Paul Sartre.
9. Shari Benstock, *Women of the Left Bank* (1986), University of Texas Press and Virago.
10. The other is *House of All Nations* (1938); sadly, out of print in the UK and US.
11. *Malina* is published by Holmes & Meier, New York, in an English translation by Philip Boehm (1990).
12. Catherine Clément, *Opera, or the Undoing of Women*, translated by Betsy Wing, University of Minnesota Press (1988) and Virago (1989).
13. From an interview with Marguerite Duras in *Signs*, Winter 1975, reprinted in *New French Feminisms*, Shocken (1987), Elaine Marks and Isabelle de Courtivron (eds), Harvester Press (1980).

TRANSITION
1900–1918

B ETWEEN 1900 and the outbreak of World War I, the century was busy drawing blueprints for the future. New movements in art and politics took the measure of the dawning machine age as they turned their backs on the past. The final decade of the nineteenth century had been one of accelerating change for industry and for labour; it had seen a massive rise in trade unionism in Britain, then the world's leading industrial power. In Russia 1905 brought the first, failed, revolution; in Italy the Futurists proclaimed their manifestos; in the USA the IWW (the Industrial Workers of the World, otherwise known as the Wobblies)[1] spread the word of the international proletariat, the word being solidarity. In the USA and Europe women pursued their struggle for the vote, after New Zealand had led the way, legislating for women's suffrage in 1893.

The pieces in this section connect with the world prior to World War I. Even though Sandel's Alberta trilogy was published in the twenties and thirties, the Paris of *Alberta and Freedom*, which appeared in 1931, is that of Sandel's own years there. It is a Paris whose transport is still horse-drawn, until the novel's final pages, when Alberta and her lover Sivert board the new St Michel-Montmartre motorbus; and its characters are at one point engrossed in the heated debates provoked by the publication of 'Gleize and

Metzinger's Book' (*Du Cubisme*, 1912). In the international
Montparnasse enclave of penurious artists and models,
aesthetic debates flourished, along with the discussion and
practice of 'free love', as they did among the bohemians of
Greenwich Village. Djuna Barnes' satirical sketch of
Greenwich Village (where she herself lived) appeared in
1916 in *Pearson's Magazine*; Barnes was at the time a
prolific and widely published journalist, writing on the hoof
as a peripatetic observer of New York life.

The political and intellectual ferment of this period is
experienced by Miriam Henderson in *Pilgrimage*, through
her encounters with Fabian Socialism and the Suffrage
Movement, and in her frequent skirmishings with male
versions of the function of literature and art. Miriam not
only wrestles with ideas continually, but with the whole field
of language and its relation to a masculine-dominated
culture that subordinates women with, among other things,
words. The egotism of *Pilgrimage*'s entirely subjective single
viewpoint is striking not least because it is a woman's – an
exclusively female (indeed feminist) viewpoint, seething with
the intense selfconsciousness engendered by the city.

Pilgrimage was published as thirteen separate novels
between 1915 and 1935. It seems appropriate to place these
extracts in the period where the sequence begins and for
which it represents such an innovation.

NOTE

1. A radical left-wing trade union movement that flourished in the
   decade before World War I, and whose members included many
   immigrant and migrant workers. Through international contacts
   the IWW also had activists in Australia, South America,
   Scandinavia and other parts of the world.

DJUNA BARNES NEW YORK

Greenwich Village As It Is

A friend once told me of an artist who had committed suicide because his colors had begun to fade. His canvases were passing like flowers. People looking upon them sighed softly, whispering, 'This one is dying,' while someone in the background added, 'That one is dead'. It was the unfulfilled fortune of his future. If he had been less enthusiastic, if he had studied what constitutes permanent color and what does not, he might have left some of those somber pictures that seem to grow daily more rigid and 'well preserved'. The earliest nudes executed with the most irreproachably permanent colors seem to be clothing themselves slowly with that most perdurable costume – the patina of time. Turner is among those who live by the death of his canvases.

And so people are standing before Greenwich Village murmuring in pitying tones, 'It is not permanent, the colors will fade. It is not based on good judgment. It is not of that sturdy and healthy material from which, thank providence, we of the real Manhattan have been fashioned.' There are a few who sigh, 'It is beautiful in places!' while others add, 'That is only an accident.'

How charming an answer it was of Nature to make most of her mistakes lovely. Christianity seems to be quite a reprehensible experiment; yet what brings tears so quickly to the eyes as two pieces of wood shaped as a cross?

Why has Washington Square a meaning, a fragrance, so to

speak, while Washington Heights has none? The Square has memories of great lives and possibilities therefore; while the Heights are empty, and Fifth Avenue is only a thoroughfare. Here on the north side are stately houses inhabited by great fortunes, the Lydigs and Guinesses and all those whose names rustle like silk petticoats, and on the other side a congeries of houses and hovels passing into rabbit warrens where Italians breed and swarm in the sun as in Naples, where vegetables and fruits are sold in the street as on the Chiaja, and ice cream is made in the bedrooms and spaghetti on the cellar floor. Here is the den where the gunmen conspired recently to shoot down the free-trade butcher and here the row of houses whose inhabitants provide the Women's Night Court with half its sensations. Satin and motorcars on this side, squalor and push carts on that: it is the contrast which gives life, stimulates imagination, incites to love and hatred.

The greater part of New York is as soulless as a department store; but Greenwich Village has recollections like ears filled with muted music and hopes like sightless eyes straining to catch a glimpse of the beatific vision.

On the benches in the Square men and women resting; limbs wide-flung, arms pendent, listless; round the fountains and on the corners children, dark-eyed Italian children shrieking now with Yankee-cockney accent, a moment later whispering to their deep-bosomed mothers in the Tuscan of Dante. Here a bunch of Jewish girls like a nosegay, there a pair of Norwegian emigrants, strong of figure and sparing of speech; a colored girl on the sidewalk jostles a Japanese servant and wonders whether he, too, is colored or if he is thought to be white like 'dem dagos'.

On every corner you can see a new type; but strange to say, no Americans are to be discovered anywhere. New York is the meeting place of the peoples, the only city where you can hardly find a typical American.

The truth has never been penned about Washington Square and Greenwich Village – names which are now synonymous. To have to tell the truth about a place immediately puts that place on its defense. Localities and atmospheres should be let alone. There are so many restaurants that have been spoiled by a line or two in a paper. We are in that same danger. What can we do? Nothing. The damage has been done, we find, and the wing of the butterfly is already crumbling into dust.

I, personally, have never seen one really good article on Washington Square. The commonest spot is not recognizable. The most daring designs in the shops have all been wrongly colored. As for the long hair of the men and the short hair of the women, that type is to be found on Broadway. Cigarette smoking goes on uptown just as much as it does here; the drinking of wine is just as public; the harmless vanities are displayed in other places quite as blatantly as they are here. The business of making love is conducted under the table beyond Fourteenth Street, but does that establish a precedent forbidding the business of holding hands above the table? Is the touch of kid more harmful than the pressure of boot leather? Of course there are pretenders, hypocrites, charlatans among us. But where are the records that state that all malefactors and hypocrites have been caught within the limits of what we call our Bohemia? And as for crime, have all its victims been found murdered in the beds of Waverley Place and Fourth Street?

Oh! out upon it, this silly repetition about the impossible people living here. Because we let you see us in our curl papers, must you perforce return to your paternal oil stove crying that you never in your life have done your own front hair up in a bang? And must you play forever the part of the simpering puritan who never heard of sex relations? What little story is it that is ringing in your ears, told you one night by your mother about Dad as she sat in the evening yielding up reminiscences, which by day appear to be right or wrong but at night are only clever little anecdotes, timid or sweet adventures of a man now too old for his youth and too wise to try to repeat those things that have made youth the world over the finest and saddest part of life? So forever we rob ourselves of ourselves. We should be born at the age of seventy and totter gracefully down into youth.

Is the beggar of Paris or of Naples any better off than the beggar of Washington Square? And is it not by our beggars that the similarity of a race as well as a group shall be known? These beggars who are the city's finger bowls, wherein the hands of greed have dipped!

What then? We have our artists, but we also have our vendors. We have our poets, but we also have our undertakers. We have our idlers, but have we not also our scrubwomen? We have our rich and our poor. We are wealthier by a mendicant and wiser by a poet.

In reality, Washington Square and Greenwich Village are not one. They have become one above the pavement at the height where men's heads pass; but measured out in plain city blocks the Village does not run past Sixth Avenue. It begins somewhere around Twelfth Street and commits suicide at the Battery.

There are as many artists living off the Square as on it. Some shops are mentioned as these artists are mentioned, because they have caught a certain something that for want of a better word we call atmosphere!

We always speak of Daisy Thompson's shop, of the Treasure Box, of the Village Store and of the Oddity Cellar. Just as many pretty things, however, are to be seen in a small shop on Eighth Street between Fifth and Sixth Avenues. Why is it not also mentioned? Because it is in, and not of, the Village.

There is the pleasant night life of the Café Lafayette. The Brevoort is loved for its basement, where one can catch the lights gleaming between the shrubbery. There, too, is the waiter who has been serving you for ten years past. There is a certain familiarity in everything you eat. You can tell just where you are by closing your eyes. The cold cuts of the Lafayette are superior to those of the Brevoort; the New Orleans 'fizzes' are abominable at the latter and delightful at the former. There is a chance that you may meet someone you do not like, as there is a probability that you will meet someone that you do. You decide beforehand what kind of a sneer you are going to throw Billy, just how coldly you are going to look past Bobbie or freeze the spinal column of Louise, who has been your next-door neighbor for months.

The cholera scare populated the place, but the atmosphere entered not much earlier than the advent of one Bobbie Edwards. In nineteen hundred and six he turned what was then the A Club into what later was known as the Crazy Cat Club or the Concolo Gatti Matti – at a restaurant run by Paglieri at 64 West Eleventh Street.

Edwards introduced the habit of pushing the tables back and organizing an after-dinner dance. He sent out cards of invitation to his friends, and they in their turn sent out invitations to their acquaintances. Leroy Scott, Howard Brubaker, and Mary Heaton Vorse were among its earliest members. Thus came the first filterings of what was to be Bohemia.

Yet what does one know of a place if one does not know its people intimately? I know of nothing that I can offer as a substitute that will fit unless it is an anecdote – the skeleton of life.

This is the story of a dancer who came down here on a bus one day last summer, to live here. What she had done in her past we did not ask – what her eyes did not tell we knew was not worth knowing – yet she was vastly frank. One night this girl arose from the table (it was at Polly's) to answer the phone. At her side sat a young Russian, and as she went out she said to him, 'Now remember, none of your dirty Slavic tricks, don't you put your fingers in my coffee while I'm gone – mind!' and someone at the other side of the table called out to the boy thus addressed, 'Well, you Cossack you, what are you going to do about that?' Instantly the dancer ran back and, flinging her arms about the boy's neck, cried, 'A Cossack, how glorious! I have heard of your brutalities.'

And so now, having eased my mind by having made at

Greenwich Village As It Is

least an attempt to dispel some of the false notions, I can find heart to give this place a body.

On Macdougal Street just above the Dutch Oven is the Liberal Club. It is one more of those things that have come to us from uptown. Margaret Wilson was one of its founders, but needless to say it has changed its tone since its change of locality. Members may bring their friends if they do not bring them too often. Many people have met here, fought, loved, and passed out. The candles of many intellects have been snuffed here to burn brighter for a space until they, too, have given place to newer candles. Here Dreiser has debated and Boardman Robinson sketched, and Henrietta Rodman has left the sound of her sandaled feet. Harry Kemp has posed for his bust only to find on turning round that no one was doing it. Jack Reed and Horace Traubel have been seen here; Kreymborg, Ida Rauh, Max Eastman, Bob Minor, and Maurice Becker; a hundred others.

Whitman dinners are held every thirty-first of May in a private room of the Brevoort. Two seasons ago the heart of the Washington Square Players began to beat here, though the theatre itself was located uptown. A little later Charles Edison – who can really afford to be known for himself, only wearing his father as a decoration – started the Little Thimble Theater with the great Guido Bruno for manager. If they had no successes aside from *Miss Julia*, that was of sufficient importance to have warranted the venture.

Bruno started to make a personal paper, entitled *Greenwich Village*. Allen Norton soon followed with the harmless little *Rogue*, which went out for a while but which is scheduled to return in October or November. Kreymborg put out *Others*, a magazine of verse, blank – the moods of many; a sort of plain-bread-of-poetry – called *vers libres*; and though it was printed in the Bronx it was reeking with the atmosphere of the studios along the south side of the square.

Clara Tice burst into print, and so did Bobbie Locher. The Baron de Meyer began to be seen above a glass of yvette in the cafes, among a score of faces that may have had addresses out of the Village itself but were Bohemians. After all, it is not where one washes one's neck that counts but where one moistens one's throat. And still things are coming, expanding. The very air seems to be improving. There is a rumor that 'King' McGrath – or otherwise Jack – backed by some society people, is going to open a tavern on Sheridan Square and, Jack adds to those who will listen, '*With* a license.'

George Newton is also planning to erect a Toy Theatre on the same Square. Newton has started a new paper, selling at two cents. The first issue will be out in August. Ah, you see! after all you cannot put out the sun by spitting on its shadow.

And our studio buildings? Our apartment houses? The Judson on the south side of the Square, the hotel Holly, the hotel Earle, the Washington; the promised building where now stands the Village soda fountain and Guido Bruno's garret. The Washington Mews has already been partly demolished to arise again. And of recent past history, what of Louis's at 660 Washington Square South? It is held in the memory, as only a dead woman or a past hostelry can be held: the one for its clasp on the heart, the other for its hold on the mind. Louis's had not only Louis, it also had Christine, a woman who, had she not been born in this century, would have been some great heavy goddess whose presence would have been justice without word of mouth. Louis's was closed because it was running without a license. Perhaps that was one of its charms! Drink there was not mere drink, it was wine *libre*.

And there is the Candlestick Tea Room, and there is Gonfarone's, and there is the Red Lamp, Mori's, Romano's, the Red Star, and Mazzini's.

And so you of the outer world, be not so hard on us, and above all, forbear to pity us – good people. We have all that the rest of the world has in common commodities, and we have that better part: men and women with a new light flickering in their eyes, or on their foreheads the radiance of some unseen splendor.

DOROTHY RICHARDSON

from
Pilgrimage

The West End street ... grey buildings rising on either side, angles sharp against the sky ... softened angles of buildings against other buildings ... high moulded angles soft as crumb, with deep undershadows ... creepers fraying from balconies ... strips of window blossoms across the buildings, scarlet, yellow, high up; a confusion of lavender and white pouching out along the dipping sill ... a wash of green creeper up a white painted house-front ... patches of shadow and bright light ... Sounds of visible near things streaked and scored with broken light as they moved, led off into untraced distant sounds ... chiming together.

Wide golden streaming Regent Street was quite near. Some near narrow street would lead into it.

Flags of pavement flowing – smooth clean grey squares and oblongs, faintly polished, shaping and drawing away – sliding into each other ... I am part of the dense smooth clean paving stone ... sunlit; gleaming under dark winter rain; shining under warm sunlit rain, sending up a fresh stony smell ... always there ... dark and light ... dawn, stealing ...

*

Life streamed up from the close dense stone. With every footstep she felt she could fly.

The little dignified high-built cut-through street, with its sudden walled-in church, swept round and opened into brightness and a clamour of central sounds ringing harshly up into the sky.

The pavement of heaven.

To walk along the radiant pavement of sunlit Regent Street, for ever.

She sped along looking at nothing. Shops passed by, bright endless caverns screened with glass ... the bright teeth of a grand piano running along the edge of a darkness, a cataract of light pouring down its raised lid; forests of hats; dresses, shining against darkness, bright headless crumpling stalks; sly, silky, ominous furs; metals, cold and clanging, brandishing the light; close prickling fire of jewels ... strange people who bought these things, touched and bought them.

She pulled up sharply in front of a window. The pavement round it was clear, allowing her to stand rooted where she had been walking, in the middle of the pavement, in the midst of the pavement, in the midst of the tide flowing from the clear window, a soft fresh tide of sunlit colours ... clear green glass shelves laden with shapes of fluted glass, glinting transparencies of mauve and amber and green, rose-pearl and milky blue, welded to a flowing tide, freshening and flowing through her blood, a sea rising and falling with her breathing.

*

The edge had gone from the keenness of the light. The street was a happy, sunny, simple street – small. She was vast. She could gather up the buildings in her arms and push them away, clearing the sky . . . a strange darkling, and she would sleep. She felt drowsy, a drowsiness in her brain and limbs and great strength, and hunger.

A clock told her she had been away from Brook Street ten minutes. Twenty minutes to spare. What should she do with her strength? Talk to someone or write . . . Bob; where was Bob? Somewhere in the West End. She would write from the West End a note to him in the West End.

There were no cheap shops in Regent Street. She looked about. Across the way a little side street, showing a small newspaper shop, offered help.

She hurried with clenched hands down the little mean street ready to give up her scheme at the first sight of an unfriendly eye. 'We went through those *awful* side streets off the West End; I was *terrified*; I didn't know *where* he was driving us,' Mrs Poole had said, about a cabman driving to the theatre . . . and her face as she sat in her thick pink dress by the dining-room fire had been cunning and mean and full of terror. The small shop appeared close at hand, there were newspaper posters propped outside it and its window was full of fly-blown pipes, toilet requisites, stationery and odd-looking books. 'Letters may be left here,' said a dirty square of cardboard in the corner of the window. 'That's all right,' thought Miriam, 'it's a sort of agency.' She plunged into the gloomy interior. '*Yes!*' shouted a tall stout man with a red coarse face, coming forward as if she had asked something that had made him angry. 'I want some notepaper, just a little, the smallest quantity you have, and an envelope,' said Miriam, quivering and panic-stricken in the hostile atmosphere. The man turned and whisked a small packet off a shelf, throwing it down on the counter before her. 'One penny!' he bellowed as she took it up. 'Oh, thank you,' murmured Miriam ingratiatingly, putting down twopence. 'Do you sell pencils?' The man's great fingers seemed an endless time wrenching a small metal-sheathed pencil from its card. The street outside would have closed in and swallowed her up for ever if she did not quickly get away.

'Dear Mr Greville,' she wrote in a clear bold hand . . . He won't expect me to have that kind of handwriting, like his own, but stronger. He'll admire it on the page and then hear a man's voice, pater's voice talking behind it and not like it. Me. He'll be a little afraid of it. She felt her hard self standing there as she wrote, and shifted her feet a little, raising one heel from the ground, trying to feminize her attitude; but her hat was hard against her forehead, her clothes would not flow . . . 'Just imagine that I am in town – I could have helped you with your shopping if I had known I was coming . . .' The first page was half filled. She glanced at her neighbours, a woman on one side and a man on the other, both bending over telegram forms in a careless preoccupied way – wealthy, with expensive clothes with West End lines . . . Regent Street was Salviati's. It was Liberty's and a music shop and the shop with the chickens. But most of all it was Salviati's. She feared the officials behind the long grating could see by the expression of her shoulders that she was a scrubby person who was breaking the rules by using one of the little compartments, with its generosity of ink and pen and blotting-paper, for letter writing. Someone was standing impatiently just behind her, waiting for her place. *'Telle est la vie,'* she concluded with a flourish, 'yours sincerely,' and addressed the envelope in almost illegible scrawls. Guiltily she bought a stamp and dropped the letter with a darkening sense of guilt into the box. It fell with a little muffled plop that resounded through her as she hurried away towards Brook Street. She walked quickly, to make everything surrounding her move more quickly. London revelled and clamoured softly all round her; she strode her swiftest, heightening its clamorous joy. The West End people, their clothes, their carriages and hansoms, their clean bright spring-filled houses, their restaurants and the theatres waiting for them this evening, their easy way with each other, the mysterious something behind their faces, was hers. She, too, now had a mysterious secret face – a West End life of her own . . .

EXTRACT TWO

An ABC appeared suddenly at her side, its panes misty in the cold air. She went confidently in. It seemed nearly full of men. Never mind, City men; with a wisdom of their own which kept them going and did not affect anything, all alike and thinking the same thoughts; far away from anything she thought or knew. She walked confidently down the centre, her plaid-lined golf-cape thrown back; her small brown boat-shaped felt hat suddenly hot on her head in the warmth. The shop turned at a right angle showing a large open fire with a fireguard, and a cat sitting on the hearth-rug in front of it. She chose a chair at a small table in front of the fire. The velvet settees at the sides of the room were more comfortable. But it was for such a little while to-night, and it was not one of her own ABCs. She felt as she sat down as if she were the guest of the City men, and ate her boiled egg and roll and butter and drank her small coffee in that spirit, gazing into the fire and thinking her own thoughts unresentful of the uncongenial scraps of talk that now and again penetrated her thoughts; the complacent laughter of the men amazed her; their amazing unconsciousness of the things that were written all over them.

The fire blazed into her face. She dropped her cape over the back of her chair and sat in the glow; the small pat of butter was not enough for the large roll. Pictures came out of the fire, the strange moment in her room, the smashing of the plaque, the lamplit den; Mr Orly's song, the strange, rich, difficult day and now her untouched self here, free, unseen, and strong, the strong world of London all round her, strong free untouched people, in a dark lit wilderness, happy and miserable in their own way, going about the streets looking at nothing, thinking about no special person or thing, as long as they were there, being in London.

Even the business people who went about intent, going to definite places, were in the secret of London and looked free. The expression of the collar and hair of many of them said they had homes. But they got away from them. No one who had never been alone in London was quite alive . . . I'm free – I've got free – nothing can ever alter that, she thought, gazing wide-eyed into the fire, between fear and joy. The strange familiar pang gave the place a sort of consecration. A strength was piling up within her. She would go out unregretfully at closing time and up through wonderful unknown streets, not her own streets, till she found Holborn and then up and round through the squares.

EXTRACT THREE

She wandered about between Wimpole Street and St Pancras, holding in imagination wordless converse with a stranger whose whole experience had melted and vanished like her own, into the flow of light down the streets; into the unending joy of the way the angles of buildings cut themselves out against the sky, glorious if she paused to survey them; and almost unendurably wonderful, keeping her hurrying on pressing, through insufficient silent outcries, towards something, anything, even instant death, if only they could be expressed when they moved with her movement, a maze of shapes, flowing, tilting into each other, in endless patterns, sharp against the light; sharing her joy in the changing same same song of the London traffic; the bliss of post offices and railway stations, cabs going on and on towards unknown space; omnibuses rumbling securely from point to point, always within the magic circle of London.

EXTRACT FOUR ═══════════════

At six o'clock the front door closed behind her, shutting her out into the multitudinous pattering of heavy rain. With the sight of the familiar street shortened by darkness to a span lit faintly by dull rain-shrouded lamps, her years of daily setting forth into London came about her more clearly than ever before as a single unbroken achievement. Jubilantly she reasserted, facing the invitation flowing towards her from single neighbourhoods standing complete and independent, in inexhaustibly various loveliness through the procession of night and day, linked by streets and by-ways living in her as mood and reverie, that to have the freedom of London was a life in itself. Incidents from Mrs Orly's conversation, pressing forward through her outcry, heightened her sense of freedom. If the sufferers were her own kindred, if disaster threatened herself, walking in London, she would pass into that strange familiar state, where all clamourings seemed unreal, and on in the end into complete forgetfulness.

EXTRACT FIVE ═══════════════

And then *London* came, opening suddenly before me as I rode out alone from under a dark archway into the noise and glare of a gaslit Saturday night.

Trouble fell away like a cast garment as I swung forward, steering with thoughtless ease, into the southernmost of the four converging streets.

This was the true harvest of the summer's day; the transfiguration of these northern streets. They were not London proper; but to-night the spirit of London came to meet her on the verge. Nothing in life could be sweeter than this welcoming – a cup held brimming to her lips, and inexhaustible. What lover did she want? No one in the world would oust this mighty lover, always receiving her back without words, engulfing and leaving her untouched, liberated and expanding to the whole range of her being. In the mile or so ahead, there was endless time. She would travel further than the longest journey, swifter than the most rapid flight, down and down into an oblivion deeper than sleep; and drop off at the centre, on to the deserted grey pavements, with the high quiet houses standing all about her in air sweetened by the evening breath of the trees, stealing down the street from either end; the sound of her footsteps awakening her again to the single fact of her incredible presence within the vast surrounding presence. Then, for another unforgettable night of return, she would break into the shuttered house and gain her room and lie, till she suddenly slept, tingling to the spread of London all about her, herself one with it, feeling her life flow outwards, north, south, east, and west, to all its margins.

CORA SANDEL

from

Alberta and Freedom

TRANSLATED BY ELIZABETH ROKKAN

Alberta's hand was shaken first by Mrs and then by Mr
Digby. And she hurried across the neat courtyard. White
shingle, newly spread, difficult to walk on, forcefully accen-
tuated its length and breadth. Budding box bushes, clipped
low, framed a centre bed. Small-leaved ivy, trimmed and
refined, covered the walls with an even, monotonous green,
and, clipped as if with a ruler, framed handsome doors with
shining brass plates and large studio windows with raw-silk
curtains inside. A concierge, looking like the housekeeper of
an elegant residence, appeared watchfully at her window. She
nodded to Alberta, because although Alberta obviously had
to be considered a questionable character, she was not the
worst kind, but on the contrary looked comparatively
respectable.

The wind blew in gusts. It was one of those March days
when sharp, warm sunshine alternates with cold wintry
blasts. Along the road, which was bordered by low walls
with gardens behind them, naked branches tossed in confusion against racing clouds and sudden depths of ultramarine
sky; at the edge of the pavement on a corner was a handcart
full of violets and mimosa, like a festive cockade on the
ragged clothing of the day.

Alberta turned another corner and found herself beneath
the tall iron skeleton of the Métro, between barrack-like
blocks of flats that cast clammy shadows. A train passed

noisily above her head. Soon afterwards she was sitting in one herself, travelling high in the air between earth and sky over Passy bridge, across the Seine.

There was a rustle along the benches as newspapers were lowered and people looked out. Far below lay Paris, bright in sudden sunshine beneath a tremendous sky full of moving banks of cloud. People, cars, *fiacres* bustled about like toys. To the north-east above Menilmontant was a coal-black shower of rain; directly beneath, the Seine like flowing metal. A tug with a string of barges behind it, working its way upstream, hooted piercingly and belched out thick black smoke, making the sharp light even sharper.

A wave of expansiveness passed through Alberta, washing away fatigue and stale cold. She felt her face changing to an expression that men found disquieting. God knows how it came about. It was suddenly there, making them turn their heads towards her, jerkily, hurriedly, as if in surprise. It was no special distinction, for it can happen to almost any woman. But at least it was a kind of guarantee that she was reasonably like other people, not remarkably ugly, not directly repulsive. And if the person in question was not himself an affront, it sometimes helped her to expand a little more.

The train rattled through the Grenelle district, alongside broad avenues with tree-lined walks down the middle. Some of the buildings were old-fashioned and squat, a bit decayed, a bit rotten with damp, some were brand new in *Jugend* style, shining like butter in the sun. Suddenly it was all gone. White tiled walls and arched roofs, variegated posters darkly illuminated, slid past. An intrusive reek of cellars and disinfectant filled the carriage. And Alberta again felt the fatigue in her limbs. Underground she flickered out.

She alighted at Montparnasse, coming up into the daylight again behind the railway station, in the shadow of the high wall and of the bridge that carried the trains out of the city on a level with the second floors of the houses. Here the pleasant parts of town ended, here the large, depressing working-class districts on the other side of the Avenue du Maine began. One was always met by a gust of greyness and narrow circumstances. Here Alberta could not help thinking of death sentences and executions. Perhaps it was because of the wall.

She paused and looked up at one of the houses in the Rue de l'Arrivée. 'Hôtel des Indes' was written in huge gold letters on a balcony railing right across the façade.

From a railing several storeys higher something white fluttered for a moment, a cloth, a handkerchief, fastened up there. It was carried outwards by the wind and then slackened again. Alberta made certain it was there, then hurried away underneath the bridge where there was a blaze of fruit, flowers and vegetables on handcarts in the semi-darkness. She bought violets and a spray of mimosa, made a couple of other purchases, went into a dairy.

Then she disappeared inside the Hôtel des Indes.

To come up from the hard street. To kick off one's shoes and stretch out one's whole length on something, a bed, a divan. To relax in every limb, while the little spirit stove hums gently. To have a cup of tea, or perhaps two, some biscuits, marmalade, a couple of cigarettes – and the numbness arrives: that blessed state of indifference out of which the will towards life is born anew.

Hungry? Yes . . .

But not as when she used to come home from skiing as a child and grabbed something or other on the way through the kitchen, because she could not wait until her ski clothes were off and she was seated at table. Not that healthy, demanding voraciousness that made all food taste good and satisfying. No – now there was the eternal dissatisfaction of the body, which remained after she had eaten, which could not be quieted, only deadened and diverted. With tea, for instance, and cigarettes.

Alberta lay on her elbow on Liesel's bed, listening to the singing of the spirit stove and smoking a Maryland. Liesel came and went, fetching cups and spoons from the wardrobe, wiping them and arranging them in the sunlight on a chair with a towel over it. Her black dress, poorly cut in one piece, tended to hang askew. She pulled at it repeatedly and stuck her nose into Alberta's flowers now and again as she passed them. They stood resplendent on the mantelpiece and were multiplied by the mirror behind them. '*Reizend*,' said Liesel. '*Wunderbar. Wie freundlich Albertchen.*'

The balcony doors were ajar. The narrow, oblong room, which obtained all its light through them, was filled with muffled noises from the street, smoke from nearby chimneys and the steadfast old bedroom smell that goes with cheap hotels. It is no use trying to air it out, it seeps back in again from the staircase.

Only now did Alberta realise how tired she was, a tiredness like disintegration. It would take at least two hot cups of strong tea to pull her together again. She exhaled small puffs of smoke and exchanged everyday remarks with Liesel. Brief as a code they dropped from them both: 'Well? . . . Oh, all right . . . No news . . . *Gar nichts*.'

On the washstand lay a quarter of a pound of butter wrapped in paper, because, as Liesel said in her housewifely manner, it keeps better on marble. There were also mandarin oranges and two small cream cheeses, which were Alberta's contribution. Liesel's wash-bowl bristled with paintbrushes put to soak.

EXTRACT TWO

A hundred in the shade.

The asphalt was like over-heated metal, the air out in the sun a burning helmet. The trees died, curling up their leaves in a last painful spasm, and letting them fall. Alberta felt she knew how the roots in the tiny round patch of soil allocated to each of them sought vainly in all directions after escape and salvation.

Horses collapsed, humans too. Every day the newspapers reported many cases of prostration. The half-naked labourers engaged in the inevitable summer road repairs were reminiscent of penal colonies in the tropics, of atrocities and merciless torture. Their eyes looked dead under their straw hats, the sweat streamed off them. But their brown torsos were bronze against the dark corduroy trousers and the flaming-red scarves that held them in place. The invincible Sivert was sure to be out painting them.

In the Seine the fish floated belly upwards, dying in their thousands in the thick, slimy water, which stank of rottenness and chlorine. When Alberta crossed the bridges in the evenings on her horse-bus ride, her body pressed up against the weak, scarcely noticeable draught made by their speed, she saw them and listened to the other passengers discussing them and the possibility of epidemics. They could be brought about by less.

In front of the small shops and the house doors chairs were dragged out, forming a continuous chain through the city. Low-voiced, almost silent people sat out there, thousands upon thousands of people of small means, their faces pallid from the heat and the still air. On the benches under the singed trees there was not an empty seat. Working folk ate their supper there, tearing at their long loaves with their teeth and drinking their wine straight from the bottle.

Alberta was seized by uncomfortable longing. She was suddenly reminded of the slap of water against the piles of a jetty, long, shining breakers, the smell of salt water and the newly-ebbed tide; of sitting in the prow of a boat on a night of sunshine, turned away from the others, one hand in the water, watching the smooth, cool shape of the displaced water round the boat, the shoal of coalfish leaping like silverfish in the sun, boats further off, the oars at rest, with gold in their wake and accordions in the prow.

Or she remembered how the air had tasted sometimes

when one went out of doors. Mild air with the thaw in it; air in transition, just as the cold was about to set in. It lay sparkling on the tongue, fresh and mild as water.

She pitched home again, the streets were quieter. Small stumps of conversation reached her from the pavement, settling in her mind like a sediment composed of other lives. A mother's: 'If only you had finished your soup — people who don't finish their soup . . .' An elderly man's: 'It's the fault of the Government. France is governed by idiots. If only we had another Government . . .' A young woman's angry 'Nothing doing tonight, *mon ami*. I shall turn my back on you, and serve you right.'

At intervals a flutter of relief seemed to go through the atmosphere, like the last gasps of a sea animal on land. From the Pont Neuf she could see the moon rising in the south-west over Charenton, a red, drunken, crazy August moon.

When she finally alighted from the tram-car at Porte d'Orléans and walked home along the fortifications it was sailing high above the roofs and the silent treetops, shining, yellow, in the company of a small star.

It was a fortnight since Alberta had spoken to a soul besides the *épicier* and the concierge. With them she discussed the temperature, agricultural prospects, their children's and grandchildren's conditions, endeavours and expectations, the occasional newspaper scandal, the behaviour of the cat, the dog and the canary since yesterday, and the blunders of the Government, which Alberta did not understand and on which she commented in the dark. Whereupon it was over for the day. The studios round her were deserted. No one came any longer to the water-tap and remarked on the flowers.

With the window and door open, naked, her kimono slung across a chair-back within reach, she sat in Eliel's broken basket chair with one of his books and a Maryland, got up now and then, poured water over herself and sat down again. The air in the room was stationary, an evil-smelling mass.

The large clay sculpture in its cloths was stinking. It caught at the throat as one came in.

The cat, too, rose occasionally from its favourite position on one of the stands, stretched itself, walked round itself a couple of times and lay down again. Or it went to its saucer on the floor, where the milk quickly turned sour.

It was an effort to go out when evening came. A kind of fear of doing so began to creep over her. But she knew it of old, knew it must not get the upper hand. And she went; a little dizzy and uncertain to begin with, a little wry in the face. She sat on a bench in the Parc de Montsouris.

This was where the summer found sanctuary. Heavy and dark with maturity the trees and bushes trailed their foliage on the ground. The twilight was scented, people sat silent on the benches. A late bird flew home, the first bat flitted soundlessly past. Arc-lamps were lighted here and there, hidden behind the enormous crowns of the chestnut trees, casting large circles of greenish light over the lawns. Someone ought to have danced in that light, fauns and nymphs, the Russian ballet.

Occasionally someone would whisper, 'Are you alone, Mademoiselle?' She would reply politely and evasively, and betake herself in a little while to another part of the park.

Alberta's limbs became as cool as marble in the heat; if she put her hand into the neck of her low-cut dress her shoulder was as cold and smooth as polished stone. But it opened up sores in her mind. She came home to the stinking studio, and suddenly tears misted her eyes and she hid her face in her hands.

And the night took its course: a torturing confusion of waking dreams; a series of painful, insecure sojourns in mysterious border regions with an occasional violent, brutal jerk back to reality, splashing ammonia on stinging collar-bones, feverishly writing on scraps of paper that were thrown unread into the trunk; a painful awakening as if from the dead when the cat mewed to be let out.

There was something she should have experienced, something besides this. There was a path somewhere that she could not find. It was and it was not her own fault.

'The ignorant man watches every night, anxious about many things. He is exhausted when morning breaks, but his sorrow is the same as before.'

His sorrow is the same as before. It was written in the *Edda*, in Eliel's copy between the stones on the table. An old truth, therefore.

THE TWENTIES

THE PAST was shattered by the cataclysm of the First World War, in which the 'metropolitan' societies of Europe had fought to conclude their nineteenth-century scramble for colonies and influence. With the Russian Revolution and the break-up of Austro-Hungary, Europe's empires began to crumble, its cities re-aligned in importance. The war brought a crisis of belief in certain kinds of progress, but it also brought new freedoms for women, and the vote for many in Europe, ushering in the 'flapper decade', when skirts and hair were shortened and the birth control movement grew.

If this global re-ordering marked the real cusp of the twentieth century, in literary terms the century shifted with the publication in Paris in 1922 of James Joyce's great novel of city consciousness, *Ulysses*. The face of the city changed with the driven new technologies the war had created, re-adjusting visual perspectives, as bridges were built and skylines rose. The movies opened up the world too, relaying the city's speed and fragmentation. From city to city, voices and images multiplied, street rhythms quickened.

The impact of the war and its aftermath on literature was complex, variously hopeful and despairing, depending on its context. Paris, Moscow and Berlin took different routes through modernism. Unlike Paris, London had no avant-garde, nor did it feel the upheavals of revolution.

The dislocations and losses of the war underlie Virginia Woolf's London novel, *Mrs Dalloway* (1925), its shocks invading a reticent nineteenth-century sensibility and modifying its qualities of memory and perception. In Jean Rhys's story, 'Night Out 1925', Paris is seen as a territory that is wearily familiar, the night's planned entertainment of sexual tourism replaced by a muted chuckle at the expense of a man and his wallet. The tone is knowing, a laconic, modern voice that sums up this nocturnal city's tawdry chic, the lopsidedness of male-female transactions, and hints at the suppression of an active female desire (the phantom of a hatless, therefore scarlet woman, like the stray hat – in the gutter).

The Tokyo of Hayashi Fumiko and Hirabayashi Taiko's stories (both published in 1927) may seem disconcertingly less remote to Western eyes than in decades since. Having repelled Western colonial incursion, Japan remained a culture with its own integrity of tradition. But, as Junichiro Tanizaki shows in his novel *Naomi* (1924), a classic of the period, Japanese city dwellers were infatuated with Western culture, its fashions in dress, dancing and movies. This infatuation was one distinctly visible aspect of a cultural and political openness that clearly had enormous significance for women. It was not only Western style, but the repercussions of revolution in the West that spread to Japan. Socialist and anarchist movements produced their own highly influential 'proletarian school' of writing, which looked to Western literature for inspiration. Active in these movements were women writers like Taiko and Fumiko. Both wrote about marginal women – prostitutes, bar girls and factory workers – drawing on their own working-class experiences. But their horizons were global. Taiko started writing while working as a waitress; her impoverished, unemployed city wanderer in 'Vagabond's Song' reads 'a tattered copy of Eugene O'Neill' (one of those Greenwich Villagers) and wonders how Baudelaire and Heine managed to make a living. With its passion for poetry and ideas, its lyrical vision as antidote

to present squalor, 'Vagabond's Song' has a tonic
utopianism of spirit that makes it startlingly modern.
Taiko's narrator is more embittered, more mutinous, a
deviant bent on being seen in all her degradation as she
traverses the city. For both protagonists, the claimed space
of the streets seems to correspond to the preservation of an
interior freedom.

In *Early Spring*, Tove Ditlevsen's backward look at
Copenhagen through her childhood eyes, the working-class
streets around her home are imaginatively mapped out as a
woman's body. The streets are a route to knowledge of adult
things: politics and unemployment, drunkenness and
prostitution, the newspaper billboards with their images of
Sacco and Vanzetti, Italian anarchists, scapegoated as US
immigrants, whose sentence of execution united the great
cities of the world in desperate and futile protest.

VIRGINIA WOOLF LONDON

from

Mrs Dalloway

For having lived in Westminster – how many years now? over twenty, – one feels even in the midst of the traffic, or waking at night, Clarissa was positive, a particular hush, or solemnity; an indescribable pause; a suspense (but that might be her heart, affected, they said, by influenza) before Big Ben strikes. There! Out it boomed. First a warning, musical; then the hour, irrevocable. The leaden circles dissolved in the air. Such fools we are, she thought, crossing Victoria Street. For Heaven only knows why one loves it so, how one sees it so, making it up, building it round one, tumbling it, creating it every moment afresh; but the veriest frumps, the most dejected of miseries sitting on doorsteps (drink their downfall) do the same; can't be dealt with, she felt positive, by Acts of Parliament for that very reason: they love life. In people's eyes, in the swing, tramp, and trudge; in the bellow and the uproar; the carriages, motor cars, omnibuses, vans, sandwich men shuffling and swinging; brass bands; barrel organs; in the triumph and the jingle and the strange high singing of some aeroplane overhead was what she loved; life; London; this moment of June.

EXTRACT TWO

She had reached the Park gates. She stood for a moment, looking at the omnibuses in Piccadilly.

She would not say of any one in the world now that they were this or were that. She felt very young; at the same time unspeakably aged. She sliced like a knife through everything; at the same time was outside, looking on. She had a perpetual sense, as she watched the taxicabs, of being out, out, far out to sea and alone; she always had the feeling that it was very, very dangerous to live even one day. Not that she thought herself clever, or much out of the ordinary. How she had got through life on the few twigs of knowledge Fräulein Daniels gave them she could not think. She knew nothing; no language, no history; she scarcely read a book now, except memoirs in bed; and yet to her it was absolutely absorbing; all this; the cabs passing; and she would not say of Peter, she would not say of herself, I am this, I am that.

Her only gift was knowing people almost by instinct, she thought, walking on. If you put her in a room with some one, up went her back like a cat's; or she purred. Devonshire House, Bath House, the house with the china cockatoo, she had seen them all lit up once; and remembered Sylvia, Fred, Sally Seton – such hosts of people; and dancing all night; and the waggons plodding past to market; and driving home across the Park. She remembered once throwing a shilling into the Serpentine. But every one remembered; what she loved was this, here, now, in front of her; the fat lady in the cab. Did it matter then, she asked herself, walking towards Bond Street, did it matter that she must inevitably cease completely; all this must go on without her; did she resent it; or did it not become consoling to believe that death ended absolutely? but that somehow in the streets of London, on the ebb and flow of things, here, there, she survived, Peter survived, lived in each other, she being part, she was positive, of the trees at home; of the house there, ugly, rambling all to bits and pieces as it was; part of people she had never met; being laid out like a mist between the people she knew best, who lifted her on their branches as she had seen the trees lift the mist, but it spread ever so far, her life, herself. But what was she dreaming as she looked into Hatchard's shop

window? What was she trying to recover? What image of
white dawn in the country, as she read in the book spread
open:

> Fear no more the heat o' the sun
> Nor the furious winter's rages.

JEAN RHYS

Night Out 1925

It had been raining and the green and red reflections of the lights in the wet streets made Suzy think of Francis Carco's books. She was walking with a man called Gilbert, known to his acquaintances in Montparnasse as 'stingy Bertie'.

Gilbert, pointing out that the rain had stopped and that the fresh air would do them good, was taking her to a place which he said was great fun and a bit of a surprise.

They crossed the Seine and went on walking. Suzy was about to tell him that she was getting tired and must have a taxi when he stopped half-way up a quiet side street. They went down a few steps into a long narrow room lined with tall mirrors, and a woman dressed in black came forward.

'Bonsoir Madame,' said Gilbert familiarly. 'Comment allez vous? I've brought a friend to see you.'

'Bonsoir Madame, bonsoir Monsieur,' said the woman showing her teeth.

She doesn't know him from Adam, Suzy was thinking when she lost sight of her and they were surrounded by a crowd of girls in varying stages of nakedness. They arranged themselves in a pattern, the ones in front kneeling, the ones at the back standing. Their spiky eye-lashes stuck out. They opened their mouths and fluttered their tongues at the visitors, not in derision as might be supposed, but in invitation.

I bet they are giving us the bird too, Suzy told herself.

'Choose one,' said Gilbert. Suzy chose a small dark girl who she thought less alarming than the rest. Gilbert chose a much taller girl with red hair and a long chin. Rather like a mare.

The others melted away, presumably to wait for the next clients.

Suzy, Gilbert and their girls went to sit at one of several small empty tables at the other end of the room. A very old waiter shuffled up and asked what they'd have to drink.

'What sort of a man takes a job as waiter in a place like this?' said Gilbert in English but without lowering his voice. The girls asked for 'deux cerises', Suzy and Gilbert for Pernod.

'He'll soon be dead,' said Suzy when the waiter had gone. 'You needn't be so virtuous about him. He can hardly walk as it is.'

'A good thing too,' said Gilbert.

The music of a java reached them from some other room. The drinks arrived and the girls began to chat in an animated way but Gilbert answered briefly or not at all and Suzy was silent because she felt shy and couldn't think of anything appropriate to say. After this had gone on for some time the mare began to look sulky but the other girl seemed worried – a hostess who feared the party was going to be dull, trying to imagine a way to liven it up.

Eventually she turned to Suzy, lifted her skirt and kissed her knee.

'Tu es folle,' said the mare.

'Mon amie n'aime pas ça,' said Gilbert.

'Ah!' said the girl. She was wearing a very short white tunic, white socks and heelless black strap shoes. A brass medal hung round her neck. Her face was quite round. She looked rather stupid but sweet, Suzy thought, smiling and putting her hand on the small plump hand.

'Tut tut,' said Gilbert. 'What am I to make of this?'

'I suppose,' said Suzy looking at him, 'that if she got fed up here she could clear out. Could she?'

'Of course she could,' said Gilbert. 'I'll ask her.'

'Mais certainement,' said the girl. 'Naturellement. Pourquoi pas?' When no one spoke, she added in a low voice, 'seulement, seulement . . .'

'Seulement what?' said Suzy. 'Seulement what?'

'Oh do shut up Suzy,' said Gilbert. 'What's the matter with you? Why these idiotic questions?'

'Come upstairs,' said the mare. 'Come and see us do our "cinéma". You won't be disappointed.'

She also had on a white tunic, white socks and black slippers, but the tunic was open to the waist in front.

'No,' said Gilbert. 'I think not.' He went on speaking to Suzy: 'This place has gone off dreadfully. It really used to be fun, it had an atmosphere. It's not the same thing at all now. Of course we are much too early. But still . . .'

'We might give you a few ideas,' said the mare. 'You look as if you need them.'

'Come along Suzy.' He sounded vexed. 'Finish your drink and we'll try somewhere else.'

'I'm all for that,' said Suzy, 'because I really don't think I'm going down very well here. One of the girls at the other end of the room is going to come across and slap my face any minute.'

'Which one?' said Gilbert turning to look. 'Where?'

'The one with the magnificent breasts,' said Suzy.

A girl with beautiful breasts and a very slim body was staring at her with an extremely angry expression.

'Very bad tempered,' said Gilbert.

'She's getting quite het up,' Suzy said.

'Yes I see,' said Gilbert.

'She thinks I'm here to stare and jeer. You can't blame her.'

The woman who had first met them came up to their table. 'Are any of these girls annoying you?'

'Why no,' said Suzy. 'Absolutely not. We think them charming, don't we Gilbert?'

Gilbert didn't answer.

63

The woman glanced meaningly at the two girls and walked away.

'Venez donc,' said the mare. 'Come upstairs. For you it will be only three hundred francs. And the champagne.'

'No,' said Gilbert. 'I regret but no. Not this evening,' and in English, 'That's quite enough of that. Let's depart.'

The girls knew that the clients were dissatisfied and intended to leave.

The dark girl was silent. But the mare began a long rapid speech to which Gilbert listened with a wry smile.

'She wants us to stump up, of course,' he said at last. 'I suppose she thinks it a good idea to harp on the difficulties of her profession. Same old miseries. No splendours. Not any more. Sad, isn't it?' He laughed.

The dark girl jumped up and hit the table with her fist so hard that her glass fell over.

'Et qu'est-ce que tu veux que ça leur fasse?' she said loudly. 'Qu'est-ce que tu veux que ça leur fasse?'

'Drama!' said Gilbert. 'What do you think it matters to them, she said.'

'Yes. Gilbert, we can't walk out and not give these girls a sou.'

'They've had their drinks,' said Gilbert.

'Two cherries in brandy. Not much. Let me give them something, will you?'

'Well,' said Gilbert, 'if I do, will you promise to come on somewhere else? Somewhere where they'll put a bit more pep into it.'

'Yes,' said Suzy, 'if you want me to.'

'All right. Here you are then.' He handed her his wallet. 'Give them each – ' He marked 10 on the table with his cigarette. 'That's quite enough.' He turned away to look at the angry girl.

Suzy opened his wallet and took out two notes. She folded them carefully and gave one to each girl. Each smiled and slipped the note into the top of her sock.

'You permit me?' said the dark one. She took off the medal

and, giving it to Suzy, kissed her warmly. 'I will be happy to see any friend of yours who visits Paris.'

Dédé was printed on one side of the medal; on the other the address.

'Alors,' said the mare briskly. 'Merci bien m'sieur et dame. Au 'voir. A la prochaine.'

'I wish they'd go away,' Suzy said.

'Allez-vous-en,' said Gilbert.

No one took any notice of them as they walked down the long room.

'Bonsoir Madame. Bonsoir Monsieur,' said the woman at the door.

They were outside.

'That was rather a fiasco,' Gilbert said. 'Sorry. It won't be difficult to find a more amusing place. I'll get a taxi.'

'Yes,' said Suzy. 'But perhaps I ought to tell you that I gave those girls a fiver each.'

'You did what?' Gilbert said. He opened his wallet and was silent. His silence lasted so long that Suzy couldn't bear it any longer. She said excitedly: 'Why shouldn't they have some money? Why shouldn't they have some money?'

'If you feel like that about it,' said Gilbert, 'why don't you try giving away your own instead of making free with someone else's?'

'Because I haven't got any,' said Suzy. 'That's easy.'

'Of course,' Gilbert said. 'Other people are always expected to pay for your oh-so-beautiful ideas. And all such bloody hypocrisy. You don't care at all really. When you'd given those girls my money you were only too anxious to see the last of them, weren't you?'

'Oh no, it wasn't that,' Suzy said. 'I thought we'd better go before there was any chance of your finding out.'

'What did you imagine I'd do? Make a row? Try to get the money back?'

'I didn't know what you'd do,' Suzy said. 'So it seemed best to get away quickly.'

'Well thanks a lot.' He walked on, to Suzy's relief, still talking in a level voice.

'And it shows how little you know about these things. If those girls had done all their stunts, all their stunts, a hundred francs would have been a royal tip. A royal tip. You've given them ten pounds for nothing at all. I'll be a laughing stock. That bit at the end was a fake. It was the "cinéma" for the clients who can't be persuaded upstairs. And you fell for it. I'll be a laughing stock,' he repeated.

'No, I don't think it was a fake,' Suzy said.

But she remembered how confidingly he had handed her his wallet and began to feel guilty.

'Ten quid isn't so very much. And you had a wad of fivers in that wallet. Was what I did so awful? Just think how you'll be received when you go back. The tall handsome Englishman who gives ten quid for nothing at all. You'll be a legend not a laughing stock.'

They'd reached the end of the street.

'A bus that will take you back to Montparnasse stops near here,' said Gilbert stiffly.

They waited. A woman's scarlet hat was lying in the gutter.

'Poor old hat,' said Suzy. 'Poor poor old hat. Someone ought to write a poem about that hat.' She was still holding Dédé's medal.

'Just a word to the wise before we part,' Gilbert said. 'Don't hang onto that medal. I know you, you'll leave it on your night table and whoever brings up your breakfast will see it. Better not.'

'They won't care either,' said Suzy.

'That's what you think. Better not. Believe you me.'

Suzy began to giggle. She arranged the medal carefully under the red hat and holding up her hand said solemnly, 'Rest in Peace in the name of Allah the Compassionate, the Merciful.'

'Here comes your bus,' said Gilbert. 'It stops quite near the Dôme and I suppose that you can find your way from there.'

'Yes I'll be all right. Au 'voir Gilbert. A la prochaine.'

'There's not going to be a next time,' said Gilbert as he walked away.

Suzy got into the bus relieved that it was half empty. She sat down and listened to the voices in her head as she thought about the evening.

'Same old miseries. No more splendour. Not now. Et qu'est-ce que tu veux que ça leur fasse?'

HAYASHI FUMIKO TOKYO

from

Vagabond's Song

TRANSLATED BY ELIZABETH HANSON

A song of sorrow
Becomes a song
Of mere smoke

Women are tossed about like flags in a breeze, I think as I wait in this long line. These women around me wouldn't be here if their circumstances were better. It is their need for work that binds them.

Unemployment is an assault, your life becomes confused like that of an unchaste woman. What does it mean, that I can't get a job that pays a mere thirty yen per month? With five yen I could buy some good quality Akita rice. I would cook it to the right fluffiness and eat it with *takuan* pickles. This is all I ask. Can't something be done for me?

The line grows shorter; some come out of the door smiling, others look disappointed. Those of us still waiting by the door gradually become irritable. More than a hundred of us are waiting to apply for two jobs available at this wholesale grain store. Finally it is my turn. In comparing our qualifications, the employer looks first at appearance, build, and weight. Exposed to stares for a few moments, I am told I will be notified by mail. I'm used to this procedure, but still, it's distasteful. How unfortunate that I was born. If one is exceptionally beautiful, that is fortune enough. I have nothing. Nothing except this strong body.

I always fail miserably at making a living, this most important of human occupations. I'm like a cheap ready-made dress, bound to fall apart. The boss has very keen eyes. He won't hire a woman like me.

But if I were to get the job, I'd work so hard for my thirty yen a month that I'd cough blood. I'm tired of spending evenings working at that stall. I'm truly sick of it. I'm tired of breathing dust, I'm tired of looking up at people standing in front of me, I'm tired of forcing smiles. It's humiliating. More than anything I want to go to huge Russia. Hey, Mr Barin, Barin. Russia is much, much larger than Japan. How pleasant it must be, if it's a country with fewer women than men.

I'll buy some ink on my way home.

'I would like very much to see you.
   'How I would like some money.
   'Even ten yen would be most adequate.
   'I long to eat a bowl of Chinese noodles.
   'I want to visit the theater.
   'I'd love to go to Korea, even to Manchuria, to work.
   'It would be wonderful to see you, even once.
   'And I truly would like some money.'

I wrote to him, but nothing will come of it. He's already married. To console myself I compose some lyrics to a song.
   Nighttime.
   I can't sleep, so I turn on the light and read a tattered copy of Eugene O'Neill. The landlord, who is a carpenter, works late into the night with his lathe, making toy tops out of wood. In this world we all must work day and night in order to eat. The mosquitoes buzz noisily but I can't afford a mosquito net. I try burning a heap of sawdust on a plate to get rid of them. Hardy mosquitoes, noisy mosquitoes. I wish I could buy my mother a new summer kimono, but I can't.

*

August — .

A bright day. The trees around the Junija Shintō shrine are a blinding green. A man leads the shrine horse, unsaddled, around the pond. The horse, covered with sweat, looks like velvet. The cries of cicadas rise.

The banner in front of the shaved ice shop doesn't stir.

Mother and I walk along with bundles on our backs. It's dreadfully hot. Summer in Tokyo is stifling.

We walk to Shinjuku to save streetcar fare and then buy five skewers of grilled dumplings from a place called Miyoshino in Narukozaka. Drinking cup after cup of tea, for a few moments I feel content.

O'Neill was a nameless sailor, who spent his time wandering; as a child he was incorrigible, and as an adult he boarded a ship bound for Buenos Aires and led a life full of adventure. After he became famous, such tales of his life didn't sound particularly strange. Maybe I will write a play. A fantastic, highly original play. Or perhaps a sad one. I wonder if O'Neill was always tragically sad.

No doubt there were times when he felt happy enough to hum a tune to himself.

Staggering under her load, the pretty little thing walks the streets of the hot city. I don't care what happens. I'm desperate. My shadow, reflected sharply on the street, creeps along like a toad.

Why did my poor mother give birth to me? It doesn't matter that I'm illegitimate, that's not my mother's fault. How can I blame her? You find illegitimate children no matter where you go in the world. That's the way life is. Women live to have children. They don't worry about formalities. If a woman likes a man, she surrenders her body to him.

At a barbershop at Kagurazaka I'm given a drink of water.

Today is the temple festival. I should be busy at the stall this evening.

I watch groups of pretty geisha pass; the man who sells *shinobu* grass and the goldfish vendor are setting up their stands. Today I have a spot next to a woman who sells those paper flowers that expand when you put them in a glass of water.

After setting up my stall, I sit on a mat under an umbrella. A blazing sunset. Where does it come from, I wonder? Heat like a sizzling calm on an ocean. A ridiculous number of people are passing by this evening, but it doesn't look like I'll sell many pairs of socks or underwear. Mother has gone on an errand to Shitaya.

In front of a hardware stall, a man has put out his checkered awning and is selling fancy beetles that children like to keep in little bamboo cages. A vendor of Chinese medicine passes.

A man in a cotton kimono, a towel around his neck, rides his bicycle down the sloping street, holding a polished wooden box with handles.

Scenes of a bustling city – no one pays any attention to a lone woman crouched below an umbrella.

EXTRACT TWO

January –

A clear, crisp day. The snow is almost blinding. A woman in her forties sits on her bed, enjoying a cigarette. The cotton quilt, which has no cover, looks greasy. The walls are covered with newspaper, the tatami mats are balding and yellowed, the ceiling is stained. Melting snow runs in the gutters. If I listen carefully, the snow dripping from the eaves sounds like the beats of a festival drum. Everyone is up, transients getting themselves ready for the day. I open the window, reach out and take a handful of snow from the roof, then wash my face with it. I put some cold cream on my face, then rub two circles of powder into my cheeks. My hair I arrange so that my covered ears look like small dumplings. I feel itchy around my ears.

A bird is singing. The railroad tracks vibrate. In the morning the streets are a mass of mud. Even so, everyone is alive, this poor part of town where people imagine setting off on journeys.

The woman in her thirties who slept beside me has a silver watch. Last night she told me again and again about how well-off she once was. Now her purple velveteen *tabi* socks are filthy and torn.

Mother and I have three useless bundles wrapped in scarves. Without any particular goal in mind, I leave Tamaga. This cheap boarding house has become my haven, my Palermo.

The brilliance of wide open spaces. Nothing is obscure. Only my heart is heavy as I go out into the slushy, muddy streets. The telephone poles, like thin crucifixes, shine in the sunlight. These poles and the streets are all convenient companions for travelling into degradation. I'm tired of this life of nakedness. Perhaps I should throw myself at the car of some rich aristocrat and then I'll be summoned to him . . . How lonely it is to be young. There's nothing so great about it . . . My hands are swollen like dumplings. At the base of my fingers are dimples. When I was in school, the teacher called these my 'dimpled hands'. Smiling hands. Even now my hands are smiling.

Doesn't anyone have a use for a girl who looks as if she just came from a mountain village? There is no point in asking for an advance from houses in the red-light district.

I leave Mother at our lodgings and set off into the muddy streets, going from café to café. In the morning the back entrances are dirty and depressing. Courage, courage, I tell myself, but it doesn't help. I decide to take a job at a rundown place called the Golden Star, better suited to a name like 'Star of Hades'. Here, I'll set off fireworks. Nearby is a group of brothels; they say the café does a good business. A little girl in the kitchen gives me a cracker. I feel tears well suddenly in my eyes. At a shop I buy a pair of new *tabi* socks for fifteen sen.

Our room costs thirty-five sen apiece. Since we were able

to pay seventy sen in advance, I feel secure there. I buy an order of fried oysters and white rice to share with mother.

That evening I go to work at the Golden Star. Myself included, there are three waitresses. I'm the youngest. I wonder if I can find my Nevrodov. If I try to look agreeable and carefree, I should be able to earn some decent tips, even if I am a bit plump. I'm as determined as most bargirls. Ah, what is a tip, anyway? No different from begging. A transaction that requires you to look agreeable with all your body, all your strength. How far I am from making my living with my writing. In the dark, stinky bathroom, I stick my tongue out, saying I can't see any longer. I have no hope of writing anything. I can't do anything. Writing poetry is complete foolishness. What about Baudelaire? Heine's big, loose neck-tie was only a decoration. I wonder how those two managed to make a living.

'Nous avons, vous avez. Pardon, monsieur.' This means something like 'Please excuse me'. Isn't that right?

I leave my kimono jacket with the landlady and borrow two yen. One yen, fifty sen I give to Mother, then I go to the public bath on the main street. Looking in the mirror at myself, I see first a healthy child. My skin is plump and pink, nothing like an adult's. From my neck up I look as if I have a kettle on my head. Waitresses come swarming in, chatting with each other. The bathhouse attendant is busily massaging a woman's shoulders. I notice a painting of a waterfall and posters advertising face powder and obstetricians. It has been so many days since I've taken a bath, it feels strange.

The dim neon signs look out of place in the snowy streets. For my pen name, should I try Yodogimi? Or Kōmori no Yasu? I imagine the stage of Sadanji in the play *Kirihitoha*. Tokyo is a place where many things happen. Even though these are mostly painful, fortunately I forget them quickly. I'll call myself Yumiko, which means Miss Archer. A bow is tough, a consolation. Please hit right on the mark.

A strange customer gives me two yen. An auspicious occasion. At a used book stall beside the muddy road I spend

73

fifty sen on a book of memoirs by Tolstoy and Chekhov. These were published on March 18, 1924. I wonder if I too could write such a book . . .

'I believe that anyone who writes stories must know the beginning and the end. We novelists are excellent liars. And one must be brief. As brief as possible . . .' Chekhov wrote this.

By eleven o'clock there are no customers in the café. As I sit reading in a corner, the big woman, Katsumi, says 'You're nearsighted, aren't you?' The other waitress is Oshin. She has two children and commutes back and forth from the shop. Katsumi has dark skin and so rubs it with peroxide. I have decided not to use face powder. I have no interest at all in tampering with my face. Katsumi is the only waitress who boards at the café. This morning, the little girl who gave me the cracker came to the shop, wearing a muslin vest. A thin, sickly child.

Katsumi asks me if I want to go to a circus the next day at Taisōji Temple. There is supposed to be a freak show as well.

I return to the boarding house at two a.m., exhausted. The same lodgers are here tonight.

Unable to sleep, I read by the small lamp beside my pillow.

HIRABAYASHI TAIKO TOKYO

from
Self-Mockery

TRANSLATED BY YUKIKO TANAKA

With a hand on my shabby winter kimono pressing against my left breast, I walk with faltering steps. I have been walking like this for some time, resisting the temptation to open the front of the kimono to see what might be causing the pain. It seems to be coming from somewhere deep inside the breast. The street stretching in front of me is covered by a thin mask of dust: it has the look of a second-hand furniture store. When I get to the corner bakery where a khaki awning hangs all the way down to prevent the dust from coming in, I stop and look at my breast, unable to resist the temptation any longer. Like a balloon that's lost its air, it hangs there loosely. Just as an old scar tells of pain once endured, my breast shows that it has once nursed. I hate looking at these breasts, for I see there, on the sagging skin, the clear image of my ugly self. But I don't find anything wrong with my left breast now. As I close the front of the kimono and resume walking, I again feel the surge of self-disgust whirling up inside of me.

Perhaps I've been walking with a faint sneer on my face, exposing my yellow teeth. People turn around as they pass, to take another look at me, a strange-looking woman. 'Who could stop a boulder rolling down from the top of a mountain?' I utter these words which come to my mind out of nowhere. Repeating the words over and over, I walk aimlessly. My eyes fix on the faces of the passersby with the rudeness of a fly that stays on your skin. This keeps the scenes of the last night and this morning from coming back to my mind like a ball of yarn spitting out an endless thread.

A brown streetcar covered by a layer of dust approaches, ringing a loud bell to warn the man who is digging up the ground between the rails. The man swings his pickax up and down mechanically as if he were a doll on a spring; he does not hear the bell and the expression on his sweaty face, languid as a high noon of late spring days, does not change.

'Watch out, you fool,' shouts the conductor, showing his irritation as he winds the emergency brake. The streetcar has momentum and does not stop right away; the old conductor becomes desperate. When I come out of my reverie, I am staring at the streetcar which has stopped in the middle of the street right in front of the construction worker. They are within touching distance from each other.

'A brake that cannot stop the car,' I say to myself. Both this expression and the one about the boulder that cannot be halted are apt descriptions of my present circumstances. Then, remembering the desperate look on the face of the conductor, I smile and say to myself, 'My own brake cannot stop anything, even if I try harder than that old conductor.' I want to burst out laughing.

Ever since I left Yada's apartment I've been walking, not knowing exactly where I was heading, but now it looks like I'm near Dōgenzaka. Divided by the stream of cars, pedestrians are walking down both sides of the street, loathsome expressions on their faces, moving their sweaty bodies and kicking the skirts of their full-length winter kimonos.

In my eyes this busy street filled with greasy faces of hot, excited people is a vivid pattern of many colours. I feel I am the only one who doesn't harmonize. I am a solid, grey thread.

The face powder that stains the collar of my kimono bothers me. Not having had enough sleep the previous night, I am exhausted. Although I have a one yen bill in my pocket – the money Yada gave me – I don't feel like spending it on train fare. But at the top of the hill I can no longer walk and so I wait at a streetcar stop.

Inside, the streetcar is stuffy, filled with the odour of sweating young men. Hanging onto a strap, I call forth Yada – his face and his scant hair – and I draw his image on the steamy windowpane. I find, surprisingly, that the evocation of his face is no longer so disturbing. It could just as well have been a picture of a total stranger drawn on a piece of paper by someone else.

'Is this my true self: an ugly woman?' I ask myself calmly.

The streetcar jerks, throwing me toward the young man holding the strap next to me. The movement is so sudden that most of the standing passengers lose their balance. The young man, too, falls sharply against the man standing on his other side. The way I totter, however, is ridiculous. The young man is wearing a fine spring suit and he carries a walking stick on his left arm. He gives me a quick glance and then straightens his head and concentrates on the advertisement in front of his eyes. He might be sneering, I think as I look up at the side of his face. I have often seen young men sneer the minute they passed by me, disappointed at what they have just seen. This young man seems to be the kind who classifies women by their appearance, who enjoys golf and going to parties at the Imperial Hotel.

When the streetcar stops at the next station, I lean over him, and when it starts up, I press my face against his arm, feeling the soft fabric of his suit. When he finally realizes that the shabby-looking woman next to him is leaning against him deliberately, the young man frowns, stares at me for a second, then moves to the next strap. I move down one strap too, pretending it is a natural course of action. Shocked, the young man looks around as if seeking witnesses to my peculiar act. When the passenger who was sitting in front of him gets off, the young man takes the empty seat in an ungentleman-like way, pushing me away with his elbow. So, when the streetcar makes another jerky movement, I place my hand right on his thigh, pretending that I simply couldn't help it. The young man, hate clearly showing on his pale face, looks at me for a moment, stands up and walks to the door. I take his seat, feeling pleased, as if something refreshing flowed down into my chest.

The conductor comes around to sell tickets; I give him the crumpled one yen bill Yada gave me, muttering to myself, 'I wonder if you know how this bill came to me.' I feel strange somehow, and stare at the conductor.

'One yen bill, eh? I'm not sure I have change,' he says, holding the bill in one hand and opening his purse with the other.

'Where are you going?'

'To . . .'

'And where did you get on, Miss?'

'At Ōhashi,' I respond smoothly.

'Ōhashi?' he says, giving me a quick glance. Then he starts counting coins onto my palm. I lose my composure and feel the blood surging up to my head. Seeing that I'm upset, the conductor seems to have decided that I lied about where I got on. He gives me another sharp look before he moves on. I did not lose my composure because I had told him a lie. When he gave me that sparkling look typical of young men, I hesitated, sensing that he had seen everything I had pushed away to the back of my mind. The conductor wore a silver-coloured medal around his neck and his long hair showed under his hat. The contour of his face, with his well-shaped nose, was pleasing. All in all he was quite good-looking. I feel relieved after he leaves; I am able to fold my arms and relax.

'But that was a legitimate one yen bill, properly issued by the Bank of Japan,' I tell the conductor silently as I get off the streetcar. Instead of verbalizing it, I smile at him.

After I get off the streetcar, I walk away from the main street and come to a fish store. Inside the dark store I stand for a long time, staring at the fish displayed with their glittering scales. The proprietor of the store stands patiently, waiting for me to say something. But I don't say a word, feeling sick at the sight of the red salmon fillets that have two yellow flies on them. The man looks at me doubtfully and starts walking toward the back of the store.

'Oh, I want this one, please,' I say abruptly. The man waves a few sticks of burning incense over the fish to get rid of the flies. Some dried-out fish scales stick to his hand. I leave the fish store, and as I'm walking along, I think about my strange conduct in the streetcar. I cannot help smiling.

It's late afternoon when I return, my face grey with dust, to the barber shop behind a bamboo field, where I rent a room on the second floor. My mind is stretched out, vacant. I tell myself, 'Something will work out. I just have to go on doing what I can.' I cannot find any other words of consolation for myself. I go inside without making any noise and take off my *geta* clogs. Koyama sees me when he comes down to use the bathroom.

'Where have you been? Wandering around all this time?' he says, not realizing that the old landlady is working in the next room. His voice is surprisingly loud. I do not respond, but the old woman lifts her inflamed eyes from her sewing and looks at me, a woman who did not come home the night before.

'I was out there doing things you can't imagine, simply to keep us together; I did it because I want to be with you.' Composing sentences like these in my mind, I go up the stairs, silent. Since morning I have repeated these words to myself, the words with which someone who understands my actions might console me. I have even secretly enjoyed the sense of beauty that accompanies this dark despair of mine. Now my legs are heavy as if they were chained.

The woman who casts her chastity away in order to save her marriage has been approved throughout our history. Her sacrifice has even been praised as a sign of womanly virtue. In my case, however, it is different. I do not have a claim upon Koyama that warrants such sacrifice. Besides, I am a woman who has known three men, each of whom I left without much agony. Koyama, who abandoned a communist group after two imprisonments, has been writing and producing large numbers of unsolicited manuscripts over the past four years. He sends them off tirelessly; they are, however,

79

all returned one after another as if there were rubber bands attached to them. He is a wretched man who conceals his real reason for living with me, namely to live off my earnings.

'Can't you go to someone you know and ask for just a little? I won't ask again,' he pleads every time we find ourselves with no money. He looks at me, narrowing his attractive eyes in an attempt to read my mind. Each time he promises 'not again' or 'only this time', but there have been too many 'the last time's'.

'I can't do that,' I tell him curtly and look straight into his face, scornfully. By 'someone' he means the men I had sexual relationships with in the past. Yesterday, too, we exchanged the same words till I got impatient and decided to do exactly what he asked me to. I had already told him that Yada had refused to loan me money. No sense giving money to a woman who lives with another man, Yada said.

Still wearing my dirty socks, I sit on the tatami floor which is old and discoloured, a pale yellow. From the window I see the strong afternoon sun through the bamboos, casting lines on the wet soil. I listen for the footsteps of Koyama coming up the stairs but there is no sound. Perhaps he has gone somewhere. While I sit and gaze outside the window, I become aware of how thirsty I am. Many thoughts go through my mind.

I wanted to believe the axiom which states that 'the just are poor'. I once knew a working-class woman who had no understanding of her husband's position; everytime he joined a strike, she railed against him. 'Only fools are agitated into destructive action,' she would say, scornfully. Though the husband was not the type to be easily affected by his wife's words, there were times when I saw he was deeply disturbed. The invisible pressure that such women exert upon their husbands must help the workers lose many a battle against the capitalists. Those women cannot help themselves – the pressure of the old customs, internalized, encourages their conservative views – but I found it difficult to suppress my disgust whenever I encountered one of them. I had wondered on occasion if I shared their attitudes. But in the case of my relationship with Koyama, the situation was reversed. In fact I nearly called him a waif once in order to humiliate him. Although my past was not without stains, that should not allow Koyama to get the upper hand in our relationship. He puts the burden of bringing in money on my shoulders because he looks down on me. To him I am a woman who has so many blemishes that she has no choice but to please her man in whatever way she can.

And as for me, I have worn myself out trying to find a man who lived up to my idealistic notions. In the process I have lost a fresh attitude toward my own life. I feel wretched; I am a woman who has lost self-control, who is persuaded by the trifling force of a hair. I had a child by the man who was my first love. The child, born on a rusty bed in a dismal charity hospital room in Manchuria, died, like a candle blown out, while I was bedridden with post-delivery beriberi. The child's father had been taken to prison, accused for something he himself had not quite understood. That happened on the morning of my first labour pains. My life of restless wandering began then.

The sagging skin of my abdomen is evidence that I delivered a child. My breasts are as limp as the dead body of a cat. At the bottom of my suitcase is a small box containing an urn wrapped in a piece of imitation brocade. I, a woman who left her first lover in a cold prison cell and then went from one man to another as if guided by some unknown force, have not been able to discard this small box which, when I shake it, makes a faint rattling sound as a toy would. More than a few times Koyama and I have exchanged foul words over this little box. He has accepted my past in his rational mind, but his weak nature dictates that he return to that time in my life whenever he needs to defend his position in our relationship.

TOVE DITLEVSEN COPENHAGEN

from

Early Spring

TRANSLATED BY TIINNA NUNNALLY

It's fall and the storm rattles the butcher's signs. The trees on Enghavevej have lost nearly all of their leaves, which almost cover the ground with their yellow and reddish-brown carpet that looks like my mother's hair when the sun plays in it, and you suddenly discover it's not totally black. The unemployed are freezing, but still standing erect with their hands deep in their pockets and a burned-out pipe between their teeth. The streetlamps have just been lit, and now and then the moon peeks out between racing, shifting clouds. I always think there is a mystical understanding between the moon and the street, like between two sisters who have grown old together and no longer need any language to communicate with each other. We're walking in the fleeting dusk, Ruth and I, and soon we'll have to leave the street, which makes us eager for something to happen before the day is over. When we reach Gasværksvej, where we usually turn around, Ruth says, 'Let's go down and look at the whores. There are probably some who have started.' A whore is a woman who does it for money, which seems to me much more understandable than to do it for free. Ruth told me about it, and since I think the word is ugly, I've found another in a book: 'Lady-of-the-evening'. It sounds much nicer and more romantic. Ruth tells me everything about those kinds of things; for her, the adults have no secrets. She has also told me about Scabie Hans and Rapunzel, and I can't comprehend it, since I think Scabie

82

Hans is a very old man. And he has Pretty Lili, besides. I wonder whether men can love two women at once. For me the grownups' world is still just as mysterious. I always picture Istedgade as a beautiful woman who's lying on her back with her hair near Enghaveplads. At Gasværksvej, which forms the boundary between decent people and the depraved, her legs part, and sprinkled over them like freckles are the welcoming hotels and the bright, noisy taverns, where later in the night the police cars drive by to pick up their scandalously intoxicated and quarrelsome victims. That I know from Edvin, who is four years older than me, and is allowed to be out until ten o'clock at night. I admire Edvin greatly when he comes home in his blue DUI shirt and talks politics with my father. Lately they're both very outraged over Sacco and Vanzetti, whose pictures stare out from the poster displays and the newspaper. They look so handsome with their dark foreign faces, and I also think it's too bad they're going to be executed for something they didn't do. But I just can't get as excited about it as my father, who yells and pounds the table whenever he discusses it with Uncle Peter. He's a Social Democrat like my father and Edvin, but he doesn't think that Sacco and Vanzetti deserve a better fate since they're anarchists. 'I don't care,' yells my father furiously and pounds the table. 'Miscarriage of justice is miscarriage of justice, even if it concerns a conservative!' I know that's the worst thing you can be. Recently, when I asked whether I could join the Ping Club because all the other girls in my class were members, my father looked at my mother sternly, as if I were a victim of her subversive influence in political matters, and said, 'There, you see, Mutter. Now she's becoming a reactionary. It will probably end with us subscribing to *Berlingske Tidende*!'

Down by the train station life is in full swing. Drunken men stagger around singing with their arms around each other's shoulders, and out of Café Charles rolls a fat man whose bald head strikes the pavement a couple of times before he lies still at our feet. Two officers come over to him and kick him emphatically in the side, which makes him get up with a pitiful howl. They pull him roughly to his feet and push him away when he once again tries to go into the den of iniquity. As they continue down the street, Ruth puts her fingers in her mouth and sends a long whistle after them, a talent I envy. Near Helgolandsgade there's a big crowd of laughing, noisy children, and when we go over there I see that it's Curly Charles, who is standing in the middle of the road, putting the steaming horse droppings in his mouth. All the while he's singing an indescribably filthy song that makes the children scream with laughter and give him shouts of encouragement in the hope he'll provide them with more entertainment. His eyes roll wildly. I find him tragic and horrifying, but pretend he amuses me because of Ruth, who laughs loudly along with the others. Of whores, however, we see only a couple of older, fat women who energetically wiggle their hips in an apparently vain attempt to attract the favours of an audience driving slowly by. This disappoints me greatly, because I thought all of them were like Ketty, whose evening errands in the city Ruth has also explained to me. On the way home, we go through Revalsgade, where once an old woman who owned a cigar store was murdered. We also stop in front of the haunted house on Matthæusgade and stare up at the fourth floor window where a little girl was murdered last year by Red Carl, a stoker my father worked with at the Ørsted Works. None of us dares go past that house alone at night. In the doorway at home, Gerda and Tin Snout are standing in such a tight embrace that you can't tell their figures apart in the dark. I hold my breath until I'm out in the courtyard because there's always a rancid stench of beer and urine. I feel oppressed as I go up the stairs. The dark side of sex yawns toward me more and more, and it's becoming harder to cover it up with the unwritten, trembling words my heart is always whispering. The door next to Gerda's opens quietly as I go by, and Mrs Poulsen signals to me to come inside. According to my mother, she's 'shabby-genteel', but I know that you can't be both shabby and genteel. She has a lodger who my mother contemptuously calls 'a fine duke' even though he's a mailman and supports Mrs Poulsen just as if they were married; they have no children, however. I know from Ruth that they live together as man and wife. Reluctantly, I obey the command and step into a living room exactly like ours except that there's a piano that is missing many keys. I sit down on the very edge of a chair and Mrs Poulsen sits on the sofa with a prying look in her pale blue eyes. 'Tell me something, Tove,' she says ingratiatingly. 'Do you know whether many gentlemen come to visit Miss Andersen?' I immediately make my eyes blank and stupid and let my jaw drop slightly. 'No,' I say, feigning astonishment, 'I don't think so.' 'But you and your mother are over there so much. Think a little. Haven't you ever seen any gentlemen in her apartment? Not even in the evenings?' 'No,' I lie, terrified. I'm afraid of this woman who wants to harm Ketty in some way. My mother has forbidden me to visit Ketty anymore, and she only goes over there herself when my father is not around. Mrs Poulsen gets nothing else out of me and lets me go with a certain coolness. Several days later a petition goes around in the building and because of it, my parents have a fight when they come to bed and think I'm asleep. 'I'm going to sign it,' says my father, 'for the children's sake. You can at least protect them from witnessing the worst filth.' 'It's those old bitches,' says my mother hotly. 'They're jealous because she's young and pretty and happy. They can't stand me, either.' 'Stop comparing yourself to a whore,' snarls my father. 'Even though I don't have a steady job, you've never had to earn your own living – don't forget that!' It's awful to listen to, and it seems as though the fight is about something totally different, something they don't have words for. Soon the day arrives when Ketty and her mother are sitting out on the street on top of all their plush furniture, which a policeman, pacing back and forth, is guarding. Ketty looks right through all the people, full of contempt, holding her delicate umbrella up against the rain. She smiles at me,

though, and says, 'Good-bye, Tove. Take care of yourself.'
A little later they drive away in the moving van and I never
see them again.

THE THIRTIES

D OROTHY PARKER'S 'The Standard of Living' is
about female friendship and shopping. Aptly for
this post-Crash, Depression decade, it ends on an
inflationary note.

Shopping needn't imply actually buying things; just
looking, an activity that forms a significant part of city life.
Annabel and Midge mince along impervious to male
onlookers, their fantasies and mutually-enhanced confidence
their only collateral on Fifth Avenue.

Shopping has been women's best pretext for dawdling in
the city. The dazzling profusion of the department store
bewildered Virginia Woolf's time-travelling androgyne,
Orlando, on arrival in Oxford Street in 1928: '. . . Each time
the lift stopped and flung its doors open, there was another
slice of the world displayed with all the smells of that world
clinging to it . . .', stirring memories of her/his centuries-long
past, and re-splintering a tenuous identity. It may well be
that shopping is about nostalgia, perhaps some blissful
infant plenitude unconsciously evoked by all that
abundance. But it is most of all about potential
transformation: 'This is a beginning. Out of this warm room
that smells of furs I'll go to all the lovely places I've ever
dreamed of. This is the beginning', Anna tells herself at the
dress shop in Jean Rhys's *Voyage in the Dark* (1934). Anna
notices women's faces in Oxford Street: '. . . when they

stopped to look you saw that their eyes were fixed on the future. "If I could buy this, then of course I'd be quite different."'

In the fifties the post-war boom turned shopping into consumerism. Disillusionment with this aspect of city life, the individual's seduction by the glossy images of advertisements and women's magazines, will haunt Elsa Triolet's sixties trilogy, *L'Age de nylon* (*The Age of Nylon*), whose first volume *Roses à crédit* (*Roses on Credit*) laments a Paris of hire purchase and rising tower blocks, and cafés with plastic décor and alienating atmosphere. By contrast, the 'Paris Dreaming' of 1938 is a city to fight for and belong to (Triolet was herself a voluntary exile, a rootless Russian who took Paris as her home).

The dreamy imagery of this piece is clearly surrealist-influenced. Triolet was never active in the Surrealist movement, but she had known those who were, and she married one of its former leading members, Louis Aragon. This oneiric vividness conjures the Paris of 'deserted streets in which whistles and shots dictate the outcome' which Walter Benjamin evokes in his essay on the significance of Surrealism.[1] For the Surrealists, not only is the city of Paris itself 'the most dreamed-of of their objects . . .', but 'only revolt exposes its Surrealist face'. It is interesting that Triolet's title just happens to be 'Paris qui rêve' (*Paris Dreaming*) and not *Paris Revé(e)* (*Paris Dreamed-of*); the active verb makes the city the masculine dreamer rather than the often feminine dreamed-of of the masculine imagination.

Its foggy, filmic dream language nonetheless constructs this Paris as a mythic place, though by this stage in the decade its scenario of violence was becoming increasingly real. The violence is there too in *The Beauties and Furies*, which depicts the city a few years earlier, in the upheavals prior to the Popular Front government of 1936. Stead, though a radical, was not one to take any myths at face value, however anti-Fascist. As far as myths are concerned, *The Beauties and Furies* is a novel of merciless deconstruction. The Paris described in these extracts from it becomes increasingly a matter of imaginative projection. First the city offered to the runaway wife, Elvira, who has just arrived from London to be with Oliver, her lover. Later, there is Oliver's romantic contemplation of the river and the city from the Pont des Arts, everything seen in radiant distance that accords with his sense of momentary omnipotence – his overwrought pride at having marched with the proletariat, his feverish sense of masculine freedoms, suggesting a Beat *avant la lettre*, restless to be on the road. Then, with the mysterious young Coromandel, Oliver's Paris assumes shadowy, Gothic outlines. The city is protean, yet Oliver sees Elvira and Coromandel with the same subsuming optic.

For Stead, there is no easy place to be in a world so unjust; no place, be it a city or an ideology, where anyone has the right to feel cosily at home, if this means appropriating the difficult realities of others into a comfortable version of the self, as Oliver so blindly does. Of course this is what fiction so often does and is, this ordering of experience through a narrow individual filter. Stead continually reminds the reader of the denial implicit in this, the exclusion and exploitation, the triumph at the expense of others' loss.

In this decade of nascent dictatorships violence erupted in many of Europe's cities. The very meaning of the city was a source of ideological conflict. To the Nazis it represented a hateful modernity, embodied in the figure of the Jewish intellectual, the Communist and the insubordinate woman. In Irmgard Keun's *After Midnight* (1937), a novel whose darkness is lightened with wit and the elations of youth, nineteen-year-old Sanna spots the bogusness of Nazi pastoralism: 'They keep building bigger and bigger cities . . .' Here, the city, which Sanna frankly prefers to the countryside, is Frankfurt, with memories of Cologne. The novel ends with Sanna's flight into exile. Keun herself had been forced to flee, escaping from the Gestapo after arrest, though returning later to live in hiding, apparently willing to risk danger rather than life where ' "The roofs that you see are not built for you. The bread that you smell is not baked for you. And the speech that you hear is not spoken for you." '

In a century of migrations and exiles, the thirties stands out. The American Agnes Smedley found her way to China in 1929 after some years in Berlin, where she was involved in setting up the city's first birth control clinic. She became a China correspondent for the *Frankfurter Zeitung*. But Smedley was no journalistic bystander. Having been active in the Indian nationalist movement and the German Left, she worked alongside women revolutionaries in Shanghai. 'A Moving Picture of Shanghai' is indeed that, a cinematic montage which cumulatively indicts the imperialism by which this internationally split city is multiply brutalised.

NOTES

1. Surrealism, the Last Snapshot of the European Intelligentsia, in Walter Benjamin, *One Way Street and Other Writings*, translated by Edmund Jephcott and Kingsley Shorter, New Left Books, 1979.

DOROTHY PARKER   NEW YORK

The Standard of Living

Annabel and Midge came out of the tea room with the arrogant slow gait of the leisured, for their Saturday afternoon stretched ahead of them. They had lunched, as was their wont, on sugar, starches, oils, and butter-fats. Usually they ate sandwiches of spongy new white bread greased with butter and mayonnaise; they ate thick wedges of cake lying wet beneath ice cream and whipped cream and melted chocolate gritty with nuts. As alternates, they ate patties, sweating beads of inferior oil, containing bits of bland meat bogged in pale, stiffening sauce; they ate pastries, limber under rigid icing, filled with an indeterminate yellow sweet stuff, not still solid, not yet liquid, like salve that has been left in the sun. They chose no other sort of food, nor did they consider it. And their skin was like the petals of wood anemones, and their bellies were as flat and their flanks as lean as those of young Indian braves.

Annabel and Midge had been best friends almost from the day that Midge had found a job as stenographer with the firm that employed Annabel. By now, Annabel, two years longer in the stenographic department, had worked up to the wages of eighteen dollars and fifty cents a week; Midge was still at sixteen dollars. Each girl lived at home with her family and paid half her salary to its support.

The girls sat side by side at their desks, they lunched together every noon, together they set out for home at the end of the day's work. Many of their evenings and most of their Sundays were passed in each other's company. Often they were joined by two young men, but there was no steadiness to any such quartet; the two young men would give place, unlamented, to two other young men, and lament would have been inappropriate, really, since the newcomers were scarcely distinguishable from their predecessors. Invariably the girls spent the fine idle hours of their hot-weather Saturday afternoons together. Constant use had not worn ragged the fabric of their friendship.

They looked alike, though the resemblance did not lie in their features. It was in the shape of their bodies, their movements, their style, and their adornments. Annabel and Midge did, and completely, all that young office workers are besought not to do. They painted their lips and their nails, they darkened their lashes and lightened their hair, and scent seemed to shimmer from them. They wore thin, bright dresses, tight over their breasts and high on their legs, and tilted slippers, fancifully strapped. They looked conspicuous and cheap and charming.

Now, as they walked across to Fifth Avenue with their skirts swirled by the hot wind, they received audible admiration. Young men grouped lethargically about newsstands awarded them murmurs, exclamations, even – the ultimate tribute – whistles. Annabel and Midge passed without the condescension of hurrying their pace; they held their heads higher and set their feet with exquisite precision, as if they stepped over the necks of peasants.

Always the girls went to walk on Fifth Avenue on their free afternoons, for it was the ideal ground for their favorite game. The game could be played anywhere, and, indeed, was, but the great shop windows stimulated the two players to their best form.

Annabel had invented the game; or rather she had evolved it from an old one. Basically, it was no more than the ancient sport of what-would-you-do-if-you-had-a-million dollars? But Annabel had drawn a new set of rules for it, had narrowed it, pointed it, made it stricter. Like all games, it was the more absorbing for being more difficult.

Annabel's version went like this: You must suppose that somebody dies and leaves you a million dollars, cool. But there is a condition to the bequest. It is stated in the will that you must spend every nickel of the money on yourself.

There lay the hazard of the game. If, when playing it, you forgot, and listed among your expenditures the rental of a new apartment for your family, for example, you lost your turn to the other player. It was astonishing how many – and some of them among the experts, too – would forfeit all their innings by such slips.

It was essential, of course, that it be played in passionate seriousness. Each purchase must be carefully considered and, if necessary, supported by argument. There was no zest to playing wildly. Once Annabel had introduced the game to Sylvia, another girl who worked in the office. She explained the rules to Sylvia and then offered her the gambit 'What would be the first thing you'd do?' Sylvia had not shown the decency of even a second of hesitation. 'Well,' she said, 'the first thing I'd do, I'd go out and hire somebody to shoot Mrs Gary Cooper, and then . . .' So it is to be seen that she was no fun.

But Annabel and Midge were surely born to be comrades, for Midge played the game like a master from the moment she learned it. It was she who added the touches that made the whole thing cozier. According to Midge's innovations, the eccentric who died and left you the money was not anybody you loved, or, for the matter of that, anybody you even knew. It was somebody who had seen you somewhere and had thought, 'That girl ought to have lots of nice things. I'm going to leave her a million dollars when I die.' And the death was to be neither untimely nor painful. Your benefactor, full of years and comfortably ready to depart, was to slip softly away during sleep and go right to heaven. These embroideries permitted Annabel and Midge to play their game in the luxury of peaceful consciences.

Midge played with a seriousness that was not only proper but extreme. The single strain on the girls' friendship had followed an announcement once made by Annabel that the first thing she would buy with her million dollars would be a silver-fox coat. It was as if she had struck Midge across the mouth. When Midge recovered her breath, she cried that she couldn't imagine how Annabel could do such a thing – silver-fox coats were common! Annabel defended her taste with the retort that they were not common, either. Midge then said that they were so. She added that everybody had a silver-fox coat. She went on, with perhaps a slight toss of head, to declare that she herself wouldn't be caught dead in silver fox.

For the next few days, though the girls saw each other as constantly, their conversation was careful and infrequent, and they did not once play their game. Then one morning, as soon as Annabel entered the office, she came to Midge and said that she had changed her mind. She would not buy a silver-fox coat with any part of her million dollars. Immediately on receiving the legacy, she would select a coat of mink.

Midge smiled and her eyes shone. 'I think,' she said, 'you're doing absolutely the right thing.'

Now, as they walked along Fifth Avenue, they played the game anew. It was one of those days with which September is repeatedly cursed; hot and glaring, with slivers of dust in the wind. People drooped and shambled, but the girls carried themselves tall and walked a straight line, as befitted young heiresses on their afternoon promenade. There was no longer need for them to start the game at its formal opening. Annabel went direct to the heart of it.

'All right,' she said. 'So you've got this million dollars. So what would be the first thing you'd do?'

'Well, the first thing I'd do,' Midge said, 'I'd get a mink coat.' But she said it mechanically, as if she were giving the memorized answer to an expected question.

'Yes,' Annabel said, 'I think you ought to. The terribly dark kind of mink.' But she, too, spoke as if by rote. It was too hot; fur, no matter how dark and sleek and supple, was horrid to the thoughts.

They stepped along in silence for a while. Then Midge's eye was caught by a shop window. Cool, lovely gleamings were there set off by chaste and elegant darkness.

'No,' Midge said, 'I take it back. I wouldn't get a mink coat the first thing. Know what I'd do? I'd get a string of pearls. Real pearls.'

Annabel's eyes turned to follow Midge's.

'Yes,' she said, slowly. 'I think that's kind of a good idea. And it would make sense, too. Because you can wear pearls with anything.'

Together they went over to the shop window and stood pressed against it. It contained but one object – a double row of great, even pearls clasped by a deep emerald around a little pink velvet throat.

'What do you suppose they cost?' Annabel said.

'Gee, I don't know,' Midge said. 'Plenty, I guess.'

'Like a thousand dollars?' Annabel said.

'Oh, I guess like more,' Midge said. 'On account of the emerald.'

'Well, like ten thousand dollars?' Annabel said.

'Gee, I wouldn't even know,' Midge said.

The devil nudged Annabel in the ribs. 'Dare you to go in and price them,' she said.

'Like fun!' Midge said.

'Dare you,' Annabel said.

'Why, a store like this wouldn't even be open this afternoon,' Midge said.

'Yes, it is so, too,' Annabel said. 'People just came out. And there's a doorman on. Dare you.'

'Well,' Midge said. 'But you've got to come too.'

They tendered thanks, icily, to the doorman for ushering them into the shop. It was cool and quiet, a broad, gracious room with paneled walls and soft carpet. But the girls wore expressions of bitter disdain, as if they stood in a sty.

A slim, immaculate clerk came to them and bowed. His neat face showed no astonishment at their appearance.

'Good afternoon,' he said. He implied that he would never forget it if they would grant him the favor of accepting his soft-spoken greeting.

'Good afternoon,' Annabel and Midge said together, and in like freezing accents.

'Is there something – ?' the clerk said.

'Oh, we're just looking,' Annabel said. It was as if she flung the words down from a dais.

The clerk bowed.

'My friend and myself merely happened to be passing,' Midge said, and stopped, seeming to listen to the phrase. 'My friend here and myself,' she went on, 'merely happened to be wondering how much are those pearls you've got in your window.'

'Ah, yes,' the clerk said. 'The double rope. That is two hundred and fifty thousand dollars, Madam.'

'I see,' Midge said.

The clerk bowed. 'An exceptionally beautiful necklace,' he said. 'Would you care to look at it?'

'No, thank you,' Annabel said.

'My friend and myself merely happened to be passing,' Midge said.

They turned to go; to go, from their manner, where the tumbrel awaited them. The clerk sprang ahead and opened the door. He bowed as they swept by him.

The girls went on along the Avenue and disdain was still on their faces.

'Honestly!' Annabel said. 'Can you imagine a thing like that?'

'Two hundred and fifty thousand dollars!' Midge said. 'That's a quarter of a million dollars right there!'

'He's got his nerve!' Annabel said.

They walked on. Slowly the disdain went, slowly and completely as if drained from them, and with it went the regal carriage and tread. Their shoulders dropped and they dragged their feet; they bumped against each other, without notice or apology, and caromed away again. They were silent and their eyes were cloudy.

Suddenly Midge straightened her back, flung her head high, and spoke, clear and strong.

'Listen, Annabel,' she said. 'Look. Suppose there was this terribly rich person, see? You don't know this person, but this person has seen you somewhere and wants to do something for you. Well, it's a terribly old person, see? And so this person dies, just like going to sleep, and leaves you ten million dollars. Now, what would be the first thing you'd do?'

ELSA TRIOLET

from *Bonsoir Thérèse*

Paris Dreaming

TRANSLATED BY LIZ HERON

I can see a street, many streets, I can see cafés, shops, people in a hurry and people strolling, I can hear conversation, I can taste wine and the flavour of brioche, and this is why I'm losing sight of Paris. Paris, open up! I don't know the magic word that would make Paris open . . .

Paris, a name that moves us, promising the best of all there is, all that is most forbidden. Paris dreaming, Paris angered . . .

Defying description, defying even love, Paris grey-lipped, tasting of ashes and fire, Paris clasps you to its bosom, its tenderness stifling. Don't waken the sleepwalkers, you would make them fall from the roof whose edge they walk upon; sleep on, people of Paris.

Paris made by men's hands and become a force of nature, which men's hands can no longer hold back. With every brick in house walls, with every chubby-faced cupid in its fountains, with every single column of its monuments, men have given it a measure more of life. You willed this Galatea in the image of a monster unknown.

This fog is unusual for Paris. Menacingly, it envelops the busy streets, the everyday streets, the shops and passersby. Everything is as always in the Métro, people going about their business, reading the evening papers . . .

Wide boulevard Magenta is almost deserted. The street-lamps and windows gleam through the drawn curtains of the fog. Passersby hasten towards the Métro. Figures are caught in outlined isolation, held fast inside the fog. The café windows cast a bright malignant light. Shops that are not already closed have their metal shutters halfway down. The shopkeepers poke out their heads from under them, looking in the direction of place de la République. House doors are ajar; people lurking behind them peer through the cracks. There is nothing happening.

Near the square, on the pavement's edge, are some men. Which men are they? The fog is thick . . .

Now the first capes loom up on the surface of the fog. Many of them.

Place de la République is covered in a milky, cataract-like fog. The square is empty. Black walls surround it.

Thud, thud, thud . . . The riot police block off a street leading to the square. Then a second, then a third. The whole square is encircled with a crown of black thorns. The black metal helmets, black gaiters, shiny and hard; the metallic clop of horses' hooves. Men cast in iron, with skulls cast in iron and bullets of steel . . .

A couple under the trees in the square, a pair of lovers. They have noticed nothing . . . Hey there, you lovers, wake up! The Republic beckons you under cover of the fog. 'Be off, make yourselves scarce,' says an officer.

No more lights in the streets. All the doors have been shut. People have come out of the cafés; they cluster in small groups. Something ripples through the darkened street: a detachment of winged policemen going past at a run.

A young fellow in velvet trousers steps out of one of the groups:

'Well, boys, shall we?'

He points an ungloved hand towards the wall of iron.

Next to a Métro entrance locked as if for the night, speech tears through the fog. But sound rises to cover up this voice;

people running ... A whirlwind cloud of shadows sweeps by.

A man all alone in the quite deserted street holds his head in his hands: '... I was there,' he murmurs, to no one but himself, 'I was doing nothing ...' Blood flows from a broad wound on his brow. Then shadows again: 'Comrades!' ... A chant comes in answer from a small neighbouring street. From the direction of the station rhythmic footfalls announce a marching column. The street is filled ...

Elsewhere, Paris, its corners softened by the fog, sits down at table. It is deaf to its heart, beating so as to burst through its ribs. It eats steak and potatoes.

Near the gare de l'Est, the fat proprietress of a big, blazing-lit café shuts the glass doors herself: 'Get out,' she yells, 'I'm scared stiff! We're closing!' ... 'Murderers!' shouts a smart-looking gentleman in the doorway of the café, 'they ran him over deliberately, they drove their van straight onto the pavement. Murderers! I saw it, with my own eyes! Murderers!'

'Mur-der-ers! Mur-der-ers!' people chant in chorus on the square.

Two black vans draw up on the corner:

'Defend yourselves!'

Stones rain down, pieces of asphalt from the broken roadway. A Vesuvius that wasn't to be taken lightly!

In the middle of the square, in front of the station – small black silhouettes, three, four of them ... There's the sound of rattling fire. The small silhouettes flap their arms, they fall into the cottonwool softness. A policeman's hand firing a revolver. A man arguing as he is held by police, a man being pushed towards a van already full.

Rat, tat, tat ... Five, eight, ten ... Endlessly. Now it ends. The curtain falls. The square is plunged into darkness, nothing disturbs the soft stillness of the fog. A few men on the pavement, at the edge of the blind, muffled cloud, smoke as they wait: 'Did you see? They ran over one of their own, and didn't even pick him up; too scared to get out!' They laugh.

The black vans patrol the streets, the police stay inside them as they fire and hit. They lean out, truncheons in hand, as the cossacks once did from their saddles. Men fall. 'This way, comrade, up this street; take it easy, the cops are like dogs, they run on your tail if you're running . . .'

In the Bois the trees swing to and fro like the bears in their cage. They bend to speak to one another. Then, with a great rustling sound, they start to talk all at once, tossing their heads, shaking their bare branches. In this strange weather the avenues are empty. The Champs-Elysées stretches out its long arms of light towards the Concorde, that great sky starred with terrestrial constellations.

Ambulances make their way through the milky ways of Paris that murmurs as it dreams . . . The fog stops up your ears.

Behind the black railings of the station is a silent crowd of people, suitcases in their hands. They cannot leave. The door of the nearby pharmacy is ajar, a man in a white overall lets in some men supporting others.

Police vans. Here's one drawing up. Some officers leap to the ground and club the bystanders. A man falls. Three of them are beating him. The one in plain clothes shouts: 'No point in taking him with us . . .' He kicks the body and climbs back into the car with the others.

The body lies there, face down. The sound of the van dies away. What's this? The prostrate body stirs, gets up, shakes himself, hitches up his trousers and makes off.

Faced with this miracle, as unlikely as it is incredible, the woman who had been hiding behind a billboard pillar and was about to rush to help the man, now breaks into hysterical laughter.

This evening people in the gare de l'Est neighbourhood were not able to take out their dogs until nearly midnight:

basset hounds, fox terriers, a large sheepdog. They walk them through the still streets. A little risky, but think of the rugs and the parquet flooring. The dogs get the scent of the blood. In the night and fog that are sovereign again, on the cobblestones and pavements lie caps and walking canes, a handbag ... Lit up by a streetlamp as if by a floodlight, a puddle with an elasticated shoe lying sodden in it.

As it slumbers, Paris turns, crushing in its sleep the children who gave it its life, the blood that flows in its veins of stone . . .

CHRISTINA STEAD PARIS

from

The Beauties and Furies

―――――――――――――――――

'Oh, no,' she said in her soft metallic voice, 'no, I just learned music, with geography, fancy-work and painting, in the ordinary way, for five or six years, but I have no real talent for it: we learned painting from an RA and music from a composer, I forget his name: when I'm lonely I play Chopin's Nocturnes, the Moonlight Sonata – '

' – in C sharp minor, Op. 27, no. 2,' murmured Marpurgo.

'I don't know,' said Elvira. 'I don't know that the name matters.'

Oliver, who had been dreaming, only said:

'I love to hear a woman playing in a house: it's always been a dream of mine, a woman's hand wandering over the ivories – when I have a house – a woman, a soft, reluctant voice, music, flowers.' He turned and smiled into Elvira's eyes.

She took her hand from his arm with irritation, looking for her powder-puff in her purse. 'A woman is a human being, not an aesthetic gratification.' There was silence: Marpurgo smiled.

The advertisements in red, blue and green neon tubes bloomed softly in and out, crowds passed along the grisette boulevards, the boulevards with open lap, decked out and beckoning. The broad, blue-crayoned streets were full of hoots, horns and wind instruments of motor-cars, hurried animals hailing as they passed. The rue Laffitte thundered, the cafés were full, their terraces, glassed-in against the cold, were planted with clients, like conservatories with pot-plants, the stoves burned bright. The gutters were frozen black, heaps of snow still lay under the trees. Friends let out of work met each other and hurried by, men with evening papers, girls with neat belted waists, streamed along. Marpurgo expanded, sniffing up a thousand details with the animal delight of a dog reconnoitring fenceposts. He made them sit down in a small bar in the rue du 4 Septembre opposite a great bank, saying if they were not going to the theatre, they had plenty of time, it was best not to eat till eight o'clock. He ordered two drinks for them, but himself took Perrier water, and described the profession, character and intentions of various persons who passed, old sleuth and boulevardier.

EXTRACT TWO

She opened her eyes wide and looked up at the ceiling.

'I am bitter and perverse: no one wants me when they know me; and I am egotistic, too. I like to spend money, I like to eat chocolates, I like to waste time. Now you know me: there's no more to me!' She laughed provocatively. She would have liked, though, to sleep all night alone wrapped in her gold-embroidered coat, with Oliver in another bed, but near: it was appropriate to the dark and glorious turrets of the Louvre, the coronet of the Champs-Elysées, the great translucent clocks of the Gare d'Orsay, the neon tubes. She was so tired that she wished Oliver had not been there and she had been able to sleep all night alone wrapped in glory, an immured citadel busy with the traffic of dreams. A sleepy glutton, doped with foretaste, she would have put off the moment of joy. She wanted so to keep him enslaved, not to gratify him.

When they woke in the morning she wished still to lie and stretch, but Oliver got up, rang the bell, poured out her coffee, arranged her pillow, brought her her dressing-gown, eventually pulled her out of bed and made her dress.

The bells of Paris rang nine o'clock as they set out. It was cold in the frosty March air, the snow lay in the corners, groins and niches, on the turrets and cornices, and hung on the breasts and noses of the statues in the Tuileries. In the garden of the Beaux-Arts a shivering dove with feathers blown the wrong way sat on the neck of a dirty, mossy torso with snow on its back. Elvira's eyes hurt, her colourless cheeks reddened, she was cross at being waked so early and having coffee poured into her and being dragged out by the scruff of the neck, and being rushed along at this pace to see a romantic commonplace like the Latin Quarter. It was there before: it had been there since Abelard: it would be there this afternoon. There were no bounds to Oliver's enthusiasm. She thought, I hope he won't be like this all the time and completely spoil the town for me.

He showed her the engravings and bookbindings on the Quai Voltaire, and half-sang as he went. 'When I was here, when we were here, the chaps and I, two years ago, in June, Alec Bute was leaving the Beaux-Arts; they always give them a send-off and they go singing round the streets at midnight and breaking a few glasses in the cafés: it's the regular thing, it's permitted . . . we had a grand time. Gee, I wish you'd been there. We drank a lovely soft Chambertin here – there they make an *entrecôte Bercy* – oo, la, la! – we ate like kings: there always used to stand a middle-aged prostitute with one leg. We used to chivvy her and stand her drinks. There a motherly old soul, with a black apron and crocheted shawl, left off drinking a mug of bread-soup to sell me a copy of Brantôme's *Gay Ladies* at thirty francs, the crook. A lot she cared what was in it: she saw a young forny fool!'

His gay laughter rang on the air. He saw that she was cold and took her to a bar where they stood up at the zinc counter and had coffee. He got into a halting conversation with a workman speaking atrocious slang on the subject of German rearmament and the funeral of a young workman killed in an encounter with the police; he was in agreement with him, with everyone: he was outrageously, indecently merry. 'And all on account of me,' thought Elvira, 'because he slept with me last night: aren't men childish? I slept with him, am I giving war-whoops?' She widened her united brows, made her semi-mongol face candid and austere, cast a wistful glance from her china eyes up at the moulding of the ceiling. Oliver was recalled by her silence and the infolding of her beauties from his boyish gallopading: he became silent, his hand crept down and found hers. He ordered another glass of coffee and drank it, with a wary eye on her, and without a word. Then they went on – bookshops, schools, famous old streets, gardens, the École de Droit, the Luxembourg, Montparnasse. To please him she submitted to it, hanging on to his arm until eleven-thirty, and then peevishly quit and sat down on a café terrace. He was all solicitude. 'What a stupid child I am! I have no consideration, to drag you like that: I'm used to hoofing it about with great hulking students. It shows I haven't squired too many ladies, at least . . .' He chattered and looked brightly into her face for approval.

She smiled and said, when they had ordered another coffee to set them up: 'What about the concierge the time you fell asleep in the street?'

EXTRACT THREE

Oliver returned from the great United Front meeting at the Mur des Fédérés on May 27 on foot, with a group of French workmen. He had been called 'camarade' so often during the day, had seen so many red flags and so many sinewy arms lifted into the air, had heard the 'Internationale' and 'The Young Guard' so often, that he was no longer himself, a piecemeal student grubbing on collegiate benches, but a glorious foot-soldier in an army millions strong, sure of battery, but sure of victory.

He left the workmen near the Pont des Arts, and stood there in the cool breeze for a while, his cheeks burning and his chestnut hair on end. The sun setting gilded the windows of the Louvre; the dark chlorophyll had now filtered through all the trees of the Tuileries: the polished automobiles budged quickly towards the Champs-Elysées like hard-shelled plant-bugs. Some of the trees along the Seine were thickly tapestried, and the air was full of floating pollen and small brown fluffs: the boulevard trees were all lace. The Île de la Cité, an enchanted city, with bastions and bridges, barges and shallops, called soundlessly downstream. On the brick quays men were still fishing for the Seine's small fry, rust-trousered unemployed were bivouacking with small fires, an artist was painting the river-scene, and a dark-haired woman in her thirties was suckling a child. Oliver leaned over the bridge in a dream. His eyes wandered from the dome of the Académie Française to the enchanted isle, to the flittering fires, the oleaginous hues of the tide, and rested on the sand-coloured breast of the woman. 'A woman is the least individual of creatures,' he thought to himself. 'To think, in the winter I shall have a child!' He smiled to himself at the idea that if he took a boat then and there, and skipped to any South American port, to Canada or the South Seas, to Majorca or Egypt, he was free to go. 'The solutions are so easy and we can't take them. Fear, pride or indecision?' He thought: 'She takes it just as if it were natural, but for me it's a new universe: so, I am sending my seed from generation unto generation, a man full of humility.'

He was in his oldest clothes, striding with the tough easy stride of thousands of miles of walking, walking all through his life, to save money, for the pleasure of it, to school and back, to the University and back, to the houses of students he tutored and back, hiking in the week-ends. He thought: 'I'd like to take a rucksack now and bum for two years. I'd come back a changed man. You can't learn in libraries, you can only learn through men. Today I'm a changed man. Can I go back to this fusty setting after this afternoon? What can I do with a house and a position? I'll take a cattle-boat to Canada and go across the provinces in the summer: I'll get across to the USA at Niagara and ride goods-waggons across to California, then down, Mexico and south. I'll get mixed up in some good old South American fight and have a good time – perhaps get shot, but have a good time. Elvira will sit at home and nurse my child.' He thought that the child would have dark eyes like his own and hers. 'With those eyes,' he thought, 'she can get away with anything – she'll never want for a home. Look how everyone befriends her, is sorry for her, runs around doing messages for her. It's a gift. Paul will be her faithful slave till death – the big, tender, kind mug.'

He leaned over the stone parapet of the quay again, under the rustling new leaves. In the distance the Seine curled by the Great Palace and the Trocadéro towers towards the open green country beyond Saint-Cloud.

EXTRACT FOUR

Coromandel went down wearing a large hat which obtruded her pose upon Oliver. She repelled him by her mannerisms, dominated him by her wilfulness.

They walked towards the rue Dauphiné, reached the banks of the river again, and so on across the river and across the court of Notre-Dame de Paris. It was now full night: out of one of the smoking turrets of that hill of stones rose a white moon, baleful, full of sorcery, turning into a fabulous ruin the columns and flying buttresses. They passed behind this ruin, the garden of the fountain and the débris of gargoyles: so to the Île Saint-Louis and back by the new bridge of Sainte-Geneviève, past the wine market to the ancient seat of the University of Paris. Oliver drew closer irresistibly to the rue Thouin, in which his apartment with Elvira was. He looked up from rue Thouin and saw a light in their apartment. At the same moment Elvira came to the open window, and behind her Paul: they were waiting for him. What now? Oliver laughed low, rebelliously, clutched Coromandel's arm.

They turned about and walked down by the École Polytechnique to the river again. Coromandel said:

'The couples in furnished rooms on a hot night filling an hour or two with talk till they can go to bed together – it's romantic, isn't it? I like these warm nights, when all these intimacies flower along the footpaths, don't you? I like love, I like to see it: I feel happy every time I see a woman embraced.'

Oliver was silent. She looked at him in surprise.

The criss-crossing bridges between the islands were dark, silent, cool, and often traversed by soft-footed, low-voiced lovers enlaced and stopping to kiss every few footfalls. In a grand house at the apex of the Île Saint-Louis, where they came once more, two negresses from the southern states of the USA, turbanned, dressed in red and blue, sang from the window of the servants' room. In another room, the masters picked small bones off porcelain under candles too rare for the old-fashioned space of the eight walls; shadows chased each other over the painted clouds on the ceiling. The willows meditated over the river; the water sounded on the moored barges. They looked back to the lights of central Paris and at the Louvre, a great forecastle sliding across the lights of the Place de la Concorde. They passed the 'street of the Woman without a Head' (now the 'rue Le Regrattier'). Oliver's voice began in the living dark, peopled by street lamps and high walls as they passed palaces and hotels made foetid by the traffic of centuries; his voice was dry and crackling.

'Every woman is the headless woman: we love the Venus without an arm, the leaf-winged hamadryad, the mermaid with only a tail, a torso without any limbs or head, but never without breasts. We are suckling babes, in fact: the bosom is everything. In that respect, you are the perfection of woman.'

Coromandel drooped.

'You treasure yourself as a sculptor his model: every muscle you have ripples towards the perfecting of your body.'

She withdrew her hand angrily from him. 'I don't care for my body.'

She laughed. 'You men! We suffer universally from an unbearable ambition. That's all. You're so smug, smirking there,' she flung at him violently.

Oliver looked pale. 'Then why haven't they ever done anything in the world's history? You can't explain that away.'

She caught hold of him. 'Oh, I could break your arm, I could choke you. Look at the vanity! Why haven't the plebs done anything in the world's history? Because they're weak, vain, and sensual too, I suppose.'

IRMGARD KEUN

from

After Midnight

TRANSLATED BY ANTHEA BELL

I'd far rather live in a city. You're not supposed to say that
kind of thing these days, on account of World Outlook and
the government. Right-thinking people don't prefer cities or
think they're nicer than the countryside. And all the poets
nowadays write things saying the only kind of Nature you
must love is your original natural background. They keep
building bigger and bigger cities all the same, and laying main
roads over the redolent soil. The point of the redolent soil is
that poets have to sing its praises so as to avoid thinking any
stupid thoughts, like what is going on in our cities, and
what's happening to the people. You also need the redolent
soil for making films about country life which the public do
not flock to see. Heini once explained all this to me and
Liska. Liska is in love with Heini. I don't always understand
him myself, but that doesn't make *me* fall in love with him.

EXTRACT TWO

They executed some Communists in the Klingelpütz prison
in Cologne. They screamed – I heard them. I was going to
the cathedral on the Number 18 tram – what's the street
called? What *is* it called? . . . Unter-Sachsenhausen. Thank
God I remember. Unter-Sachsenhausen. I was on the Number
18 tram – why was I going to the cathedral? What did I want
there? When the tram was driving past the side street where

111

that dreadful prison stands, the Klingelpütz, we could hear the screaming. Screams that made the air shake with pain. 'That's the Communists being executed in the Klingelpütz,' said a young SA man standing near the tram driver. He sounded proud that he knew what was going on. I couldn't make out how we could hear them all this way off. 'I knew one of 'em, quite a young fellow he was, eighteen at the most,' said the tram driver. He sounded proud too. He drove on, and the screaming went with us. One man took his hat off in a gesture of solemn and devout respect, as you might at the funeral of someone much loved and well esteemed. He put it on again hastily, with a hand that shook, when the SA man gave him a sharp, suspicious glance. A child laughed, and its mother wept. One fat woman clutched her left breast with both hands, breath coming short, a desperate look in her eyes. The screaming still hung in the air, though we couldn't hear it any more, but we could see it. We all saw it and felt it, and for a second we were united in fear and grief. For life had been taken, and we had been there. Then everything in the world was still. A young man got out of his seat, dropped to his knees and prayed. The SA man and the tram driver preferred to suppose he was mad, rather than have to rebuke him. They took great pains not to hear what he was praying. So we drove on to the cathedral, where we all got out.

A Moving Picture of Shanghai

A tiny, chubby Chinese child is running races with a black puppy along a Shanghai street. It is summer and the child is clothed in a tiny red apron that just covers its stomach. It has been sitting in the dirt. About its fat little ankle is fastened a tiny bell on a cord, and about the neck of the puppy is also a little bell on a cord. The two little creatures run races on the pavement before a flower-shop, back and forth from one telephone pole to another. Tiny, lovely little fellows. The puppy does not always know when to stop, but when he learns that his companion is not at his side he pauses and looks back. The child, with laughter that rivals the tinkling of the bell on its ankle, waits for him, and then they run together. With each jump the puppy's big ears flop up and down and the child laughs in joy. The little feet and paws beat a soft patter, patter, patter on the pavement. Nothing in all Asia can equal such beauty as this.

The dinner is finished. A highly respectable dinner, with evening suits and low-necked dresses. The men now lean over the bar in a club, and one asks the other: 'Well, what did you do last night?' – and winks. The other makes a desperate effort to play up and gives an answering devilish wink. In the corner someone slams a table with the flat palm of his hand and utters a classic expression often used by fine gentlemen and stable boys. The curse has taken on the colour of Asia and mentions someone's mother, grandmother, and spirit of the grandmother.

The speaker has had enough of Shanghai. Afterwards he will go to a night café and dance with a very young dancing girl. For he is growing old. He will dance round and round in a rolling, old-fashioned waltz, his eyes closed to recall memories of many dead Mays. The young men sitting at side tables will smile, and later the dancing girls will go to their tables and laugh under their breath as they talk of them.

It is five o'clock in the morning. The factory siren sounds shrill and loud and long. The grey streets become filled with little children, mingling with tired women and a few men. All are going to work or returning from a night's heavy labour. The hands of the little children are small and tender. Their soft black eyes crowd the streets – eyes filled with experience and suffering beyond their years.

Under protection of foreign flags and in the full glare of the lights of the city at night, stand rows of girls and women offering themselves for sale – twenty or thirty cents an hour, fifty cents or a dollar a night. Many are no older than twelve or fourteen – half-grown children. Near by stand old women – their owners or guards. For these girls are slaves, many of them peasant women and girls sold into slavery from the famine districts. Now they make a living for their owners. Sometimes they bargain with men alone; sometimes the old women bargain for them.

A slender girl of some sixteen bitter summers, clad in a grey cotton gown, stands alone in the same place night after night. No old woman is with her. By her side is always a little girl of eight or ten, playing with a wooden bird on a rubber string. This child may be a young sister or an 'apprentice' slave, learning the profession. The older girl watches her tenderly, always watching, her head inclined downwards towards the child. Men pause and bargain and the child listens. Men bargain with other women standing about waiting, and often a girl will follow after a man, as a dog follows his master, her eyes on the pavement.

Two tall working-men swing down the street. An old woman prompts two girls, one a child not more than twelve. The girls cling to the arms of the working-men. The men shake them off roughly and say: 'You have the wrong men!' The girls fall back, abashed. The old woman again speaks to them, and again they rush forward, clasping the men by their arms. And again they are shaken off, roughly and decisively.

A ricksha coolie, ragged and crouching, does not see the traffic signal and starts to cross the street. The policeman does not arrest him, merely beats him with a long club over the shoulders and then permits him to pass. The coolie cowers under the blows like an animal, then bows his head and runs on. He is blind in one eye and one leg is diseased. His old trousers hang in long rags about his legs, flapping up and down as he runs.

A high Chinese official, his wife, and friends are at tea.

'No,' he says, 'I don't read. You see, I graduated in nineteen-thirteen.'

'My library is also out of date,' his wife remarks. 'I graduated in nineteen-fifteen.'

Another official speaks: 'I don't have to read to know what we need in China. We need education. If, instead of spending money on wars, we should use it all for thirty years for education, we would become the strongest nation on earth. The right thing to do is to stop fighting and make every person go to school right up through the universities – coolies and beggars also. I wrote a thesis on this when I was in college and I still hold to it.'

A Chinese woman very active in the Kuomintang interrupts: 'I think reading books only confuses one. The best way to keep the mind clear is to talk out every idea you have.'

115

A Chinese writer sits at the table and listens in silence. Afterwards he goes into the street, kicks the gravel before him, and speaks harshly: 'This is our ruling class. One hasn't thought a new thought for twenty years; one has never thought – or if she has, has treated her one idea like a laxative.'

A German business man asks over a dinner table: 'And would you free the ricksha coolie also?' His face is a picture of disgust at the very idea. 'The coolie is only half human,' a French physician of the rich declares: 'My Chinese patients will tell you that also' ... An American editor, who cannot get near his desk because of his stomach, exclaims: 'Gawd! How I hate weak, backward peoples!' His face is hateful with disgust ... An English editor with the long face of a horse tells of the countless sacrifices England has made for China, and a Japanese editor says that Japan is protecting Chinese sovereignty in Manchuria ... A Chinese financier trained in Harvard explains the reasons China should not develop state-owned industries. 'Look at America!' he says decisively. 'What is wrong with China,' he complains, 'is that no man is willing to sacrifice himself. China needs a Gandhi, content with a loin-cloth and a bowl of rice. China needs men who do not care for money.' As he speaks he climbs into his limousine, with his initials embossed on the door, and rolls away.

In one of the countless night dancing halls an American sailor slaps a Japanese dancing girl. She dashes a glass of water in his face, then cringes in a corner. Men interfere. Infuriated, the sailor yells: 'I'm three times seven and *white* – see? No yella woman in all Asia can do that to me!' A marine police enters the scene. His head is shaved and he wears his little white cap perched right down over his eyes. His face is like a potato. Cheerfully and vigorously he beats the sailor over the head with his club. Afterwards he drinks a glass of beer and remarks: 'Aw! I don't beat 'em any more'n I'd expect to be beat up if I was them.'

From the prison in the French Concession the news percolates through that four working-men have died under torture. And from the Chinese military court in the Chinese city comes the news that a girl student, arrested by the British police in the YWCA as a Communist, has died under torture. One of her hands was burned off, but still she would tell no names of her comrades.

Secrecy hides the torture, but her brother comes stealthily to a foreign woman in the YWCA and asks her to deliver to him the trunk of his sister. The foreign woman does it, but she says: 'Be careful! I have seen the contents. Your sister was a Communist and the trunk is filled with literature.' The youth answers: 'I know – give me the trunk! My sister is dead. They have tortured her to death.' He takes the trunk and disappears in the vast life of Shanghai, where revolutionaries are born and killed, but where new ones advance always to fill the breach.

A strike-leader on a tramway is arrested. He is an honest worker and refuses to be terrorized by the gangsters who work with the Kuomintang. It takes about ten minutes for the French Court to sentence him to ten years' hard labour. 'You are a Communist,' they say. 'How can you say that?' he protests. A detective is put in the witness-box and shows a pamphlet about Communism. This, says the detective, he took from the strike-leader's room. 'I have never seen the thing! It was never in my room – this is a plant,' the worker angrily interrupts. 'Ten years' hard labour!' the Judge decides. And the worker disappears for ever from the scene in Shanghai.

Five Korean revolutionaries are caught and will be delivered to the Japanese. Spies seek out the desperate wives, sisters, and daughters of the arrested men and say: 'Give me a thousand dollars and I will use my influence to save him.'

The women give all their hard-earned savings and borrow on every hand, burying themselves in debt. The spies take the money and disappear. And the prisoners are turned over to the Japanese. Frail, gentle, crushed into half-death, the women bow their heads.

A ricksha coolie falls to his knees in the middle of the street and begs, with folded hands, before a policeman. The policeman drives him to the kerb. There the coolie again falls on his knees in terror and raises his clasped hands to the small group that gathers and watches. A working-man explains to a stranger: 'He new man. He from country . . . He peasant. He no understand Shanghai . . . He make mistake and policeman take his cushion from ricksha. He must pay fifty cents to get back cushion . . . He no got fifty cents.'

Along the streets come a trio – man, wife, child. The man, dressed in the blue cotton trousers of a working-man, carries a bamboo pole across his shoulders and at each end of the pole hang bamboo baskets, heavily filled. As the man walks he utters the rhythmical sing-song: 'Hai-ho, Hai-ho, Hai-ho!' Clinging to the basket in the back the little child patters along, singing also in a childish high voice: 'Hai-ho, Hai-ho, Hai-ho.' The mother watches him and smiles.

A German tells his story. Thirty years in China and for seventeen years he has been planning to go home. He never gets beyond that. Every night he goes to the dancing halls, drinks, dances with Japanese, Korean, Chinese, or White Russian dancing girls, and spends all his money. 'Long ago,' he tells, 'we used to know when we were going to the dogs . . . now we no longer know.'

A foreign woman tourist stands in the entrance of one of the wealthiest foreign hotels and bargains with a Chinese flower vendor for a bunch of carnations. The man asks twenty cents; the woman offers ten, and bargains and bargains. She has heard that one must bargain in China, and she does not intend to be cheated just because she is a stranger.

News reaches Shanghai of a new nationalist wave in India. Hindu merchants close their shops and spend hours in prayer. Foreigners laugh, and the British remark: 'Let 'em keep on praying!' On Nanking Road appear proclamations in an Indian language. A British policeman tries to soak one of them off, remarking: 'These bastards are up to something again!'

A White Russian lies dead drunk on the streets. A crowd of Chinese surround him, and one reaches out with his foot and kicks him. A German pauses and remarks: 'I am sorry . . . he is a white man . . . but I wouldn't give him a penny.' The White Russian turns over and slobbers.

White Russians roam up and down the China coast. They beg, rob, steal, kidnap, and fill the spy ranks of all the nations in China; they smuggle opium, forge, murder; they act as strike-breakers against Chinese workers and are guarded by foreign police. There are White Russian regiments in British uniforms in Shanghai. They march and sing Czarist songs. The French detective force is filled with White Russian detectives, and White Russian spies write daily reports to their masters and are paid a few dollars.

White Russian women, too proud to work in the Soviet Union, fill the brothels and night cafés of Shanghai. They compete with all the prostitutes of Asia. They are found in the harems of Chinese war-lords. Chinese coolies on the streets of Shanghai will follow men and whisper: 'Wanchee Russki girl? Tall girl, short girl, fat girl, little girl? Black girl, white girl?'

The other foreigners complain that the White Russians have ruined the prestige of the white race in Asia. But they help them ruin it further by using them as strike-breakers, as mistresses and prostitutes, as mercenary soldiers and spies.

*

In an old Chinese theatre a wealthy young Chinese bows politely to a man across the aisle. 'Who is that?' he is asked. He replies: 'That is the gang leader of Shanghai – the king of kidnappers ... No, he does not do this kidnapping himself, but he finances it and, of course, gets the money.' The young man mentions his name – Tu Yulh-seng – a name known to every person in Shanghai, a powerful official name. An old-fashioned Chinese comes in, bows to the gang leader, sits by his side, and engages him in intimate conversation. 'Who is that?' the rich young man is asked again. 'That is the president of the Chamber of Commerce; he is a close friend of the gang leader.'

'Does the gang leader have many such friends?'

The young man answers: 'The gang leader's friends are the highest ministers and commanders in the Government. He holds more than one official position. He is the chief anti-Communist suppression agent of Shanghai. And he is the chief of opium traffickers also.'

A woman gives a ricksha coolie twice as much money as he expected. Gratefully he bows with clasped hands: 'Thank you, missie, thank you!' He is a big man, a peasant fresh from the land. He has searched for work in the factories and found nothing. The peasants are becoming ricksha coolies. They sleep on the pavements of the city, in dark corners, on the foot-boards of their rickshas. Shanghai was once a city of hope for them. But now they know it is a city of despair.

Foreign women drink tea languidly and gossip. One remarks: 'Yes, China would be a lovely country if it were not for the Chinese.' The others nod approvingly.

Another group of foreign women are gossiping over their tea. One is soon to have a baby. She is the wife of a Chinese, and two other women present are also foreign wives of Chinese.

'Who will attend you at confinement?' the expectant mother is asked. She answers, giving the name of a foreign physician. 'No,' she explains, 'I could not possibly have a Chinese physician at an event so intimate as this!'

A high British official calls Shanghai a 'pearl of a city'. And the daily press in Shanghai reports that thirty-six thousand dead bodies were picked up in the streets of this city in the year of our Lord, nineteen hundred and thirty, and thirty-two thousand in the year of grace nineteen hundred and thirty-one. The city maintains an ambulance that goes about the city just to pick up the dead. For Shanghai is a 'pearl of a city' and the dead can't be left lying about the streets like that.

The dead – laconically the press says they consist of children thrown away because the parents could not support them and of men and women who had starved to death or died of cold.

Along the great boulevards in western Shanghai where the rich foreigners and Chinese have built their villas, high brick walls enclose the villas and the lovely gardens surrounding them. Here, on the street, when it is not too cold, sleep the poor of the city. At night one can walk along the boulevard, meandering here and there to avoid stepping on the dark, exhausted forms of men who have worked all day and then sunk to the pavements to sleep at night. Some have their tools under their heads – their only earthly possessions.

Beyond the wall live the wealthy, who gamble, dance or banquet all night, sleep all day, as it pleases their fancy, their limousines rolling in and out of the great iron gates that open and close at their bidding. Their victims litter the streets far and wide – the victims out of whose bodies their wealth is drawn, the victims who have built these villas, these walls, and laid out these gardens, the victims on whose prostrate bodies all of Shanghai rests.

On the walls are often chalked the slogans: 'Support the Chinese Soviet Republic!' 'Join the Red Army of Workers and Peasants!' 'Down with the imperialists!' 'Down with the

Kuomintang, the running dog of the imperialists!' Just like that – on the walls surrounding the homes of the wealthy! How shocked the foreigners and rich Chinese are!

There are other walls in the city of Shanghai. They enclose convents and monasteries and behind them walk black-robed priests and nuns. On the side of the sacred walls facing the street the police or someone like them have printed these words in French: 'Commit no nuisance against this wall.' But the Chinese poor are without places to commit nuisances, so they commit them against these walls. Now this, perhaps, proves that the Chinese are heathens, for they do not know the difference between a sacred and a profane wall.

In another part of the city live the Japanese and the Chinese together. And there is no love lost between them. There is no wall between the foreign-controlled International Settlement and the Chinese-controlled city. So a Japanese steps out three steps into the Chinese city and stands with his face to a wall. A group of Chinese get hold of him at a critical moment. He yells bloody murder and a policeman comes running and rescues him. 'Why do you molest the man?' the policeman bawls. A coolie spokesman proudly steps forward and presents the case for China. 'Why he no water in the foreign settlement? Why on Chinese soil?'

The Japanese mark down this incident, and it forms one of the more than three hundred so-called insults suffered by 'Japan' at the hands of 'China'.

Here is a rich German merchant who has lived in Shanghai for twenty years. He owns a mansion surrounded by a great garden. His initials, M.K., appear in iron characters on the iron gate leading into the garden. He is a Fascist, and the old monarchist flag of Germany flies over his property. He is short and very fat, with a big bulging belly and a neck that rolls over his collar. His head is as round and naked as a billiard ball and his face as red as a spanked baby's bottom. In the hot summer months he walks around his house and garden clad only in tight-fitting bathing-shorts. Above the shorts his belly heaves and rolls and on his knob of a head is perched a stiff straw hat.

Often he goes to Germany for a year's vacation. As a violent German nationalist he finds this proper. But in Germany one must pay taxes after six months' residence. This rich man, under his nationalist flag, always lives five and a half months in Germany, then announces his departure for Switzerland, where he lives for one month, making a break in the six-months' period. Then he returns to Germany and takes up his 'new' residence. He has avoided paying taxes. He says he would live in Germany always except that the taxes are too high.

So he lives in China where he pays practically nothing. And if in either China or Germany a poor man steals a loaf of bread, this Fascist patriot is the first to shout him down as a thief and call for his imprisonment for breaking the law. For he is a nationalist and believes in 'law and order'.

Through the streets of a Chinese section of the city races a boy some twelve years of age, followed by a man. The boy is stricken with terror, the man is filled with murderous hatred. The boy wears the miserable cotton cloth, dirty and patched, of a small coolie worker. The man catches him, throws him to the earth, and is in the process of murdering him when others interfere and pull the man off. It is a scene of dirt, squalor, and bestiality. About are the small, one-storey houses and shops, disorderly, patched with old tin cans, rags and bits of stone; rags hang over wash-lines over the street. Murder belongs to this street – nothing but murder could take root and grow here.

It is in the French Concession late at night. A ricksha coolie fails to observe some petty traffic regulation. Although there is no life on the street except a foreign man and woman walking near, the policeman raises his long club and follows the usual police habit of beating the coolie. The foreign man and woman watch the brutal scene, then interfere. When the coolie sees sympathy, he kicks back at the policeman with his bare foot. Then the 'arm of the law' is upon him like a wild beast, beating him as if he were a dog, and when he is bleeding and broken, arrests him for 'obstructing traffic'.

The foreign man and woman accompany the coolie and the policeman to the French police station. They complain in defence of the coolie. The French police sergeant, short, fat, cynical, hears them and then remarks: 'The policeman only did his duty.' And when they protest violently, the sergeant again remarks: 'You see, the policeman is a Chinese. He knows how to treat his own people. You are wasting breath to bring in your sentimentalism when the law is at stake.'

In bitterness the woman says as she walks away: 'I want to leave China – I can endure it no more.'

But there is no leaving China for the masses of the oppressed. They must stand and be beaten or shot to death as serfs, or they must die fighting for their freedom. The foreigners can run away; or those who do not, remain and join the ranks of those who do the beating – only one in a hundred thousand joins the ranks of the oppressed.

THE FORTIES

T HE SECOND World War entered Europe's cities
with convulsive force. Bombs were dropped on
them and battles fought within them. In Leningrad,
a third of the city's population of three million died
of starvation during a seige that lasted more than two years.
Lidia Ginzburg's picture of Leningrad bombarded and
encircled, its people starving, acutely conveys the relentless
process whereby a city under such pressure reinvents a sense
of normality. What is normal is what enables survival.
Ginzburg records these extreme circumstances with an
analytic eye; what do they reveal about human behaviour
and human psychology in its allegedly 'normal' forms,
among them differences between men and women? In this
context certain aspects of women's experience acquire an
upgraded value, while women still have to contend with
ingrained notions of superior male status.

Of the different wars that came to different cities
London's was a war of Blitz devastation, but in this
unoccupied capital the Home Front had its moments of
respite and liberating transformation. We know the ghostly,
moonlit London of the blackout from Bill Brandt's
photographs of the period. In a notable piece of London
wartime fiction, Elizabeth Bowen's 'Mysterous Kôr' (not
included here but much anthologised), a story where
wartime passions and regrets are already embedded in young

lives, London is evoked as a place of the imagination, a city drained of its millennial reality and belonging only to an intense and timeless poetic present. Bowen wrote and published this story in wartime, which also produced her novel, *The Heart of the Day* (1949). But much writing that concerns the everyday extremes of war in continental Europe was, often by necessity, retrospective. Much of it too takes the form of journals or memoirs, works of imaginative reconstruction.

The war changed the face of continental cities. Few were as ravaged as the Warsaw visited by Storm Jameson at war's end, when only four buildings remained intact. Marguerite Duras worked in the French Resistance; in her fictional memoir, *La Douleur* (1985), she describes the hiatus between Liberation and peace with a sense of betrayal. Although Paris is now lit up at night, the visibility of peace is 'like a great darkness falling, it's the beginning of forgetting'. This means oblivion for those who suffered and died; 'The lit-up city means only one thing to me: it is a sign of death, of a tomorrow without them. There's no present in the city now except for us who wait. For us it's a city they won't see.' This darkness is also the fast rewriting of history, as new balances of power are established. It took Duras forty years to write *La Douleur* (just as Ginzburg took many years to complete her account of the siege). The war, a rupturing of time and history, has needed a very long reckoning.

In New York the war is experienced as happening elsewhere, profitably for the skimmers, in Christina Stead's *A Little Tea, A Little Chat*: 'Everyone scooped greedily in the great cream pot of war . . . The town reeked of easy, greasy "dough".'

Up in Harlem things are not so easy for Lutie Johnson, the struggling single mother in Ann Petry's *The Street* (1946), whose grim naturalism is very much a feature of the black protest fiction of the period. Lutie is alone not through the separations of war, but because of a husband's infidelity,

126

giving her a perspective that accentuates the glaring
oppressions of the ghetto street, the extra burdens borne by
black women. Yet the disruptions of the war raised
expectations of old fixities shifting, of poverty yielding to
will and hard work. Reminiscent of *The Street*'s vision of the
city's promise tantalisingly but desperately just out of reach,
is another North American novel of working-class life,
Gabrielle Roy's *Bonheur d'Occasion* (1945, translated as
The Tin Flute 1947), which has Montreal as its setting.

The war seems already remote in Shirley Jackson's 'Pillar
of Salt' (1948), a story whose dating immediately lends it
overtones of Eisenhower-era allegory. The unspoken trauma
of McCarthyism infected much of the period's cultural life.
It seems cognate with the dislocations of a woman
accustomed to a traditional domestic role and panic-stricken
by New York's erasure of all that is familiar, and familial.
The city as a paralysing nightmare, the alienating effect of
New York's speed and indifference are recurring literary
images, just as urban threat and anxiety permeate the mood
of Hollywood *film noir*. Madness, a fatally inchoate
rebellion, is of course a classic female response to social
repression.

It is impossible not to find allegory in Carmen Laforet's
Nada (1945), just as in many of the fictions constricted by
Francoist ideology, particularly in the years immediately
after the Civil War. Where the Spanish Republic had
enlarged the scope for women's freedom, Fascism reinstated
a brutally hierarchical regime of the sexes. Censorship and
the diaspora of many pro-Republican writers saw to it that
the experience of Spain's Civil War was kept at fictional
distance until many years later. Among the writers who were
to make the war the subject of their novels are Susana
March – in *Algo muere Cada día* (1955) – and Mercè
Rodoreda, a writer whose stream of consciousness technique
has prompted critical comparisons with Virginia Woolf. Her
best-known novel, *Time of the Doves* (1962), written in
exile, narrates life in Barcelona from the viewpoint of a

young working-class woman who marries, has children, loses her husband at the front and lives through a crisis of identity in the aftermath of defeat.

Nada's young protagonist, Andrea, arrives in Barcelona to study, under the supervision of an aunt and other relatives. This household carries an atmosphere of repression and fraught secrets, from which Andrea finds relief in Barcelona's streets, her restless footsteps taking her in search of identity.

LIDIA GINZBURG

from
The Siege of Leningrad

... At the beginning of the war the city began to acquire
unusual details. First of all cross-shaped strips of paper began
to appear on windows (to keep the glass from flying out).
The authorities had suggested this measure to the citizenry
during the very first days of the war. Amid the fluctuating
anguish of those first days, when the new mode of life had
not yet taken shape, this mechanical activity had a calming
effect and distracted people from the emptiness of anticipation. But there was also something agonizing and strange
about it, as, for example, in the sparkle of a surgery ward
where there were as yet no wounded but undoubtedly would
be.

Some people pasted these strips in quite intricate patterns.
Somehow or other the rows of glass covered with paper strips
created an ornamental design. Seen from a distance on a
sunny day, it looked cheerful. Like the gingerbread trim that
adorns the cottages of well-to-do peasants. But everything
changed if you peered at the strips on the lower windows
during bad weather. The yellowness of the damp newspaper,
the paste stains, the print showing through like dirt, and the
jagged edges formed a symbolism of death and destruction
that simply had not yet had time to take hold, to attach itself
to the cross-shaped strips.

Later on, people began to board up the windows of homes
and stores. Some covered their windows because the glass

had already shattered and others so that it wouldn't shatter. Sometimes they used fresh, practically white sheets of plywood for this purpose and sometimes rough, very somberlooking boards. A boarded-up window symbolizes an abandoned building. But in the fall the apartment houses were not yet empty; the population of three million, encircled by the blockade, still filled them to the brim. During those autumn days the symbol of a boarded-up window acquired a horrible reverse meaning – it became the symbol of people cooped up together, buried alive and perishing in darkness. It contained the funereal symbolism of boards, the tomblike feeling of basements, and the weight of a multi-story building falling on someone.

The city was filled with a monotonous diversity of details that were expressive and individually different but that blended into one. Dank walls displayed windows covered with fresh plywood, boarded up with rough planks, sealed with paper – blue wrapping paper, colored paper, newsprint – and blocked up with bricks. Sometimes one window combined sections of plywood, bricks, glass, and glued-on paper. Symbols varied and became muddled; onerous associations ran together without managing to take shape. Then it no longer made any difference. The windows became covered with ice. People on the street didn't look at buildings anymore. They looked down at their feet because the sidewalks were iced over and they were afraid that the slipperiness and their own weakness would make them fall. They were especially afraid of falling with containers full of soup.

. . . We saw everything in Leningrad during the siege, but we saw fear least of all. People scarcely listened to artillery shells whistling overhead. To wait deliberately until a shell exploded was much more difficult, of course; but everyone knew that you could hear a shell explode only if you weren't hit that time.

The quantitative scale of danger, or, more precisely, the probability of perishing (the degree of probability) holds key psychological significance. The distance between certain death and almost certain death is immense. The danger in Leningrad was constant and relentless, and its relentlessness was designed to wear on people's nerves, but statistically it was not especially great. The danger from bombing and shelling, verified by daily experience, was overshadowed by the enormous number of deaths from malnutrition. This slow kind of death required a completely different sort of inner preparedness. People in Leningrad naturally had a different attitude toward shells and bombs than did front-line soldiers or, later on, the inhabitants of cities that were burned to ashes by aerial attacks.

Few people in Leningrad were afraid of bombings – only those with a special physiological predisposition toward fear. Calmness became the universal and typical standard of behaviour, and not to conform to it was more difficult and more frightening than the real dangers. You must be practically a hero to retain your composure in the midst of universal panic. But just try to scream and tear around when everyone else is going about his business – that takes a lot of audacity.

When beauty parlours were still operating normally, I once happened to be stranded at the hairdresser's during an air raid and I observed how ordinary young women continued to give six-month perms amid the noise of anti-aircraft fire, exchanging remarks all the while about how terribly frightening it was.

Death can be successfully put out of mind for the simple reason that it is beyond human experience. Death is either the abstract concept of nonexistence or the emotion of fear. In the first instance it belongs to the category of the unimaginable (like eternity and infinity). In order to think concretely about the instantaneous transition from a person in a room to the chaos of brick, metal, meat, and, most importantly, nonexistence, the imagination must work harder than many people's imaginations are capable of working.

*

. . . From the days of old to the present the word *coward* has had a magical ring. It is all right to be afraid of the common cold, but to fear death is considered shameful. How did such a notion become instilled and ingrained in humankind when the instinct of self-preservation is so strong? Probably because society, the nation-state, could not possibly exist without it and threw all its weight into instilling it.

. . . People from the outside world who ended up in Leningrad would become distressed. 'Why aren't any of you afraid?' they would ask. 'What do you do to keep from being afraid?' The answer would be: 'When you've lived here for a year and a half, starving and freezing . . . well, there's no way to explain it.'

Habit alone was not enough. Habit merely weakened the impulses of fear and self-preservation; it helped you suppress them and replace them with others. To avoid being afraid you had to acquire other impulses that were so powerfully primordial as to suppress and consume all the rest.

The siege survivor of the fall of 1941 gave way to the survivor of the winter of 1941–42. He is the person who walks down the street during an artillery barrage. He knows that this is very dangerous and frightening. But he's going to the cafeteria for dinner. And instead of being afraid, he is irritated (they won't even let him have dinner in peace); instead of being afraid of dying, he's afraid of being stopped along the way, of being detained and driven into a shelter so that he won't endanger his life. This person is conscious of the possibility that he might perish, but his immediate sensations are of starvation, more particularly the fear of starvation, and of a hunger-induced haste rushing blindly toward its goal. You can be aware of various things simultaneously, but you can't desire them to the same extent at the same time.

A person wakes up in the night at the sound of an air alert. His hopes for a *quiet* alert are short-lived. The anti-aircraft guns are firing closer and closer. What a shrill strike! Or is that actually a bomb? By this time, he no longer thinks about getting up, finding his overshoes, and going to the freezing basement. He's thinking that he shouldn't fall asleep. He doesn't want *that* to happen while he's sleeping. He doesn't want to wake up with the world caving in on him just to witness his own death in one very brief flash that instantly goes out. It's better to be prepared. It's better to lie there listening to the explosions as they come closer and closer. It's better when there's a lead-in to disaster. He is thinking that he shouldn't fall asleep, but in a few minutes he does fall asleep, because he's tired.

What's happening is very frightening. Right now, at any moment – before he can pull up the blanket, before he exhales the air that is expanding his chest – right now reality as he knows it might give way to some other incredible reality that is wailing, ringing, falling from utmost suffering into extinction.

All this could happen, but he doesn't have the strength to be afraid. He wants to sleep. He is amazed at what he was like at the beginning of the siege. Then he would wake up at 1 or 2 a.m. at the sound of an air-raid warning. That sound was enough to make him instantly forsake his warm bed in favour of the frozen basement. It was a naive wholeness and a fresh instinct of self-preservation not yet eaten away by fatigue and by a constant struggle with suffering. As a result of this struggle, the bed warmed by his body, his body lying peacefully in bed, became a blessing, an object of desire that not even the intellectual stuff of terrible thoughts could overpower.

I know that this is frightening. I want to live. If the worst happens, I will spend my last instant of consciousness cursing myself for being so reckless. I know that I should be afraid and take precautions. But I'm not afraid and can't be afraid, because I want to sleep.

Subtle changes occurred in the reactions of the siege survivor during the summer of 1942. By then he responded only out of habitual nervous tension, which would disappear along with the irritant that had caused it. The moment he heard the all-clear signal, he felt a sort of physical satisfaction, a sense of relief like the sudden cessation of a toothache. This explains people's strange mood swings, strange because of their swiftness. One minute they would be listening for death, while the next they would be chattering away, repeating office gossip; women who were still coming back to life made plans to get hold of stockings or redo a dress.

Stable feelings and imagination no longer played any part in determining nervous reactions, and conscious will did not stand in the way. The powerful impulses of the capacity to resist had managed to reshape everything. People in whom these impulses were not working found themselves in the same position as the sick.

Why was starvation the most powerful enemy of the ability to resist? (The Germans realized this.) Because starvation is continuous and can't be turned off. It persisted and constantly took its toll (though not necessarily through the desire to eat); its most excruciating and depressing effect was felt at mealtime as the food came to an end with frightening speed, bringing no satiety.

The object of the morning excursion outside is the daily trip to the store. A grocery store has now replaced the bakery. An announcement even hangs on the door: 'This store sells bread.' Can it possibly be trying to attract customers? At this moment the store is empty and quiet. The clerks are wearing white jackets, sample displays sparkle on the shelves, irritating the customers, that is, those registered to shop here, while the groceries that have not yet been distributed and can't be purchased are laid out on the counter.

. . . During the winter, when bread was apt to run out (this situation was later rectified), lines made sense. But there were also other lines – the result of famine madness. On the day they announced the distribution of fat and 'confections', a crowd would already be waiting at the store by 5 a.m. People would endure all the agonies of standing in line for hours, knowing that by 10 or 11 a.m. the store would be empty. It was psychologically impossible to sleep, to become occupied with anything else, or simply to exist without entering the process of drawing near the fat and sweets as soon as they became a possibility.

A line is a collection of people doomed to a communality of enforced idleness and intrinsic divisiveness. Idleness, if not construed as recreation or entertainment, is suffering and punishment (prison, lines, waiting in reception rooms). A line is a combination of complete idleness and a heavy expenditure of physical strength. Men are especially poor at enduring lines beause they are accustomed to having people appreciate and value their time. It's not even a matter of the objective state of things but, rather, of inherited experience. Working women have inherited from their mothers and grandmothers the notion that their time is worthless. And daily life does not allow this atavism to die out. A man thinks that after work he should amuse himself or relax; when a woman gets home from work, she works at home. During the siege of Leningrad, lines joined the long-standing tradition of distribution and acquisition, the habitual irritability and the habitual patience of women.

In contrast, almost every man who shows up at a store tries to bully his way to the counter without waiting. Men can't explain where they get this feeling that inwardly they are right when outwardly their conduct is clearly wrong. But they know for certain that waiting in line is a woman's job. Perhaps they have some vague notion that their claims are justified because there are so few men in line. But they don't give any reasons; they either behave boorishly or utter the classic phrase: 'I'm late for work.' 'And aren't we late for work?' (Women invariably say *we*. A man standing in line thinks of himself as an isolated individual whereas a woman regards herself as the representative of a group.) 'Nowadays everybody's late for work,' a woman with a briefcase replies angrily. The man furtively hides the bread he has gotten by this time. There is nothing he can say, but deep down inside he's convinced that even if a woman actually works as much or more than he does, her attitude toward time, toward the value, use, and allocation of time, is different from his. And his attitude gives him the right to receive bread without standing in line. The clerk, a woman with no stake in the outcome, understands this and usually encourages these male claims of privilege.

Extremely few people read books or even newspapers while waiting in line. This comes as a surprise only to those who have never stood in line for hours at a time, day in and day out. The basis of line psychology is a nervous, wearisome yearning for the end, for some inner means of pushing empty time forward; weariness drives out everything that might dissipate it. The psychological state of someone standing in a long line is not usually conducive to other activities. An educated person has naively brought along a book, but he prefers to follow what's happening around him. Pushing up to the counter sideways, he watches the clerk hand out rations to those standing in front of him. If her gestures slow down, he responds by pushing forward with an inner shudder (if the clerk leaves the counter for a moment, the torment is akin to that of a train stopping suddenly). Or he finds satisfaction in closely watching the precise rhythm of her work or rejoices when some time is gained unexpectedly (as, for example, when someone's ration cards are given back to him because he's not assigned to this store).

A person becomes genuinely hysterical when some claimant wedges in ahead of him and then, after receiving his dole, immediately strikes up a conversation with an acquaintance for half an hour, now conversing like a free person, as though he were here on his own initiative. As long as he's in line, he, along with the whole line, is seized by a physical craving for movement, even if it's illusory. The ones behind yell at the ones ahead of them, 'Get a move on! What's holding you up?' And then some philosophizer who doesn't understand the mechanics of everyone's mental state will invariably respond, 'Where can they possibly go? We won't get there any faster this way.'

In the winter the lines of people suffering from malnutrition were morbidly silent. In the spring the habits of those waiting in line gradually changed as the bread ration increased, the weather grew warmer, and greens appeared (people bought beet leaves and boiled them). The lines started to converse.

Humans abhor a vacuum. The immediate filling of a vacuum is one of the basic functions of speech. Meaningless conversations are no less important in our lives than meaningful ones.

The course of every conversation is, in its own way, predetermined, but the springs that propel it are hidden from the participants. Subjectively they are committing an act that is almost independent of any resistance from the objective world that hangs over every *deed*. Conversation is an unrestrained substitute for action, which must always conform to rules. It is a distant prototype of art, which is also a special kind of reality, and people themselves create and destroy the objects that populate it.

Conversation is a replica of passions and emotions; love and vanity, hope and animosity find in it an illusory realization. Conversation is the fulfillment of desires. In conversation over a cup of tea or a glass of wine, insurmountable barriers are broken down and goals are achieved that in the world of actions would cost a great amount of time, failure, and effort.

Conversation is a form of release, and it is also the objectivization of desires, values, ideals, abilities, and possibilities, whether cognitive, aesthetic, or volitional. Above all, conversations with fellow mortals are the most powerful means of self-assertion, a declaration of one's own worth. Something stated becomes real and acquires a social existence – this is one of the fundamental laws of behaviour.

While engaged in dialogue with his neighbour, a person asserts himself both directly and indirectly, by head-on and circuitous routes – from out-and-out bragging and naive talk about himself and his concerns to secret admiration for his own views on science, art, and politics, for his own wittiness and eloquence, for his power over the listener's attention. Self-assertion hides itself in something that is objectively interesting; it buries itself in information or in something aesthetically significant. Sometimes information is only a pretext, and sometimes self-assertion merely accompanies information. One way or another, self-assertion is the imperishable heart and soul of conversation.

There are situations – the existentialists call them borderline situations – when it would seem that everything must change. In reality the eternal motive forces continue their monumental labour (as Tolstoy established once and for all). What was hidden, however, becomes obvious, what was approximate becomes literal, and everything becomes condensed and revealed. This is what happened to conversation during the siege of Leningrad – in editorial offices, in cafeterias, in bomb shelters, and in lines.

A line is an involuntary combination of people who are simultaneously irritated with one another and focused on a single, common circle of interests and goals. This leads to a mixture of rivalry, hostility, and collective sentiment, a constant readiness to close ranks against a common enemy – anyone who breaks the rules. Conversations among people waiting in line unravel because of the enforced idleness and at the same time hang together because of the fixed nature of their content, for they are tied to whatever the line is all about.

Understandably, the business of obtaining food requires statements that have a communicative function ('Who is last? What kind of coupon do we need? How many? Do they have "Southern" candy today? Is it true that "Iran" candy comes in wrappers? Then it's not worth it!') and statements devoted to the battle against rule breakers. Formally speaking, the latter are also communicative (they aim for a practical result). But in actual fact the practical element in such statements is just as insignificant as the value of the housewife's time that is expended on the interloper who has wormed his way into line. The sense of justice she appeals to in her usual emotional manner is also insignificant. The practical bent of heckling comments masks a release of irritation, impatience, and all sorts of accumulated passions. Their emotional essence is borne out by the unprovoked rudeness and animosity in replies to perfectly innocent questions like 'Do you happen to know how many coupons they take for a worker's ration?' or 'How do you cook that?' The answers might be: 'What's the matter? Is this the first time you've ever gotten food here?' or 'What's your problem? Haven't you ever cooked before?' (Here you begin to suspect that you're dealing with an aristocrat who considers herself above all this.) In the winter you couldn't ask anybody anything: any question was a longed-for excuse to give a savage reply that would relieve hostility and torment. In better times, along with rude answers one would encounter wordy, substantial replies when the speaker enjoyed playing the role of advisor and guide.

But the soul of a line lies in another kind of conversation, the kind that fills the vacuum of inactivity and is thoroughly predetermined and only ostensibly free. Conversations about food (about life and death) come in the plain brown wrapper of housewives' professional interests.

For intellectuals, for young people, even for men in general this is a fresh topic of conversation from which the ban has just been lifted, and they invent new clumsy and expressive turns of phrase. They are powerless to resist this topic but are ashamed of it as a sign of degradation. For housewives this is simply the continuation of their age-old conversations. For housewives of the immediate prewar period there is nothing new about standing in lines, carrying ration cards, or asking, 'What are they handing out?' And so they didn't have to update their terminology in any radical way.

Still, some things did change. First, conversations about food crowded out all other housewifely topics of discussion (school, shopping, domestic help). Second, conversations that were once despised by men and working women (especially young ones), that housewives were forbidden to thrust upon such know-it-alls – these conversations triumphed. They acquired a universal social significance and meaning, the price of which was the terrible experience of winter. A discussion of the best way to cook millet – without salt, because then it *stretches* farther – became a conversation about life and death (for people learned how to increase their millet). Conversations narrowed in scope (to siege cuisine), but they were enriched by the peripeteia of difficulties to be overcome and problems to be solved. And being the most important discussions in the given life-and-death situation, they encompassed all imaginable interests and passions.

When people in line carry on conversations about food, their discussions contain everything: emotional release in reproaches and complaints, cognitive generalization in debates about the best way to obtain, prepare, and divide up food, the recounting of 'interesting stories', and all means of self-assertion.

. . .'Oh, dear, I've started eating my bread. Now I'm afraid there won't be any left when I get home.'

'You should never start eating here.'

A third woman (standing in line for sweets):

'The calmest time is when you've finished it. As long as it's there, it draws you like a magnet. Like a magnet.'

'You can't calm down until you've eaten it all. And you can't forget about it.'

'It draws you like a magnet.'

'Why, I used to clean out the candy bins. I'd buy it a hundred grams at a time.'

'And half a kilo of bread and butter is gone in a flash. It's just awful to have to carry it home.'

The satisfaction of talking about yourself is duplicated by the satisfaction obtained from intellectual processes. Self-observation turns into generalization based on experience.

'You should never start eating it here' is actually a maxim; 'It draws you like a magnet' is an artistic image.

'Well, then, my kid and I will eat this right up.'

'In one day?'

'What do you mean in one day? In an instant. Before the war we used to go through two hundred grams of butter a day.'

'Yes, that was perfect for three people.'

'You can't imagine what my kids used to be like. Suddenly they wouldn't want to eat buckwheat porridge. They wanted me to make them oatmeal. Both oatmeal soup and oatmeal porridge. I'd say, "Pick one or the other, either soup or porridge . . ." "No, make both of them." "All right, I'll make porridge – "'

'And my boy – he's only seven, but these days kids know everything there is to know about food. Whenever they announce the children's allocation on the radio, he's all ears. "Children under twelve can get sugar . . ." He says, "Mama, that's my sugar. I'm not going to give you any." And I say to him, "Then I won't give you any candy."'

A story about yourself, about your family, specifically about how your family ate in the past, has objective, universal appeal. This is confirmed when a listener responds with a question ('In one day?'). The story about how people used to eat contains a subtext of self-assertion: See how high my family and I could and still can rise above the forces that rule us. The reaction this elicits shows understanding; it indicates that the listener is also above it all and belongs to the same circle, that very circle of people in which a family of three used to go through two hundred grams of butter a day.

The story about buckwheat porridge and oatmeal has an underlying theme: The family lived so well that the children demanded not something better but something a little worse just to be different (out of satiety, the way the gentry used to eat rye bread).

After that would come the eternal female topic of children, now based on new and frightening material. The story of the boy who already knows everything there is to know 'about food' has a certain amount of artistic, thematic appeal; but the main point, to be sure, is that this boy is mature for his tender age, that he'll manage to survive, and that he already acts like an adult while still retaining a sweet, childish naivete. But this child who is so well adjusted to life immediately suffers defeat. For a listener suddenly begins talking about another boy who also behaved like an adult.

'No, my boy, who's dead now, always shared everything. It was amazing. His father and I couldn't take it. But he would hide candy in his pocket. He'd pat his pocket and say, "That's enough for now." And he was so unselfish. He would give away his own food. He'd say, "Mama, you're still hungry. Take some of my bread."'

... Food mania and maniacal conversations about food would intensify greatly whenever there was a breather. People were very quiet during the days of severe starvation. All resources were completely cut off, leaving no room for psychological enrichment with facts, for the use of facts by the eternal human will to affirm one's system of values.

A great amount of suffering leads to a different order of sensations. Thus the critically wounded experience no pain at first and people who are freezing to death fall into a pleasant state at the end. Real starvation, it is well known, does not resemble the desire to eat. It has various guises. It could turn into anguish, indifference, mad haste, and cruelty. It was more like a chronic disease. And, as with any disease, the psyche played a very important role. Those who were doomed were not the darkest, most emaciated and swollen people but the ones whose faces had an alien expression, a wildly concentrated look, who would begin to tremble before a bowl of soup.

STORM JAMESON

from
Journey from the North

In the morning I stared from my single pane of glass at sprawling pyramids of rubble under a hard blue sky. So far as I could see there was nothing else, only these ossuaries of fractured stone and brick. A great tangled arc of steel sprang from the collapsed skeleton of some large building to hang grotesquely in mid-air. Nothing we had seen on the way across had prepared me for a city destroyed as a human body is destroyed by a shell, a mess of torn entrails and splinters of bone.

EXTRACT TWO

Seen at eye level, the desert of dust and bricks fell apart. In the street outside the hotel, the ruins had a solemn beauty. Hard to believe they were freshly made, they had every air – except the deep peace of age – of having decayed slowly through centuries: defaced carvings and the crumbling heads of statues clung to the façades, which might be a whole roofless front, or part of one, or only a few feet of jagged wall, or a single broken column in sunlight. The prevailing colour of the stone was a greyish rose fading to soft cindery pink or darkening to rust. Behind the disembowelled fronts, cataracts of rubble and dark dust. The wide street itself was as lively as a fair-ground. For its volume, the traffic made an incredible noise – a few lorries crammed with soldiers or

143

workers, country carts, shabby horse cabs, a few open seatless carts plying as buses, and odd wooden contraptions pushed by a bicycle, to hold two persons.

On every side narrow lanes traced the lines of vanished streets between the scorched shells of houses, each vomiting its dust-choked torrent of rubble. With only spades and bare hands, men and a few women were working headlong to clear them. The faintly sweetish stench of the bodies rotting under the rubble still clung to it. In London all these streets would have been roped off as dangerous – as they were. But to give a thought to safety would have put the whole of Warsaw behind ropes. Small stalls backed against the collapsing ruins were selling bread, a few pounds of butter, uninviting scraps of meat, eggs, cakes, and, believe it or not, flowers. On one stall, flour in German bags, loot from the new provinces. Countrywomen with bare dusty legs squatted on the rubble behind scraps of food, and bare-footed young boys, agile dirty gutter-rats, stood about with trays of cigarettes monstrously too dear to buy – who bought them was a mystery of the same order as the channels by which they reached Warsaw.

ANN PETRY

from

The Street

After she came out of the subway, Lutie walked slowly up the street, thinking that having solved one problem there was always a new one cropping up to take its place. Now that she and Bub were living alone, there was no one to look out for him after school. She had thought he could eat lunch at school, for it didn't cost very much – only fifty cents a week.

But after three days of school lunches, Bub protested, 'I can't eat that stuff. They give us soup every day. And I hate it.'

As soon as she could afford to, she would take an afternoon off from work and visit the school so that she could find out for herself what the menus were like. But until then, Bub would have to eat lunch at home, and that wasn't anything to worry about. It was what happened to him after school that made her frown as she walked along, for he was either in the flat by himself or playing in the street.

She didn't know which was worse – his being alone in those dreary little rooms or his playing in the street where the least of the dangers confronting him came from the stream of traffic which roared through 116th Street: cross-town buses, post-office vans, and newspaper delivery cars that swooped up and down the street turning into the avenues without warning. The traffic was an obvious threat to his safety that he could see and dodge. He was too young to recognize and avoid other dangers in the street. There were, for instance, gangs of young boys who were always on the lookout for small fry of Bub's age, because they found young kids useful in getting in through narrow fire-escape windows, in distracting a storekeeper's attention while the gang light-heartedly helped itself to his stock.

Then, in spite of the small, drab flat and the dent that moving into it had made in her week's pay and the worry about Bub that crept into her thoughts, she started humming under her breath as she went along, increasing her stride so that she was walking faster and faster because the air was crisp and clear and her long legs felt strong and just the motion of walking sent blood bubbling all through her body so that she could feel it. She came to an abrupt halt in the middle of the block because she suddenly remembered that she had completely forgotten to shop for dinner.

The butcher's shop that she entered on Eighth Avenue was crowded with customers, so that she had ample time to study the meat in the case in front of her before she was waited on. There wasn't, she saw, very much choice – ham hocks, lamb cutlets, bright-red beef. Someone had told Granny once that the butchers in Harlem used embalming fluid on the beef they sold in order to give it a nice fresh colour. Lutie didn't believe it, but like a lot of things she didn't believe, it cropped up suddenly out of nowhere to leave her wondering and staring at the brilliant scarlet colour of the meat. It made her examine the contents of the case with care in order to determine whether there was something else that would do for dinner. No, she decided. Hamburger would be the best thing to get. It cooked quickly, and a half-pound of it mixed with bread-crumbs would go a long way.

The butcher, a fat, red-faced man with a filthy apron tied around his enormous stomach, joked with the women lined up at the counter while he waited on them. A yellow cat sitting high on a shelf behind him blinked down at the customers. One of his paws almost touched the edge of a sign that said, 'No Credit'. The sign was fly-specked and dusty; its edges curling back from heat.

'Kitty had her meat today?' a thin, black woman asked as she smiled up at the cat.

'Sure thing,' and the butcher roared with laughter, and the women laughed with him until the butcher's shop was so full of merriment it sounded as though it were packed with happy, carefree people.

It wasn't even funny, Lutie thought. Yet the women rocked and roared with laughter as though they had heard some tremendous joke, went on laughing until finally there were only low chuckles and an occasional half-suppressed snort of laughter left in them. For all they knew, she thought resentfully, the yellow cat might yet end up in the meat-grinder to emerge as hamburger. Or perhaps during the cold winter months the butcher might round up all the lean, hungry cats that prowled through the streets; herding them into his back room to skin them and grind them up to make more and more hamburger that would be sold well over the ceiling price.

'A half-pound of hamburger,' was all she said when the butcher indicated it was her turn to be served. A half-pound would take care of tonight's dinner and Bub could have a sandwich of it when he came home for lunch.

She watched the butcher slap the hamburger on a piece of waxed paper; fold the paper twice, and slip the package into a brown paper bag. Handing him a dollar bill, she tucked the paper bag under her arm and held her pocket-book in the other hand so that he would have to put the change down on the counter. She never accepted change out of his hand, and watching him put it on the counter, she wondered why. Because she didn't want to touch his chapped roughened hands? Because he was white and forcing him to make the small extra effort of putting the change on the counter gave her a feeling of power?

Holding the change loosely in her hand, she walked out of the shop and turned toward the grocer's next door, where she paused for a moment in the doorway to look back at 116th Street. The sun was going down in a blaze of brilliant colour that bathed the street in a glow of light. It looked, she

147

thought, like any other New York city street in a poor neighbourhood. Perhaps a little more down-at-heel. The windows of the houses were dustier and there were more small shops on it than on streets in other parts of the city. There were also more children playing in the street and more people walking about aimlessly.

She stepped inside the grocer's, thinking that her flat would do for the time being, but the next step she should take would be to move into a better neighbourhood. As she had been able to get this far without help from anyone, why, all she had to do was plan each step and she could get wherever she wanted to go. A wave of self-confidence swept over her and she thought, I'm young and strong, there isn't anything I can't do.

Her arms were full of small packages when she left Eighth Avenue – the hamburger, a pound of potatoes, a tin of peas, a piece of butter. Besides six hard rolls that she bought instead of bread – big rolls with brown crusty outsides. They were good with coffee in the morning and Bub could have one for his lunch tomorrow with the hamburger left over from dinner.

She walked slowly, avoiding the moment when she must enter the flat and start getting dinner. She shifted the packages into a more comfortable position and feeling the hard round-ness of the rolls through the paper bag, she thought immediately of Ben Franklin and his loaf of bread. And grinned thinking, You and Ben Franklin. You ought to take one out and start eating it as you walk along 116th Street. Only you ought to remember while you eat that you're in Harlem and he was in Philadelphia a pretty long number of years ago. Yet she couldn't get rid of the feeling of self-confidence and she went on thinking that if Ben Franklin could live on a little bit of money and could prosper, then so could she. In spite of the cost of moving the furniture, if she and Bub were very careful they would have more than enough to last until her next pay-day; there might even be a couple of dollars over. If they were very careful.

The glow from the sunset was making the street radiant. The street is nice in this light, she thought. It was swarming with children who were playing ball and darting back and forth across the pavement in complicated games of tag. Girls were skipping double dutch rope, going tirelessly through the exact centre of a pair of ropes, jumping first on one foot and then the other. All the way from the corner she could hear groups of children chanting, 'Down in Mississippi and a bo-bo push! Down in Mississippi and a bo-bo push!' She stopped to watch them, and she wanted to put her packages down and jump with them; she found her foot was patting the pavement in the exact rhythm of their jumping and her hands were ready to push the jumper out of the rope at the word 'push'.

You'd better get your dinner started, Ben Franklin, she said to herself and walked on past the children who were skipping. All up and down the street kids were shining shoes. 'Shine, Miss? Shine, Miss?' the eager question greeted her on all sides.

She ignored the shoeshine boys. The weather had changed, she thought. Just last week it was freezing cold and now there was a mildness in the air that suggested early spring and the good weather had brought a lot of people out on the street. Most of the women had been marketing, for they carried bulging shopping bags. She noticed how heavily they walked on feet that obviously hurt despite the wide, cracked shoes they wore. They've been out all day working in the white folks' kitchens, she thought, then they come home and cook and clean for their own families half the night. And again she remembered Mrs Pizzini's words, 'Not good for the woman to work when she's young. Not good for the man.' Obviously she had been right, for here on this street the women trudged along overburdened, overworked, their own homes neglected while they looked after someone else's while the men on the street swung along empty-handed, well dressed and carefree. Or they lounged against the sides of the buildings, their hands in their pockets while they stared at the women who walked past, probably deciding which woman they should select to replace the wife who was out working all day.

And yet, she thought, what else is a woman to do when her man can't get a job? What else had there been for her to do that time Jim couldn't get a job? She didn't know, and she lingered in the sunlight watching a group of kids who were gathered around a boy fishing through a grating in the street. She looked down through the grating, curious to see what odds and ends had floated down under the pavement. And again she heard that eager question, 'Shine, Miss? Shine, Miss?'

She walked on, thinking, That's another thing. These kids should have some better way of earning money than by shining shoes. It was all wrong. It was like conditioning them beforehand for the role they were supposed to play. If they start out young like this shining shoes, they'll take it for granted they've got to sweep floors and mop stairs the rest of their lives.

Just before she reached her own door, she heard the question again, 'Shine, Miss?' And then a giggle. 'Gosh, Mum, you didn't even know me.'

She turned around quickly and she was so startled she had to look twice to be sure. Yes. It was Bub. He was sitting astride a shoeshine box, his round head silhouetted against the brick wall of the apartment house behind him. He was smiling at her, utterly delighted that he had succeeded in surprising her. His head was thrown back and she could see all his even, firm teeth.

In the brief moment it took her to shift all the small packages under her left arm, she saw all the details of the shoeshine box. There was a worn piece of red carpet tacked on the seat of the box. The brassy drawing pins that held it in place picked up the glow from the sunset so that they sparkled. Ten-cent bottles of shoe polish, a worn shoe-brush and a pad, were neatly lined up on a little shelf under the seat. He had decorated the sides of the box with part of his collection of book matches.

150

Then she slapped him sharply across the face. His look of utter astonishment made her strike him again – this time more violently, and she hated herself for doing it, even as she lifted her hand for another blow.

'But Mum – ' he protested, raising his arm to protect his face.

'You get in the house,' she ordered and yanked him to his feet. He leaned over to pick up the shoeshine box and she struck him again. 'Leave that thing there,' she said sharply, and shook him when he tried to struggle out of her grasp.

Her voice grew thick with rage. 'I'm working to look after you and you out here in the street shining shoes just like the rest of these little niggers.' And she thought, You know that isn't all there is involved. It's also that Little Henry Chandler is the same age as Bub, and you know Little Henry is wearing grey flannel suits and dark blue caps and long blue socks and fine, dark brown leather shoes. He's doing his homework in that big, warm library in front of the fireplace. And your kid is out in the street with a shoeshine box. He's wearing his after-school clothes, which don't look too different from the ones he wears to school – shabby knickers and stockings with holes in the heels, because no matter how much you darn and mend he comes right out of his stockings.

It's also that you're afraid that if he's shining shoes at eight, he will be cleaning windows at sixteen and running an elevator at twenty-one, and go on doing that for the rest of his life. And you're afraid that this street will keep him from finishing at high school; that it may do worse than that and get him into some kind of trouble that will land him in a reform school because you can't be home to look out for him because you have to work.

SHIRLEY JACKSON NEW YORK

Pillar of Salt

For some reason a tune was running through her head when she and her husband got on the train in New Hampshire for their trip to New York; they had not been to New York for nearly a year, but the tune was from further back than that. It was from the days when she was fifteen or sixteen, and had never seen New York except in movies, when the city was made up, to her, of penthouses filled with Noel Coward people; when the height and speed and luxury and gaiety that made up a city like New York were confused inextricably with the dullness of being fifteen, and beauty unreachable and far in the movies.

'What *is* that tune?' she said to her husband, and hummed it. 'It's from some old movie, I think.'

'I know it,' he said, and hummed it himself. 'Can't remember the words.'

He sat back comfortably. He had hung up their coats, put the suitcases on the rack, and had taken his magazine out. 'I'll think of it sooner or later,' he said.

She looked out the window first, tasting it almost secretly, savoring the extreme pleasure of being on a moving train with nothing to do for six hours but read and nap and go into the dining-car, going farther and farther every minute from the children, from the kitchen floor, with even the hills being incredibly left behind, changing into fields and trees too far away from home to be daily. 'I love trains,' she said, and her husband nodded sympathetically into his magazine.

152

Two weeks ahead, two unbelievable weeks, with all arrangements made, no further planning to do, except perhaps what theatres or what restaurants. A friend with an apartment went on a convenient vacation, there was enough money in the bank to make a trip to New York compatible with new snow suits for the children; there was the smoothness of unopposed arrangements, once the initial obstacles had been overcome, as though when they had really made up their minds, nothing dared stop them. The baby's sore throat cleared up. The plumber came, finished his work in two days, and left. The dresses had been altered in time; the hardware store could be left safely, once they had found the excuse of looking over new city products. New York had not burned down, had not been quarantined, their friend had gone away according to schedule, and Brad had the keys to the apartment in his pocket. Everyone knew where to reach everyone else; there was a list of plays not to miss and a list of items to look out for in the stores – diapers, dress materials, fancy canned goods, tarnish-proof silverware boxes. And, finally, the train was there, performing its function, pacing through the afternoon, carrying them legally and with determination to New York.

Margaret looked curiously at her husband, inactive in the middle of the afternoon on a train, at the other fortunate people traveling, at the sunny country outside, looked again to make sure, and then opened her book. The tune was still in her head, she hummed it and heard her husband take it up softly as he turned a page in his magazine.

In the dining-car she ate roast beef, as she would have done in a restaurant at home, reluctant to change over too quickly to the new, tantalizing food of a vacation. She had ice cream for dessert but became uneasy over her coffee because they were due in New York in an hour and she still had to put on her coat and hat, relishing every gesture, and Brad must take the suitcases down and put away the magazines. They stood at the end of the car for the interminable underground run, picking up their suitcases and putting them down again, moving restlessly inch by inch.

The station was a momentary shelter, moving visitors gradually into a world of people and sound and light to prepare them for the blasting reality of the street outside. She saw it for a minute from the sidewalk before she was in a taxi moving into the middle of it, and then they were bewilderingly caught and carried on uptown and whirled out on to another sidewalk and Brad paid the taxi driver and put his head back to look up at the apartment house. 'This is it, all right,' he said, as though he had doubted the driver's ability to find a number so simply given. Upstairs in the elevator, and the key fit the door. They had never seen their friend's apartment before, but it was reasonably familiar – a friend moving from New Hampshire to New York carries private pictures of a home not erasable in a few years, and the apartment had enough of home in it to settle Brad immediately in the right chair and comfort her with instinctive trust of the linen and blankets.

'This is home for two weeks,' Brad said, and stretched. After the first few minutes they both went to the windows automatically; New York was below, as arranged, and the houses across the street were apartment houses filled with unknown people.

'It's wonderful,' she said. There were cars down there, and people, and the noise was there. 'I'm so happy,' she said, and kissed her husband.

They went sight-seeing the first day; they had breakfast in an Automat and went to the top of the Empire State Building. 'Got it all fixed up now,' Brad said, at the top. 'Wonder just where that plane hit.'

They tried to peer down on all four sides, but were embarrassed about asking. 'After all,' she said reasonably, giggling in a corner, 'if something of mine got broken I wouldn't want people poking around asking to see the pieces.'

'If you owned the Empire State Building you wouldn't care,' Brad said.

They traveled only in taxis the first few days, and one taxi had a door held on with a piece of string; they pointed to it and laughed silently at each other, and on about the third day, the taxi they were riding in got a flat tire on Broadway and they had to get out and find another.

'We've only got eleven days left,' she said one day, and then, seemingly minutes later, 'we've already been here six days.'

They had got in touch with the friends they had expected to get in touch with, they were going to a Long Island summer home for a weekend. 'It looks pretty dreadful right now,' their hostess said cheerfully over the phone, 'and we're leaving in a week ourselves, but I'd never *forgive* you if you didn't see it *once* while you were here.' The weather had been fair but cool, with a definite autumn awareness, and the clothes in the store windows were dark and already hinting at furs and velvets. She wore her coat every day, and suits most of the time. The light dresses she had brought were hanging in the closet in the apartment, and she was thinking now of getting a sweater in one of the big stores, something impractical for New Hampshire, but probably good for Long Island.

'I have to do some shopping, at least one day,' she said to Brad, and he groaned.

'Don't ask me to carry packages,' he said.

'You aren't up to a good day's shopping,' she told him, 'not after all this walking around you've been doing. Why don't you go to a movie or something?'

'I want to do some shopping myself,' he said mysteriously. Perhaps he was talking about her Christmas present; she had thought vaguely of getting such things done in New York; the children would be pleased with novelties from the city, toys not seen in their home stores. At any rate she said, 'You'll probably be able to get to your wholesalers at last.'

They were on their way to visit another friend, who had found a place to live by a miracle and warned them consequently not to quarrel with the appearance of the building,

155

or the stairs, or the neighbourhood. All three were bad, and
the stairs were three flights, narrow and dark, but there was
a place to live at the top. Their friend had not been in New
York long, but he lived by himself in two rooms, and had
easily caught the mania for slim tables and low bookcases
which made his rooms look too large for the furniture in
some places, too cramped and uncomfortable in others.

'What a lovely place,' she said when she came in, and then
was sorry when her host said, 'Some day this damn situation
will let up and I'll be able to settle down in a really decent
place.'

There were other people there; they sat and talked com-
panionably about the same subjects then current in New
Hampshire, but they drank more than they would have at
home and it left them strangely unaffected; their voices were
louder and their words more extravagant; their gestures, on
the other hand, were smaller, and they moved a finger where
in New Hampshire they would have waved an arm. Margaret
said frequently, 'We're just staying here for a couple of
weeks, on a vacation,' and she said, 'It's wonderful, so
exciting,' and she said, 'We were *terribly* lucky; this friend
went out of town just at the right . . .'

Finally the room was very full and noisy, and she went
into a corner near a window to catch her breath. The window
had been opened and shut all evening, depending on whether
the person standing next to it had both hands free; and now
it was shut, with the clear sky outside. Someone came and
stood next to her, and she said, 'Listen to the noise outside.
It's as bad as it is inside.'

He said, 'In a neighbourhood like this someone's always
getting killed.'

She frowned. 'It sounds different than before. I mean,
there's a different sound to it.'

'Alcoholics,' he said. 'Drunks in the streets. Fighting going
on across the way.' He wandered away, carrying his drink.

She opened the window and leaned out, and there were
people hanging out the windows across the way shouting,

and people standing in the street looking up and shouting, and from across the way she heard clearly, 'Lady, lady.' They must mean me, she thought, they're all looking this way. She leaned out farther and the voices shouted incoherently but somehow making an audible whole, 'Lady, your house is on fire, lady, lady.'

She closed the window firmly and turned around to the other people in the room, raising her voice a little. 'Listen,' she said, 'they're saying the house is on fire.' She was desperately afraid of their laughing at her, of looking like a fool while Brad across the room looked at her blushing. She said again, 'The *house* is on *fire*,' and added, 'They say,' for fear of sounding too vehement. The people nearest to her turned and someone said, 'She says the house is on fire.'

She wanted to get to Brad and couldn't see him; her host was not in sight either, and the people all around were strangers. They don't listen to me, she thought, I might as well not be here, and she went to the outside door and opened it. There was no smoke, no flame, but she was telling herself, I might as well not be here, so she abandoned Brad in panic and ran without her hat and coat down the stairs, carrying a glass in one hand and a package of matches in the other. The stairs were insanely long, but they were clear and safe, and she opened the street door and ran out. A man caught her arm and said, 'Everyone out of the house?' and she said, 'No, Brad's still there.' The fire engines swept around the corner, with people leaning out of the windows watching them, and the man holding her arm said, 'It's down here,' and left her. The fire was two houses away; they could see flames behind the top windows, and smoke against the night sky, but in ten minutes it was finished and the fire engines pulled away with an air of martyrdom for hauling out all their equipment to put out a ten-minute fire.

She went back upstairs slowly and with embarrassment, and found Brad and took him home.

'I was so frightened,' she said to him when they were safely in bed, 'I lost my head completely.'

'You should have tried to find someone,' he said.

'They wouldn't listen,' she insisted. 'I kept telling them and they wouldn't listen and then I thought I must have been mistaken. I had some idea of going down to see what was going on.'

'Lucky it was no worse,' Brad said sleepily.

'I felt trapped,' she said. 'High up in that old building with a fire; it's like a nightmare. And in a strange city.'

'Well, it's all over now,' Brad said.

The same faint feeling of insecurity tagged her the next day; she went shopping alone and Brad went off to see hardware, after all. She got on a bus to go downtown and the bus was too full to move when it came time for her to get out. Wedged standing in the aisle she said, 'Out, please,' and, 'Excuse me,' and by the time she was loose and near the door the bus had started again and she got off a stop beyond. 'No one *listens* to me,' she said to herself. 'Maybe it's because I'm too polite.' In the stores the prices were all too high and the sweaters looked disarmingly like New Hampshire ones. The toys for the children filled her with dismay; they were so obviously for New York children: hideous little parodies of adult life, cash registers, tiny pushcarts with imitation fruit, telephones that really worked (as if there weren't enough phones in New York that really worked), miniature milk bottles in a carrying case. 'We get our milk from cows,' Margaret told the salesgirl. 'My children wouldn't know what these were.' She was exaggerating, and felt guilty for a minute, but no one was around to catch her.

She had a picture of small children in the city dressed like their parents, following along with a miniature mechanical civilization, toy cash registers in larger and larger sizes that eased them into the real thing, millions of clattering jerking small imitations that prepared them nicely for taking over the large useless toys their parents lived by. She bought a pair of skis for her son, which she knew would be inadequate for the New Hampshire snow, and a wagon for her daughter inferior to the one Brad could make at home in an hour.

Ignoring the toy mailboxes, the small phonographs with special small records, the kiddie cosmetics, she left the store and started home.

She was frankly afraid by now to take a bus; she stood on the corner and waited for a taxi. Glancing down at her feet, she saw a dime on the sidewalk and tried to pick it up, but there were too many people for her to bend down, and she was afraid to shove to make room for fear of being stared at. She put her foot on the dime and then saw a quarter near it, and a nickel. Someone dropped a pocketbook, she thought, and put her other foot on the quarter, stepping quickly to make it look natural; then she saw another dime and another nickel, and a third dime in the gutter. People were passing her, back and forth, all the time, rushing, pushing against her, not looking at her, and she was afraid to get down and start gathering up the money. Other people saw it and went past, and she realized that no one was going to pick it up. They were all embarrassed, or in too much of a hurry, or too crowded. A taxi stopped to let someone off, and she hailed it. She lifted her feet off the dime and the quarter, and left them there when she got into the taxi. This taxi went slowly and bumped as it went; she had begun to notice that the gradual decay was not peculiar to the taxis. The buses were cracking open in unimportant seams, the leather seats broken and stained. The buildings were going, too – in one of the nicest stores there had been a great gaping hole in the tiled foyer, and you walked around it. Corners of the buildings seemed to be crumbling away into fine dust that drifted downward, the granite was eroding unnoticed. Every window she saw on her way uptown seemed to be broken; perhaps every street corner was peppered with small change. The people were moving faster than ever before; a girl in a red hat appeared at the upper side of the taxi window and was gone beyond the lower side before you could see the hat; store windows were so terribly bright because you only caught them for a fraction of a second. The people seemed hurled on in a frantic action that made every hour forty-five minutes long, every day nine hours, every year fourteen days. Food was so elusively fast, eaten in such a hurry, that you were always hungry, always speeding to a new meal with new people. Everything was imperceptibly quicker every minute. She stepped into the taxi on one side and stepped out the other side at her home; she pressed the fifth-floor button on the elevator and was coming down again, bathed and dressed and ready for dinner with Brad. They went out for dinner and were coming in again, hungry and hurrying to bed in order to get to breakfast with lunch beyond. They had been in New York nine days; tomorrow was Saturday and they were going to Long Island, coming home Sunday, and then Wednesday they were going home, really home. By the time she had thought of it they were on the train to Long Island; the train was broken, the seats torn and the floor dirty; one of the doors wouldn't open and the windows wouldn't shut. Passing through the outskirts of the city, she thought, It's as though everything were traveling so fast that the solid stuff couldn't stand it and were going to pieces under the strain, cornices blowing off and windows caving in. She knew she was afraid to say it truly, afraid to face the knowledge that it was a voluntary neck-breaking speed, a deliberate whirling faster and faster to end in destruction.

On Long Island, their hostess led them into a new piece of New York, a house filled with New York furniture as though on rubber bands, pulled this far, stretched taut, and ready to snap back to the city, to an apartment, as soon as the door was opened and the lease, fully paid, had expired. 'We've had this place every year for simply ages,' their hostess said. 'Otherwise we couldn't have gotten it *possibly* this year.'

'It's an awfully nice place,' Brad said. 'I'm surprised you don't live here all year round.'

'Got to get back to the city *some* time,' their hostess said, and laughed.

'Not much like New Hampshire,' Brad said. He was beginning to be a little homesick, Margaret thought; he wants to yell, just once. Since the fire scare she was apprehensive about large groups of people gathering together; when friends began to drop in after dinner she waited for a while, telling herself they were on the ground floor, she could run right outside, all the windows were open; then she excused herself and went to bed. When Brad came to bed much later she woke up and he said irritably, 'We've been playing anagrams. Such crazy people.' She said sleepily, 'Did you win?' and fell asleep before he told her.

The next morning she and Brad went for a walk while their host and hostess read the Sunday papers. 'If you turn to the right outside the door,' their hostess said encouragingly, 'and walk about three blocks down, you'll come to our beach.'

'What do they want with our beach?' their host said. 'It's too damn cold to do anything down there.'

'They can look at the *water*,' their hostess said.

They walked down to the beach; at this time of year it was bare and windswept, yet still nodding hideously under traces of its summer plumage, as though it thought itself warmly inviting. There were occupied houses on the way there, for instance, and a lonely lunchstand was open, bravely advertising hot dogs and root beer. The man in the lunchstand watched them go by, his face cold and unsympathetic. They walked far past him, out of sight of houses, on to a stretch of grey pebbled sand that lay between the grey water on one side and the grey pebbled sand dunes on the other.

'Imagine going swimming here,' she said with a shiver. The beach pleased her; it was oddly familiar and reassuring and at the same time that she realized this, the little tune came back to her, bringing a double recollection. The beach was the one where she had lived in imagination, writing for herself dreary love-broken stories where the heroine walked beside the wild waves; the little tune was the symbol of the golden world she escaped into to avoid the everyday dreariness that drove her into writing depressing stories about the beach. She laughed out loud and Brad said, 'What on earth's so funny about this Godforsaken landscape?'

'I was just thinking how far away from the city it seems,' she said falsely.

The sky and the water and the sand were grey enough to make it feel like late afternoon instead of midmorning; she was tired and wanted to go back, but Brad said suddenly, 'Look at that,' and she turned and saw a girl running down over the dunes, carrying her hat, and her hair flying behind her.

'Only way to get warm on a day like this,' Brad remarked, but Margaret said, 'She looks frightened.'

The girl saw them and came toward them, slowing down as she approached them. She was eager to reach them but when she came within speaking distance the familiar embarrassment, the not wanting to look like a fool, made her hesitate and look from one to the other of them uncomfortably.

'Do you know where I can find a policeman?' she asked finally.

Brad looked up and down the bare rocky beach and said solemnly, 'There don't seem to be any around. Is there something we can do?'

'I don't think so,' the girl said. 'I really need a policeman.'

They go to the police for everything, Margaret thought, these people, these New York people, it's as though they had selected a section of the population to act as problem-solvers, and so no matter what they want they look for a policeman.

'Be glad to help you if we can,' Brad said.

The girl hesitated again. 'Well, if you *must* know,' she said crossly, 'there's a leg up there.'

They waited politely for the girl to explain, but she only said, 'Come *on*, then,' and waved to them to follow her. She led them over the dunes to a spot near a small inlet, where the dunes gave way abruptly to an intruding head of water. A leg was lying on the sand near the water, and the girl gestured at it and said, 'There,' as though it were her own property and they had insisted on having a share.

They walked over to it and Brad bent down gingerly. 'It's

a leg all right,' he said. It looked like part of a wax dummy, a death-white wax leg neatly cut off at top-thigh and again just above the ankle, bent comfortably at the knee and resting on the sand. 'It's real,' Brad said, his voice slightly different. 'You're right about that policeman.'

They walked together to the lunchstand and the man listened unenthusiastically while Brad called the police. When the police came they all walked out again to where the leg was lying and Brad gave the police their names and addresses, and then said, 'Is it all right to go on home?'

'What the hell you want to hang around for?' the policeman inquired with heavy humor. 'You waiting for the rest of him?'

They went back to their host and hostess, talking about the leg, and their host apologized, as though he had been guilty of a breach of taste in allowing his guests to come on a human leg; their hostess said with interest, 'There was an arm washed up in Bensonhurst, I've been reading about it.'

'One of these killings,' the host said.

Upstairs Margaret said abruptly, 'I suppose it starts to happen first in the suburbs,' and when Brad said, 'What starts to happen?' she said hysterically, 'People starting to come apart.'

In order to reassure their host and hostess about their minding the leg, they stayed until the last afternoon train to New York. Back in their apartment again it seemed to Margaret that the marble in the house lobby had begun to age a little; even in two days there were new perceptible cracks. The elevator seemed a little rusty, and there was a fine film of dust over everything in the apartment. They went to bed feeling uncomfortable, and the next morning Margaret said immediately, 'I'm going to stay in today.'

'You're not upset about yesterday, are you?'

'Not a bit,' Margaret said. 'I just want to stay in and rest.'

After some discussion Brad decided to go off again by himself; he still had people it was important to see and places he must go in the few days they had left. After breakfast in the Automat Margaret came back alone to the apartment, carrying the mystery story she had bought on the way. She hung up her coat and hat and sat down by the window with the noise and the people far below, looking out at the sky where it was grey beyond the houses across the street.

I'm not going to worry about it, she said to herself, no sense thinking all the time about things like that, spoil your vacation and Brad's too. No sense worrying, people get ideas like that and then worry about them.

The nasty little tune was running through her head again, with its burden of suavity and expensive perfume. The houses across the street were silent and perhaps unoccupied at this time of day; she let her eyes move with the rhythm of the tune, from window to window along one floor. By gliding quickly across two windows, she could make one line of the tune fit one floor of windows, and then a quick breath and a drop down to the next floor; it had the same number of windows and the tune had the same number of beats, and then the next floor and the next. She stopped suddenly when it seemed to her that the windowsill she had just passed had soundlessly crumpled and fallen into fine sand; when she looked back it was there as before but then it seemed to be the windowsill above and to the right, and finally a corner of the roof.

No sense worrying, she told herself, forcing her eyes down to the street, stop thinking about things all the time. Looking down at the street for long made her dizzy and she stood up and went into the small bedroom of the apartment. She had made the bed before going out to breakfast, like any good housewife, but now she deliberately took it apart, stripping the blankets and sheets off one by one, and then she made it again, taking a long time over the corners and smoothing out every wrinkle. '*That's* done,' she said when she was through, and went back to the window. When she looked across the street the tune started again, window to window, sills dissolving and falling downward. She leaned forward and looked down at her own window, something she had never thought of before, down to the sill. It was partly eaten away; when she touched the stone a few crumbs rolled off and fell.

It was eleven o'clock; Brad was looking at blowtorches by now and would not be back before one, if even then. She thought of writing a letter home, but the impulse left her before she found paper and pen. Then it occurred to her that she might take a nap, a thing she had never done in the morning in her life, and she went in and lay down on the bed. Lying down, she felt the building shaking.

No sense worrying, she told herself again, as though it were a charm against witches, and got up and found her coat and hat and put them on. I'll just get some cigarettes and some letter paper, she thought, just run down to the corner. Panic caught her going down in the elevator; it went too fast, and when she stepped out in the lobby it was only the people standing around who kept her from running. As it was, she went quickly out of the building and into the street. For a minute she hesitated, wanting to go back. The cars were going past so rapidly, the people hurrying as always, but the panic of the elevator drove her on finally. She went to the corner, and, following the people flying along ahead, ran out into the street, to hear a horn almost overhead and a shout from behind her, and the noise of brakes. She ran blindly on and reached the other side where she stopped and looked around. The truck was going on its appointed way around the corner, the people going past on either side of her, parting to go around here where she stood.

No one even noticed me, she thought with reassurance, everyone who saw me has gone by long ago. She went into the drugstore ahead of her and asked the man for cigarettes; the apartment now seemed safer to her than the street – she could walk up the stairs. Coming out of the store and walking to the corner, she kept as close to the buildings as possible, refusing to give way to the rightful traffic coming out of the doorways. On the corner she looked carefully at the light; it was green, but it looked as though it were going to change.

Always safer to wait, she thought, don't want to walk into another truck.

People pushed past her and some were caught in the middle of the street when the light changed. One woman, more cowardly than the rest, turned and ran back to the curb, but the others stood in the middle of the street, leaning forward and then backward according to the traffic moving past them on both sides. One got to the farther curb in a brief break in the line of cars, the others were a fraction of a second too late and waited. Then the light changed again and as the cars slowed down Margaret put a foot on the street to go, but a taxi swinging wildly around her corner frightened her back and she stood on the curb again. By the time the taxi had gone the light was due to change again and she thought, I can wait once more, no sense getting caught out in the middle. A man beside her tapped his foot impatiently for the light to change back; two girls came past her and walked out into the street a few steps to wait, moving back a little when cars came too close, talking busily all the time. I ought to stay right with them, Margaret thought, but then they moved back against her and the light changed and the man next to her charged into the street and the two girls in front waited a minute and then moved slowly on, still talking, and Margaret started to follow and then decided to wait. A crowd of people formed around her suddenly; they had come off a bus and were crossing here, and she had a sudden feeling of being jammed in the center and forced out into the street when all of them moved as one with the light changing, and she elbowed her way desperately out of the crowd and went off to lean against a building and wait. It seemed to her that people passing were beginning to look at her. What do they think of me, she wondered, and stood up straight as though she were waiting for someone. She looked at her watch and frowned, and then thought, What a fool I must look like, no one here ever saw me before, they all go by too fast. She went back to the curb again but the green light was just changing to red and she thought, I'll go back to the drugstore and have a Coke, no sense going back to that apartment.

The man looked at her unsurprised in the drugstore and she sat and ordered a Coke but suddenly as she was drinking it the panic caught her again and she thought of the people who had been with her when she first started to cross the street, blocks away by now, having tried and made perhaps a dozen lights while she had hesitated at the first; people by now a mile or so downtown, because they had been going steadily while she had been trying to gather her courage. She paid the man quickly, restrained an impulse to say that there was nothing wrong with the Coke, she just had to get back, that was all, and she hurried down to the corner again.

The minute the light changes, she told herself firmly; there's no sense. The light changed before she was ready and in the minute before she collected herself traffic turning the corner overwhelmed her and she shrank back against the curb. She looked longingly at the cigar store on the opposite corner, with her apartment house beyond; she wondered, How do people ever manage to get there, and knew that by wondering, by admitting a doubt, she was lost. The light changed and she looked at it with hatred, a dumb thing, turning back and forth, back and forth, with no purpose and no meaning. Looking to either side of her slyly, to see if anyone were watching, she stepped quietly backward, one step, two, until she was well away from the curb. Back in the drugstore again she waited for some sign of recognition from the clerk and saw none; he regarded her with the same apathy as he had the first time. He gestured without interest at the telephone; he doesn't care, she thought, it doesn't matter to him who I call.

She had no time to feel like a fool, because they answered the phone immediately and agreeably and found him right away. When he answered the phone, his voice sounding surprised and matter-of-fact, she could only say miserably, 'I'm in the drugstore on the corner. Come and get me.'

'What's the matter?' He was not anxious to come.

'Please come and get me,' she said into the black mouthpiece that might or might not tell him, 'please come and get me, Brad. *Please.*'

CARMEN LAFORET \quad BARCEL

from
Nada

TRANSLATED BY INEZ MUÑOZ

Angustias examined the wrinkled leather of my shoes (which, like a human face, betrayed their age), noticed the holes that let in the dampness, and said I had taken cold from wetting my feet. 'And besides,' she went on, 'when one is poor and lives on charity, my child, one must be more careful of one's personal belongings. You mustn't go for so many walks, and you must tread more carefully . . . Don't look at me like that: I might as well tell you that I know perfectly well what you do when I am at the office. I know you go out and come back before I do, so that I shan't find you out. May I ask where you go?'

'No special place. I like to see the streets – and the city.'

'But you like to go about alone, my dear, as if you were a street urchin, exposed to men's impertinences. Do you think you are a servant girl? . . . When I was your age, I wasn't allowed to go as far as the front door. I know you have to walk to the University and back . . . but this wandering about like a stray dog . . . When you are alone in the world you can do as you please. But now you have a family, a home, a name. Obviously your country cousin didn't teach you how to behave. Your father was a very peculiar man. Not that your cousin is not a excellent person, but she lacks refinement. Anyhow, I hope you didn't gad about the village streets all day.'

'No.'

169

'Well, please do so even less here. Do you hear me?'

I didn't say anything more. What could I say?

Suddenly, just as she was leaving, she turned with a horrified look and asked:

'I hope you haven't been along the Ramblas towards the port?'

'Why not?'

'My child, if a lady were to go into some of those streets, she'd lose her reputation for ever. I'm referring to the Chinese quarter. You don't know where it begins . . .'

'Yes, I know perfectly well; I haven't been there. What is it like?'

Angustias looked at me angrily:

'Full of women, thieves and the devil's own glitter.'

(At that moment I pictured the Chinese quarter sparkling with beauty.)

The moment for an explanation with Angustias was approaching, like an inevitable storm. I knew the first time I talked with her that we would never understand one another. My astonishment at that first, disagreeable encounter had given my aunt an advantage over me. But after this new conversation I thought, 'That's all over now.' I saw myself beginning a new life and doing what I pleased, and I smiled at Angustias with secret irony.

EXTRACT TWO

The University clock was striking half-past twelve as we reached the square. Juan crossed it and stopped at the corner opposite – where the Ronda de San Antonio runs into the darkness of the calle de Tallers. A stream of bright light came from the calle de Pelayo below. The electric signs were winking as if taking part in a stupid game. Trams passed in front of Juan. He glanced about as if to get his bearings. He was so thin that his coat hung round him loosely and flapped against his legs in the wind. I was standing almost beside him, not daring to speak to him. What would have been the use?

My heart was beating after running so fast. I followed him as he took several steps towards the Ronda de San Antonio. Suddenly he turned round so quickly that we were almost face to face. However, he did not notice me and passed me in the opposite direction. We came again to the Plaza de la Universidad and he turned into the calle de Tallers. It was quite empty. The street lights were dimmer here, and the pavement was very uneven. Juan stopped again where the street forked. I remember a drinking-fountain with a dripping tap, which made puddles on the ground. Juan looked for a moment towards the square of light where the street opens into the noisy Ramblas. Then he turned into the equally dark and twisting calle de Ramalleras. I had to run to keep up with him. A smell of fruit and straw came from a shut shop. The moon rose over a wall. I felt my blood rushing through my veins.

Whenever we came in sight of the Ramblas from a side street Juan stopped and looked round, with hollow eyes, biting his lips. At the corner of the calle de Carmen, which was better lighted than the others, I saw him stand still with his right elbow in the palm of his left hand, stroking his face, as if under stress of some great mental effort.

It seemed that the chase would never end. I had no idea where he wanted to go and I did not care. I was obsessed with the need to follow him although I did not know why I was doing it. Later I realized that we could have come by a much shorter way. We went through part of the San José market, our footsteps echoing under the high roof. The great building, with its multitude of empty stalls, looked dead and sad under its few yellow lamps. Large rats, with eyes as bright as cats, fled noisily from us. A few very big ones stopped a moment, as if they might attack us. There was an indescribable smell of rotten fruit and remains of fish and meat ... A night-watchman eyed us suspiciously as I ran after Juan into one of the narrow back streets.

When we reached the calle del Hospital, Juan dashed towards the lights of the Ramblas which he had previously seemed to avoid. We were in the Rambla del Centro and I had nearly caught up to him. He seemed to be instinctively aware of me, and kept looking back; but although his gaze fell upon me he appeared not to see me. He looked like a suspicious character, like a thief running away, bumping into passersby. I think someone flung an obscene remark at me, but I am not certain, although I was probably insulted and laughed at many times. I did not stop to think how this adventure might end, nor what I could do to calm a man whose violent outbursts I knew so well. The knowledge that he was unarmed was a relief. I was so agitated that my thoughts were in confusion, and my throat ached.

Juan went into the brilliantly lit, crowded calle del Conde de Asalto. I realized that this was the beginning of the Chinese quarter. The 'devil's brilliance' which Aunt Angustias had told me about was squalid and tawdry, displaying itself in a great number of posters of men and women dancers, and stalls like those of a fair. Harsh, discordant music came from all sides and filled the air. Making my way quickly through a crowd of people who got in my way exasperatingly and prevented my following Juan, I vividly remembered a carnival I had seen as a child. These people really were grotesque. A man in a wide hat passed by, his face rouged and his eyelashes thick with paint. They all seemed to be wearing fancy dress in the worst of taste, and my senses were assailed by the noise, and by the smell of wine. I was not even afraid, as I had been long ago, when, holding on to my mother's skirts I had listened to the laughter and watched the absurd contortions of the masqueraders. It was all part of a nightmare in which the only real fact was my pursuit of Juan.

To my consternation I lost sight of him. Someone pushed me. I raised my eyes and at the end of the street I saw the Montjuich clothed in greenery, in the purity of the night . . .

EXTRACT THREE

The air outside was warm. I stood at the top of the long calle Muntaner, not knowing what to do. Above, the almost blue-black, cloudless sky looked heavy and menacing. There was something awe-inspiring in the classical beauty of the sky weighing down upon the silent street, something which made me feel small and as if caught in the midst of cosmic forces, like the heroine of a Greek tragedy.

I felt stifled by so much light, by the thirsty expanses of asphalt and stone. I walked as if I were retracing the deserted path of my life. I saw the shadows of other walkers flit by and could not stop them. At every moment I felt more hopelessly alone.

Cars passed me. A crowded tram went up the street. In front of me was the via Diagonal with its pavements, its palm trees, its benches. A moment later I found myself sitting huddled on one of these benches. I was exhausted and aching as if after a great effort. How useless it seemed to struggle along, without ever being able to leave the shut-in path of one's own personality! Some people are born to live; others to work; others to contemplate life. My role was the insignificant one of a spectator and I could not free myself from it. At the moment the only reality was my own misery.

The world began to tremble behind a soft grey mist, made opalescent by the sun. My face welcomed my streaming tears. My fingers dried them angrily. I continued to weep for a long time in the privacy of the indifferent street, and gradually I felt my spirit becoming cleansed.

My childish grief at a disappointment was not really worth so much display. I had rapidly turned over one page of my life and it was not worth while thinking of it again. I had often laughed unfeelingly at greater sorrow in others . . .

On my way home I walked the whole length of the calle de Aribau. I had been so long engrossed in my own thoughts that the sky was turning pale. The street was coming alive with the dusk and the shop windows were like a long row of yellow and white eyes peering from their deep sockets . . . A thousand smells, sorrows, and memories rose from the pavements and crept up to the windows and doors of the calle de Aribau. A wave of lively humanity was coming down from the fashionable world of the Diagonal to meet the crowds of the Plaza de la Universidad. A mingled stream of different lives, characters, tastes, flowed down the calle de Aribau. I myself was one drop in it, small and lost.

EXTRACT FOUR

I walked down the Ramblas towards the port. I grew calmer as I thought fondly of Ena. Her own mother had assured me of Ena's devotion to me. She, who was so brilliant and universally beloved, admired and liked me. I was proud to think that Ena's mother had entrusted me with a mission on her behalf. But I did not know if my intervention would serve any purpose. Gloria's news of Ena's projected visit that afternoon filled me with anxiety.

I had reached the port. The shut-in patch of sea was bright with spots of oil, and a smell of rope and tar penetrated my lungs. The tall sides of the ships looked enormous. Now and again the water quivered under the movement of a fish or the oars of a rowing-boat. There I stood this summer noon. Perhaps, from the deck of a ship, blue Nordic eyes were looking at me as a tiny dot in a picture of a foreign shore . . . A Spanish girl, with dark hair, standing on the quay at Barcelona. In a moment life would go on and carry me on to some other point; I would find myself in another setting . . . 'Eating somewhere, perhaps,' I thought at last, as hunger gripped me. I had very little money, but still I had some. I went slowly towards the gay restaurants and bars of Barceloneta. Painted in blue or white, they strike a cheerful, marine note on sunny days. Some have terraces where people sit and eat rice and shell-fish, their appetites stimulated by the rich warm summer smells coming from the beach and the neighbourhood of the docks.

A hot, grey wind was blowing from the sea that day. I heard someone say it was the season for storms. I ordered beer and cheese and almonds. The bar where I was sitting was a two-storied affair, painted indigo and decorated with nautical instruments. I sat at one of the little tables outside and the ground seemed to sway beneath me propelled by some hidden engine, as if to carry me far away . . . to new horizons. This daydream of mine was one which used to crop up, without rhyme or reason, all my life long.

I sat there for a long time . . . My head ached. At last, very slowly, I dragged myself home, with the clouds weighing on my shoulders like sacks full of wool. I turned aside once or twice. But as the time passed, I stood still for a while. An invisible thread seemed to be pulling me in the direction of the calle de Aribau, to the front door, to Román's room at the top of the house . . . When the afternoon was half over I could no longer resist and entered our door.

As I went up the stairs the familiar dull silence hung about me. On one of the landings the sound of a servant girl singing in the courtyard reached me through a broken window-pane.

THE FIFTIES

S YLVIA PLATH'S novel *The Bell Jar* (1963) opens in
New York on the sultry July day in 1953 when Julius
and Ethel Rosenberg were executed as Soviet spies.
'The idea of being electrocuted makes me sick, and
that's all there was to read about in the papers – goggle-eyed
headlines staring up at me on every street corner and at the
fusty, peanut-smelling mouth of every subway. It had
nothing to do with me, but I couldn't help wondering what
it would be like, being burned alive all along your nerves,'
recalls the young Esther Greenwood. The novel ends with
Esther's breakdown and hospitalisation.

Like Shirley Jackson's 'Pillar of Salt', *The Bell Jar* seems to
distil the period's airlessness, the oppressive family values
absorbing the daily tensions and treasons of McCarthyism.
This is an urban landscape peopled by figures lost to
themselves, a hallucinatory reality where women feel more
than can be borne.

Carol, the novel Patricia Highsmith published
pseudonomously in 1952, gives yet another take on this
prohibitive and persecutory climate, with its story of a
lesbian love affair that begins in a New York department
store. Elsewhere, in Greenwich Village, now the enclave of
the Beats, free-falling revolt from family conformities
relegated women to the role of hangers-on or supports.
Wives, lovers, surrogate mothers for men to go home to

after a spell on the road. And leave, without scruple, as adolescents in flight from a mother's stifling embrace.

Chronologies, always uneven, whether within or between cultures, seem particularly haywire in the fifties, as the war's chaotic aftermath soon led to different forms of stabilisation across the world. New orders were set up, old ones re-asserted. We view the fifties as a period of rigidity, with its emphatic polarising of masculine and feminine roles. Yet the changes wrought by the war went too deeply for women to accept wholesale redefinition as keepers of the hearth and home. In any case, in many parts of Europe post-war reconstruction needed their labour.

The independence relished by Olivia Manning's Ellie Parsons – who buoyantly regards the city as a place for self-invention – is more problematic for Irene and Adriana, the two friends in Alba de Céspedes' novel *Between Then and Now*. Rome in the fifties did not offer London's scope for independent living. In a little-industrialised economy with scant demand for women's paid labour, women were expected only to leave the family home on marriage. As rare refugees from solid bourgeois expectations, Irene and Adriana have become conscious outsiders in a way that Ellie Parsons need not within London's bedsit universe.

De Céspedes stands out as a feminist writer in the Italian context of the time. Articulating women's discontent and frustrations, she wrote very much against the traditional gender grain in her novels. The single writer who can be regarded as her predecessor in this respect is Sibilla Aleramo, whose autobiographical novel *A Woman* (1906) remains a landmark of feminist fiction, in which the city represents politics, future and freedom, its protagonist leaving a harshly imposed marriage to embark on involvement in feminist and literary circles in Rome.

In 'The Sea is not Naples', and in other stories in the collection *The Bay is not Naples* (1953), Anna Maria Ortese employs a first-person narrator who speaks with a gender-neutral voice that could easily be assumed to be male –

precisely because it is the voice of the detached observer bearing witness. Ortese's context was one in which a male voice would have carried more authority as a commentator, and it has come readily to many women writers in both the nineteenth and twentieth centuries to adopt either a masculine name or tone.

Naples is a vast city whose poverty is legendary, as is its vitality. After visiting Naples in 1936, Simone de Beauvoir said of it that there 'Human life is exhibited in its organic nudity, in its visceral warmth; it is under this aspect that it astonished and saddened us'. Ortese too is saddened by the drastic effects of war on the city, and the humiliating effects of its dependence on the presence of the military after Liberation.

The distance between this Naples and the São Paulo of the *favelas* inhabited by Carolina María de Jesús is not so far. Within Europe, Naples still has the status of a Third World city, despite a changing Italy.

The story of Carolina María de Jesús is one where a resolve to rise above the city's monumental weight of oppression seems to have triumphed. After discovery by a journalist, her diaries describing the struggles of shanty-town life were edited and published, a media phenomenon earning her enough money to leave the miseries of the *favelas* behind.

OLIVIA MANNING   LONDON

from

The Doves of Venus

Walking home one night, taking a round-about route to add
to experience, to stay awake a little longer and meet, perhaps,
some curiosity of life not met before, Ellie Parsons, aged
eighteen, independent, employed person, living in Chelsea,
passed, near the Victoria Coach Station, a couple from her
home town. She recognised the shape of them. She hurried.
She thought herself safely past, when the husband called:

'Why, Ellie Parsons!'

His tone showed that he was struck by seeing among eight
million strangers someone known to him. Ellie had not the
courage to ignore him. She paused and faced them, pretending surprise.

'The Ripleys,' she said.

The Ripleys, not on their own ground, looked unsure of
themselves, but they were, as usual, armed with disapproval.
Overcoming his surprise, Mr Ripley asked: 'How are you
getting on?' He was a lay preacher at the Pratt Hill Baptist
Chapel, Eastsea, and publicly held it shameful that Ellie
Parsons should have left home against the wish of a widowed
mother. His face became stern: 'You're going to Eastsea for
Christmas, I hope?'

Ellie, standing two yards away from him, said: 'Yes,' then,
suddenly defiant, added: 'I have a job in a studio. I'm doing
my own work. It's wonderful!' Unable to control her voice,
she shouted like a schoolgirl: 'I've never been so happy before
in my life.'

A smile appeared unexpectedly on the young-old face of the wife. She put her hand on her husband's arm, prompting him to say 'Good-night,' then, as they moved off, she whispered: 'That girl's in love.'

Ellie heard her, and did not care. As she turned her back on them, London was about her again and she felt her own freedom.

It was a mild December night, pretending spring. The sky, lacquer-black and peppered with small stars, looked as though blown clean by a gale, but the breeze that came from the side streets was tender as the breath of a fan. The road before her was empty. At the triangle where it joined Ebury Street, it looked as spacious as a ballroom. Ellie broke into a run. At that moment it seemed to her, were she to leap up, she would rise from the moorings of earth and sail between the stars; and if she called out, her voice would fill the sky.

On an impulse, she jumped and called: 'Hey!' As she landed, the pavement smacked sharply through her thin soles; her cry came out like a mouse-squeak. She looked over her shoulder, but there was no one who might have heard her. She burst out laughing. It was true. She was in love.

That evening while Quintin Bellot and she had been gazing at one another across the restaurant table, his expression had changed. She had felt between them not merely that sharp-edged, sparking attraction, but tenderness. She had felt it like a supernatural glow in the air about them. She touched his hand with her finger-tips and he gathered her fingers into his hand, then he laughed and gave her hand an impatient shake and said: 'You must choose something from the menu.'

She tried to give her attention to the menu. It was a pity she was not hungry in the evenings. She took her main meal at mid-day and the occasional evening meal that Quintin bought her, seemed to her wasted. She wished she could say: 'Give me the money instead so that I can have a real meal tomorrow.'

He started explaining the items to her: '*Langue de Boeuf en Paupiettes* – that's ox-tongue done with a sort of meat

stuffing and bacon; in *paupiettes*, in ... oh, you know! ...
in slices. *Côtes de veau foyot* – veal cutlets done in white
wine with grated cheese and breadcrumbs. Very nice. Would
you like that? Or some sort of chicken?'

She suddenly became annoyed that he should take her
ignorance for granted. She said: 'But all this is nonsense.
These French names don't mean anything.'

'But of course they do.' He laughed at her: 'If they didn't,
how could you tell one dish from another?'

Her mother, who kept a restaurant in Eastsea, was always
telling her customers that the French on menus was meaningless, invented to impress simpletons. 'We write in English,'
she would say. 'We've nothing to hide.'

Quintin said: 'Or would you like some kebabs – they're
pieces of meat put on a skewer and cooked over a charcoal
fire.'

Disconcerted, Ellie asked stupidly: 'But how do you
know?'

He pushed her hand away. Still laughing at her, he said:
'Don't be silly.'

Suddenly she said so loudly that people turned their heads:
'How marvellous everything is!'

He raised an eyebrow: 'I believe you're the first person I've
heard say that since 1939.'

'Why 1939?'

'That was when the war started.'

'Oh, the war!' – she had almost forgotten it. 'I was
evacuated.'

'Evacuated! I thought you girls were all conscripted.'

'I was too young.'

'So you were. So you were.' Quintin let his eyelids droop
with a look of melancholy, rather comical: 'And I? Even
then, I was middle-aged.'

It was for that reason, among other reasons, when later in
the evening he had roused himself and said with a yawn:
'Well, I suppose I must dress and see you home,' that she

pushed him back against the pillows and said: 'No, stay there. You look so comfortable.'

Not moving, he protested: 'But I must put you into a taxi.'

'Oh no.' Anything but that. Once before he had put her into a taxi and the fare had beggared her for a week. 'You just stay there,' she said.

He sighed and said weakly: 'This is disgraceful. I'm being spoilt.'

Ahead of her, traffic lights changed in an empty world. When she reached them, she gazed down Chelsea Bridge Road to observe the infernal splendour of the Battersea Power Station. It was flood-lit. The rosy cameo of chimneys, seeming incandescent against the black sky, billowed smoke wreaths, glowing, massive, majestical as the smoke of hell. She loved them. They were a landmark of home. They remained at hand as she passed the cemetery. An icy dampness came from the earth where the old soldiers lay buried. She knew these old soldiers. On her Saturday afternoon walks she came here and read the inscriptions to the Master Builder, the surgeon and the mysterious Sixpennyman; to the cook who had died aged twenty-nine and the officers who had died of their wounds. She had sketched into a notebook the tomb that bore so lavish a collection of trophies of war, and had written beneath her sketch 'Decoration for a bed-head', hoping that one day at the studio she would be required to decorate a bed-head. It was familiar ground, yet now, in the darkness, she was unnerved by the glimmer of the headstones. At the thought of the dead who lay there in the cold of winter, the darkness of night, she was touched by mortality. Life was wonderful, but men died.

She looked up at the sky and was reminded of a night – she thought of it as some hour near midnight but it must have been early on a winter evening – when she had walked with her father along the Eastsea promenade. The invisible sea had scratched on the pebbles below. Her father had pointed out stars to her – Orion's Belt, the Plough, the Bear, the Dog. He had said: 'They are worlds, like ours.'

'With people?'

'Perhaps. Why not?'

For the first time in her life she had realised the sky was not a solid, light-pricked canopy, but infinite space.

The night before he was taken to the sanatorium they had walked by the sea for a little way, very slowly. He had said: 'You know, I may not come back.'

Hoping to seem courageous in her fear, she had asked: 'Do you mean you may die?'

He said: 'Yes, but it does not matter. Our destiny is not here.'

She had remembered that as she had remembered nothing spoken at the Pratt Hill Baptist Chapel.

That was ten years ago. Already she could look back ten years! How quickly one aged! She saw time stretching like a shadow behind her, like the long, dark, empty promenade on which the two figures, very small in her memory, pressed against the wind. Her father had known that he was dying. Perhaps it was death that had drawn his glance up to the stars.

The Embankment meant she was nearly home. When she neared Oakley Street, she crossed the road at a run. She lived here in this impressive street where the houses stood in the streetlights like façades cut upon solid rock. She had found her room advertised on a postcard in a sweetshop. Who could otherwise have guessed that such houses were boarding-houses? The long, glossy, upcurve of tarmac road was deserted. Ellie began to imagine herself a spirit, perhaps isolated in some dimension of her own – but, no, there was someone else in the world. Round the corner, in Upper Cheyne Row, a door-knocker was being furiously banged against a door. The knocking stopped. There was the squeak of a window going up. A woman's voice called out: 'The bell *is* working, dear.' There was silence, then suddenly, into

Oakley Street, walking on tall, thread-fine heels, a woman came as though in flight. She passed Ellie without noticing her. She was a delicately-shaped woman in a coat of expensive fur. A startling beauty.

Elie thought: 'She must be somebody. Perhaps she's famous.'

The woman, stumbling at times on her high heels, began to run and wave and shout: 'Taxi! Taxi!' A taxi was coming up from the Embankment. It stopped beside her: she entered it: it turned in the road. Ellie watched it until it was out of sight.

Well, that was London. Profoundly satisfied by her adopted city, Ellie found her key, entered her house and climbed to her room on the top floor. When she reached it, she opened her window and gazed down on the windows of Margaretta Terrace. She was wide awake again and excited as though, even at this last minute of the day, life might extend some new experience. What lay ahead for her? Would she ever rap on door-knockers with the urgency of important emotions? and run round a corner wearing a fur coat? and, lifting a hand to an approaching taxi, impress some other girl named Ellie and fill her with envy and ambition?

Forced by the cold to close the window, Ellie embraced her own shoulders and turned round and round. The room's size did not permit a real dance, but she moved as wildly as she could to celebrate the end of her virginity.

ALBA DE CÉSPEDES

from

Between Then and Now

TRANSLATED BY ISABEL QUIGLY

'When I was in Naples in 1944, if I had a bit of free time I used to go and see Marta at the hospital; and as there were very few nurses, she often used to give me a white overall and something to do. Simple things, you know – carrying bowls and trays, and sometimes she'd entrust me with a patient who was starting to get up, and say, "Get him to walk up and down the corridor." There was a doctor who was always eyeing me and stopped to chat every time he met me. He was young and seemed intelligent; it was a pity his hair was too long and too oily, but on the whole I liked him. One evening there was an air raid warning and Marta said to me, "Come up to the first floor, we've got to take the bad cases down to the shelter." We could already hear the noise of bombs in the distance. I was very scared as I went up the stairs; through the skylight above we could see the search-lights. I was overtaken by the young doctor hurrying up, and I must have been pale because he looked at me and said, "Go down to the shelter at once." I was trembling, and wanted to go down quickly and take cover. But I'd have been ashamed to do so, among all those people running towards the wards. I could hear people sobbing, and those who couldn't move calling for help. So I said, "I can't. I've got to help my sister." Later he asked if he could take me home, saying that it was dangerous for a woman to be out alone because there were Negroes about, and the city was blacked out. But the Negroes

186

didn't show themselves, whereas he tried to kiss me and called me "beautiful doll". I pushed him off, and he went away red-faced and simply furious. A few days later I ran into him again in the hospital and he said to me, "I've got it now: you're a fanatic." I didn't know what he meant by that word either, I just guessed it was the opposite of "beautiful doll". Since then, whenever I do something which to me seems natural or necessary, I realize that a lot of people think, "She's a fanatic."'

Little by little as we talked we had reached the Via Sistina. The restaurant we were aiming for was near the Piazza di Spagna. We had been walking for an hour, both of us obeying an unconscious impulse to tire ourselves out. It had stopped raining, but drops pattered down from the gutters and bounced off our raincoats.

'Let's hope it'll be fresher,' I said. 'I can't bear the sirocco. The air of Rome seems to have grown oppressive. Or perhaps,' I added smiling, 'I didn't notice before.'

We went to lean over the balustrade of Trinità dei Monti. After the first few steps the staircase was a dark void. I felt my unhappiness welling up and I was so exhausted I felt almost dizzy. I felt as though I were falling head first into the dark abyss of the stairs.

'I'm scared,' I said.

Adriana was silent, looking towards Via dei Condotti where the lamps were strung out in a shining straight line; I hoped she hadn't heard, but she had.

'We've been scared so many times,' she said.

We had never admitted it; yet on some evenings for no apparent reason we would say to each other: 'Ring me up; there's still so much to talk about, we could go on indefinitely. Ring me when you like, any time, even if it's the middle of the night. I've got the phone by the bed and I always read late. Anyway, I've got to work this evening.' They were casual, nonchalant words, but both of us knew that what they really meant was, 'Ring me if you can't hold out any longer, if you're on the point of taking sleeping tablets or turning on the gas.' We knew that sometimes the least thing could mean the difference between salvation and perdition. Yet we had never phoned and it was nights like these that had taught us to live.

'That's true,' I said rebelliously, 'but in the end we run down. You know, I'd like to pick up my life like a parcel and dump it in somebody's arms and say, "Now you think about it". But it's never possible, we've pulled down our own destruction upon us. Every morning you find life heavy on your shoulders and you have to start reasoning again. Pietro says that reason sets us free, but that isn't true: reason everlastingly confronts us with ourselves. That's a good joke! We're all lost and Pietro more than anyone: when I go into his study and find him writing away in his delicate handwriting I always think that outside there are people doing the pools.'

'What an idea!' Adriana exclaimed. 'Why do you think that?'

'I don't know why,' I said. 'But I always do.'

People brushed against us as they passed, and we could hear women laughing in the rain-scented air.

'Perhaps,' I went on, 'it's because I'm envious. It's very tiring to go on without believing in luck or chance; and to know that money changes nothing. It makes life easier, though, and of course I could do with it. Just think . . . this month I've got the electricity bill, the telephone account, and my income tax all at once, I don't know how I'll manage, but we always do in the end; that's what wears us out . . . I was saying that basically money doesn't matter, the only thing that matters is what happens in ourselves. And yet I'm fed up. I shouldn't like Pietro to hear me say this, because he's the only person who makes me ashamed when I don't live up to what I'd like to be . . . but I must admit I sometimes envy whores. Not the ones who . . . but those who can laugh, as you say, and go to bed with a man for the sake of a mink coat.'

Adriana slipped her hand under my arm.

'When we talk like this, it's a sign that one thing's piled up on top of another, and they're weighing us down.'

'No,' I answered after a pause. 'I suffered this afternoon; I was really hurt. Now it's over. But I'd give anything not to understand what I do understand.'

We had begun going down the damp, slippery steps. Adriana still held my arm, and I clutched her tightly; suddenly her slight body seemed fragile and weak.

'If only we could at least grow old quickly,' she sighed.

We were out in the square among the impatient cars. Men were glancing at us, trying to make out our figures under the raincoats.

'A rather distant hope at the moment,' I said maliciously.

'Have we been mistaken in everything, then?' Adriana demanded.

The fresh air, the rhythm of our well-matched steps, had cheered me: I felt self-confident again.

'No,' I answered, 'I don't think so. But we may have missed something.'

'Mink coats,' Adriana said, laughing.

EXTRACT TWO

I was alone in the street: cats fled at the sound of my footsteps. I thought I might get myself a cat, or some other animal; but the thought of its eyes staring at me, trying to fathom what I was and what I meant to do with it, put me off. The more I felt I belonged to life as a whole, the more I was afraid of watching the development of one particular life. I loved Pietro because there were no obstacles, no barriers, between us: I knew what he'd think and do on any particular occasion, at any given time. But this knowledge only increased my loneliness, because I realized that each of us, through mind or senses, in loving the other loved himself; and I wondered whether ours were really love, or whether, at a certain point, love could not be something more than that.

I walked on slowly. The great white block of flats where I

189

lived glimmered coldly in the night, and along the unmade pavements rose the black skeletons of half-built houses. Fields still lapped the street, which exhaled the weariness of a new community that must adjust itself to new ways of living and had no idea where to take refuge or find help amongst these identical houses, these dark voids of windows and of shops.

I felt as I used to feel when I first came to live there: scared of being sacked from the job I then had in a library and constantly wondering what I'd do if I were. I was still wearing clothes which my mother had bought me, elegant and well-cut, and I thought it must be these clothes that stopped me accepting my poverty. They made me feel uneasy when I ate standing up in a delicatessen: I always stood a long way from the door, so that if anyone I knew came in to buy cooked meats I wouldn't have to greet her with my mouth full. I hated being ashamed like that, as though I didn't approve of the life I led. Until then I had lived with my mother, who provided everything; so that now I blushed at having to tell the tradesmen to come back later as I had no money. I thought of all the women who did not know what it cost to say that, and reflected that if I had married Maurizio I shouldn't have known either. 'It seems impossible, but really it's just these material, practical things that make you realize you exist,' I told myself. 'You don't know you're born until you're faced with bills for which you're directly responsible – until you're the debtor, the accused, and have no one but yourself to turn to. That's when you find out that newspapers aren't just useful for the cinema programmes.' All the same, I recognized that it was precisely when I had learnt what everyone should know in order to live that my mother became convinced that I was accursed, and Maurizio that I couldn't possibly make a good wife.

I went indoors and switched on the light. My heart contracted, showing me that I had unconsciously been hoping to find Erminia waiting for me. Instead, everything confirmed her cruel desertion: there wasn't a sign of her. And yet I felt calmer; I undressed, got ready for bed, and lay down.

'Tomorrow evening I mustn't forget to fill a hot-water bottle,' I thought with a shiver. I felt I had to start all over again; and recognized the same sweet unease which had swept over me when I had to accept solitude as part of the choice I had made – a choice that might be right or might be wrong – I couldn't tell.

I had already had to face it in the past. The first time was when I returned to Rome in the summer of '44, after nearly nine months in the south, beyond the front which separated me from my mother, from my home, and from Maurizio.

During that long separation, I had often pictured the moment of my return, desiring it, dreading it, telling myself that it would never come. I lived almost a double life; I was down there in the south, but in my imagination I saw myself in Rome. And I didn't imagine the city as it really was during those months, dark and thronged with frightened, oppressed people. I saw it always full of sunshine, I saw the wide streets, the great trees, the tall houses as they had appeared to me when I was a child. I imagined my mother waiting for me at the big French window which opened from the house into the garden; I saw myself pushing the heavy iron grille and running desperately towards her, as I used to do when I was a little girl, coming back from the Pincio park; when I hugged her I hid myself against her because she was so tall, losing myself in her perfume, feeling against my cheeks the warmth of her body through her dress. 'How you've been running!' she always exclaimed. 'Aren't you tired?' – a reproof softened by the tenderness in her voice. I thought of this without ever wondering whether, on my return, I should find her fixed in that memory, or if she would come out of it to become my mother at last.

ANNA MARIA ORTESE NAPLES

from

The Bay is not Naples

TRANSLATED BY FRANCES FRENAYE

Immediately after the Allied troops had pushed their way to
the North, I went down to Naples and shut myself up in the
house for a whole year of despair.

The house was in an alley, formerly quiet and isolated,
perfumed by the lemon trees of an occasional abandoned
garden and swept by breezes from the sea. This whole alley
had been requisitioned for the bombed-out population of the
Strada del Lavinaio, one of the worst slums of the Mediterranean basin, and — according to its original inhabitants — it
had become transformed beyond recognition.

The sky above was just as radiant as it had been in better
years; and the sea, in the background, just as blue as when,
in our days of youth, we had beat our fledgling wings on its
shore; but the atmosphere of the whole quarter had changed
terribly — as perhaps was the case with the whole of the rest
of the city. Neapolitans have never been what you might call
really happy, and their blood seemed to have become black
and congealed; their mildness and childlike simplicity shattered; the graceful turn of their speech lost, like that of a girl
who has turned to walking the street; and, in the same way,
their amiable habit of gesticulating, which made them so
endearing to everyone, gone or even lost altogether. Their
well-known vivaciousness was now a form of restless anxiety,
and their superficial gaiety concealed a wild melancholia, a
sinking sensation of defeat and the end of everything they

knew. A face suddenly struck by paralysis could have been no harder and no more pitiful; it was the expression of someone profoundly shocked, one eye wandering, like a blind man's, towards the sky, and the other nailed, smiling, to the ground.

The city was still filled with gardens and that spring they bloomed more gloriously than ever. The bay ran, a dark blue paradise, from one end of the city to the other, quite detached from the sordid sorrows of the human masses miserably grouped upon its shore. For I am speaking of the poor, of the army of the poor, which in no other city has ever marched in such great numbers or under such tattered flags. The wealthy, aristocrats or shopkeepers, as they may be, form a separate race; they live in modern houses in handsome streets stretching up over the hills; they have joys, sorrows, hopes and ambitions of their own. The poor, to whom hope and ambition are denied, the humble of heart, the good thieves, frail young prostitutes, savagely maternal mothers and their appealing but neglected children, these make up the real and regal population of Naples.

The city, then, was radically changed. These people, among whom I had grown up, had slipped down nine steps of the ten which form the gamut of their lives. They had lost their old houses and had no desire to build new ones. Eight or ten persons slept, fully dressed, in a room containing only one bed; others, even less fortunate, huddled on some filthy landing on a public staircase, while from a grating in the pavement there exuded the odours of a rich man's kitchen; and there were yet others who subsisted in shelters made from the boughs of trees in the public parks, where bright fires marked their bivouacs. All their ambitions could be summed up in the single word *money*. The whole city was one diabolical market-place, where everything – cigarettes, bread, women, and saddest of all, even children – were for sale.

All this because nobody had the inclination or the opportunity to get steady employment; if chances were bad yester-

193

day, they were worse to-day – and in such a vast city too, a city which seemed to have risen from a dream of a succession of exhausted generations, and which by sheer chance had been sited amid a countryside of fabled enchantment. The people of the city had become utterly effete and idle, feeding their hunger and thirst on song, and careless of the lengthening shadows springing up round their superfluous bodies. Even their religion and the churches, packed with effigies of innumerable saints, indulgent to every type of sin, were but further testimonials to the general weakness and inertia; they claimed to offer salvation, but instead brought nothing but damnation. Many churches had fallen out of use, but no schools or factories had taken their place; there was no attempt to encourage a belief in the dignity of honest work, or to offer hope for that physical and spiritual regeneration which leads to the possession of God.

Beggars, beggars everywhere; beggars buying and beggars selling. Even the rich were beggars, without any kindness to give away, as they sat walled up in their cool oases. Most were completely idle, and the few who were dreamers were considered traitors to their class or downright crazy.

The culture of the common people now embraced a knowledge of English, just a smattering, but enough to facilitate a profitable contact with the army of clean-limbed, fair-haired men who had come upon them from the sea in 1943. Almost everyone had picked up some notion of the language, particularly the women and children. The men seemed to find it less easy, and for that reason they inspired the more pity.

I didn't know English, either. And perhaps it was the feeling of inferiority and humiliation which beset me, as I wandered about a city no longer my own, and heard its people debasing themselves in a strange tongue that caused me to shut myself up in my own house and look no farther than the patch of blue sky visible above the dark surrounding walls, a patch of sky reminiscent of times long past.

But where had these times gone? I could not recapture them. Even the remnant of the people that did not mouth English was in a state of muddy metamorphosis near to delirium. I shivered as I watched them, like a man who sits down after a long journey, on the edge of a chasm, and stares dully into the blank space beyond, searching vainly for the red chimneys and roof-tops of his beloved native village, to which he can now never return.

CAROLINA MARÍA DE JESÚS

from
Beyond All Pity

TRANSLATED BY DAVID ST CLAIR

May 19 I left the bed at 5 a.m. The sparrows have just begun their morning symphony. The birds must be happier than we are. Perhaps happiness and equality reigns among them. The world of the birds must be better than that of the *favelados*, who lie down but don't sleep because they go to bed hungry.

What our President Senhor Juscelino has in his favour is his voice. He sings like a bird and his voice is pleasant to the ears. And now the bird is living in a golden cage called Catete Palace. Be careful, little bird, that you don't lose this cage, because cats when they are hungry think of birds in cages. The *favelados* are the cats, and they are hungry.

I broke my train of thought when I heard the voice of the baker: 'Here you go! Fresh bread, and right on time for breakfast!'

How little he knows that in the *favela* there are only a few who have breakfast. The *favelados* eat only when they have something to eat. All the families who live in the *favela* have children. A Spanish woman lives here named Dona Maria Puerta. She bought some land and started to economize so she could build a house. When she finished construction her children were weak with pneumonia. And there are eight children.

There have been people who visited us and said: 'Only pigs could live in a place like this. This is the pigsty of São Paulo.'

I'm starting to lose my interest in life. It's beginning to revolt me and my revulsion is just.

I washed the floor because I'm expecting a visit from a future deputy and he wants me to make some speeches for him. He says he wants to know the *favelas* and if he is elected he's going to abolish them.

The sky was the colour of indigo, and I understood that I adore my Brazil. My glance went over to the trees that are planted at the beginning of Pedro Vicente Street. The leaves moved by themselves. I thought: they are applauding my gesture of love to my country. I went on looking for paper. Vera was smiling and I thought of Casemiro de Abreu, the Brazilian poet who said: 'Laugh, child. Life is beautiful.' Life was good in that era. Because now in this era it's necessary to say: 'Cry, child. Life is bitter.'

I went on so preoccupied that I didn't even notice the gardens of the city. It's the season for white flowers, the predominating colour. And in the month of May the altars must be adorned with white flowers. We must thank God or Nature, who gave us the stars that adorn the sky, for the flowers that adorn the parks and the fields and the forests.

When I was going up Southern Cross Avenue I saw a woman with blue shoes and a blue handbag. Vera told me: 'Look, Mama, what a beautiful woman. She is going in my car.'

My daughter Vera Eunice says she is going to buy a car and will only drive beautiful people in it. The woman smiled and Vera went on: 'You smell so good!'

I saw that my daughter knew how to flatter. The woman opened her bag and gave me 20 cruzeiros.

Here in the *favela* almost everyone has a difficult fight to live. But I am the only one who writes of what suffering is. I do this for the good of the others. Many look in the garbage for shoes to wear. But the shoes are weak and only last six days. In the old days, that is from 1950–1958, the *favelados* sang. They had parties. 1957, 1958 life was getting tougher and tougher. Now there isn't even money for them to buy *pinga*. The parties were shortened until they snuffed themselves out. The other day I met a policeman. He asked me: 'You still live in the *favela*?'

'Why?'

'Because your family has left the Radio Patrol in peace.'

'There's no money left over to buy booze!' I snapped.

I put João and Vera to bed and went looking for José Carlos. I telephoned the Central Police Station. The phone doesn't always resolve things. I took a streetcar and went there. I didn't feel cold. I felt as if my blood was 40 degrees. I spoke with the Female Police who told me that José Carlos was at Asdrubal Nascimento Street (juvenile court). What a relief! Only a mother could appreciate it.

I went towards Asdrubal Nascimento. I don't know how to walk at night. The glare of the lights turns me around. I have to keep asking. I like the night only to contemplate the shining stars, to read and to write. During the night it is quieter.

I arrived at Asdrubal Nascimento and the guard told me to wait. I looked at the children. Some were crying but others were furious with the interference of a law that didn't permit them to do as they pleased. José Carlos was crying. When he heard my voice he became happy. I could feel his contentment. He looked at me and it was the tenderest look I have ever received in my life.

At 8:30 that night I was in the *favela* breathing the smell of excrement mixed with the rotten earth. When I am in the city I have the impression that I am in a living-room with crystal chandeliers, rugs of velvet, and satin cushions. And when I'm in the *favela* I have the impression that I'm a useless object, destined to be forever in a garbage dump.

May 20 Day was breaking when I got out of bed. Vera woke up and sang and asked me to sing with her. We sang. Then José Carlos and João joined in.

The morning was damp and foggy. The sun was rising but its heat didn't chase away the cold. I stayed thinking: there are seasons when the sun dominates. There's a season for the rain. There's a season for the wind. Now is the time for the cold. Among them there are no rivalries. Each one has a time.

I opened the window and watched the women passing by with their coats discoloured and worn by time. It won't be long until these coats which they got from others, and which should be in a museum, will be replaced by others. The politicians must give us things. That includes me too, because I'm also a *favelado*. I'm one of the discarded. I'm in the garbage dump and those in the garbage dump either burn themselves or throw themselves into ruin.

The women that I see passing are going to church begging for bread for their children. Brother Luiz gives it to them while their husbands remain home under the blankets. Some because they can't find jobs. Others because they are sick. Others because they are drunk.

I don't bother myself about their men. If they give a ball and I don't show up, it's because I don't like to dance. I only get involved in fights when I think I can prevent a crime. I don't know what started this unfriendliness of mine. I have a hard cold look for both men and women. My smile and my soft smooth words I save for children.

There is a teenager named Julião who beats his father at times. When he hits his father it is with such sadism and pleasure. He thinks he is unconquerable. He beats the old man as if he were beating a drum. The father wants him to study law. When Julião was arrested the father went with him with eyes filled with tears. As if he was accompanying a saint in a procession. Julião is a rebel, but without a cause. They don't need to live in a *favela*; they have a home on Villa Maria hill.

Sometimes families move into the *favela* with children. In the beginning they are educated, friendly. Days later they use foul language, are mean and quarrelsome. They are diamonds turned to lead. They are transformed from objects that were in the living-room to objects banished to the garbage room.

For me the world instead of evolving is turning primitive. Those who don't know hunger will say: 'Whoever wrote this is crazy.' But who has gone hungry can say: 'Well, Dona Carolina. The basic necessities must be within reach of everyone.'

How horrible it is to see a child eat and ask: 'Is there more?' This word 'more' keeps ringing in the mother's head as she looks in the pot and doesn't have any more.

When a politician tells us in his speeches that he is on the side of the people, that he is only in politics in order to improve our living conditions, asking for our votes, promising to freeze prices, he is well aware that by touching on these grave problems he will win at the polls. Afterward he divorces himself from the people. He looks at them with half-closed eyes, and with a pride that hurts us.

When I arrived from the Palace that is the city, my children ran to tell me that they had found some macaroni in the garbage. As the food supply was low I cooked some of the macaroni with beans. And my son João said to me: 'Uh huh. You told me we weren't going to eat any more things from the garbage.'

It was the first time I had failed to keep my word. I said: 'I had faith in President Kubitschek.'

'You had faith, and now you don't have it any more?'

'No, my son, democracy is losing its followers. In our country everything is weakening. The money is weak. Democracy is weak and the politicians are very weak. Everything that is weak dies one day.'

The politicians know that I am a poetess. And that a poet will even face death when he sees his people oppressed.

May 21 I spent a horrible night. I dreamt I lived in a decent house that had a bathroom, kitchen, pantry, and even a maid's room. I was going to celebrate the birthday of my daughter Vera Eunice. I went and bought some small pots that I had wanted for a long time. Because I was able to buy. I sat at the table to eat. The tablecloth was white as a lily. I ate a steak, bread and butter, fried potatoes and a salad. When I reached for another steak I woke up. What bitter reality! I don't live in the city. I live in the *favela*. In the mud on the banks of the Tieté River. And with only nine cruzeiros. I don't even have sugar, because yesterday after I went out the children ate what little I had.

Who must be a leader is he who has the ability. He who has pity and friendship for the people. Those who govern our country are those who have money, who don't know what hunger is, or pain or poverty. If the majority revolt, what can the minority do? I am on the side of the poor, who are an arm. An undernourished arm. We must free the country of the profiteering politicians.

Yesterday I ate that macaroni from the garbage with fear of death, because in 1953 I sold scrap over there in Zinho. There was a pretty little black boy. He also went to sell scrap in Zinho. He was young and said that those who should look for paper were the old. One day I was collecting scrap when I stopped at Bom Jardim Avenue. Someone had thrown meat into the garbage, and he was picking out the pieces. He told me: 'Take some, Carolina. It's still fit to eat.'

He gave me some, and so as not to hurt his feelings, I accepted. I tried to convince him not to eat that meat, or the hard bread gnawed by the rats. He told me no, because it was two days since he had eaten. He made a fire and roasted the meat. His hunger was so great that he couldn't wait for the meat to cook. He heated it and ate. So as not to remember that scene, I left thinking: I'm going to pretend I wasn't there. This can't be real in a rich country like mine. I was disgusted with that Social Service that had been created to readjust the maladjusted, but took no notice of we marginal people. I sold the scrap at Zinho and returned to São Paulo's back yard, the *favela*.

The next day I found that little black boy dead. His toes were spread apart. The space must have been eight inches between them. He had blown up as if made out of rubber. His toes looked like a fan. He had no documents. He was buried like any other 'Joe'. Nobody tried to find out his name. The marginal people don't have names.

201

Beyond All Pity

Once every four years the politicians change without solving the problem of hunger that has its headquarters in the *favela* and its branch offices in the workers' homes.

When I went to get water I saw a poor woman collapse near the pump because last night she slept without dinner. She was undernourished. The doctors that we have in politics know this.

Now I'm going to Dona Julita's house to work for her. I went looking for paper. Senhor Samuel weighed it. I got 12 cruzeiros. I went up Tiradentes Avenue looking for paper. I came to Brother Antonio Santana de Galvão Street, number 17, to work for Dona Julita. She told me not to fool with men because I might have another baby and that afterward men won't give anything to take care of the child. I smiled and thought: in relations with men, I've had some bitter experiences. Now I'm mature, reached a stage of life where my judgement has grown roots.

I found a sweet potato and a carrot in the garbage. When I got back to the *favela* my boys were gnawing on a piece of hard bread. I thought: for them to eat this bread, they need electric teeth.

I don't have any lard. I put meat on the fire with some tomatoes that I found at the Peixe canning factory. I put in the carrot and the sweet potato and water. As soon as it was boiling, I put in the macaroni that the boys found in the garbage. The *favelados* are the few who are convinced that in order to live, they must imitate the vultures. I don't see any help from the Social Service regarding the *favelados*. Tomorrow I'm not going to have bread. I'm going to cook a sweet potato.

May 22 Today I'm sad. I'm nervous. I don't know if I should start crying or start running until I fall unconscious. At dawn it was raining. I couldn't go out to get any money. I spent the day writing. I cooked the macaroni and I'll warm it up again for the children. I cooked the potatoes and they ate them. I have a few tin cans and a little scrap that I'm going to sell to Senhor Manuel. When João came home from school I sent him to sell the scrap. He got 13 cruzeiros. He bought a glass of mineral water: two cruzeiros. I was furious with him. Where had he seen a *favelado* with such highborn tastes?

The children eat a lot of bread. They like soft bread but when they don't have it, they eat hard bread.

Hard is the bread that we eat. Hard is the bed on which we sleep. Hard is the life of the *favelado*.

Oh, São Paulo! A queen that vainly shows her skyscrapers that are her crown of gold. All dressed up in velvet and silk but with cheap stockings underneath – the *favela*.

THE SIXTIES

T HE BERLIN Wall went up in 1961. The Algerian
War, fought in the cause of independence from
France since 1954, ended in 1962, the most
immediately decisive in a growing number of such
struggles waged across Africa and Asia throughout the
decade. The most momentous of these was the war in
Vietnam, a focus for movements of protest that spanned the
western world and inspired new libertarian visions of what
solidarity could achieve in challenging hierarchies of class
and race, culture and gender. On the streets of Paris and
other western cities, these movements reached their
confrontational peak in 1968.

This is a decade that ends very differently from how it
began. After the whirlwind of 1968 the world had a
dramatically altered look about it, not so much because of
changes achieved, though changes there were; more because
of new ways of thinking, those concepts then becoming
motors of changes to come.

All kinds of discontent worked their way through the
decade towards that magic year. If the women's liberation
movement had its collective beginnings only as the seventies
dawned, it was feeling its way into being much earlier. Far
from the restlessness of Western youth, in Moscow *Novy
Mir* serialised Natalya Baranskaya's *A Week Like Any
Other*,[1] which documented a Moscow woman's routine

exertions to combine professional life and family demands –
as housewife, mother, scientist – suggesting that the
discontent crossed Cold War frontiers.

In the West this is the post-existentialist decade of
individual rebellions, of youth disaffected in the singular,
like Anne in Albertine Sarrazin's autobiographical
L'Astragale (1965). L'Astragale is the astragalus: a bone in
the ankle (which Anne breaks on her escape from prison)
but also, among other things, a genus of wild plant that has
no particular use. Written in prison, the novel records
Anne's life on the run, her love affair with Julien and her
return to prostitution as a means of independence.

The lesbian women whose lives form the London mosaic
of Maureen Duffy's *The Microcosm* (1966) are figures who
before long will emerge from their basement meeting place,
the metaphorical House of Shades, into the light of sexual
revolution. The section describing Cathy's arrival in London
reads as conventional narration; elsewhere in the novel
Duffy uses more experimental techniques: fractured interior
monologues, time shifts across centuries . . . fictional routes
for identities in uncertain movement.

Ingeborg Bachmann wrote 'A Place for Coincidences' to
be read when she was awarded the Georg Büchner prize for
her poetry, in 1964. The Wall was still a recent shock to the
city. Bachmann said that she could only write about Berlin
in symbolic terms, and the piece plays on contrasts of
'consequence' and 'inconsequence'. Berlin came to bear the
visible burden of Cold War splits; in Bachmann's jagged,
expressionistic prose with its madhouse insinuations, in her
surreal images of casual collapse and catastrophe – blood,
fire, flood, storm and ice – the city staggers under this great
weight.

Claire Etcherelli's *Elise or the Real Life* is a novel of the
city as a yearned-for 'real life' that becomes an encounter
with love and with politics. Elise's job on a factory assembly
line leads to closeness with an Arab worker. In the
atmosphere of the Algerian War the city's conflicts become

intensely a part of her experience. In *Elise*, the 'metropolis' as colonising power becomes the internal metropolis in crisis as the decade proceeds towards revolt.

NOTE

1. Published by Virago in Pieta Monks's translation, in 1989.

INGEBORG BACHMANN

A Place for Coincidences

TRANSLATED BY AGNES ROOK

> He hunted with furious speed
> his whole life through, and then he said:
> 'consequence, consequence'
> when someone spoke to him:
> 'inconsequence, inconsequence'
> – the hollow ring of irredeemable folly
>
> Georg Büchner, *Lenz*

It is ten houses past *Sarotti*, it is a couple of blocks before *Schultheiss*, it is five traffic lights away from the merchant bank, it is not at the *Berliner Kindl*, there are candles in the window, it is on the offside of the tram, it is also there in the silence, there is a cross in front of it, but it is not that close – wrong advice! It is a concern, it is not an object, it is there during the day and also at night, it can be used, there are people inside it, there are trees surrounding it, it can, must not, ought, should not, is carried, is delivered, it comes feet first, has a blue light, has nothing to do, it is, yes it is, it has happened, has been given up, is now and has been for a long time, is a permanent address, it is unbearable, it comes, it happens, it comes out, it is something – in Berlin.

In Berlin all people are now wrapped in greaseproof paper. It is a Sunday in May. Myriads of beer bottles are lined up right down to the Wannsee, many bottles are already floating in the water, pushed close to the banks by the waves created by the steamer so that the men can still fish them out. The men open the bottles with their bare hands, they press them open with the ball of their thumbs. Some men call complacently into the wood: We'll do it yet. The women in the greaseproof paper arouse compassion, some of them are allowed to get out of the paper and sit in the grass with their greasy clothes. Then the patients are also allowed to land. We've got so many sick people here cries the night nurse and fetches the patients who are leaning over the balcony and are quite damp and trembling. The night nurse has seen through everything once again and gives an injection which goes through and through and sticks in the mattress so that one cannot get up again. The last passenger plane flies in, the medication is still to come and then there must be silence, the air mail and later the air freight are barely audible. Now, every minute a plane flies through the room, passes the hook with the flannel, accelerates when a hair's breadth above the soap container. The airplanes, about to land in the landing lanes which run across the room, have to fly more silently. The hospitals have complained. The planes throttle back, but it is worse than ever, as they hum past, above the heads and the sweat-soaked hair, just below the ceiling. There is a continual excitement in the hospitals on account of all those planes which throttle their engines and then become so silent that one no longer hears them, nevertheless one tends to listen for the moment when one catches the first humming sound, almost as if one held a tuning fork close to it. Then one hears more clearly, then they are here, then they are gone, then there is a faint hum, then nothing anymore. Then the next faint sound, then one is no longer pleased that one hardly hears them at all, so that the head physician has to go out into the street to produce evidence by waving the manifold pages covered with hieroglyphs. Then for the moment this suffices, but in the next moment free from planes all the church bells in Berlin begin to ring, churches rising up from the ground, coming quite close, lots of new, bare colourless churches with clock towers, Protestant music on tape. The excitement grows because of the bell-ringing, the Mayor himself ought to come, there are cries that the churches should be abolished here, the patients scream, escape into the passages, water from the rooms is flooding the passages, there is blood in it because some people have bitten their tongues on account of the churches. The resident chaplain sits in the visitors' chair, he keeps on repeating that he used to be a naval chaplain and has sailed round the Cape of Good Hope. He does not know anything about bells, he takes the biscuit on the plate, no one dares to say anything because of the biscuit and the bells and he does not ask whether anything is amiss, just twists his green hunting hat round and round in his hand. He is asked to leave because the place has to be aired.

The burnt down walls on the Lützow Square are lit up by large floodlights, everything is smokey, the fire must be over. Torches are used to light up the clumps of grass, there is nothing left only charred bones and scorched soil, no complete skeletons, only bits of bone. The programme is already underway with ever increasing lighting on the vast wastelands, there are more and more building sites on which, however, no one is starting to build. The atmosphere is good. A large placard is being carried around. *Scharnhorst* travel agency. Everybody is in agreement, the programme continues in the *Kadewe*, the white and blue *Kadewe* banner flutters high above, everyone suddenly wants to get inside the *Kadewe*, it is quite clear already that it isn't possible, but the atmosphere gets better and better, the people become impossible to control, they crowd round the shop assistants, they suddenly all want to have their palms read, then they all want their horoscopes, they snatch each other's lottery tickets and run towards the machines, the money is thrust in so violently that the ball-bearings of the machines are destroyed and in some rooms there is a wailing for sleeping pills. But no more tonight. At least people have stopped yelling and are merely merry, the decorations are torn down and hurled from the top storeys, the escalators are jammed, the lifts are bursting with scarves and dresses and coats, but the plump cashiers are right in the middle of it all, they are almost choking and call out: that will have to be paid for, you'll pay for this.

The passages have to be mopped down again. A number of well-known people have been secretly admitted, at night when the blue lights are on, most of them are, however, close relatives unable to provide support, they have addresses but no next of kin. Most important that, next of kin. They are all lying there in silence. He is on his way, the night nurse says, he is coming from here or from there, there will be a plane any minute – rest assured, it will happen. She must mean the next of kin. The head physician is expecting the plane, he has committed himself totally on this. Then, in order to get some peace, he says that everyone may go home next week. Everyone coughs and hopes and has put the thermometer in his arm pit, under his tongue or in his anus and a ten centimeter long needle in his flesh. The dark balconies are ready for demolition, no one dares to climb the bannisters tonight or threaten the night nurse who is once again making coffee for the night duty doctor; everyone is making his own plans, a plan to build a tunnel or to make direct for the waste land, or to release the camel in the zoo, untying it, saddling it and riding off on it through Brandenburg. One can rely on a camel. Then in the middle of the night there is a rise in fees, a perspiring as never before. It is quite terrible. The room now costs a thousand gold marks. Everyone grabs the bell and pushes the button.

The disabled limp down the steps of the Bellevue S-Bahn station, the light sways as in a vault, most of the disabled wear yellow armbands with black circles, carry sticks for support, and some have foreshortened limbs in iron supports. Everyone is disabled not so much by shells but inwardly, the bodies in disarray, too short either on top or below, the flesh on their faces dull and lifeless, the angles of the mouth and eyes are crooked, while the swaying shadow in the station makes everything look worse. The ticket collector at her window has to prop up the ceiling as well as the train because it is rumbling again. The woman luckily has enormous hands and muscles so that even while handing out the tickets she is supporting the train, because the train running in the opposite direction towards Friedrichstrasse thunders above it. Then a part of the ceiling collapses, but she lifts it up again, then another part comes down, the one on which the Victory Column stands, then the train rattles past again towards Wannsee. It is a catastrophe. People seek refuge in the nearby restaurant, they crouch beneath the tables, they are expecting an attack, but the ticket collector comes and says there is no attack. All is well, it won't happen again.

The head physician must not be disturbed, the notice has been there for years, but it is not conspicuously displayed. It must be a 'disturbance'. Throughout the town something of this filters through, and everyone maintains he has read or heard of a 'disturbance', some people have even thought about it. But nothing is official. Still more trees are planted in the sand, trees used to the desert. Everyone eventually goes to work in silence. All in fresh white shirts tied at the neck. There is no longer any excitement. Everything is subdued. Most of the people are half asleep anyway.

The streets are rising at an angle of 45 degrees. The cars on their way to the horizon naturally roll backwards, the cyclists lose their balance, they skid towards you more quickly than anyone else, and it is impossible to prevent the cars from causing damage; a sports car speeds backwards right into the institution, blowing sky high – pails, spittoons, trolleys and stretchers. The head physician ignores it all, everything is quietly cleared up; he has to leave at once for town because he is due there to play cards. And it is also happening in the restaurant in the Radio Tower. The whole city is turning, the restaurant rises and falls, trembles, shakes, everything begins to skid about, Potsdam with all its houses has skidded into the Tegel houses, the pine trees are intertwined with their needles clawing each other. In the restaurant everybody clings to the chairbacks and continues talking, no one admitting what is happening and they all look at each other as if this would be the last thing they would see, many eyes are glancing at each other while the tables with their roast duck and almonds wobble as if on the high seas; the wine in the glasses starts swaying dangerously, the fork bends its prongs downwards, the knives cut haphazardly into the ketchup, the red sauce runs across the table cloth which is immediately whisked away and shown to all and sundry, then is the collapse imminent. It sobs, it is in someone's throat, cannot move forward or backward, things will never be all right again.

In the academy all the doors and windows are made of glass, there are no curtains so that everything is bright, it is light soon after midnight, only the portraits are covered with cloths. The exhibition has been opened, many heads, everyone is present in front of his picture. The exhibitors are still looking for the picture that is to be dissected. Before that there is a long and terrible wait, each one thinks he is the one to be executed. Nevertheless, everyone is crying. The fire that suddenly breaks out in the cellar saves them, everyone flees towards the entrance and the cars outside, they jump in. Some have been set alight by the fire and they run into the Tiergarten and throw themselves to the ground to extinguish the flames; they are all well-known people. They all meet up at *Kempinski*, the incident has been dismissed, the waiters bring small wash basins for the feet, everyone removes his socks and places his feet in the warm, soapy water. It is an act of mercy. The black water seeps across the floor. The waiters come back with napkins and dry the feet.

Due to politics the streets rise up at an angle of 45 degrees, the cars slide backwards, the cyclists and pedestrians whirl back on both sides of the street, it is impossible to prevent the damage caused by the cars. The pedestrians catch each other, firmly they keep their dentures in place, they do not speak, but they are looking for some support with their hands held over their mouths. One of them indicates with his eyes that it is still better to be here, that it is best to stay here, here one can stand it better than elsewhere, it is not better anywhere else. Then everything is repeated again on the Radio Tower but the marshland with its pines and willows is quite still while everything else turns. It is best to look firmly at the sand. Giddiness stops, the nurse shakes up the pillows in the back. It is still better here.

A thunderstorm has come to the lake. Two hundred counted flashes of lightning forked into the lake. The thunderstorm has spread to the nearby districts, and that is why the white birds have flown away. But some music develops by the lake, music hastily composed and quickly entrusted to the waves of the lake which soon freezes up, thaws, sludges up and freezes again. The stiff fishing rods are embedded in the ice, with notes caught on the hooks, the music too is frozen while the car race takes place on the Avus, the thunderous roar of Berlin envelops the fearful silence of Berlin at prayer, impossible to contemplate sleeping. The sweet served at supper is sent back by the patients, no one can swallow a spoonful, no one wants to count another flash of lightning and accompany this by swallowing his spoonful of sweet. The nurses, with disapproving glances, remove all the flowers from the rooms and place the vases in the passage.

On the way to Krumme Lanke (beside the Grunewald, the pearl with a flaw) lies the huge tree, hewn down, broken off one metre above ground. The patients who have had walking prescribed for them, wait nevertheless to get down to the water, but the nurse orders everybody to stop and climbs the trunk of the tree herself, lifting the branches to see whether there is any blood on them and to find out if the tree has killed anyone. She waves, one does not know whether she has discovered blood or not. People begin to get restless, everyone wants to know whether he has been murdered, things get progressively more awkward, no one has a coat, it is raining again, a clamour starts up, no one wants to return to his ward because he does not know which is the right one. 'It's got to be more than a disturbance' shout a couple of them and begin hitting each other. 'No disturbance is like this, it must be something worse!' Everyone is soaked to the skin, shirts stick to bodies, more haste now because of the cold, because of the rain in mouths, water in noses, a river across the eyes. Painless collapse under the tree.

Berlin has been tidied up. The shops have been put one on top of the other, stacked into a heap, shoes, yardsticks, some stored rice and potatoes and coal, the large amount of coal which the Senate has stored is easily recognizable lying around the perimeter. Sand is now everywhere, in shoes – on the coal. The large shop windows with their secret names written above, names like *Neckermann* and *Defaka* soar like glass domes above everything else, one can see through them yet recognize very little. A pub in the Old Moabit district is still open under the glass dome and no one can understand how this is possible. Everything has been tidied up there. The landlord pours out double Doornkaats, gives himself one, his pub was always the best, the oldest, always full of people. The people, however, are no longer in Berlin. He starts another round, it is drunk up at once and again, that is how it is with double gins, large beers and always doubles. The Spree and the Teltow canal are already overflowing with gin, the Havel is foaming with beer, no one is capable of speaking distinctly beneath the stacked glasses, everything that is being said flows almost incomprehensibly, out of the corners of mouths, anyway no one wants to talk anymore, but just mumble something out of the corners of his mouth, everything is being poured out anyway, everything double.

*

The fashionable Kreuzberg, the damp cellars and the old sofas are in demand again, the stove pipes, the rats, the view onto the backyard. Added to which one has to grow one's hair long, has to roam about and make a lot of noise, has to be drunk and scare old people from the Hallesche Tor to the Bohemian village. One has got to be simultaneously alone and among too large a crowd, converting people from one faith to the next. The new religion comes from Kreuzberg, and the revivalist beards and the orders to revolt against all this subsidized agony. Everyone has to eat from the same type of tin crockery, thin Berlin broth with brown bread, after which the strongest brandy must be ordered and still more brandy for the longest nights. The junk shops no longer sell things so cheaply because the district is becoming fashionable, the *Kleine Weltlaterne* is disbursing itself, the preachers and disciples letting themselves be admired in the evenings and not caring a garlic sausage about the curious onlookers. A century is being challenged that, here too, does not want to display itself. An entrance gate is being rattled, a lamp post is knocked down, some passersby are struck on the head. You may laugh about it in Berlin.

All the bars are crowded after midnight, the *Eierschale*, the *Badewanne*, the *Pferdestall*, the *Kleist-Casino*, the *Volle Pulle*, *Tabu*, *Chez Nous*, *Riverboat*, *Big Apple* and the *Edensaloon*. They are all places rocked and racked by music which only bursts forth in the night for a few hours. Turnover is increased immediately, there is an inflation of wet hands and glazed eyes. At night the whole of Berlin is a place for quick returns and turnover. Everything is confusion for a while, and some groups split off. Espionage thrives, each disruption is transparent. Everybody is anxious to rid himself of his secret, to broadcast his news, to break down during interrogation. Everyone is after everyone else and no one is able to check the proffered bill in the dim light. Outside it is another dawn, it is too bright. There no bill adds up right. No one knows which sex the transvestites will end up with and with what imprint on their painted lips they will return home to sleep happily through into the next day.

Anyone who enters the city uninvited, steps down into it, flys into it, walks into it, will be admitted, X-rayed, have his temperature taken and be thoroughly examined. He is led with bandaged eyes into camouflaged houses where the bandage is removed, and of course he does not know where he is and is not expected to ask questions. Everything is a secret. But they ask nothing out of the ordinary, merely his name and how he lives, always when, where and why. It is so secret that one has to repeat everything over and over again, no one takes it amiss, only rarely are divergent questions put by different questioners. It continues hour-long, day-long, until one begins to shake a bit, and until one has repeated one's name firmly and calmly for the last time. Then one is expected to forget it all, and one is taken away – blindfolded and permitted to stay. Has not betrayed a thing. Has betrayed. Hasn't lied. Has lied. In the houses there were only armchairs and tables, no black wall, not even a thumb screw. Merely a little coughing now and then, a few knuckles banging on the table, a disinterested glance. But the houses cannot be found again. The security service remains secret.

It is quite quiet, it is night-time. Since then no one has been in the streets. The old houses are covered in grime and are overgrown, they sink deeper and deeper into the gardens. At the Koenigsalle junction muffled shots are being fired at Rathenau. At Plötzensee people are being hanged. In the telephone boxes the penny pieces come out of the slot machine again, they have been inserted fruitlessly. There is no connection. From Halensee to the centre there is no one to be found. In the coffee-house *Kranzler*, where the lights are dimmed, old ladies seated at tables wearing felt hats are chewing away at their pieces of cake, frequently they put two pieces at once into their mouths because no one can see anything. The waitress catches her high heels in the whipped cream and splatters the cap on her head as well as her stomach. The old ladies guzzle and guzzle and the old men stand outside *Kranzler* with hat stands in their hands, some of them are kneeling on the pavement drawing their old wives on the concrete, they make obscene jokes with blue and pink chalk, they draw their wives squarely on the ground, naked with carbines between their heavy thighs. In *Kranzler* the women have pulled their felt hats firmly over their eyes, they chew and then help themselves to more.

The patients are allowed to go out for an hour, but they return after a few minutes. An American, presumably made of lead, wearing a short white helmet and holding a lowered machine gun is standing as if rooted at the junction of the southern by-pass. The manoeuvre lasts for hours, the muffled angry murmuring is easily discernible through the cheap curtains. The auxiliary nurse says she cannot hear anything, it is only the manoeuvres. She polishes the doorhandles and the taps, laughing and singing: that's no war. The motorcade of young red-nosed Englishmen stops, two Soviet Russian Guards go out into the street, there is much counting and talking, then neither understands the other. The auxiliary nurse interrupts. Suddenly all kinds of armoured cars arrive, one faction does not want the other faction to enter Berlin, excitement ensues. The auxiliary nurse starts to laugh and furtively passes a cigarette. Then the guards begin to go up and down again, not giving anything away, no one noticed the cigarette incident. It is permissible to smoke cigarettes in Berlin. The armoured cars eventually drive one behind the other into the city.

In the Friedrichstrasse there is yet another crossing, an entrance and an exit for ambulances and large black cars with closely curtained windows. It is dark, there is whispering, men in uniform give signals and up until midnight point out Checkpoint Charlie, always straight ahead in the opposite direction. At the correct crossing point they are not exactly annoyed to have gone to the wrong crossing point, but once again there is whispering, one thinks one has made a mistake and holds up one's passport and then pop music is played and the prettiest passports are stamped. Then one has to strip the paint from the car, it is quickly done, the paint peels off in strips like cold wax, then one has to knock three times on tin, kick the wheel once with one's foot and then one is given 1 Mark which has to be thrown to the ground, heads or tails. Everyone salutes, one salutes into the rear mirror and drives back.

The week begins with Nepal and Ghana. On Tuesday the Congolese are dragged from one side of the Friedrichstrasse to the other to the accompaniment of complaints and angry commentaries, on Wednesday Pakistan hires a coach for a round trip, on Thursday the delegation from the South Pole is acclaimed on one side and ignored on the other. The following evening the medley of visitors drive off with the wigs belonging to the Schiller theatre and they are given costumes to go with the wigs at the Schiffbauerdamm theatre, then there is a hold up, the Americans from the Middle West rip out the Brandenburg gate and take it with them as a memento, then come the Malayans and disappear with the Reichstag. Suddenly the gypsies have taken over Berlin and put up their tents, the Berlin population flees into the outer suburbs and then gypsies wash everybody's linen which can be seen to flutter as far as Lichterfelde. In the Philharmonie the Fanfares are opening in a new play, it must be Sunday. Unter den Linden rises up black, gold and red. The Gedächt-nis church ascends heavenwards.

No one believes, least of all the newcomers, that the animals really live at the station Zoo. No one is prepared for the camel. On its hump now stands the Victory Column. The platform became empty very quickly because of the animals. The men all go to the aquarium, the women to the monkey house. The men remain for hours in front of the fish, finally in front of the salamanders, they have golden green salamanders in their eyes, gentle most gentle, they would like to take them home, but the keepers at the door search even the breast pockets, there is nothing one can do about it. The women, keeping their distance from one another, suspicious of each other, visit their favourite monkey. They have brought along a silver spoon and a silk pouch and only give their favourite monkey sugar. At closing time the men and women rejoin each other at the hot house on the bridge over the suggestion of a stream. Below the crocodiles are dozing in the sticky heat. Everyone looks down with weary eyes, but the crocodiles won't perform, they are biding their time. The bridge could collapse and rouse the crocodiles, but it does not collapse. No one can fall off as long as nobody pushes on purpose. The temperature should not rise because it is carefully controlled, nevertheless, the temperature does rise. No one wants to look at the crocodiles any longer, and each pushes his way out and would like to get back for the evening visiting hour.

The children have been sent into the streets, onto the concrete barriers. They ride on the barriers and have hundreds of wishes. They want to be soldiers and pilots or spies, they want to get married and eat chicken on Sundays, they want barbed wire and pistols and liquorice and they want fairy tales in the evenings. The guards who are too grown up to have any truck with children are, however, inwardly annoyed and chase them home for lunch.

Everyone is waiting for the circus. The taut, restless ponies and the ponderous elephants slurping about in their loose skin come down the avenue, escorted by the Allies. The director of the Zoo, in an open car, waves to the passersby who have to wait, he speaks continually into his microphone, he eulogizes about his lions and monkeys but not about the camels who come last, carrying their heads high. The camels fall further and further behind, segregating themselves, they belong to the same circus but have nothing more to do with it. The patients are waiting only for the camels, move towards the camels and place themselves under their protection. Their fur smells strongly of the desert, of freedom and the open air, everyone walks with his camel and passes everywhere without hindrance, cross country he goes, through the frost, he swims with his camel through stagnant water, mounts his camel at last and crosses forests and water. The camel does not mind water, it hears no whistling, no patrol cars, no siren, no night bells, no shots. The camels move more quickly in the sand. One more forest. They are in the open.

On the Kurfürstendam at the Joachimsthaler street corner a wood pile has been erected. There are no papers. The papers which were to be used to kindle the bonfire have not appeared. The paper kiosk is empty, not even the girl who sells them is here. People hesitate, then everybody boldly picks up a log. Some people immediately take their logs home under their coats, others begin carving with their pocket-knives anything that comes to mind: signs and symbols of the sun and life. Some people make snide remarks and say the wood is damp. An old man brandishes his log, screaming: 'Sabotage. We are playing into the enemy's hands.' And sure enough the logs are being passed from one to the other, one throws a log to the next man, but no one ignites a log, everyone is sensible. Soon all the wood is gone and the traffic continues to flow. Suddenly the newspapers appear again, first the small ones with smudged letters and greasy headlines, with surplus cold grease which runs along the edges. Next the big ones, those slim, snide ones dripping with clear soup, the ones that need to be held in kid gloves.

The letter has a threatening appearance, dark green or dark blue. One is instantly suspicious. It is not the expected letter, it is another letter. It is short. The Insurance that handles Berlin announces that it is not liable for ailments incurred before signing the agreement. The pain is subjugated and because there are no doctors, because they only appear at important functions in the mornings – only during visiting hours – they all say to the nurses that it is unfair, it is not correct, because in that case everything would be incurable. The nurses do not disclose whose side they are on or how much they know. They put down the trays with the pills and the fruit juices, turn a blind eye to the occasional bottle of beer when the doctors' backs are turned, they wink, almost as if one could confidently expect that it was not incurable. Always this kindness! The nurses avoid talking about essentials, it is 'diplomacy', that is what they call it. Everyone with his subdued pain says that now it is diplomacy. There is nothing to be done. The exhaustion is too great. They all drink their fruit juices and lie down breathing heavily. The linen sheets are smoothed. For a moment everything is all right.

A Berlin room, a dusky link in the bright flight of rooms. On the high ceiling is the comforting stucco-work, a reminder that it used to be in Schöneberg. A cell for meditation among all those noisy rooms. The white lies and cobwebs that were all left behind them, that was a long time ago, it was not a long time ago. There is a celebration, everyone has been invited, there is drink and dancing; everyone has to drink in order to forget something, something which is – wrong – it is today, was yesterday, will be tomorrow, it is something in Berlin. Young people all dance silently, cheek to cheek. Then they all drink a great deal. The last guests scream at the top of their voices, they no longer know what they are saying: can I, can I, have I, have I, do I, do I! None of the cars start and they all want to spend the night in this room. The head physician will be late for his game of cards, for once he looked in and put his finger to his lips: one does not know whether there is any hope, but if there is no hope it is not quite so frightening, it is subdued, it does not have to be hope, it can be something less, does not have to be anything, it is nothing, it is past with the *Scharnhorst* past insurances, tobacconists, past sweet-shops, *Leiser*, past the fire insurance, the merchant bank, past *Bolle*, past; the last airplane has come in, the first one flies in after midnight, they all fly very high, not through the room. It was a disturbance nothing else. It will not happen again.

CLAIRE ETCHERELLI PARIS

from
Elise or The Real Life

TRANSLATED BY JUNE P. WILSON AND BENN MICHAELS

The assembly line came to a halt and the siren went off. Mustapha brought me the gasoline cloth Arezki had given him. It was a signal. He wanted to speak to me.

I picked up my coat and left for the Porte d'Italie. I felt the need to walk and talk out loud. There were gusts of wind that raised your hair on end and sliced the skin of your face, beautiful girls in warm coats who, height of injustice, were made even more beautiful by the cold and their winter clothes, Algerians walking duckfooted in spring jackets with their collars turned up; there were cops at the entrances to the Métro checking identity cards, and the windows – from the Prisunic to the most dilapidated grocer – were caught up in a fever of garlands and lights. A happy throng, well-nourished, wearing fur-lined boots and interlined coats, who spent August by the sea and wore spring clothes at Easter, a throng that paid for its leisure with the sweat of its brow, walked, sat at café tables, and looked the other way when into its territorial waters slipped ill-nourished types who wore Easter clothes in November and who, for all their brow's sweat, earned only enough for bread. These species just happened to gather in special neighbourhoods – shanty towns, run-down hotels – and, by nationalities: Algerian, Spanish, Portuguese, and, naturally, French. They also fell into other categories: alcoholics, idlers, tuberculars, degenerates. There is something to be said for the ghetto. But sometimes these types managed to sneak up on you in the Métro, in the café, and in addition, they were noisy, lost, or disgustingly drunk. And occasionally, in these caricatures of humanity, in these suffering bodies mutilated by misery, in the cold dark rooms, between the dirty laundry and the drying laundry, one of these dregs carried inside him – by luck or miracle – the gleam, the flame, the spark that made him suffer even more. The spirit breathed there as much as anywhere; intelligence either developed or died, crushed.

These thoughts, the cold, my hair blowing around my neck, Arezki's disappearance, the Magyar's blood and the smell of the factory, the four hours on the line stretching ahead, the still unread letter from Grandmother, all this is life. How gentle it had been, the previous one, a little blurred, far from the sordid truth. It had been simple, animal, rich in dreams. I said 'one day . . .' and it was enough.

I am living this day, I am living the real life, involved with other human beings, and I suffer.

EXTRACT TWO

'Listen. Take the Métro to Stalingrad. All right? Get off, take a seat, and wait for me on the platform. While you wait, read a paper folded in front of your face. If any people from here get off, they won't recognize you.'

I followed his directions. He joined me on the platform at Stalingrad where I had buried my face in the front pages of my paper. This made him laugh. He tapped on the paper and said we'd go on to Ternes.

'It's near the Etoile. I think it's a good place.'

Arezki had dressed carefully. He was wearing a white shirt, a tie hidden by his scarf, and his brown suit, shiny with wear, was spotless.

At last, I was seeing Paris by night, the Paris of postcards and calendars.

'You like it?'

Arezki was having fun. He suggested that we walk up to

l'Étoile and then come back on the opposite sidewalk. It would be easy to lose ourselves and become a part of the scene. To feel one had a place in this beautiful city, to be integrated . . .

We spent some time discussing the Magyar's accident. We were both cold. Arezki glanced toward the cafés as we walked. He must be worrying about their being expensive, I thought. Three days until payday. He must be almost broke, too.

As we turned back toward Les Ternes, he said: 'You're cold,' and we went into a café whose sidewalk terrace was heated. But he preferred the interior, picked out two places and ordered two teas. The process was always the same. Our neighbours studied us in silence for several seconds and it was easy to guess their thoughts. I tried to say to myself: 'So what? It's Paris, the city of outlaws, fugitives from all over the world. This is 1957. Am I going to come apart because of a few stares? We are a scandal in this lovely neighbourhood. Are these people responsible?'

'. . . But where are the police? Look at that guy sitting right next to you in a nice place where you've made a date with a nice girl you're going to take home in the car you've parked nearby . . . and there's an Arab with a French girl! She's French and working class for sure, you can tell right off. We're fighting a war with those guys . . . Where are the police? No, we don't want to make them suffer; we're human. There are camps, places they can be assigned to. Clean up Paris. Maybe this one has a gun in his pocket. They all have.'

Every one of their stares said that.

EXTRACT THREE ════════════════════

When Arezki joined me at Stalingrad, he stated that we wouldn't go to Les Ternes anymore. It wasn't a good neighbourhood.

'We're going to . . . the Trocadéro.'

We went to the Trocadéro. We even returned two days

later. We walked in the gardens where the freezing fog raised protective walls around us.

We went to the Opéra and circled the building several times.

We crossed the bridges.

We lost ourselves on the streets around Saint-Paul.

We walked up the boulevards toward Saint-Augustin.

Starting at Vaugirard, we ended up at the Porte d'Auteuil.

The Rue de Rivoli we did in both directions.

And the Boulevard Voltaire, and the Boulevard du Temple, and the little streets behind the Palais-Royale. And La Trinité and the Rue Lafayette.

We never returned to the same neighbourhood. The smallest incident, a gathering of people, the shadow of a police car, someone who seemed to be following us, and our walk was abruptly ended. We had to part, to go home separately. These interrupted evenings, our conversations cut short, and the anxiety – never knowing, leaving him behind, waiting until the next day to find out if anything serious had happened – these bound me to him in that well-known way where the more fleeting the thing, the dearer it is.

He saw police everywhere. I thought he exaggerated. I protested a bit when he'd say:

'Look. See that guy in front of the window. He's a cop. You don't believe me? I tell you it's so.'

'So what? What does it matter?'

We continued our walk.

There were lots of police raids. Arezki dreaded them.

'But you don't break any laws.'

'You think that satisfies them?'

And the next night, we changed neighbourhoods. I asked no questions. Time passed, we met almost every day. I tried to address him as 'tu', for he became angry one night at my continual 'vous'. I loved to hear him talk. His tongue made a soft little roll when he pronounced his 'r's'. We passed from serious to gay, we made fun of our friends on the assembly line. I told him about Lucien's youth, I often talked of

227

Grandmother. She had become familiar to him; he knew her faults, her expressions, her manias. Mustapha, Grandmother, Lucien – these people who made up our company helped us to discover each other. Out of shyness, we made use of them to talk about ourselves.

One evening, we were walking in the gardens of the Trocadéro. We found a hole in the shadows and Arezki kissed me violently. With my new ideas, I thought, this is it, now he's going to take me to his room. But nothing happened. Our understanding was miraculous: anyone else would have been more impatient, more audacious. If he wasn't, it was because to the difficult circumstances that already hampered us had been added the calculated pleasure of our moving forward together.

We observed each other for a long time with growing tenderness. In front of others, we feigned indifference, that game where the smallest gesture, a blink of the eye, an inflection of the voice, takes on intense meaning.

Each time we separated, Arezki swore me to secrecy, which annoyed me a little. Actually, it suited me perfectly.

Rain, sleet, we walked. Paris was an enormous ambush through which we moved with ludicrous precautions. Our love heightened the background of our wanderings. Nothing was ugly. The rain polished the pavement and the lone light of an alley made a prism of the shimmering stones. The squares had a provincial charm and the broken-down sheds took on the look of old abandoned windmills. Our happiness transformed Paris.

EXTRACT FOUR

'Here's Paris.' The cloth tears. The countryside and the soft wind in the trees, anticipating the summer to come, prolonged still further the funeral ceremony and its capacity to appease. But here begins the city's overflow. A clock marks the time. The streets are rectilinear and without mystery. The horizon now is a fragment of sky between the many buildings. It is decidedly blue. It is going to be hot, and the women are wearing dresses without collars or sleeves. Some Arabs are digging a sidewalk. Once we've passed the viaduct at Auteuil, the traffic grows heavier. This is Paris. Delivery trucks, trailer trucks, buses, it's the start of a day. From the Porte de Versailles, we move slowly and I examine the people on the sidewalk to my right, as if they could answer my questions. It's because here, in the noise of the city, in its colours and mixtures, I've found Arezki again.

Now the buildings of the 'Cité Universitaire'. The red brick of their walls reminds me of the English colleges, the way they looked in my brother's school books. Between two pavilions, a garden gives to the whole a quality of fullness. Lecture halls, rooms from which it must be possible to see the distant roses amidst the green . . . because of that, because of the old stones and a few students walking toward the boulevard, I tell myself that Arezki risks nothing. Farther along, coming out of the Moroccan pavilion, a boy yawns, his collar open. He stretches his free arm. And even if Arezki didn't come back, I'd rouse Paris. There are lawyers, news-papers. A man's life, that matters here. A few would rise up to cry out, protest, make demands. The 28th of May was not a dream.

At the Porte de Gentilly, the road goes gently downhill. The concrete of the stadium steps is blinding in the sun. On a sign, I read 'Poterne des Peupliers'. It reminds me of gallows. Articles 76 and 78: 'Attack on the internal and external security . . .' They won't let go all that fast.

We pass a monument made of white stones: 'TO FRENCH MOTHERS'. The homage, the veneration, they come later, when it's too late. The slope flattens out toward the Place d'Italie. I know it too well; I barely look to the left toward this old whore of a factory where I read the inscription 'Automobiles; Wood-working machines'. I feel as if the unnerving noise of the assembly line were reaching out for me. I smell the warm metal.

When we begin the descent towards Charenton, the vibrating motions of the car – the boulevard is being repaired – throw me from hope back to anguish. And memories are mixed in as we pass the square of La Limagne. Arezki used to say 'de la Limace'. He also said: 'Le Mont de Pitié', and I loved this last word.

On the Pont National, at the sight of the water, I think about the bodies that float under it. Bodies that are thrown in on nights of big riots, in the paroxysm of hatred; the bodies of the weak who have talked too much and whom death punishes. Out of place in this area, L'Auberge du Régal watches those pass whom no red light stops.

On the Boulevard Poniatowski, buildings rise to circle Paris with their pre-war ugliness. Unfriendly houses with rough façades, dull stones, shapeless doorways, large interior courts no sun could ever reach; there lives the workers' aristocracy aspiring to the bourgeoisie. Crushed and constricted by indifference, by new ideas, what price the life of an Arab here? The love of order oozes from these buildings. He's been sent away, sent back into the war. I could cry, but who would hear me? If he's alive, where is he? If he's dead, where is his body? Who will tell me? You've taken his life, yes, but what have you done with his body? At the Porte de Vincennes, the boulevard comes to an end and a vast housing project takes over: new apartment buildings with terraces shaded by blue and orange awnings. They suggest hot afternoons where you drink from frosted glasses while listening to a record. Who will think of Arezki?

Henri slows down still more. We're behind a truck that belches its exhaust. Montreuil is at my right and the Rue d'Avron opposite. The stalls of les Halles challenge a painter's palette. The rows of fruit, the pyramids of vegetables tear the fabric of my hopes. In front of the mounds of garden produce, thousands of ants act as a rampart before the displays.

On the hill between Bagnolet and Les Lilas, the car struggles between two buses. A road gang at the Porte de Ménilmontant is taking time off for a drink. Tomorrow, one of them won't be back and fifty will appear to pick up his shovel. There are so many, there are too many, inexhaustible reserves, forever replenished.

After Les Lilas, on the curve going down toward the Pré-Saint-Gervais, you see before you Aubervilliers, pale in the heat haze. On the barren esplanade, a curious solitary church attracts me. But now Henri is driving very fast and it's only after the Porte de Pantin that we reach the slums of that other Paris that comes to Paris only for the 28th of May. Not dangerous, easy to control, easy to satisfy. We enter the tunnel under the Porte de la Villette. I have a presentiment that I will never see Arezki again.

ALBERTINE SARRAZIN

from

L'Astragale

TRANSLATED BY LIZ HERON

It's my first Paris wander beyond Annie's boulevard for years. I stop at the junction: the traffic cop, the pedestrian crossings, the Métro, then the jigsaw of streets and houses stretching to infinity. If I step over this boundary, if I go down underground or on to the next boulevard, how could I put up with going back to Annie's, to her rotten coffee, and her piecework ties, Annie and the Santé nick, Annie and her gloomy old Sébastopol?

But to keep Julien I have to keep Annie: I begin to see myself in all the people he describes to me, but I haven't a single address, a single name that isn't a nickname or an alias, I have no way of contacting him. Except Annie.

For a moment Julien parts the fog, and I step through it with him, my lips gauze-soft; then he dissolves, and I'm facing the sunless day again, looking for what he has taken with him and I can't reach now.

I lean against the ironwork of the Métro entrance to count what's left in my pocket. It's okay, I have enough change for a ticket.

When I get back up into the open air, every detail of this neighbourhood hits me in the face, instantly familiar: I know every last shop window, every single sign and its lettering big or small, I know which ones glitter in the solitary winter streets, promising the night. The years drop back and I'm sixteen, dragging my espadrilles in the roadway; there I am, with my hair left loose and my breasts bare under my sweater; like the Gitane on the posters, I've got clouds beneath my feet. Paris caresses me with a thousand glances, offering itself just as I do: 'Hey, I can walk where I like, can't I? Scram, that's what I'm saying.'

'Why you not nice to me, bad French girl?'

Yup, those blackies are still there too, ogling with their syrupy eyes, as well as the no-nonsense ones 'walk on ahead, I'll follow you', and the little guys and the big old guys, the guys all got up smart and the ones in overalls. What's the difference between the ones then and the ones now, the ones today walking alongside me, in front of me and behind me, whispering: 'How'd you like to have a drink?'

We'd have a drink, put down the glass, back in ten minutes . . . I'm not sure anymore, I haven't got the nerve.

Sometimes one of my drinking companions would give me a nod from behind his glass of calva; from the covered café terrace we would watch the world go by, the crowd gradually gathering around the door: men who would walk on a few yards and come back again, making their own little commotion inside the big one. 'I think there's somebody waiting for you,' my pal would say, 'don't let me keep you . . .'

My old convoy has gathered round again, surrounding me. But I walk without slowing my step, eyes on the ground; I'm scared. If there's a cop on the patch. If . . . Come on Anne, look up, make a choice, shake out those fingers again . . .

'Is it for a short-time?' asks the girl upstairs, who hasn't recognized me.

The lock on the door. The first garments sliding off, the pause: Ah, your little present, is that it? That's exactly it.

I am miles away, passive, my mind a blank. I won't even be late for lunch.

And I won't have my eye on Annie's pockets any more.

EXTRACT TWO

Around four o'clock I get ready, doing my clothes and make-up carefully, to see me through until the evening: run-proof stockings, smudge-proof mascara, a get-up that looks smart but is comfortable; I fold things and dust things, tidying my room like a boarding-school girl, first because chambermaids make me jumpy, and in the second place because maybe I'll never come back again.

('Come on, on your feet, no lounging about for tarts like you; hey, would you take a look at this block-head!')

When I give up after hours of questioning and let them have my address, all the fuzz will find here is some panties drying on the radiator, and to safeguard anything that seems too nice to them not to be stolen, a sheaf of receipts: receipts for the radio, the watch, the travelling iron.

You have to be ready for it, every moment, every step of the way . . .

I seldom sleep out; usually, boredom sets in before the time of night when I could ignore sleep, become a shadow and find myself all-nighters, more lucrative clients than the quickies. Anyway, I've only ever heard about nights at thirty or fifty thousand francs in the slammer, where bullshit puts no limits on fancy ideas. Probably the price should be even higher for nights with a girl on the run, but night covers day, and all twenty-four hours are coloured the same, the livid colour of danger. I swallow my tiredness and disgust until I've scored my target, then I wash them away in delicious undisturbed sleep.

In the bars where prostitutes hang out I've come across a few minors from Fresnes, either hustling on the sly until they're old enough to be registered, or who've reached that age and turned professional. In spite of my new style, my figure a good twenty pounds slimmer and my civilian togs, they've recognized me: 'Hey, Anne! So you're out then?'

I reply that my name isn't Anne, and I'm making 'my début' in Paris, as I scan the gallery of faces for the ones back in the slammer. Thick, cumbersome dresses in grey or brown: those were the winter faces; striped or checked smocks, threadbare, their fullness and pleating worn thin: those were the summer faces. But summer or winter alike, my little sisters wore the same mask, skin pale or flushed or blotchy, dark-circled eyes, and that dull, featureless look they all had. Sometimes, attention would be caught by shining eyes, well-contoured lips, really white teeth; but how was I to remember any names, how was I to know from which chrysalis these girls were born, who were now unrecognizable in a different uniform: heavy make-up, tight clothes, dyed hair?

They stay in the bar waiting for the tricks to come to them; they've got nothing else to do. They wait, slumped against the jukebox or hunched at the bar in front of their glasses, just the way shopkeepers wait for business in their doorways, hands behind their back, up there, past the kingdom of the whores, with its network of alleyways, out in the bright-lit space of the boulevard. Their business takings depend on the time of year, on the way they're dressed or have done their hair: 'My dear, when I wear this dress I have no problem.'

'I only do good business when I'm in trousers.'

As for me, I walk. I don't loiter, I haven't got time, I don't like the pavement and I'm no more a tart than I'm anything else. I use this method because it's fast, it doesn't go by fixed hours or take much practice – or very little: I was saving my skin from pimps' paws and shifty clients when I was only sixteen, and nothing much has changed . . . All I'm really afraid of is the fuzz, since I haven't got a single piece of identification to show them if I'm stopped; but I keep on changing my street, my hotel, my appearance; I sniff out the passing trade before I give them an answer; some unfathomable but sure intuition holds me back or draws me on, lights blinking on in my head, red for a warning, green okay, go on, wait, don't wait, get out of here fast, smile, yeah. Through the streets I glide with brisk, hurried steps, hardly limping at all and walking as fast as I can; this apparent lack of interest, this 'you don't look the type' type, works as both shield and come on.

'Can I see you again?'

'Why not, if it turns out that way?'

'Thing is though, where can I find you? You must have some place, a regular bar?'

'Me? . . . I just walk.'

Whenever they're particularly generous or pathetic, to keep them happy I sketch out my movements and jot down an appointment in my diary – a scribbled note for that evening, best not to leave things in writing, so who's this one then, miss block-head? Be a fluke if the guy runs into me again, Paris is a big place. What's it to me, anyhow? You say you waited an hour? I've waited two hours. It was somewhere else and it wasn't for you, but so what? That's an hour one of you owes me.

MAUREEN DUFFY LONDON

from
The Microcosm

And the trains pulls in, draws its length along the platform
kerb, brakes wheezing with the effort, doors flung open,
watch that door, opening on the foam of fairy seas, breaking
against the barrier white surf of faces, all your tickets please,
and the station booming like the public baths with echoes of
feet, voices, slamming metal bouncing off the glass and girder
roof. A female voice amplified as if the deity speaks from the
throat of some brass idol sends its commands flying in
scattered fragments of sound incomprehensible as the delphic
oracle to strike the inattentive with apprehension and trembling. Step through, give up your ticket, all tickets please.
Where do we go from here? Up to now it's been easy. Get on
a train and the machine will make all the decisions, carry you
across country once you've set its wheels in motion, and spill
you out of its tired belly at the appropriate time, a little late
perhaps as the timetable shows but time enough for you with
nothing in front of you. Almost as you draw through the
suburbs you would hold the wheels back now with a braking
will but set going like a sentence half spoken and regretted
there's no drawing back and now you're on your own,
beyond the man in uniform taking away your pass to security
the decisions are all yours; resume responsibility for the feet
that move you into the dour entrance hall, the place of transit
where even the tramps and the meths drinkers, the hooked at
the end of a visionary high who clog the benches for a little,

237

are only passing through though they sit humped, motionless as statuary, limp hands crossed, or shuffle uneasily in their stale clothes, migrants brought down on this draughty perch by a sudden squall of down on your luck. Leave them; continue up the ramp and pause at the top of the steps. At your feet thunders the river of the Euston Road. You stand on the bank, held above the flood that sweeps along cars, buses, lorries; straws, leaves, logs whose waters are the dark waves of hurrying taxis. Go down, immerse yourself in the stream that can hide your past in the anonymous swirl of its waters until you no longer even remember yourself, the hurts soothed, the edges smoothed away.

'Taxi Miss?'

She shook her head and began to move aimlessly in any path that her feet would take, down the row of parked cabs with their drivers reading newspapers, a fat man leaning in at a window in sidelong furtive talk, and down towards the street, the roar increasing with every step and breaking over her as she passed through the ungated portal, blanketing out all thought, all ability to decide anything until she was brought to a stop again like a stupefied hunted animal and leant against the wall, holding on tight to the case and breathing quick and shallow.

But it's no good, she thought, I can't just stand here, must move, get somewhere. The address, find the address. She dug in her pocket, wanting to put the case down and search properly but what was it they said at home? Never put your case down in a London street or they'll whip it away from under your nose before you've time to look round. So she hung on and struggled, aware she was wearing too many clothes and it wasn't as cold down here. Still I couldn't have packed them anyway and they had to get here somehow. I can't imagine them sending anything on.

It came out at last, the scrubby back of an envelope where she'd written it down as Babs had given it to her. 'There's the Y.W. of course,' she'd said, 'if you're really stuck or the cops will always find you somewhere but I always try to keep clear of them. Well you never know do you? Not that I ever but anyway that's all over now and I'm a respectable married woman. But you, what're you after down there? I mean you're not the type. You're clever? Funny how we hardly spoke at school and now I'm telling you all this.' 'I've no one else to ask and you promised not to tell them anything.' 'And neither I won't. Besides it's a big place London is. They tell me there's like eight million there and I can believe it. You'll see when you get there. Like looking for a French letter on Hollheath. What you going for, Cathy? Won't you ever come back? You will, you see, just like me, when you're ready to settle.'

Southgate Terrace, it said, Bayswater. She looked up at the buses but they were bowled along in the stream and none of them said Bayswater on the front, not even in the smaller print and they might be going in the opposite direction. Best to walk on the way she was going until she came to a policeman or to another station and it was a good day for walking even with a suitcase heavy with all your life up to that point, and a bit of a sun shining although far away through the haze of fumes and smoke and everyone seemed very brisk and busy as she passed a huge building site where men in orange tin hats drove tractors, mixed and poured concrete or simply walked about with plans and schedules clipped to bits of board looking purposeful under the raking shadow of the giant crane that lowered a ton of steel girder as gently as a woman picking strawberries. 'Aye, there're always building summat down there like kids with a box of bricks but dammall we get done up here and where would they be wi' out us any road?' she heard her father saying and she would have liked to have stopped on the observation platform, provided by the company for the amusement of passersby with a bird's eye view, among the smart poster men in their bowler hats that she'd thought had all gone long ago apart from the picture house since foremen had given up the fashion and her father had put his carefully away in a brown paper bag at the top of the wardrobe.

Then, across the road, she saw the station, Warren Street it said, with people coming and going like ants from the nest on a summer's day and she crossed the road waiting first for the stream to be dammed by the red light. What does this remind me of, this going down a hole in the ground? How do I know where to go? That's where you get your ticket, phone boxes, a map. You are here. Now if I stand here and just look through all the places eventually I'll find it. There's the river Thames. Would it be North or South of that? There doesn't seem to be much in the South. Nowhere in the middle; they're all famous names. The Right will be the East End and it isn't there. Somewhere near the park, she said. Which park? Hyde Park? That's the only one I know of. There ought to be an easier way of doing this. Supposing I get lost among eight million people. Well I just find a station and try again. Hyde Park Corner, Marble Arch, Queensway, Bayswater. There it is. Now how do I get there? Go back to square one. You are here. I'll write it all down so I don't forget. From here to Tottenham Court Road, then the red line, where's the key, that's the Central to Notting Hill Gate, then the yellow line, that's the Inner Circle to Bayswater. Go West young man is the answer.

Her voice sounded high and strange as she asked for her ticket and she put down half-a-crown and pushed it towards the man thinking that would be enough if she didn't understand what he said. A dark skinned girl in the official uniform clipped her ticket, the first time she'd seen one off the screen though she thought they had them in Bradford, and she stepped on to the moving staircase, all luggage dogs and perambulators must be carried, and they had one of those in Bradford too in a big store. The platform seemed very narrow and the drop on to the glinting rails almost enticing so she drew her eyes away and looked at the other travellers who were all shapes, sizes and colours as she'd noticed up in the street. Well among all of them who'll notice me; eight million and all looking so different like hundreds and thousands of dolly mixtures.

The journey was long and nerve-racking because like a sailor at night she had to continually check her course by the points of the compass and by the fixed star of Bayswater. Emerging into daylight again she felt tired and hungry, the case too heavy, and she still had to find the road. Once again she was bewildered by the different faces of the crowds hurrying past. No one looked like a resident, someone who could be trusted with directions. Like the people in the station they seemed to be just passing through. Then she saw the policeman waving his arms at the traffic and dragged her case across to his island. He brought out his little book and thumbed over the pages. 'You'd have done better to go to Queensway.' Her mind staggered and then steadied itself to concentrate on the directions. He seemed fairly cheerful about her prospect of getting to Southgate Terrace and carried along by his optimism and her first communication with another human being in this city, she walked down two streets, changing hands on her case at every sixth lamp-post and turned right into a row of high white houses with late classical porches at the top of shallow steps.

'How long did you want it for?' the woman asked staring at Cathy round the half-open door.

'I thought perhaps four days.'

'Nights; we go by nights here. A guinea a night, twenty-one shillings, in advance. All right?' The girl nodded. 'You look very young to me. Not run away? I don't want no trouble, no men in your rooms after twelve o'clock.'

'I'm nineteen.'

'That's all right then. Long as you're over age. I'll show you your room.' She opened the door fully, let the girl step past her into the hall and shut it again after her. 'How did you find us? Someone recommend you?' She led the way upstairs.

EXTRACT TWO

At night and on her days off she wanders the city, peering into amusement arcades where the lost play pintables, fruit machines, stare through sights out of alignment for a bull's eye, top score, jackpot, the answer that comes when the bell rings, lights flash, the world comes crowding to see the tarnished silver leaping into the cupped hands, overflowing onto the floor among the fag-ends, blown paper, dust, or dive clubs where children of her own age dance bound together, caught up in the present, seeing nothing while the music holds them. She walks swiftly like someone with a destination but she is searching. Somewhere there must be, they are here I know, there was that article. Never believe all you read in the papers, catchpenny, catch you too if you don't look sharpish. Once on a tube train a woman stared her down, the eyes full of question; once she followed a couple through the streets until they disappeared through a discreet door and she caught a brief glimpse of steps leading down, heard music and voices laughing but it closed against her and she hadn't the courage to push it open again and walk in. She searched the faces of crowds too, dreaming of the small incident, the sudden happening that would unlock her isolation but the miracle never came. All around her were signs, hints, a way of walking or speaking, a style of dress or gesture, the question in the eyes but they were as indecipher-able as a tramp's message scratched on a gatepost, under-stood only by the fraternity.

THE SEVENTIES

W OMEN'S WRITING became a presence to be
reckoned with in the seventies. For one thing,
there was more of it taking up space in
bookshops, as the infant feminist presses began
rediscovering forgotten writers and encouraging new ones.

Most visible was Movement fiction – those best-selling
novels and their progeny, wherein the chrysalis of
oppression was eventually thrown off to reveal the winged
creature of liberation. Its progress was often picaresque and
likely to dispense with the grounding of place, shifting from
campus to city, from city to country, from one country to
another – movement fiction in more ways than one.

This largely confessional genre was of its moment, the
moment of consciousness-raising and new-found feminist
identities. If a lot of it now seems simplistic, it still has the
value of registering how much there was to be challenged or
reinvented. Verena Stefan's *Shedding* (1975) sits firmly
within this literature of collective awakening.

For *Shedding*'s narrator the city space she feels the right to
claim is everywhere invaded, whether in her own Berlin
district, in London, or hitch-hiking on the road between
countries and cities. These are intimate invasions: touches
from strangers on the street, whistles, unwelcome sexual
advances. Stefan's book made an impact on publication,
precisely because such prohibitions on dress or mobility

were familiar experiences to women, though a reality largely invisible to men.

Women's scope for travel, and even for adventurous travel in the mode the Beat boys had jealously inscribed as male, became much greater in the seventies. In Europe and North America a whole student generation, much enlarged by expanded higher education, took to the road. The world opened wider, both for travellers in motion and for the armchair variety, by way of the post-colonial literature gradually reaching western readers, the Latin American writers finding their way into translation.

It is difficult to represent the urban experience of women in the cities of Africa and Asia because such a literature is slight in societies that are still predominantly rural, and where within the urban setting women's possibilities are scarcer. In her novel *Return to Beirut*, Andrée Chedid writes of Paris as a liberation from the constraints imposed on women's movement in the Egyptian capital: 'In Cairo I scarcely knew the streets, and public transport was a forbidden sphere. I came and went within a closed world of private houses . . .' The fictions of women in the Indian sub-continent reflect life lived within family walls, or often, as in the Arab world, in the space of an inner courtyard. Varying cultural factors influence how women in these societies relate imaginatively to their urban environment. Lagos is black Africa's fastest growing city. In Flora Nwapa's story, from her collection *This Is Lagos and Other Stories* (1971), the city disrupts rural patterns and social conventions. It is the marketplace writ large as Vanity Fair.

Angela Carter travelled to Japan at the start of the decade, looking hard at things made all the more cryptic by particularly tricky language barriers, treating her stay there, she wrote, as 'an involuntary apprenticeship in the interpretation of signs'. 'Tokyo Pastoral' is one of several bulletins she sent back from this realm of the strange, among them an account of working as a bar hostess. That sharp use of her outsider's eyes on the arresting oddities of an utterly foreign landscape must indeed have been invaluable for Carter, whose fiction relentlessly probes the distinction between what is natural and what is cultural, and how much we live through representations *as* reality.

This was the decade when Latin America became prominent in global perceptions; not only through the export of its literature and cinema. Political terror reigned in many of its cities. The 1968 Olympics in Mexico City coincided with the massacre of student demonstrators there. Marta Traba's *Mothers and Shadows* is a novel that roves between cities in the continent's Southern Cone, charting the responses of different women characters to the states of emergency around them. In the extract here, women relatives of Argentina's 'disappeared' gather in what was a regular protest in the Plaza de Mayo of Buenos Aires, a protest always eerily bereft of witnesses. Another South American writer, Luisa Valenzuela, wrote of those years: 'Back in Buenos Aires after two years in Europe, I found that my city had turned on me. My secretive, friendly city was no longer. The chiaroscuro had muddied, giving way to sheer darkness and repression . . .'[1]

NOTE

1. From a paper given at the International Writers Conference in Dublin, 1988.

VERENA STEFAN

from

Shedding

TRANSLATED BY JOHANNA MOORE AND BETH WECKMÜLLER

I come unexpectedly out of winter into the cascade of greening birches. In Berlin, this birch green erupts overnight, yellow-tinged, phosphorescing out of another world. During the usual morning walk to the subway, something appears changed. Not until I am able to relate the onset of numbness back to greening birch trees can I recognize what it is. The first pleasure – the anticipation of perpetual warmth from the sun – lets me breathe freely again and smile. But at second glance, the green strikes my eyes like a neon light.

What did I do last year after the first days of birch greening? Was I even alive between April of last year and March of this? I had forgotten that this kind of green existed. I had not forgotten the sun, nor the cold, nor the longing for warmth, but had forgotten that spring brings with it something more than sun, forgotten that there are birch trees which open their floodgates of green.

Each year I find it disconcerting. In other places anemones crocuses daisies already bloom, forsythia as well, but not here on the streets where I live, on these streets the birches are the first to blossom forth overnight. Time, the past, the uncertain future, the year whizzing past – nothing else reminds me of these things as sharply and as painfully. Seven years in Berlin, every year this birch episode. Two, three years ago the green began to hurt my eyes. I hurry through these interludes. I must try and remember. What else can I hold onto now? This is when my new year begins. In my chronology it is this iridescent green shock which signals that which the calendar shows as New Year's Eve. I am filled with anxiety because I cannot remember the past year.

This birch greening, the energy which flows from it is no everyday event. I cannot live this way every day – young woman suddenly bursts into flames on the street.

Weeks later and again overnight, when the chestnut trees blossom forth like burgeoning candelabra, I have calmed down a bit. Later still, by the time we can sit beneath the towering chestnut tree and drink a beer without feeling chilly, I will have been swept along by the tide of everyday events; soon the first snowfall will come without my even noticing.

On the way home I pass a tavern. Two men and two women are sitting at a table right next to the sidewalk. Noticing me, one of the men is taken aback. He remarks to the others. They turn to stare at me.

I am wearing a long skirt and a sleeveless teeshirt. In one hand I carry a shopping bag which holds three bottles of wine. The man leans over the railing and stares fixedly at me as I approach. Something about this situation alarms me more than usual. The man's expression is not lustful or lewd, but instead quite righteously indignant. As I pass him he says, incensed: Hey baby, what happened to your boobs?

My spine stiffens. The man is twice my size and half drunk besides. The others laugh in agreement. Two steps later I hear the shrill catcall whistling past my ears. From the corner of my eye I see the men's legs and hear, after the whistle: Jesus, what knockers!

I crouch, ready to pounce. And then what? I ready myself to lash out. How to attack? Only five more steps until I can push open the heavy door to the building, rest the shopping bag next to the mailbox, take out the mail, go through the inner courtyard to the side entrance, climb the two flights of stairs, unlock the apartment door, enter the kitchen, open the refrigerator, carefully place the three bottles of wine on the shelf, let the door close and look about the kitchen, arms hanging down at my sides. My breasts hang against my ribcage, warm, sun-filled gourds. Under them, tiny rivulets of sweat had gathered and now dissolve, one drop at a time.

EXTRACT TWO

I am standing at Wittenbergplatz waiting for the traffic light to turn green. In my left hand I am carrying a shopping bag filled with groceries, in my right a jumbo package of toilet paper. I can sense two men approaching me from behind, and I glance back over my shoulder. Just then the man on the left gets hold of a handful of my hair, which is tinted red and shoulder length; he scrutinizes the strands gliding through his fingers and says to his friend: terrific hair! I whirl around and hit him in the face with the toilet paper, using it as a club to extend my reach. Then drained of strength, knees shaking, I cross the street. My arm is now heavy as lead, I can no longer lift it. The two men follow me, cursing angrily and calling me names for having had the audacity to stand up to them. On the other side of the street I turn around once more, hiss at them to shut up. They would really like to come after me, but it is broad daylight and there are people on the street, the two of them are foreigners. Sitting in the subway, I woefully study my small hands. With them alone, I could not have landed even one blow. An everyday occurrence. The everyday treatment of a woman, second-class citizen not only in the third world. I probably have a nicer apartment, more social contacts, better working conditions than most of the foreign workers in West Berlin. But every man – foreign or native – can, regardless of living or working conditions, mistreat me at any time he pleases. Do I have better living conditions simply because I may have a nicer apartment than my oppressor?

At that time I had long hair. I've always been slight, it's always been easy to put an arm around me. It was obvious that I couldn't hitchhike alone, I would have to find another woman if I wanted to come through more or less unscathed. There was no other woman. How could I get to know the world on my own? It was dangerous. To get entangled with a man would mean becoming a participant in his sex life, whatever that might involve. That was just as dangerous. Why couldn't I travel without fear of being molested, why was this direct access to the world closed off to me? At that point I was still inquisitive enough to attempt to experience the world on my own. But later on I realized I could only gain access to the world with the help of middlemen. I made it to Athens without having to have intercourse.

In the youth hostel I finally met up with other women who were travelling alone. A black woman from the US and a woman from India. But I found no one who wanted to go to Northern Europe. Athens in August, waves of heat washing over me. To be able to lose my self in the south, dissolve into a day without end, to end this vacation from the north and begin instead an endless day of perpetual warmth!

This feeling of contentment was short-lived. I was gradually overcome by the fear of not finding anyone with whom I could hitchhike back. It would have been inconceivable for me to go and stand alone beside one of the roads leading out of Athens. Seeing no other way out, I fell in love with a guy who was bumming around the world. With him I travelled all the way across Europe and up to London. I had once spent a few pleasant weeks there with Ines, a summer without entanglements, without fear. This time, the city was closed to me.

I felt myself being swept along through London's streets, but the city itself remained inaccessible. I began searching for people who had already gained access. At Piccadilly Circus I attached myself to an easygoing group and went with them to their house. We drank tea, smoked hash and listened to music. That same evening they left on vacation. I kept edging along the city, constantly losing my sandals.

In the subway – I filled my lungs with the black, tar-like odour, at least that was real – an American commented on the faded blue shirt I was wearing. I smiled, relieved. We made a date for that evening. Changing trains, as he stood on the step shifting his weight from one foot to the other, he suddenly kissed me. I drew back, he chuckled in gleeful anticipation: only kidding, Baby. Watch out for the doors! To spend just one evening in this city with one of them instead of being hassled by all the rest, is that asking too much? I stood there pleading with myself.

'That's hard to believe, a girl on vacation all by herself and not in the mood for it?' one of the men who had given me a ride in Saloniki had said, perturbed. 'Are you sure I can't help you out?' I didn't understand why he said that. I didn't want sex. I wanted to see foreign countries.

FLORA NWAPA

This is Lagos

'They say Lagos men do not chase women, they snatch them,' Soha's mother told her on the eve of her departure to Lagos. 'So my daughter, be careful. My sister will take care of you. You should help her with her housework and her children, just as you have been doing here.'

Soha was fond of her aunt. She called her Mama Eze. Eze was her aunt's first son. And Mama Eze called Soha my sister's daughter. She too was fond of Soha whom she looked after when she was a little girl.

Soha was a sweet girl. She was just twenty when she came to Lagos. She was not beautiful in the real sense of the word. But she was very pretty and charming. She was full of life. She pretended that she knew her mind, and showed a confidence rare in a girl who had all her education in a village.

Her aunt and her family lived in Shomolu in the outskirts of Lagos. There was a primary school nearby, and it was in the school that her uncle by marriage got her a teaching job. Soha did not like teaching, but there was no other job, and so, like so many teachers, the job was just a stepping stone.

In the morning before she went to school, Soha saw that her aunt's children, five in all, were well prepared for school. She would see that they had their baths, wore their uniforms, and looked neat and tidy. Then she prepared their breakfast, and before seven each morning, the children were ready to go to school.

Everybody in the 'yard' thought how dutiful Soha was. Her aunt's husband who was a quiet man praised Soha, and told his wife that she was a good girl. Her aunt was proud of her. Since she came to stay with them, her aunt had had time for relaxation, she did less housework, and paid more attention to her trade, which was selling bread.

For some time, everything went well with them. But Mama Eze did not like the way Soha refused to go on holiday when the school closed at the end of the first term. She was surprised when Soha told her that she did not want to go home to see her mother, despite the fact that her mother had been ill, and was recovering.

'Why don't you want to go home, my sister's daughter?'

'Who will look after the children if I go home?' she asked. Mama Eze did not like the tone of Soha's voice. 'Who had been looking after the children before you came, my sister's daughter? Your mother wants you to come home. You know how fond she is of you. I don't want her to think that I prevented you from coming home.'

'She won't think so. I shall go during the Christmas holiday. This is a short holiday, only three weeks. And the roads. Remember what Lagos-Onitsha road is like.' But she did not go home during the Christmas holiday either.

It was that argument that sort of did the trick. Mama Eze remembered the accident she witnessed not long ago. She was returning from the market, a huge load on her head, when, just in a flash it happened. It was a huge tipper-lorry and a Volkswagon car. She saw blood, and bodies, and the wreck of the Volkswagon. She covered her face with her hands. When she opened them, she looked the other way, and what did she see, a human tongue on the ground.

When she returned home, she told her husband. She swore that from thenceforth she would travel home by train.

She did not suggest going home by train to her niece. Soha had long rejected that idea. She did not see the sanity of it all. Why should a man in Lagos, wishing to go to Port Harcourt decide to go up to Kaduna in the North first, then down south to Port Harcourt, and to take three days and three nights doing the journey he would do in a few hours if he were travelling by road.

One Saturday, during the holiday a brand new car stopped in front of the big 'yard'. The children in the 'yard' including Mama Eze's children trooped out to have a closer look. A young man stepped out of the car and asked one of the children whether Soha lived there. 'Yes, sister Soha lives here. Let me go and call her for you,' Eze said, and ran into the house.

Soha was powdering her face when Eze pushed open the door and announced, 'Sister Soha, a man is asking for you. He came in a car, a brand new car. I have not seen that car before. Come and see him. He wants you.' Eze held her hand and began dragging her to the sitting room. 'No Eze, ask him to sit down in the sitting room and wait for me,' Soha said quietly to Eze. Eze dropped her hand and ran outside again. 'She is coming. She says I should ask you to sit down in the sitting room and wait for her,' he said to the man. The man followed him to the sitting room.

The children stood admiring the car. 'It is a Volkswagon,' one said. 'How can that be a Volkswagon? It is a Peugeot,' another said. 'Can't you people see? It is a Record,' yet another child said. They were coming close now. Some were touching the body of the car and leaving their dirty finger-prints on it when Eze came out again and drove them out. 'Let me see who says he is strong, dare come near this car.' He planted himself in front of the car, looking bigger than he really was.

'Does the car belong to Eze's father?' a child asked.

'No. It belongs to sister Soha's friend,' one of Eze's brothers replied without hesitation.

'I thought it belonged to your father,' the same child said again.

'Keep quiet. Can't my father buy a car?' Eze shouted standing menacingly in front of the child.

Soha was still in front of the mirror admiring herself. She

was not in a hurry at all. Her mother had told her that she should never show a man that she was anxious about him. She should rather keep him waiting as long as she wished. She was wearing one of the dresses she sewed for herself when she was at home. She suddenly thought of changing it. But she changed her mind, and instead came out. She was looking very shy as she took the outstretched hand of the man who had come to visit her.

'Are you ready?'

'For . . .'

'We are going to Kingsway Stores.'

'Kingsway Stores?'

'Of course. But we discussed it last night, and you asked me to come at nine-thirty,' the man said looking at his watch.

'I am sorry. But I can't go again.'

'You can't go?'

'No.'

'Why?'

'Can't I change my mind?'

'Of course you can,' the man said quietly, a little surprised.

'I am going then.'

'Already?'

'Yes.'

'Don't you work on Saturdays?'

'No.'

'Go well then,' Soha said.

'When am I seeing you again?'

'I don't know. I have no car.'

'Let's go to the cinema tonight.'

'No, my mother will kill me.'

'Your aunt.'

'Yes. She is my mother. You said you will buy something for me today.'

'Let's go to the Kingsway Stores then. I don't know how to buy things for women.'

'Don't you buy things for your wife?'

'I told you, I have no wife.' Soha laughed long and loud. The man watched her.

'Who are you deceiving? Please go to your wife and don't bother me. Lagos men, I know Lagos men.'

'How many of them do you know?' She did not answer. She rather rolled her eyes and shifted in the chair in which she sat.

'I am going,' he said standing up.

'Don't go now,' she said. They heard the horn of a car.

'That's my car,' he said.

'So?'

'The children are playing with the horn.'

'So?'

'You are exasperating! I like you all the same. Let's go to this shopping, Soha. What is wrong with you? You are so stubborn.'

'No, I won't go. I shall go next Saturday. I did not tell Mama Eze.'

'You said you would.'

'So I said.'

He got up. It did not seem to him that there would be an end to this conversation.

'You are going?'

'I am going.'

'Wait, I'll come with you.' He breathed in and breathed out again.

'Go and change then.'

'Change. Don't you like my dress?'

'I like it, but change into a better dress.'

'I have no other dress. I might as well stay. You are ashamed of me.'

'You have started again.'

'I won't go again. How dare you say that my dress is not respectable. Well, maybe you will buy dresses for me before I go out with you.' He put his hand in his back pocket and brought out his wallet. He pressed a five pound note into her hand. She smiled and they went out.

'Eze, you have been watching his car?' Soha said.

Eze nodded. He dipped into his pocket and gave Eze a shilling. Eze jumped with joy.

'We watched with him,' the other children chorused.

'Yes. They watched with him,' Soha said. He brought out another shilling and gave it to them. Then he drove away.

Mama Eze did not know about the young man who visited Soha. Soha warned the children not to tell their parents. But it was obvious to her that Soha had secrets. It was easy for a mother of five children who had watched so many girls growing up in the 'yard' to know when they were involved in men. At first, she thought of asking Soha, but she thought better of it until one day when Soha told her she was going to the shops and did not come back until late in the evening. She called her in. 'Where did you go, my sister's daughter?'

'I told you I went to the shops.'

'Many people went to the shops from this 'yard', but they returned long before you.'

'Well, we did not go to the same shops,' Soha said. Mama Eze did not like the way Soha talked to her. She smiled. 'Soha,' she called her. That was the first time Mama Eze called her by her name. 'Soha,' she called again. 'This is Lagos. Lagos is different from home. Lagos is big. You must be careful here. You are a mere child. Lagos men are too deep for you. Don't think you are clever. You are not. You can never be cleverer than a Lagos man. I am older than you are, so take my advice.'

Soha said nothing. She did not give a thought to what her aunt told her. But that night, Mama Eze did not sleep well. She told her husband. 'You worry yourself unnecessarily. Didn't she tell you before she went to the shops?'

'She did.'

'Well then?'

'Well then,' Mama Eze echoed mockingly. 'Well then. Go on speaking English, "well then". When something happens to Soha now, you will stay there. This is the time you should do something.'

'Why are you talking like that, Mama Eze? What has the girl done? She is such a nice girl. She doesn't go out. She has been helping you with your housework. You yourself say so.'

Mama Eze said nothing to him any more. One evening when Soha returned from school, she asked her aunt if she would allow her to go to the cinema. Her aunt clapped her hands in excitement, and rushed out of the room. 'Mama Bisi, come out and hear what Soha is saying.'

Mama Bisi who was her neighbour came out. 'What did she say?' she asked clasping her chest. She was afraid.

'Soha, my sister's daughter, wants to go to the cinema.' Mama Bisi hissed. 'Is that all? You are excited because she has told you today. What about the other nights she has been going?'

'Other night? Other nights?'

'Go and sit down *Ojari*. You don't know what you are saying. Soha, your sister's daughter, has been going out with different men for a long time now. You don't even see the dresses she wears, and the shoes. Do they look like the dresses a girl like her would wear?'

Mama Eze said nothing. Soha said nothing. 'When Papa Eze returns, ask him whether you can go to the cinema,' Mama Eze finally said after looking at her niece for a long time.

It wasn't long after this that Soha came to her aunt and told her that she wanted to move to a hostel.

'To a hostel, my sister's daughter. Who will pay for you?'

'I receive a salary.'

'I see. I know you receive a salary. Those of us who have never received salaries in our lives know about salaries. But why now? Why do you want to leave us now? Don't you like my home any more? Is it too small for you? Or too humble? Are you ashamed of entertaining your friends here?'

'I want to start reading again. That's why I want to move to a hostel. It will be more convenient for me there.'

'That is true. When you sing well, the dancer dances well. I understand my sister's daughter. I have to tell my husband

and my sister. Your mother said you should stay with me. It is only reasonable that I tell her that you are leaving me to go to a hostel. What hostel is that by the way?'

'The one at Ajagba Street.'

'I see.'

When Soha went to school, Mama Eze went over to Mama Bisi and told her what Soha said. 'I have told you,' Mama Bisi said. 'Soha is not a better girl. Do you know the kind of girls who live in that hostel at Ajagba Street? Rotten girls who will never marry. No man will bring them into his home and call them wives. You know that my sister who is at Abeokuta whom I went to see last week?'

'Yes, I know her. Iyabo.'

'That's right. Iyabo. One of her friends who stayed in that hostel, nearly took Iyabo there. I stopped it. As soon as I heard it, I went to her mother at Abeokuta and told her. She came down, and both of us went to her. After talking to her, she changed her mind. So that's the place Soha wants to go and live. I no tell you, they say to go Lagos no hard, na return. Soha will be lost if she goes there.'

Mama Eze returned home one evening from the market and was told that Soha had not been home from school. She put down her basket of unsold bread and sat down. 'Didn't she tell you where she went?' she asked Eze. Eze shook his head. 'And where is your father?' Mama Eze asked Eze.

'He has gone out.'

'Where has he gone?'

'I don't know.'

'You don't know. Every question, you don't know. Do you think you are still a child? Let me have some water quickly.' Eze brought the water. Then Eze's father returned.

'They say Soha has not returned home,' Mama Eze said to her husband.

'So Eze told me.'

'And you went out, because Soha is not your sister. If Soha were your sister you would have been hysterical.'

Then Mama Bisi came in, and sat down. She had heard of course.

'Eze, why not tell them the truth?' Mama Bisi said. Eze said nothing.

'Eze, so you know where Soha went?' Mama Eze asked. 'I don't know,' Eze protested vehemently.

'You helped Soha with her box, I saw you,' Mama Bisi accused.

She did not see Eze do this, but what she said was true. Mama Eze and her husband were confused.

'Mama Bisi, please, tell me what you know.'

'Ask your son there. He knows everything. He knows where Soha went.'

'I don't know. You are lying, Mama Bisi.' Mama Eze got up and slapped Eze's face. 'How dare you, how dare you say that Mama Bisi is lying, you, you good-for-nothing child.'

'Ewo, Mama Eze, that will do. If you slap the boy again, you'll have it hot.'

'*Jo* don't quarrel,' Mama Bisi begged. She went over to Papa Eze. 'Please don't. But Eze, you are a bad child. Why are you hiding evil? A child like you behaving in this way.'

Eze knew a lot. He helped Soha pack her things, and it was the gentleman with the car who took Soha away. Soha told him not to breathe a word to anybody. She also told him that she and her husband would come in the night to see his parents.

As they were wondering what to do, Eze slipped out. He was the only one who heard the sound of the car. He had grown to like Soha's friend since the day he watched his car for him. And he had also had many rides in his car as well, for anywhere Soha's friend saw Eze, he stopped to give him a lift, and he had enjoyed this very much.

Soha and the gentleman stepped out of the car, Soha leading the way. Mama Eze, Mama Bisi and Papa Eze stared at them. Soha and her friend stood. They stared at them.

'Can we sit down?' Soha asked as she sat down. The gentleman stood.

'Sit down,' Papa Eze said. He sat down.

None found words. Soha's gentleman was completely lost.

'Is Soha living with you?' Papa Eze asked after a long time.

'Yes,' he said.

'In fact we were married a month ago,' Soha said.

'No,' Mama Eze shouted. 'You, you married to my sister's daughter. Impossible. You are going to be "un-married". Do you hear? Mama Bisi, is that what they do here?'

'This is Lagos. Anything can happen here,' Mama Bisi said. Then she turned to the gentleman and spoke in Yoruba to him. It was only Papa Eze who did not understand.

'It is true, Papa Eze. They are married. What is this country turning into? Soha, you, you who left home only yesterday to come to Lagos, you are married, married to a Lagos man, without telling anybody. It is a slight and nothing else. What do I know? I didn't go to school. If I had gone to school, you wouldn't have treated me in this way.'

'So you pregnated her,' Mama Bisi said to Soha's husband in Yoruba. He did not immediately reply. Soha's heart missed a beat. 'So it is showing already,' she said to herself. Mama Bisi smiled bitterly. 'You children. You think you can deceive us. I have seven children.'

'What is your name?' Mama Bisi asked Soha's husband in Yoruba.

'Ibikunle,' he replied.

'Ibikunle, we don't marry like this in the place where we come from . . .' Mama Eze did not finish.

'Even in the place where he comes from *kpa kpa*,' Mama Bisi interrupted. 'It is Lagos. When they come to Lagos they forget their home background. Imagine coming here to say they are married. Where in the world do they do this sort of thing?'

'You hear, Mr Ibikunle, we don't marry like that in my home,' Mama Eze said. 'Home people will not regard you as married. This is unheard of. And you tell me this is what the white people do. So when white people wish to marry, they don't seek the consent of their parents, they don't even inform them. My sister's daughter,' she turned to Soha, 'you have not done well. You have rewarded me with evil. Why did you not take me into confidence? Am I not married? Is marriage a sin? Will I prevent you from marrying? Isn't it the prayer of every woman?'

'It is enough Mama Eze,' Mama Bisi said. 'And besides . . .'

'You women talk too much. Mr Ibikunle has acted like a gentleman. What if he had run away after pregnating Soha. What would you do?'

'Hear what my husband is saying. I don't blame you. What am I saying? Aren't you a man? Aren't all men the same? Mr Ibikunle, take your wife to your house, and get ready to go home to see your father and mother-in-law. I'll help you with the preparations.'

Husband and wife went home. Mama Eze went home and told Soha's parents what had happened. A whole year passed. Mr Ibikunle did not have the courage, or was it the money to travel to Soha's home to present himself to Soha's parents as their son-in-law.

Tokyo Pastoral

This is clearly one of those districts where it always seems to be Sunday afternoon. Somebody in a house by the corner shop is effortlessly practising Chopin on the piano. A dusty cat rolls in the ruts of the unpaved streetlet, yawning in the sunshine. Somebody's aged granny trots off to the supermarket for a litre or two of honourable saki. Her iron-grey hair is scraped into so tight a knot in the nape no single hair could ever stray untidily out, and her decent, drab kimono is enveloped in the whitest of enormous aprons, trimmed with a sober frill of cotton lace, the kind of apron one associates with Victorian nursemaids.

She is bent to a full hoop because of all the babies she has carried on her back and she bows formally before she shows a socially acceptable quantity of her gold-rimmed teeth in a dignified smile. Frail, omnipotent granny who wields a rod of iron behind the paper walls.

This is a district peculiarly rich in grannies, cats and small children. We are a 60 yen train ride from the Marunouchi district, the great business section; and a 60 yen train ride in the other direction from Shinjuku, where there is the world's largest congregation of strip-shows, clip-joints and Turkish baths. We are pretty bourgeois enclave of perpetual Sunday wedged between two mega-highways.

The sounds are: the brisk swish of broom on tatami matting, the raucous cawing of hooded crows in a nearby willow grove; clickety-clackety rattle of chattering house-wives, a sound like briskly plied knitting needles, for Japanese is a language full of Ts and Ks; and, in the mornings, the crowing of a cock. The nights have a rustic tranquillity. We owe our tranquillity entirely to faulty town planning; these streets are far too narrow to admit cars. The smells are: cooking; sewage; fresh washing.

It is difficult to find a boring part of Tokyo but, by God, I have done it. It is a very respectable neighbourhood and has the prim charm and the inescapable accompanying ennui of respectability.

I can touch the walls of the houses on either side by reaching out my arms and the wall of the house at the back by stretching out my hand, but the fragile structures some-how contrive to be detached, even if there is only a clearance of inches between them, as though they were stating emphat-ically that privacy, even if it does not actually exist, is, at least, a potential. Most homes draw drab, grey skirts of breeze-block walls around themselves with the touch-me-not decorum of old maids, but even the tiniest of gardens boasts an exceedingly green tree or two and the windowsills bristle with potted plants.

Our neighbourhood is too respectable to be picturesque but, nevertheless, has considerable cosy charm, a higgledy-piggledy huddle of brown-grey shingled roofs and shining spring foliage. In the mornings, gaudy quilts, brilliantly patterned mattresses and cages of singing birds are hung out to air on the balconies. If the Japanese aesthetic ideal is a subfusc, harmonious austerity, the cultural norm is a homey, cheerful clutter. One must cultivate cosiness; cosiness makes overcrowding tolerable. Symmetrical lines of very clean washing blow in the wind. You could eat your dinner off the children. It is an area of white-collar workers; it is a good area.

The absolute domestic calm is disturbed by little more than the occasional bicycle or a boy on a motorbike delivering a trayful of lacquer noodle bowls from the café on the corner for somebody's lunch or supper. In the morning, the men go off to work in business uniform (dark suits, white nylon shirts); in the afternoon, schoolchildren loll about eating ice-cream. High school girls wear navy-blue pleated skirts and sailor tops, very Edith Nesbit, and high school boys wear high-collared black jackets and peaked caps, inexpressibly Maxim Gorki.

At night, a very respectable drunk or two staggers, giggling, down the hill. A pragmatic race, the Japanese appear to have decided long ago that the only reason for drinking alcohol is to become intoxicated and therefore drink only when they wish to be drunk. They all are completely unabashed about it.

Although this is such a quiet district, the streets around the station contain everything a reasonable man might require. There is a blue movie theatre; a cinema that specialises in Italian and Japanese Westerns of hideous violence; a cinema that specialises in domestic consumption Japanese weepies; and yet another one currently showing *My Fair Lady*. There is a tintinnabulation of chinking *pachinko* (pinball) parlours, several bakeries which sell improbably luxurious European pâtisserie, a gymnasium and an aphrodisiac shop or two.

If it lacks the excitement of most of the towns that, added up, amount to a massive and ill-plumbed concept called Greater Tokyo, that is because it is primarily a residential area, although one may easily find the cluster of hotels which offer hospitality by the hour. They are sited sedately up a side street by the station, off a turning by a festering rubbish tip outside a Chinese restaurant, and no neighbourhood, however respectable, is complete without them – for, in Japan, even the brothels are altogether respectable.

They are always scrupulously clean and cosy and the more expensive ones are very beautiful, with their windbells, stone lanterns and little rock gardens with streams, pools and water lilies. So elegantly homelike are they indeed, that the occasional erotic accessory – a red light bulb in the bedside light, a machine that emits five minutes of enthusiastic moans, grunts and pants at the insertion of a 100 yen coin – seems like a bad joke in a foreign language. Repression operates in every sphere but the sexual, even if privacy may only be purchased at extortionate rates.

There are few pleasant walks around here; the tree-shaded avenue beside the river offers delight only to coprophiles. But it is a joy to go out shopping. Since this is Japan, warped tomatoes and knobbly apples cost half the price of perfect fruit. It is the strawberry season; the man in the open fruit shop packs martial rows of berries the size of thumbs, each berry red as a guardsman, into a polythene box and wraps each box before he sells it in paper printed with the legend, 'Strawberry for health and beauty.'

Non-indigenous foods often taste as if they had been assembled from a blueprint by a man who had never seen the real thing. For example, cheese, butter and milk have such a degree of hygienic lack of tang they are wholly alienated from the natural cow. They taste absolutely, though not unpleasantly, synthetic and somehow indefinably obscene. Powdered cream (trade-name 'Creap') is less obtrusive in one's coffee. Most people, in fact, tend to use evaporated milk.

Tokyo ought not to be a happy city – no pavements; noise; few public places to sit down; occasional malodorous belches from sewage vents even in the best areas; and yesterday I saw a rat in the supermarket. It dashed out from under the seaweed counter and went to earth in the butchery. '*Asoka*,' said the assistant, which means: 'Well, well, I never did,' in so far as the phrase could be said to mean anything. But, final triumph of ingenuity, Megapolis One somehow contrives to be an exceedingly pleasant place in which to live. It is as though Fellini had decided to remake *Alphaville*.

Up the road, there is a poodle-clipping parlour; a Pepsi-Cola bottling plant heavily patrolled by the fuzz; a noodle shop which boasts a colour TV; a mattress shop which also sells wicker neck-pillows of antique design; innumerable bookshops, each with a shelf or two of European books, souvenirs of those who have passed this way before – a tattered paperback of *The Rosy Crucifixion*, a treatise on budgerigar keeping, Marx and Engels on England; a dispenser from which one may purchase condoms attractively packed in purple and gold paper, trademarked 'Young Jelly'; and a swimming pool.

I am the first coloured family in this street. I moved in on the Emperor's birthday, so the children were all home from school. They were playing 'catch' around the back of the house and a little boy came to hide in the embrasure of the window. He glanced round and caught sight of me. He did not register shock but he vanished immediately. Then there was a silence and, shortly afterwards, a soft thunder of tiny footsteps. They groped round the windows, invisible, peering, and a rustle rose up, like the dry murmur of dead leaves in the wind, the rustle of innumerable small voices murmuring the word: '*Gaijin, gaijin, gaijin*' (foreigner), in pure, repressed surprise. We spy strangers. *Asoka*.

MARTA TRABA

from

Mothers and Shadows

TRANSLATED BY JO LABANYI

The two women walk one behind the other because of the narrow pavement and the odd person sitting out on the doorstep with legs protruding, in time-honoured indifference to the passersby. She would rather have gone down another street, Florida for example, but Elena presumably wanted to avoid the risk of bumping into someone she knew. She looked down the first side-street towards the port, and with a twinge of nostalgia recognised the distant outlines of the ships at anchor. It was as if she'd flashed back to the childhood days when ships and ports dizzied her with an attraction nothing else could equal, rescuing her from the urban greyness of Buenos Aires. They went on walking in silence till they came out into the square.

She stopped short, dazzled by the whiteness of that vast, bleak, open space, with its ludicrous obelisk sticking up in the middle. 'It must be the light reflecting on the paving stones,' she thought, confronted by a stream of images in which she crossed the square again and again, first as a child and then as a girl. She began to make her way falteringly across the horrid square, squinting at the blinding light. When finally she opened her eyes wide, she saw the sun was still high overhead, in an unblemished sky without a hint of cloud. She felt irritated by that conjunction of blue and white, evoking the national colours and flag. Argentine nationalism was, it seemed, doomed to belong to the category of the kitsch. Give her the tropics any day, with their stormy skies perpetually rent by the play of warring elements. She noted that a handful of people, no more than that, were dotted around the middle of the square. But something felt wrong. She looked and looked again, trying to work out what was out of place in that provincial square whose every detail she knew so well. Her eyes went from the Cabildo to the Cathedral, and back again. The Casa Rosada, as unspeakably hideous as ever, was blocking the view of the river. When would they pull that pink monstrosity down? Everything was as it had always been, drab, bare and ugly. And then it hit her; apart from the groups of women arriving for the demonstration, there was nobody in the square. No sightseers were standing around, no school children or men going about their daily business were hurrying across it, no old people were sunning themselves on the park benches. There were no street vendors anywhere to be seen. 'I'm going mad like the other women,' she thought, and looked round the square again, surveying it inch by inch. The gathering in the middle of the square was growing; women on their own or arm-in-arm were streaming out of the side-streets. 'I can't believe it,' she said to herself again. 'Why is there no one here?' She turned round and saw four women coming towards her, knotting their scarves under their chins. On the corner behind them, a little girl was tying her scarf round her neck. She looked up at the windows overlooking the square. No one was looking out. With a puzzled frown, she took her white scarf out of her bag and put it on. Elena was watching the demonstration grow from the pavement at the edge of the square. But her mind was completely taken up with the fact that, at half past four in the afternoon, there was not a single person there except for the women taking part in the demonstration. Elena took Victoria's photograph out of her handbag and started to study it; it looked somewhat the worse for wear, though she did her best to flatten it out and straighten the corners. She felt embarrassed to ask if she could have a look at it. From what she could make out, it seemed that Victoria was standing on a beach though wearing a polo-neck sweater and trousers. Did she have her hands in her pockets? But Elena lowered the photo and started to walk towards the centre of the square. In the fraction of a second that she was left stranded not knowing quite what to do, a woman dashed past with a bundle of duplicated lists and handed her one. It went on for twenty-three pages; she felt an urge to count the names and started to run her forefinger down the columns to work out how many names were on each page. She'd got to the forty-fifth line when someone stopped at her elbow and said: 'You needn't bother to count them, sister, there are about a thousand names down here, but the actual number who've disappeared is much higher than that. We've only just started compiling the lists. The job is complicated by the fact that a lot of people are unwilling to give the full names and ages, or the parents' names and phone numbers.' She shrugged her shoulders and walked on. She felt annoyed with the woman for calling her 'sister' and poking her nose into what was none of her business, but she took another glance at the list. Only now did she notice the ages; they mostly ranged from fifteen to twenty-five; she went on going through it page by page. A woman of sixty-eight, another of seventy-five. She shuddered. A four-month-old baby, a two-year-old girl, another of five, a brother and sister of three and four. The list in her hand began to quiver. How can a four-month-old baby disappear? The entry read: Anselmo Furco, four months, disappeared on . . . Parents: Juan Gustavo Furco, 23, Alicia, 20, also missing. It was followed by the name, address and telephone number of the grandparents. A violent lurch in the pit of her stomach made her grope for the nearest wall to lean against. Someone came up to her and said: 'Come on now, you mustn't give up.' They steered her back to the square. She felt better in the open air and looked around her. So these were the Madwomen of the Plaza de Mayo . . . The number of women was incredible and so was the silence; apart from the rapid footsteps and muffled greetings, there was not a sound. Not

269

a single prison van, not a single policeman, not a single army jeep was in sight. The Casa Rosada looked like a stage set, with thick curtains drawn across its windows. There were no grenadier guards on sentry duty at the gates either. It was the realisation that the grenadier guards were not there that gave her a sudden, terrifying insight into the enemy's machinations: *every Thursday, for the two or three hours during which the demonstration took place, the Plaza de Mayo was wiped off the map.* They couldn't fire on the women or lock them all up. It would have undermined the concerted effort they'd made to project a carefree image of 'the Argentina I love'. Their ploy was simply to ignore them; to ignore the existence of the square and of the madwomen stamping their feet. Had they arrived at that degree of sophistication? And why not, if the same sophistication operated at the level of tortures and abductions? A developed nation does things properly.

She was beginning to give way to despair; more questions flooded into her head. What about the people who regularly passed through the square at that time of day? What about the bank clerks? What about the crowds permanently gathered on the corner by the Cabildo? Where the devil were they? What about the priests and parishioners who every afternoon without fail went to pray in the Cathedral? Did they sneak out of the back door or stay waiting inside in the dark? What about the people who at that precise moment had to get an important document signed at the solicitor's offices bordering the square? How had they managed to get such a motley collection of people, who couldn't possibly have come to a joint agreement, to melt into thin air? What had provoked this reaction of blind terror in each and every one of them? Or were they unanimously shunning this vast array of desperate women because it brought them face to face with a grief that words could not convey? And the same cowards who would not risk setting an immaculately shod foot in the square would loudly proclaim, contented citizens all, that they were avid football fans, that they ate meat every day, that they holidayed at Mar del Plata whenever the fancy took them, that they wouldn't dream of missing a Sunday on the beach despite all those dreadful rumours – put around by the enemies of the fatherland – of bodies floating in the River Plate. Or did they sleep uneasily at night?

Meanwhile more and more women kept on arriving; by now the square was so packed they were spilling out into the roadway. She lost sight of Elena and knew there was no point trying to look for her in such a crowd, but she plunged into it all the same, edging her way forward as best she could.

THE EIGHTIES

I N TONI MORRISON'S *Tar Baby*, Jadine represents sophistication and urbanity, while her lover Son – 'the anxiety-ridden man in a Hilton bathtub' – stands for the rural past of black America. It is a reversal of the classic gender division whereby black women are kitchen-rooted custodians of folk memory; a rewriting of the paradigm that matches woman's nature to man's culture.

Jadine's zestful homecoming to New York reads like a proclamation of ownership. The city belongs to women at last. However it treats them, it can't disown them, for they are its life blood too.

Jadine's arrival in New York is preceded a few pages earlier by Son's. He waits for her at the Hilton, lost in the city, nostalgic for another New York he hazily remembers – physically rather like the one Ann Petry depicted in *The Street* some thirty-five years before. This present city is alien to him, the once-reliable gender boundaries around black men and women now slipping, the children less like children, more street-wise than he ever was. Jadine, not Son, has 'city-sense', and he is the one whose mind is on her making babies. As his name suggests, Son is one of those men who sees women as mothers. Regardless of how they see themselves.

Neither of the two other New York fictions extracted here could be said to celebrate the city, but in *On the Stroll*

(1981) and *The Colorist* (1989), novels which bracket the decade, Alix Kates Shulman and Susan Daitch have an authorial gaze which encompasses the city, perceiving it as a totality (as Morrison does in Jadine's concise train of New York images). In both, the urban labyrinth is entered at its deepest and most dangerous subterranean points. Daitch treats the city as a maze of signs; the city means living with the Minotaur, confronting it rather than remaining at a fearful distance. Women are no longer Ariadne holding the thread for Theseus, they venture into the maze themselves; naively, as young Robin Boots does in this, Shulman's opening chapter; with alert intelligence, like Daitch's Julie; or with a violent, wilful and self-jeopardizing rage, like Elfriede Jelinek's Erika Kohut in Vienna.

The sexual dangers of the city are not only faced more directly in women's fiction by the eighties, as elements in characters' experience; but sex is also a reality into which characters like Erika Kohut insert themselves as onlookers/ voyeurs, displacing the male gaze and refusing the position assigned to women in the sexual domain, as merely the 'looked-at' commodity. These sexual terms assume a mythic dimension, so open does the conflict for the space of the city become.

In other fictions the space of the city assumes mythic conflictual proportions in relation to the destructive forces of history. Both Christa Wolf and Giuliana Morandini evoke images of the ancient world. For Wolf, Athens inspires imaginative speculation on the nature of cities in the modern world, their vulnerability to ecological havoc and the nuclear threat – something which was seen in the eighties as perilously close. Cassandra the seer has a foreknowledge of Troy's destruction that is paralleled in Wolf's feminist belief of a specifically female prescience about late twentieth-century dangers to the planet. The city here becomes a visionary space.

Morandini's Berlin is a city whose structures of repression are both historical and suggestively individual. The labyrinth parallels the female unconscious in images of boundaries and frontiers pushed against, in images of an archaeology whose traces are not entirely erased by new building work or weeds run riot. Roots remain, the repressed asserts itself in what is neglected or overlooked – as in Walter Benjamin's vision of the city; and indeed Morandini's angel is the angel of history, her book's epigraph Benjamin's words, which refer to Paul Klee's painting 'Angelus Novus': 'His face is turned towards the past. Where we perceive a chain of events, he sees one single catastrophe which keeps piling wreckage upon wreckage and hurls it in front of his feet. The angel would like to stay, awaken the dead, and make whole what has been smashed. But a storm is blowing from Paradise; it has got caught in his wings with such violence that the angel can no longer close them. This storm irresistibly propels him into the future to which his back is turned, while the pile of debris before him grows skyward. This storm is what we call progress.'

Both Morandini and Dea Trier Mørch lament the wound that does not heal, which the city of Berlin represents. History moved very fast at the decade's end to change what Berlin had come to stand for. It ceased to be a symbol of the unresolved post-war split in the world and became overnight the world's symbol of hope – precisely because that overnight breach in the Wall was so unexpected.

In the political vocabulary of the eighties, Life replaced Freedom as a key word, its emphasis on preserving what was threatened, a retreat from the urgencies of radical change which had characterised the politics of contestation in the seventies. In Italy the defeat of these politics was consolidated at the decade's start by a wave of state repression that divided the loyalties of a generation, and erased great tracts of collective memory. As elsewhere, the city assumed a glossy new consumerist face. Ida Faré's story consists of letters between a separated couple in Naples and Milan. Night, that zone of the unconscious, is when the city's phoney new prosperity recedes and time can breathe again. The city lived as remembering or forgetting.

The decentredness of holiday and place (Sydney is a city that seems altogether to lack European urban density) spreads across Barbara Brooks's here/there narration, which leans back and forth to catch hold of both intense subjectivity and the world out there that presses upon it. How remote are the wintry cities of the north thus viewed from their summer Antipodes, but how close too are their dangers. The world both shrinks and is vast; experience is irreducible.

TONI MORRISON

from

Tar Baby

Jadine sat in the taxi barely able to see over her luggage piled in the seat in front of her. Unlike the anxiety-ridden man in a Hilton bathtub, she wanted to giggle. New York made her feel like giggling, she was so happy to be back in the arms of that barfly with the busted teeth and armpit breath. New York oiled her joints and she moved as though they were oiled. Her legs were longer here, her neck really connected her body to her head. After two months of stingless bees, butterflies and avocado trees, the smart thin trees on Fifty-third Street refreshed her. They were to scale, human-sized, and the buildings did not threaten her like the hills of the island had, for these were full of people whose joints were oiled just like hers. This is home, she thought with an orphan's delight; not Paris, not Baltimore, not Philadelphia. This is home. The city had gone on to something more interesting to it than the black people who had fascinated it a decade ago, but if ever there was a black woman's town, New York was it. No, no, not over there making land-use decisions, or deciding what was or was not information. But there, there, there and there. Snapping whips behind the tellers' windows, kicking ass at Con Edison offices, barking orders in the record companies, hospitals, public schools. They refused loans at Household Finance, withheld unemployment cheques and drivers' licences, issued parking tickets and summonses. Gave enemas, blood transfusions and please lady don't make me mad. They jacked up meetings in boardrooms, turned out luncheons, energized parties, redefined fashion, tipped scales, removed lids, cracked covers and turned an entire telephone company into such a diamondhead of hostility the company paid you for not talking to their operators. The manifesto was simple: 'Talk shit. Take none'. Jadine remembered and loved it all. This would be her city too, her place, the place she spent a whole summer once in love with Oom. Riding the subways looking for his name, first as a talisman, then as a friend and finally as a lover in the tunnels of New York City. And now she would take it; take it and give it to Son. They would make it theirs. She would show it, reveal it to him, live it with him. They would fall out of Max's Kansas City at 4 a.m.; they would promenade Third Avenue from the Fifties to SoHo; they would fight landlords and drink coffee in the Village, eat bean pie on 135th Street, paella on Eight-first Street; they would laugh in the sex boutiques, eat yogurt on the steps of the Forty-second Street library; listen to RVR and BLS, buy mugs in Azuma's, chocolate chip cookies in Grand Central Station, drink margaritas at Suggs, and shop Spanish and West Indian at the Park Avenue Market. She would look up Dawn and Betty and Aisha and show him off: her fine frame, her stag, her man.

Jadine was so ruttish by the time she got to the Hilton, she could barely stand still for the doorman to take her bags, and when she was checked in, and had gotten his room number from information, she did not call him – she took the elevator to his floor and banged on the door. When he opened it, she jumped on him with her legs around his waist crashing him into the purple carpet.

ALIX KATES SHULMAN

from
On the Stroll

The small circle of Midtown New York surrounding the Port
Authority Bus Terminal for a radius of half a dozen blocks
goes by many names. Tour guides call it the Crossroads of
the World. The hookers who work it know it as the stroll.
Pimps call it the fast track. Three-card monte players speak
of Forty-Deuce. Maps show the neighborhood as Clinton.
But to the stagestruck and starstruck it is still Broadway, to
tourists it is Times Square, to the old people and derelicts
who live off discards from the teeming Ninth Avenue food
stalls of Paddy's Market it is more aptly Hell's Kitchen, and
to the New York City Police, Vice Squad, and Mayor's
Special Task Force on Crime it is simply the Midtown
Enforcement Area.

What you see of this amazing neighborhood depends on
the season, the hour, and your game. Are you a tourist after
entertainment? A thrill-seeker? Are you an adolescent hunting freedom, a healer searching out the damned, an aged
survivor seeking shelter and food for one more day? Whoever
you are, you will probably see what interests you and turn
away from the rest.

Here, for instance, on a weekend night, scores of theater-
goers tip their waiters at ten to eight, tuck their credit cards
into their wallets, and rush unseeing past the whores and
hustlers lounging in the doorways of the stroll. By nine, as
these innocents are applauding first-act chorus lines, second-

279

shift diners are sipping espresso in the darkened interiors of Restaurant Row, preparing for the embarrassment of checking anonymously into a midtown hotel for half a night of illicit love with someone else's spouse. Though tied to the neighborhood by passion, these desperate adulterers conduct their affairs foolishly unaware that just down the street the Live Sex Acts are pulling in the marks, the dirty book parlors of 42d Street are doing a brisk business, and one block over behind the bus station the elderly homeless and alley cats slowly circle the vegetable stalls for handouts from grocers' assistants at closing time. Taxi drivers pull up before the emptying theaters and lock their doors until they find their fares, then speed quickly away. Their passengers dissect the show, oblivious of the gang of hoodlums across the street and of the men on the corner passing around a bottle of Midnight Special in a brown paper bag. For one moment, a speeding police car racing the wrong way up a one-way street, siren screaming, may startle pedestrians, cabbies, and passengers alike into wondering what terrible act they may be forced to witness. But soon the sound disappears and they resume their talk, unaware of the shopping-bag ladies and men who, expecting rain, either make their way to St Agatha's to jockey for a bench on which to sleep or cautiously take a seat in the inadequate waiting room of the Port Authority Bus Terminal.

It was here in the bus station on a Friday night that the shopping-bag lady known to locals as Owl (and to the rookie cop patrolling the station as, simply, 'one of your cleaner types') had her second mystical vision in twenty years. The first had come to her at the gate fifteen minutes before takeoff in Chicago's O'Hare Airport. The vision, she always believed, had been set in motion by a radio playing a Spanish-from-Spain version of 'Siboney'. She never discovered the source of the music (there were no radios at the gate, no airport Muzak in those days, and they were ready to board); yet the gypsy falsetto of that slightly Oriental song had brought into perfect harmony all the inhabitants of that exotic land: the mystic saints, the imperial guards, Ferdinand and Isabella, the Moors, the beautiful black-haired Iberian peasant women washing clothes on the riverbanks, the silent young men in the bars of Madrid, flamenco dancers, and, having herself once spent several months in Spain with an international refugee unit after the war, her own humble self, together with everyone she had ever known. Like mystics down through the ages, she had seen then in a flash the perfect unity of life. She would have traded her own to have the vision continue, but once it had ended, she was both sorry and glad: she had a plane to catch and a daughter to meet.

This time, however, she was only sorry. She had nowhere to go and no daughter. This second vision, coming some twenty years later, was far more timely, for her luck had long since run out. When during her worst times she'd touched bottom, her vision had drawn her back up. Maybe now that she was sinking again she was getting another lift from Beyond.

Here is what Owl saw that early evening as she sat among her shopping bags, resting her legs, in the main waiting room of the bus station.

Around her in the circle of molded plastic seats carefully designed to preclude a snooze sat the usual array of weary travelers, hustlers, and unknowns. In the center of the circle was a row of four pay-TV sets, their swivel bases bolted to chairs. In the tan plastic chairs facing the screens, eyes glazed, mouths slightly open, sat several large, unmoving teenaged males. Occupying the surrounding seats were families with crying babies, weary commuters, madmen, and innocents. Some of these no doubt waited for buses; others, like Owl herself, simply passed the time. All were shielded from too deep a scrutiny of each other (and themselves) by a thin curtain of complacency that concealed reality.

Now suddenly, without warning, Owl saw the curtain part. For perhaps ten seconds truth was revealed to her. She saw that all the people in the waiting room, together with everyone else alive in the universe at that particular instant, were in unique possession of a rare, infinitely precious and mysterious gift casually (so casually!) called life.

The light of this knowledge filled Owl with wonder and love. Before her enchanted eyes the ordinary differences among the living she had learned to recognize over more than half a century – differences in station and temperament, in awareness and privilege, in age, health, achievement, sorrow, fate – all disappeared and became as nothing beside that one miraculous singularity they shared. They had lived! They lived! Her feet hurt her, her welfare check was late, she had no one and no place, but she was infinitely blessed. If she had believed in God she might have called her vision religious, but she had always stood firmly with the atheists in matters of theology. Sister Theresa of the Shelter and Father Glendon who fought the pimps were the best citizens of the neighborhood, and the Church that backed them up was one of the few remaining places that embraced the homeless; but nothing they did could establish the truth of their beliefs. Truth was established otherwise. Truth was . . . not what you believed, not what you proclaimed, but what you saw.

And what Owl saw as she rested in the waiting room at seven o'clock on that otherwise uneventful Friday evening was that out of the infinity of inert souls past or possible, these and no others had been chosen to live, to partake of blessed life, and among them was herself. She peered hard at reality, searching for someone she knew. Her mother? Her lost boy? But like the cats and birds Owl fed each day, all absolutely equal in her eyes, everyone there in the room, bathed in life, looked equally precious. In that clear, vivid light, cats, birds, humans were all connected. One with her. Any waif she made a home for was her child. She saw that life was a gift, a precious gift, and she swelled with happiness.

Then, as suddenly as it had parted, the curtain closed, the veil descended, and she was once again seated among her shopping bags in the uncomfortable waiting room of the bus station, alone, disconnected, without hope, awaiting the inevitable tap on the shoulder from the man in blue.

Prince sipped at his coffee and looked nervously at his watch. Time to go; the bus from Boston was due in any minute. He knew he shouldn't be drinking coffee at all, but he hated this bus station crawling with cops, it made him nervous, and he had to do something for his nerves.

That wasn't all. The place was full of scum, smelly old hags, detectives, he-shes, perverts . . . It was as bad as the sin hole of Hong Kong where he'd once spent three days' shore leave. But this was the best place to cop a girl. He'd heard there were lots of them coming through lately from Boston, and though waiting for a bus was a longshot, he had to get himself a girl, at least check it out.

Even when he spotted a likely prospect climbing off a bus and looking around, it was tricky to catch her. She might know someone already, she might be meeting her mother, she might slip away before he had a go at her, or run for a cop. Still, he had to take his chances. He was getting desperate. Today he had a pocketful of bills from last week's three-card monte game: enough to catch a bitch if his luck held out. Wasn't every chick a potential ho? And wasn't he a good-looking dude who could sweet-talk his way like the best of them? He knew how to be gentle, modest, loving; he could also be forceful, fierce, intense. He understood what women needed and what he needed. He money, they love: that winning combination.

Another time he might have blown his bucks in a day, as he and his buddies had done in each new port. He liked good clothes and good times. But in the navy with that paycheck growing all the time and nothing to spend it on at sea, life had been different. Now years had passed since he'd seen a paycheck. He was overdue on his hotel bill, his wheels were in the shop, for a long time he'd sent nothing to his mother. Since Sissy had blown he needed money fast. So instead of partying, he'd got his copping clothes cleaned and pressed, had a manicure, a shave, and a shine, and prepared the rest for flashing. A fat roll of singles topped by three twenties in a gold money clip and a handful of silver dollars to give weight even to loose change were the oil that made his charm hum. Now all he needed was the chick to go for it. And soon. His stomach, which had kept him from signing up for another hitch at sea, was acting up all the time now. He used to be able to ignore it, but it seemed to be getting worse. Since he'd been alone it seemed to him he was always thinking about it – his stomach or his bad tooth or the way his hair had started coming out in his comb. Like his mother, he had fine, black, silky Filipino hair; but his fair-haired father, he'd been told, had been half bald at thirty. His luck, he'd probably gotten all his father's bad traits. Or else he was just getting old.

Old? He never thought he'd get old, not the Prince. But he had to do his pushups every morning now, he had to watch what he ate or his nerves would give out. If he'd jumped ship in Tahiti he might never have aged. It was the street that turned you old, keeping you hustling morning to night. In Tahiti, the women were for you, not against you. When you were hungry you picked a breadfruit off a tree or caught yourself a fish. But here, he felt thirty-five, not twenty-five. Who starts losing his hair at twenty-five? The place was turning into a sewer. The fags were everywhere and spreading. Crackos pulled knives in the street, winos sprawled in the gutters and pissed on the pavement as if they owned the place, perverts came right up to you, bag ladies, panhandlers, freaks roamed the streets like they were home. Even the cops had started dressing up like old women. They all belonged in Bellevue, but no one cared. If he hadn't wrecked his wheels he would have gone to Florida long ago, found out where Sissy was, and . . . But now, unless he pawned his ring, he couldn't spare the cash for bus fare. And who could he trust? No one.

For a brief moment he imagined the future in the sparkle of the diamond in his ring. A lady with that sparkle in her eyes and brains enough to understand his needs. But he was a practical man and knew how far he could get on dreams. For now, it was enough to hope the girl wasn't so dumb that she'd let herself get picked up by the Runaway Squad. He'd try to warn her. Some of the young ones from out of state were so dumb they wound up costing you more than they gave you, even if they had no mileage on them at all. Or so scared that they got themselves addicted. And some were so smart you couldn't hold on to them long enough to make them pay off. Better, then, to cop and blow – take what you could get and cut her loose. On the other hand, if he caught one with a little money it might be better to try to disappear until she spent it, and then move on in. He'd have to figure it out carefully and play it close. It wasn't an easy game. He bent down to the shiny reflecting surface of the cigarette machine to comb his hair. Not bad, he thought. He smoothed down his mustache and flashed a smile. Handsome son-of-a-bitch. Then, bouncing on the balls of his feet like his running partner, Sweet Rudy, he sauntered down to the gate to meet the Boston bus.

Robin Ward looked out over the steamy streets of Hell's Kitchen from the Greyhound window and wondered how she'd ever find Boots. The city was so vast. Buildings, stretching as far as she could see in all directions, pressed down on her like waves on the sea; as soon as you rolled past one block of them another was upon you and another after that. Where was the shore? She felt a momentary panic, the first since she'd boarded the bus in Maine eight hours before. She'd left home so abruptly she hadn't had time to be afraid. As soon as Billy had told her that their father was sitting in the principal's office with a cop and two men, she'd run home for her backpack and money and got ready to split. On the ferry from the island she'd been terrified her father would stop her; but once the bus had taken her out of the Portland station without him on board, every turn of the wheels had brought relief, and on the highway she'd been actually happy.

'But how do you know they called him in about you?' Billy

had asked her, for Luke Ward had three kids in the school to answer for. She didn't know, but she had a good idea. She had watched Boots turn on her smile and relieve two men of several hundred dollars, then disappear. Besides, even if her father had been called in about one of the boys, chances were she'd still wind up getting the blame. With her father on the warpath, why wait and see? She was sorry to have put in most of the semester and not get credit, but if those two men were who she thought they were, running was safer than sticking around to see what developed. From the day she first ran away at eight to look for her mom to the time she'd been picked up with Boots on the highway for hitchhiking, running had always been easier. The only difference was this: the other times she'd run because she wanted to; this time she ran because she had to. This time she couldn't go back. Her past was finished, like sand pictures erased by the tide.

She pressed her nose against the window as if to squash the past. She needed a new name. She had pale skin that pinked in the sun and peeled, never tanning even in summer. Too delicate a skin for the Maine coast, said her mother. And indeed, she had a fragile look that kept her apart and made even the bullies ashamed when they teased her more than they teased others. She had a bump in her nose she hated, but otherwise she looked like an old poster for spring, with a small, delicate child's mouth that seemed smaller still when she was ready to cry and that opened into a bright disarming smile in those rare moments when she felt delight. Though her smile would now never grace the pages of any yearbook, it would carry her far, she hoped – farther than the school she had left abruptly in the middle of eleventh grade. With her mouth, her guileless hazel eyes, pale lashes, and the sweet voice that ranged from childlike innocence to haughty disdain, she hoped to pull off masterpieces of deceit. Already she had perfected a wide range of poses in her brief life and she considered herself an actress of no little talent. In a mere sixteen years she had accomplished painful and difficult deceptions. And still her full range had not begun to be tested and she had a whole life ahead of her. Once she got it together to have a portfolio made hinting at the variety of moods and ages she could do (for she could still pass for thirteen if she tried and with difficulty do twenty) she'd be on her way. Peter had suggested that New York was a little premature, that she ought to try herself out in Portland or Boston first, but she disagreed. The fare to New York was not all that much more than to Boston, and Boots, who had sent her a postcard with a New York number, had gone directly there and made it.

One thing was clear: she was not going back. In her yellow T-shirt that told the world she was 'Born to Dance' (and incidentally that this kid would not be hampered by any bra!), carrying all she needed in her backpack, ready to move with benefit of smile, palm, and thumb for traveling, her terrible past was over. Now they would never find her, and she would never go back. Never.

The finality of that *never* was so fierce that it brought tears to her eyes, mourning tears. It was a *never* of dead gulls dashed on the rocks.

The driver pulled to a stop inside a tunnel and announced: 'Port Authority.'

Though the phrase was a mystery to Robin, she knew enough to heed it. You didn't argue with authority. She slung her pack onto her shoulder, hooked the tie of her bedroll over her wrist, and lined up in the aisle behind the other passengers.

SUSAN DAITCH NEW YORK

from
The Colorist

Laurel and I got out of the subway, stopping to look at the things for sale, spread on blankets near the subway stop: toaster parts, car radios, answering machines without cords, used tweed suits with the pockets cut out, a pyramid made of tiny white plastic shoes – they even had bows and high heels – a secondhand copy of *The Thief's Journal*, old Patti Smith records; *Life, Time, Look* from 1969, 1970, 1971; Richard Nixon on one cover, Patty Hearst on another. I saw black shorts over black sweatpants. Just for an instant, as those legs leaped over a blanket spread with hundreds of fragments of glass and rhinestone jewelry, I thought of the kid from the roof, then the legs disappeared around the corner and he was gone.

We walked past empty lots filled with the winter shelters of the homeless. Constructions made of cardboard cartons (small Coke, Colgate-Palmolive, and Marlboro estates) cut into igloos; broken umbrellas stuck out like warnings or fake television antennas, sometimes real gardens sprinkled with empty amyl nitrate bottles, bags of cans and bottles that would later be counted by fives and cashed in. Soon a bulldozer will flatten all the paper and tin houses. A foundation was already being dug on the lot next door. Someone wrote on the plywood surrounding the pit: *Rich people will soon live here*. We looked through one of the holes, although it was dark out and construction had stopped for the day. If

288

I lose my job, can't pay my rent, and Eamonn disappears, what would I put into shopping bags? What would I put in a locker in Grand Central Station? Even the logic of sweaters, heavy coats, and blankets reflects the wrong kind of thinking. I couldn't carry that much.

EXTRACT TWO

The top of a building near Fantômes was lit gold. As I walked east, the red and green lights on the top of the Empire State Building appeared from behind the gold panels, seeming to move forward in the brilliantly colored fog. Like finding a badly lit cathedral with no visitors except a few faithful old women, you become a believer, even if it's just cold and raining on Thirty-sixth Street. In the misty and nearly empty streets at night, you could believe in androids, mutants, Dracula, Frankenstein, the nineteenth century, and the future. What wasn't making sense was the bit in the middle.

EXTRACT THREE

Blue-and-white roadblocks crossed Fifth Avenue. A bomb had gone off in an embassy. The avenue metamorphosed from a street whose history had always been one of order, expensive clothing, and jewelry to one of police sirens, ambulances, fire engines and camera crews. In the chaos, what had been valuable, even priceless, suffered the displacement of archaeological relics uncovered at a location where their original context has been rendered impossible to guess. A neo-Baroque façade shattered, angel body parts were found five blocks away, flying slivers of glass blinded tourists on their way to the Metropolitan, credit-card machines smashed on curbstones, bloody cuffs on mannequins. People who passed by or ran to the site from unaffected blocks had two choices: to watch or to walk away. They stood behind the cordons, some of them, and struggled to see or to be recorded by a television camera or by Eamonn. Later, at home, witnesses could repeat, *Today I saw . . .*

EXTRACT FOUR

One Sunday afternoon Martin and I were out of money and so we visited a cash machine in a small enclosed cubicle near Broadway. The glassed-in room was ankle deep in garbage: green and brown beer bottles, aluminum and plastic containers, remaining shreds of takeout food, newspapers, drugstore ads, things passed out in the street, and huddled in the corner was a solitary old sock. I wondered how or why it was there. Someone had painted the President's name near one of the cash machines, and the name was followed by the statement that he was a liar and a drug dealer. A very thin man who looked like one of the Senegalese umbrella salesmen, but who spoke without an accent, opened the door for people so they wouldn't have to use their bank cards to get in. He shook a plastic cup, the rim bitten into small flaps. A line of customers snaked around the room. A few minutes after we arrived, a chinless blond man in his twenties stood in the door, holding it open, depriving the beggar of his job. The blond man said to another black man, *It will take awhile but it will come*, then he took out a piece of paper and listed the four different kinds of prayer. The black man said he had been a POW in Vietnam, he had been there three and a half years. The proselytizer looked condescendingly surprised and told him it would take a long time to learn how to pray. People continued to get into line as he spoke. He was preventing the man with the cup from opening the door for people, and the beggar looked crushed and defeated. Martin asked the chinless man if he was going to get into line or just stand there all day, and he finally got out of the doorway. A Jamaican wearing several sweaters instructed the man with the cup what to do if the police attacked him. *If it was just a bit of a poke, forget it, but if he look crazy, sitting in his car, and like he is going to run you through with his night stick, then you run.* The beggar barely responded. A large woman with curly hair signed a check with relish, saying, *My last check from the lab,* while another talked about shopping. When we got to the machine Martin scratched an *N* after *withdraw* with a dried-out pen he had found in his pocket.

Outside, it was bright and cold. Early Christmas decorations, bits of Christmas music floated past us as we walked east. I turned around and saw the blond, chinless man a few yards behind us. I told Martin he might be following us, looking for converts. Martin looked back and said that when he saw repulsive characters like that he was afraid one of them might be a relative. I stared. Martin looked nothing like the man who seemed to be following us. We stopped and let him pass. He went into the subway, and I asked Martin what the physical resemblance might be. I didn't see it. Martin was not blond and had rather a large jaw.

EXTRACT FIVE ━━━━━━━━━━━━━

EPISODE IV

Electra Doesn't Know What to Do

Useful on Earth in some places, *the package said. It had been zippered into her suit. Inside were hundreds and thousands of dollar bills. She had read about dollars, pounds, and francs but didn't really understand what money might be; its purpose or value was unclear to her. A picture of a house, a picture of a man, a signature, numbers; there were so many bits of paper but no directions as to what they were for. She left the package on a rock in Central Park.*

She had to live on the street and grew ragged constructing her possessions from what other people threw away. Because inconspicuousness seemed desirable, Electra drifted to the southeast side of the city. A rush-hour crowd pushed her through a subway turnstile, and the hurtling motion of the trains reminded her of a primitive sort of spaceship. When the streets ceased to be numbered and stations were named

she got off. The cars were packed full of people, and she felt
claustrophobic, as if she must certainly be rushing toward a
fatal accident. She asked people who stared at her questions
about food and sleeping. Her system was to avoid people
who looked away, but she had no guarantee that those who
politely looked away would have been less anxious to explain
the city to her. Even if other citizens treated her with
equanimity, as if she were just like them, she suspected her
slip-ups, she sensed they were being polite and not mention-
ing her mistakes in social behavior. Memories of a life of
privilege, extravagant intelligence, and faintly odd looks
served to give her away to herself, if not to others. Only
vague childhood memories resisted erasure. A laboratory
whose walls were uneven rock, a little girl splashing soapy
water from test tube to Petri dish, domes of suds in the sink,
a recording of Glenn Gould playing partitas (although she
didn't clearly remember Dr Atlas, who had been in love with
him). Parts of the city looked familiar, but the familiarity
was grounded in mistaken identity. A stone-faced tunnel near
Police Plaza bore little resemblance to rooms hollowed under
the Sierra Madres. Nothing to jar presence into the absence
created by Orion's chance ray, touched off in agony.

Her glassy, translucent skin grew dirty and cracked, but
the dirt concealed the fact that Electra had the look of
someone who was born out of a tank. Layers of clothing
found in the street; jackets, trousers, skirts made her a
shapeless Père Ubu; hair matted and greased stood up
straight. It was summer and she could wash under the
hydrant at night after the children ran away, but she began
to like it, thinking smell was like a thumbprint or the sound
of voices, each peculiarly idiosyncratic. She had no concept
of what it might be to appear offensive.

Language had a chancier aspect on the streets. It wasn't
entirely neologisms she hadn't learned due to her isolation in
space but a combination of idioms and slang, and the local
habit of aposiopesis and metonymy, which confused her.

Spoken sentences never seemed finished, although she suspected the thoughts behind the broken phrases were.

Few of Electra's companions on the street were charitable or magnanimous about distributing whatever they might have scavenged. The concept of surplus didn't exist. One's body was a savings banks, a storage vault, interest cumulative depending on market value. Rubber bands were among the utilitarian rarities coveted by the homeless. Incapacity didn't eliminate the imperative of committing crimes, and there was a gluey nastiness to their fights. In the aftermath of a fight between two men, as one lay unconscious and bleeding, the other rifled through his stiff, ligneous rags. They did this to the dead as well. Useful objects – bags, safety pins, rope, rubber bands – were of value and had degrees of preciousness. Down along the line, everything changed hands, was transformed. A belt became a handle, bicycle tires became trouser suspenders, a paper bag became a hat. Possessions, bits of objects, were piled into supermarket carts. One had to maintain a balance between accumulation and mobility. They filtered through the garbage like the houilleurs of nineteenth-century Paris.

Electra lived in an old cardboard refrigerator box. The manufacturer's emblem printed on the box reminded her of her spaceship. Electra knew other citizens on other avenues looked and behaved differently, so she stayed on her street, rarely going more than a few blocks in any direction. Sometimes she moved with clots of homeless men and women, settling for a few days on the corner of a busy intersection. The men might wash cars. When her box disappeared she slept by herself on a traffic island in the middle of Allen Street, learning to ignore the sound of cars and trucks. Electra's clothing was made up of what she found, but she was selective as well as eclectic. Another homeless woman had painted her face so she looked like a Bengali princess: her eyes were ringed with black and green from makeup found in a discarded stolen suitcase, her scalp was painted red at the part, beaded silver key chains were linked together and pinned across her forehead.

One night an unhappy woman alone in her car mistook Electra for her lost sister. Electra was leaning against a chain-link fence; she had turned away from a basketball game, which made no sense to her. The car slowed down, came to a stop, window rolled down. 'Hey, you,' the unhappy woman shouted. 'Come here, please.' Electra ignored her, not out of antisocial instincts, but because salutations and requests confused her. The woman walked toward her. She was wearing a large black coat and a black fur hat. One or two of the men playing basketball yelled at her, and she said to Electra, 'I wish you hadn't made me get out of my car.' She held Electra's face in her hands for a few minutes without saying anything, then asked, 'Can't you see that we're mirror images of each other, but I can't take you home with me?' Electra's unsuitability and their similarity seemed connected, at least for the woman in black. It seemed logical that her missing sister would have turned into the kind of person she couldn't have in her home. When she had imagined the lost woman she imagined someone utterly rebellious and unconventional. That had seemed as predictable as their physical likeness would be. One of the basketball players who'd stopped to yell noticed a glimmer of recognition on Electra's glassy face. Electra initially mistook the woman in black for one of her own duplicants, but she was too well adjusted, too comfortable, and had too much self-confidence. Unless a duplicant had somehow escaped Orion and had managed to precede Electra to Earth . . . Such a woman, although a paper tiger, would not have figured the planet out by now with the apparent ease of the woman in black. She extended her left hand to Electra. The dupes were right-handed. She reached into a coat pocket and handed Electra a wallet, her husband's. She'd abandoned him at a party, in a car, anywhere, and she'd taken his wallet by mistake, or because she had no money of her own. Electra hugged her, because if this woman was a duplicant, she would fold up like an accordion. She

didn't. She remained standing. She handed Electra the keys
to her car, said she was very sorry, and walked away toward
Stanton Street, which she crossed before disappearing into
the night. Electra was utterly confused. She screamed, but
the street was deserted, no NYPD, not even a Fantômas
appeared on the Boulevard du Crime. In the middle of the
night, nobody would have looked twice. She stuffed the
wallet into her pocket, it was warm and curved, like a hot
clamshell. She guessed the keys went to the car. Electra had
seen bodies rifled through on the street before, although it
wasn't clear to her what the objects were for. She drove
down Allen Street to Pike, parked the car, put the microchip
for the lost mimetic device in the glove compartment, and fell
asleep in the back seat.

CHRISTA WOLF

from

Cassandra

TRANSLATED BY JANE VAN HEURCK

I did not know what to make of the city we first caught sight
of late the next morning, because I did not have anything to
look for there. Details of pictures filtered through, excerpts
from the unrolling film of everyday life: cats prowling
through the roof landscape of the crumbling house across the
way. The fruit seller on the ground floor of the house next
door whose displays I looked down on from above. Light-
blue venetian blinds which I viewed from our tiny balcony –
now tightly shut, now half open, then with wide-open lids.
Finally, on the third day, a black-haired, pale-skinned woman
shaking out a brilliant-coloured blanket. The mute, hard-
bitten caretaker who rode up and down with us in the
elevator cubicle. In the shop on the left, the two sisters'
patient, moonlike faces, always the same, shining out of the
darkness behind the displays of nuts, bakery goods, bread.
The huge exit road that divided our quarter of narrow streets
and little shops from the national park where the Seville
oranges glow in the dark foliage. One night, bypassing
fragrant shrubbery, we reached the foot of the Acropolis,
which I had seen all day floating in the deep-blue sky like an
airship, smaller than expected, high above the houses where
people have their home, surprising the way it abutted a row
of streets. Why not say what people expect to hear? Beautiful!
Who would want to be the monster left indifferent by the
Acropolis of Athens?

296

Surrounded by tourists I walked across Syntagma Square and for a long time watched the two marionette soldiers in front of the government buildings strutting toward and then away from each other in ridiculous slow motion, wearing grotesque berets, rifles stiffly at their shoulders, clapping their wooden shoes. I felt a compulsion to list the cities I had already walked through this way. The words and melody of the opera still stuck in my brain: 'He who values not this grace / Merits nought bu-u-t disgra-a-ce.' Then finally I was able to transfer them to Mario, Dionysus's little son, who did not understand a word of German but demanded to hear the verse every time I saw him: 'Sing the German song again!'

The spirit of place held back. Sightseeing made me feel numb, I might have known it would. On Friday, on the trip to Piraeus – what were we doing in that packed, speeding bus? – I saw nothing but stills from Spanish colour films which I galvanically impressed upon my mind. These two young men in their olive-green and cobalt-blue outfits in the dark-green garden, behind the white wall broken by a lattice gate. The gate gave a clear view of the delicate little garden table where the two men sat down and – if the films and stills were right – carried on cynical, meaningless conversations while they drank their garishly coloured drinks out of odd-looking glasses. It was the same with the vast coastal arc where the harbour lay. Although I deliberately conjured up its name more than once – Piraeus Piraeus – I heard no echo. What multitudes of ships and nations have approached this bay over the centuries. Now we are sitting here under the awnings in front of plates of the choicest fish. Expensive, expensive. N. is right, we do not yet know the value of money here. The stiffly shy Englishman behind us, who cannot defend himself against the gypsy women with their huge, artfully embroidered coverlets.

How old was Cassandra when she died? Thirty-five? Did she come to feel she had survived a lot, too much? New to me was the question of whether indifference might not be the price of survival. Indifference, the least welcome thing of all, the alien element where we are most sure to founder, even more surely than in impotence and guilt. No, I told the young gypsy woman, I do not want my hand read. That's true, isn't it? said C. — one doesn't want to know the bad things that are to come. But that noon under the bright Greek sun on the foreign coast, there was nothing I feared more than the verdict that *nothing* was to come. How hyper-alert I was the first time I crossed over the border, how greedy to hear the first words in a foreign language; how captivated by my first foreign city. Captivated by love, small wonder (I heard the ironical echo say inside me, the echo which I am used to by now). You cannot expect love from this city. The miracle of self-renewal — that can no longer be expected from any city. To be destined to walk on lifeless stone, between mutely erect stone walls, under mute and meaningless skies — that oracle seemed to me inescapable and unacceptable. After all, you can come to Greece too late.

Not only victors but victims, too, climbed up to the Acropolis. Man and beast, they took turns on the altars of the temples which stand superimposed or side by side. The lamb took over from the young man, the chicken from the captive woman. It was the same with the gods: the earlier god, the earlier goddess were always sacrificed to the later. At the very bottom, at the foot of the Athena Nike temple, is the shrine of the earth goddess Gaea, filled with rubble, covered, built over, invisible to us later-born. In exchange we have the reproduction of the renowned Phidias's colossal statue of Pallas Athena, ivory and gold and armed with helmet, shield, spear, and breastplate; with the miniature statuette of Nike, goddess of victory, in her left hand; powerful and cold. Motherless. An evil thought emerging with shield and spear from the head of her father, Zeus. Never, I think, has she been more godforsaken and more remote from her nature than in Phidias's costly idol. The desolate and mostly clueless, ant-like obtrusiveness of the tourists, who, like me, are resting on chunks of marble, glistening sharp-cornered stone, smooth to the touch. Objects ought to be speaking to me, but that fact does not loosen their tongues. The colour snapshots N. is taking will not stir my imagination when I get them home, any more than they do here. Of course, we were at the Acropolis, too (I will say). And so? A vast heap of rubble. Splendid views of a city destroyed by building. And a blinding glare of reflected light, I had never experienced the like of it; yes, really, even though it was only April.

And then we went to see the *korai* ('maidens') from the Erechtheum, which have been placed in the museum on the Acropolis to safeguard them from total destruction. They stand in a semicircle, gaze down at us spectators, and weep. The stone is weeping, and I do not mean metaphorically. Tears have streamed over the faces of the stone maidens and eaten them away. Something more powerful than grief has engraved itself in these beautiful cheeks: acid rain, polluted air. Once these faces may have been blank and expressionless; our century has forced its own expression on them, that of mourning, which finds an echo in me as if I had been kicked from inside. All the emotions that mourning brings with it begin to stir – anger, fear, dread, guilt, shame. I have arrived. I understand this mountain of stone and bones. I understand the overcrowded, hurrying, homicidal, money-chasing city that pumps out smoke and exhaust fumes, trying to catch up in a few years with what some of its Western sisters took more than a century to achieve. I understand: you, the need of the present-day city, were not compatible with the need of the stone maidens with their serene, proud bearing, who supported, for more than two thousand years, the canopy over the grave of the snake-king Cecrops, founder of Athens. The *korai*, the maidens, once the fertility goddess Persephone and her daughter, later reduced to supporting beams, now infertile, placed out of bounds. Shall I try to prevent them from appearing to my inner eye over and over in the guise of symbols, not only while I am in Greece, but afterward, too? Shall I try to name the 'meaning' they stand for, which is really a non-meaning? The barbarism of the modern age. The question that disturbs me: Was there, is there, an alternative to this barbarism?

Am I already broaching the theme?

The self-devouring city. A force has come over me. Have the sightless eyes of the *korai* opened up to me? Now I roved through the city with these ancient burning eyes, and I saw today's people, my contemporaries, as descendants. That young woman leaning in the door of the shop where she sells Turkish honey and Oriental spices: a descendant of those Achaean women who had waited away ten years of their lives by the time the heroes returned from Troy, and who – small consolation – may have modeled for the *korai*. Those men in the unique fish hall saturated with the pungent odours of the sea who toss the twitching fish onto the wooden tables with a swift sharp motion and kill it with little hatchets, cut it up with sharp knives: great-great-grandsons of the early Greek seafarers. Furrowed brown peasant faces in the meat halls, where the drawn and quartered sacrificial beasts hang in rows on meathooks, drained of blood. Who were their ancestors? Thessalians? Macedonians from the supply lines of Alexander the Great? Smoking his pipe behind a steaming roast of aromatic chestnuts: a Turk. The slender dark girls who run out from a dim school gate into the blindingly bright street are familiar to me from pictures of the Minoan Cretans, and the street vendor with his mobile glass showcase of gold jewelry is, in his gestures and the cut of his face, an Italian descended from Venetian merchants and soldiers who colonized the Mediterranean region. They all pressed toward me from the crowd hurrying away from Omonia Square, while we were struggling to reach it. I was not able to catch their eyes. Apart from a few bold, naked looks from men, which a woman learns to fend off here simply by straightening up, no attempt was made to look at each other. City-monads, I thought; who fired them off, what nucleus do they orbit, what holds them together? 'The hunt for the drachma,' says N. 'Self-interest. Each needs the other in order to sell him something, cheat him, tap him, suck him dry. And

Omonia Square is their hunting ground,' he said, 'both above and below ground.' And the heart of the preserve, where it was still as the heart of a whirlwind, was the taverna where we were sitting. Cool grotto light, as in all the Greek tavernas, emanating from the blue-green painted walls, a light which immediately seems to cool off and calm down those who enter in a fever. Their deep-dyed impatience is met by the waiters' brisk service; broad slices of fresh white bread already stand waiting; tomatoes, green cucumbers, olives, oil and vinegar are already on the table; there is a quarter liter of retsina for everyone; the aroma spreads; behind the counter, fish and meat are frying in open pans; and the innkeeper, small, massive, solemn, greets his guests with a dignified nod. The feast is ready. Show yourself worthy of it. The dignity of eating, in countries where you cannot take it for granted that everyone will be able to eat his fill every day; where avarice has not yet been able completely to suppress the gesture of hospitality, which, even if it has a price, meets with a ready welcome. We foreigners are all the more dependent on it because here we have no command of words, are incapable of deciphering even the signs outside the shops, must rely on pictures, smells.

But isn't the word the very thing that has taken over control of our inner life? The fact that I lack words here: doesn't this mean that I am losing myself? How quickly does lack of speech turn into lack of identity? A curious notion: If a Cassandra were to appear now – and from the look of things she must exist among the women here – I would not recognize her, because I would not understand her speech. Supposing that she fell into a frenzy like the first Cassandra – I would not be able to judge whether one of these smartly dressed, white-gloved police officers was entitled, up to a point, to seize her upper arm soothingly but also admonishingly, rebukingly; to draw her out of the circle of curious onlookers, who, because of the excitement they show here, seem more involved than people in cities to the north; and to deliver her to the ambulance which is already waiting in one of the side streets. A superstitious awe prevents me from thinking with her head and saying what she would say, but in my own language. For her message would apply to more than one city. That is why she was able to prophesy the doom that would befall the House of Atreus after the death of Agamemnon, after her own death – the doom that would come through Orestes, the son who was believed dead.

GIULIANA MORANDINI BERLIN

from

Berlin Angel

TRANSLATED BY LIZ HERON

She went through as she had done so many times before. Her hands felt a little cold. As usual she kept them in her pockets, in her right hand gripping her passport so as to feel safer; she could get lost, just by magic, under an evil spell.

The young soldier stared at her, while making a show of being busy with something else, as if her features were hard to pin down.

Erika took out her passport and her crossing permit and raised them fan-like in front of her cold face. The soldier took them and went back inside the hut; she saw him light a cigarette on the other side of the windowpane.

It always felt strange crossing a border. As a child she had found it quite exciting to be thrust from country to country. She would walk across the frontier, alert to the vague difference between the two territories. She could even turn back at the last minute, or go on. This either-or appealed to her.

Nowadays, crossing the frontier meant finding out for herself how the city was experiencing the split; a wound that did not heal.

You could see the broken windowpanes of the empty houses, the state of the deserted rooms in their sunlit reflections. Walled-up windows demanded freedom through the cracks widened in the brickwork by the roots of shrubs.

A baby-faced guard stood stock-still beside the sentry box;

he was holding a sub-machine gun bigger than he was, as people say; the weapon fell right across his chest and looked as if it hampered his movements. He had short arms. His superiors had disregarded the fact that killing takes promptness and skill; all they needed was a hand ready to fire, to stop people from making the crossing.

The boy soldier looked at her, knowing that with her permit she would proceed undisturbed into no-man's-land. Inside the hut the other soldier checked and stamped the documents.

A frontage disclosed that once there had been a hotel here; the building remained but was no longer recognizable. It was a dead place, even though inside it there lived offices, rooms where data was received and sent out, and where files and dossiers piled up. Soldiers went in and out, so young that none of them would pause to think what this building had once been.

Next to a window walled up after a fashion with bricks and heaped stones, some greenery tried to push its way through between two stones. The stones had been used as a machine-gun rest, and the house opposite, which was on the other side, was pockmarked from the volleys; a face that would never heal, the result of smallpox caught when young, when the tissue is delicate and the infection leaves bigger pits. The contaminated skin made the holes stand out as if in relief, and tentative sunlight settled on the ravaged surface, corroding the outlines as it scanned the more visible areas; pausing on the edges, where the virus had carved out its mark. The undamaged parts of the face – the eyelids, which by a fluke of nature emerge untouched by the disease – had sagged in the rain. The gaze beneath them was only clearer, like that of the sick before they die, when they wish to see a little longer before taking leave of life; they stare at the road they will follow, maybe someone there behind those lids pointing it out. Who is to know!

Sometimes people don't manage to keep track of the signs in no-man's-land and have the temerity to stop; just as Erika does now. She would like to pluck that flower haphazardly rising up above an empty tin can overflowing with rubbish and army bandages. It is a splendid flower, but it will never be splendid enough, for it won't have a name. It belongs to no classification, it has no place in botany's domain, science disowns it. Can we ever admire and love someone whose origins and birth are unknown to us? We feel a faint unease, and we pull the flower up then throw it away, after pausing to say, 'Here, look, what a strange flower this must be, it would be nice if . . .' It withers in our hand, we cast it down without a thought, anywhere at all. The flower lies there, knowing it is not wanted and is to be banished so that other flowers can be seen, flowers less intriguing but familiar, which we can name and can link to the fragrance of child-hood, to the loved caresses of the mother. The stranger we desire could rob us of memory, transport us back to the darkness of a past without history.

The wings no longer shine on the gilded bronze Victory of the Brandenburg Gate; they have been coated with lead, for fear she might flee on her chariot and abandon the city, leaving it without protection.

EXTRACT TWO

Berlin is a non-stop building site. A pointless race for construction, for who gets there first and who builds higher and better.

Budapesterstrasse is nothing now. Erika hated it at once. Years after the street was built the trees in the nearby Tiergarten still claim more space for their spreading roots. After the war, nothing but dust remained of the eighteenth-century garden the Elector planned; yet the plants took revenge, mingling airborne seeds and pollen and growing in the fashion once desired. Now and then bulldozers unearth roots centuries old, wound together like bodies in an embrace, crushing them.

When Erika passed by at midday the traffic had been halted. Cars were diverted, and people were stopping to watch others at work, as in days gone by. It just happened to be the midday break. The massive power-drill had come to a stop and the crane hung suspended in mid-air like an elephant's trunk. A child had been the first to look. Then, in a matter of minutes, from the highrise hotels, the doorways of airline offices, from plateglass car showrooms, and the nearby Europa Center, young people on the scene had run to see. Their first thought was some serious accident, then something comical; the zoo was nearby and maybe one of its inmates had come out to meet the public without waiting for visitors to be drawn in by the image carved on the pink stone of the entrance. Instead, it was nothing more than ancient roots, dark and twisted as if they were relics of Roman legions. 'It's an old story,' someone interjected, 'that roots look like bodies; nothing out of the ordinary.' The crane made no sound, motionless in the void.

EXTRACT THREE

The little theatre in the bierkeller, with the floodlights uncovering the marks on the walls and speaking of wounds in the mind. The young Turkish couple . . . and the music as piercing as the fragrance of Turkish delight. Images assailed her . . . Like the stubborn plants in the Sudbahnhof widening the cracks in the stonework, jostling between the rusted tracks, and the sheets of colour on the murals giving life to walls that still stood.

'It's as if I had lived through it all before, years ago . . .' The colours of the small town square, the narrow lattice-beamed houses, pink and green or grey like clouds. In spring a touch of paint brightened up the colour drained by the play of wind and ice. In the alleyways, around the red-brick churches, the same aromas – from the bierkeller, goulash spices and carp cooking in copper pans. In the square people crowded round the bright-coloured fabrics the ships unloaded at Rostock or that came from the streets of Poland and Bohemia.

Dust had settled on the warm bricks and delicate hues. The factories consumed fuels whose emissions could not be filtered; in the small town of Neuruppin, a new kind of life erased the reflections of the sky and the lakes, the avenues of cherry trees.

The chessboard had been put away too long ago, its figures slithering on some shelf or other. Smears of colour, like the Kreuzberg tower blocks, pale houses and dark balconies, iron baskets laden with secrets . . .

The pall of dust had got the better of the tiles on the uniform houses along the reborn Frankfurterstrasse. Each morning Erika looked at them; they showed her the rhythm of the seasons, heralding the spring or holding the last of the summer warmth. The Dresden and Potsdam ceramics were losing the prestige their kilns had once had. They no longer were in keeping with the times; like the clocks and dried-up fountains that the architect had thought to thread between the houses. The trees on the Frankfurterstrasse were no longer the limes Prince Friedrich Wilhelm had wanted there; they had smooth trunks and dark leaves, and in the clearing beyond the houses were sparse tufts of grass.

Erika was used to waging war with dust. Restoring monuments meant dissolving the greyness of years, the ashes of explosions, the chemical wound. Buildings reclaimed their outlines, their gildings and their clear facades. Elegant buildings, like the palace conceived with the grace of von Erlach furniture, and which Berliners re-baptised 'the chest of drawers'. Altogether decorous like the Französicher Dom and the Schauspieltheater. Majestic in their wisdom like the museums on the island. Domes laid bare, as that of the Deutscher Dom partly was, it was said, with the ribbing burned from the angels' vendetta. Could angels forgive? They did not say so, but they folded their wings once more on the stone cornices, sentinels of the void.

Erika could feel that all of this care had a bitterness at its heart. The monuments could no longer answer for themselves. The angels were the weary straggling birds of a migration. The theatre, Schinkel's masterpiece, had been rebuilt, with painstaking attention to the original plans. Nearby there rose the boxed whiteness of a hotel, a cube of glass, transparent, but taking just a blinding ray of light to make the surface shuttered and compact. Nothing gave out light, neither gold nor glass. The tall antenna transmitting to the ether had stopped the angels' flight.

The trouble Leonard had in shifting the little statue and the blood red dust around it ... The wounds that did not heal, like memories ... Life slid across gaps ... Perhaps the life of objects was the patina that one laid on them, that one fingered fondly from desire for an ancient touch. 'To see a little statue like that one emerge from the hands of an artisan, taking shape in the workshop of a church,' she thought, 'would seem lifeless to me.' Life was a clot of blood-red dust, a faint corrosion. Yes, dust is like shadow, it can animate a love of things.

She walked through the streets with Thomas, feeling the life of the city.

'I know what's on your mind,' he was saying; 'I've felt it myself. You stop in front of the monuments and palaces ... everything else seems like a hum, a background noise.'

'You are all alike,' she protested, 'you always have to convince me of something.'

'I'm not giving any advice whatsoever,' he said. 'Learn to look: it is so hard to see things as they are.'

Simple as that! The discovery amazed her.

'In my studio,' Thomas continued, 'with the desk lamps shining on the plan tilted on the drawing board, I felt suffocated.'

In those years it was different for Erika. In the morning she would step out of the front hallway thinking of reaching her office, thinking of the card indexes, the photographs and the plans rolled up on the shelves. She paid no attention to things as she walked along the pavement or rode in the bus; the details that struck her were painful. The streets were a stream of faces and the squares were shaped by the muddle of traffic. What stories did the Alexanderplatz tell but a fever of troubled projects or rather no projects at all? There were those who had spoken of fever and mentioned the disease whose symptom it was. Now people were invisibly devoured by a new fever. Erika locked herself away in the museum on the island, in the airiness of its wide rooms, in front of its great windows. The altar of Pergamus had been reconstructed, along with relics of ancient temples. Ishtar's gate in Babylon saw movement and colour, Assyria's bricked walls conveying the illusion of merging with the sand that for millennia had defended its secret.

Erika looked at the lions, brilliant in the colours of the great ceramic work. Their manes were undimmed. Thousands of tourists bred strength of will. And the lions showed the visitors the meaning of this solemn procession, recalling that strength gave protection to authority. Once over the threshold that was sacred to the goddess, power was as the lions claimed it to be: indomitable. Babylon, what have you brought from your womb? How many peoples have you infected! And what meaning guided the reconstruction of the gate that led to your bosom? Assyria is remote, the illusion of the desert sands is annulled on the faces of the hurried tourists – the visa for the heart of Berlin expires at midnight – and they have to make the whole tour, the prearranged programme, so as to be able to tell themselves they've done it all. Centuries ago the desert sun disoriented nations, annulled their mother tongue and scattered the world's speech. How much she liked those ceramics; she lost herself before their azure light. She thought of them in the desert: 'This azure blue truly challenged the light of the sun, and the azure blue enamels stayed intact all the while that languages were blended.' The ceramics laid beside them by the archaeologists to furnish continuities were pale; a faint difference in

309

colour, perhaps intentional, out of scientific discretion or so as not to compete with the terrifying goddess.

In the museum's rooms the past was set out with authority, the air did not prick it, the statues placed against the walls were untouched by the stone angels' turmoil on the pediment. History had to appear thus: tamed and coherent as philosophers and architects acknowledged it.

But in whose interest was history to be reasonable? Monuments were embalmed by restoration. Strange objects were set down in the city by construction works. The sorrow in the mind remained, objects were surrounded by a wall which thoughts and tender feelings did not cross.

DEA TRIER MØRCH

from

The Morning Gift

TRANSLATED BY CHRISTINE ENGLISH

In January they took a weekend trip by rail. By that time Signe was seven months' pregnant. The child rotated in its own hidden universe. Signe sat with her hands crossed over her stomach, looking out of the carriage window.

There was a watchtower, a border with fine sand, a forest in the distance and, suddenly, Berlin Ostbahnhof.

Through Checkpoint Charlie they moved from a silent world out into seething West Berlin to look for the hotel. They found their room. It was cramped and drab. With a large bed and a big mirror on a creaking wardrobe door. They opened their rucksacks, unpacked and put their belongings away in the wardrobe. Then down the stairs and out into Berlin.

A dark spirit joined them. With long shadowy strides down the Kurfürstendamm. Past the whipped cream. Past the glossy profusion. Past the soft traffic lines where death comes so softly.

Staring blackly, lurking at the bottom of stair wells. Running along the stippled line past children on pedestrian crossings. Waiting with folded arms on the platform in the Underground. Stealing after them up the tower. Carrying its load of bombs through the raindrops over the noisy neon city.

Accompanying them everywhere, with long, springy strides. With light, soundless steps. With outstretched arms, prepared to capture them.

A sound like a drumbeat grew in volume.

Was it their blood pounding?

Was it the air, bombarding them incessantly with its molecules?

Someone tried to grab them. In the dark between two visions. During the night between Saturday and Sunday. In the tunnel between two stations. Berlin was divided, just as we are. Between East and West. Between tears and laughter. Contempt and fear.

Suddenly everything was reversed. East became West. And West became East.

Only Jacob's soft kisses and body soothed her.

They clung to each other, like branches over dark water.

They longed to return to the great stillness in the East. They went through Checkpoint Charlie, through the Wall into an empty world.

Their luggage was in the left-luggage office. Surrounded by a sighing as of seashells, they walked, along canals and through empty palaces and heard the cackle of ducks beneath the bridge by the Museum of Egyptology. Past barracks where soldiers with red bands round their caps hung out of windows, shouting.

The weather cleared. Now the sun was glittering and smooth like a coin. A yellowish-green afterglow pricked behind their eyelids.

In East Berlin it was Sunday – there were mile-long gaps in the traffic. Workers in heavy overcoats bought cigarettes at a kiosk. Rolls of barbed wire lay on Potsdamer Platz.

Part of them stood in the tank by the Brandenburg Gate. The other half stood on a wooden platform staring out into this still, whispering world.

Where was the graphic formula, the magic symbol that could cure this poisoning, heal this rift, unite the two halves of Europe?

ELFRIEDE JELINEK

from

The Piano Teacher

TRANSLATED BY JOACHIM NEUGROSCHEL

Chasms of streets open up, then close again because Erika can't make up her mind to enter them. She simply stares straight ahead when a man happens to wink at her. He isn't the wolf, and her vagina doesn't flutter open; it clamps shut, hard as steel. Erika jerks her head like a huge pigeon, to send the man packing. Terrified by the landslide he's triggered, he loses all desire to use or protect this woman. Erika sharpens her face arrogantly. Her nose, her mouth – everything becomes an arrow pointing in one direction; it ploughs through the area as if to say: Keep moving. A pack of teenagers makes a derogatory comment about Erika, the lady. They don't realize they are dealing with a professor, and they show no respect. Erika's pleated skirt with its checkered pattern covers her knees, not one millimetre too high or too low. She's also wearing a silk middy, which covers her torso precisely. Her briefcase is clamped under her arm as usual, tightly zipped up closed. Erika has closed everything about her that could be opened.

Let's take the trolley. It runs out into the working-class suburbs. Her monthly pass isn't valid on this line, so she has to buy a ticket. Normally, she doesn't travel here. These are areas you don't enter if you don't have to. Few of her students come from here. No music lasts longer here than the time it takes to play a number on a jukebox.

Small greasy spoons spit their light at the sidewalk. Groups of people argue in the islands of streetlights, for someone has said something wrong. Erika has to look at many unfamiliar things. Here and there, mopeds start up, rattling needle pricks into the air. Then they vanish quickly as if someone were waiting for them somewhere – in a rectory, where they're throwing a party, and where they want to get rid of the moped drivers immediately for disturbing the peace and quiet. Normally, two people sit on a feeble moped to use up the space. Not everyone can afford a moped. Tiny cars are usually packed to capacity out here. Often a great-grandmother sits inside a car, amid her relatives who take her for a pleasure spin to the graveyard.

Erika gets out and continues on foot. She looks neither left nor right. Employees lock and bolt the doors of a supermarket. In front, you can hear the final, gently throbbing engines of housewife chitchat. A soprano overcomes a baritone: the grapes were really mouldy. The worst were at the bottom of the plastic basket. That's why no one bought them today. All this is spread out loudly and rattlingly in front of the others – a garbage heap of complaints and anger. Behind the locked glass doors, a cashier wrestles with her register. She simply can't track down the mistake. A child on a scooter and another child running alongside him, weeping and yammering that he'd like to ride it, the other kid promised. The rider ignores the requests of his less-privileged colleague. You don't see these scooters in other neighbourhoods anymore, Erika muses to herself. Once she got one as a present and she was so happy. Unfortunately, she couldn't ride it because the street kills children.

The head of a four-year-old is thrown back by a mother's slap of hurricane strength. For a moment, the head rotates helplessly, like a roly-poly that has lost its balance and is having a hard time getting back on its feet. Eventually the child's head is vertical again and back in its proper place. But now it emits horrible sounds, whereupon the impatient mother promptly knocks it out of plumb again. Now the child's head is marked by invisible ink and ordained for a

314

much worse fate. The mother has heavy bags to struggle with, and she'd much rather see her little girl vanish down a sewer. You see, in order to mistreat her daughter, she has to keep putting down her bags, which only adds to her drudgery. Yet the extra effort seems worthwhile. The child is learning the language of violence, though not willingly. At school, she likewise picks up very little. She knows a few words, the most necessary ones, even though you can barely understand them among her sobs and tears.

Soon the woman and the noisy child are way behind Erika. After all, they keep stopping! They can never keep up with the swiftness of time. Erika, a caravan, marches on. This is a residential neighbourhood, but not a good one. Fathers, straggling home late, lunge into building entrances, ready to pounce on their families like dreadful hammers. The final car doors slam shut, proud and self-assured, for these tiny autos can get away with anything, they are the darlings of their families. Glittering amiably, they remain behind at the curbside, while their owners hurry to supper. Anyone without a home-sweet-home may wish for one, but he'll never manage to build one, even with the help of a generous mortgage. Anyone with a home around here, of all places, would much rather spend most of his time somewhere else. More and more men cross Erika's path. The women, as if having heard a magic formula, have vanished into the holes that are called 'apartments' here. They do not venture outdoors alone at this time of night, unless accompanied by family members – adults – to have a beer or visit a relative. Their inconspicuous but so necessary activities are pervasive everywhere. Kitchen odours. Sometimes the soft clattering of pots and scratching of forks. The first early-evening sitcoms seep bluishly from one window, then another, then many. Sparkling crystals to adorn the gathering night. The building fronts become flat backdrops, behind which there is probably nothing: all these birds are of one feather. Only the TV sounds are real, they are the actual events. All the people around here experience the same things at the same time, except for some loner, who switches to the educational channel. This individualist is informed about a eucharistic congress, provided with facts and figures. Nowadays, if you want to be different, you have to pay your dues.

You can hear bellowing Turkish vowels. A second voice instantly enters: a guttural Serbo-Croatian counter-tenor. Gangs of men, on tenterhooks, small troops, hurrying here in dribs and drabs, now turning left underneath the roaring elevated train: a peepshow has been set up under one of the viaduct arches. The space is exploited so efficiently, down to every last nook and cranny, no centimetre wasted. The Turks are, no doubt, vaguely familiar with the arch shape from their mosques. Maybe the whole thing recalls a harem. A viaduct arch, hollowed out and full of naked women. Each woman gets a chance, each in turn. A miniature Venusberg. Here comes Tannhäuser, he knocks with his staff. This arch is built of bricks, and so many men have gawked at so many beautiful women here. This little shop of whorers, in which naked women stretch and sprawl, fits precisely into the arch, hand in glove. The women spell one another. They rotate, according to some displeasure principle, through a whole chain of peepshows, so that steady customers can always get to see new flesh at specific intervals. Otherwise the regulars will stop coming. After all, they bring good money here and insert it, coin for coin, into an insatiably gaping slot. Just when things are getting hot, another coin has to go in. One hand inserts, the other senselessly pumps and dumps the virile strength. At home the man eats enough for three people, and here he heedlessly scatters his energy to the winds.

Every ten minutes, the Vienna Municipal Railroad thunders overhead. The train shakes the entire arch, but, unshakable, the girls keep turning. They've got the hang of it. You get used to the din. The coin goes in, the window goes up, and rosy flesh comes out – a miracle of technology. You mustn't touch this flesh; you couldn't, because of the wall. The outside window is covered with black paper. It is decorated with lovely yellow ornaments. A small mirror is inserted in the black paper, so you can look at yourself. Who knows why. Maybe so you can comb your hair afterward.

A small sex shop is attached to the peepshow. There you can buy what you've been turned on to. No women, but, to make up for that lack, tiny nylon panties with many slits, in front and/or in back. At home, you can put them on your wife and then reach in, and your wife doesn't have to take them off. There's a matching tank top with two round holes. The woman sticks her breasts through these holes, and the rest of her torso is covered transparently. The tank top is lined with teensy frills and ruffles. You can choose between dark red and black. Black looks better on a blonde, red goes better with black hair.

You can also find books here, magazines, videocassettes, and 8mm movies in various stages of dustiness. These items don't move at all. The customers don't own VCRs or projectors. The hygienic rubbers with various kinds of ribbed surfaces sell a lot better; so do the inflatable women. First the customers look at the genuine article, then they buy the imitation. Unfortunately, the customer cannot take along the beautiful naked women in order to screw them royally in his protective little room. These women have never experienced anything profound, otherwise they wouldn't flaunt their bodies here. They'd come along nicely rather than just pretend to come. This is no work for a woman. A customer would gladly take any of them, it doesn't matter which, they're all alike. You can barely tell them apart; at most, by the colour of their hair. The men, in contrast, have individual personalities: some men like one thing, some like something else. On the other hand, the horny bitch behind the window, beyond the barrier, has only one urgent desire: that asshole behind the glass window should keep jerking until his cock falls off. In this way, the man and the woman each get something, and the atmosphere is nice and relaxed. Everything has its price. You pay your money and you get your choice.

Erika's pocketbook, which she carries along with her music

case, is stuffed with coins. Few women ever wander this way, but Erika likes getting her own way. That's the way she is. If many people do something, then she likes to do the exact opposite. If some people say go, Erika alone says stop, and she's proud of it. That's the only way she can get them to notice her. Now she wants to come here.

The Turkish and Yugoslav enclaves retreat at the approach of this creature from another world. All at once, they're practically helpless; but if they had their druthers, they'd rape any woman they could. They yell things at Erika that she doesn't understand, luckily. She keeps her head high. No one grabs at Erika, not even a drunk. Besides, an elderly man is watching. Is he the owner, the proprietor? The few Austrians hug the wall. No group bolsters their egos, and in addition, they have to graze past people whom they usually avoid. They make undesired physical contact, while the desired physical contact never comes. Unfortunately, male drives are powerful. These men don't have enough cash for a genuine wine spritzer, it's almost the end of the week. The natives trudge hesitantly along the viaduct wall. One arch before the big show, there's a ski shop, and one arch before that, a bicycle store. These places are asleep now, their interiors are pitch-black. But here, friendly lamplight shines out into the street, luring these bold moths, these creatures of the night. They want something for their money. Each client is rigourously separated from the next. Plywood booths are precisely custom-tailored to their needs. These booths are small and narrow, and their temporary inhabitants are little people. Besides, the smaller each booth, the more booths you can squeeze together. In this way, a relatively high number of men can find considerable relief within a relatively short period.

The clients take along their worries, but leave their precious semen. Cleaning women make sure the seeds don't sprout – even though each customer, if asked, would assure you how fertile he is. Usually, all the booths are occupied. This business is a treasure trove, a gold mine. The foreign workers patiently line up in little groups. They kill time by cracking jokes about women. The small space of the booth is directly proportional to the small space of their living quarters, which are sometimes only quarters of a room. They are used to cramped rooms, and they can even find privacy here between partitions. Only one man to a booth. Here, he is all alone with himself. The beautiful woman appears in the peephole as soon as he inserts his coin. The two one-room apartments with individual service for more demanding gentlemen are almost always empty. Few clients here are in a position to make special requests.

Erika, thoroughly a professor, enters the premises.

A hand hesitantly reaches out for her, but then shoots back. She does not walk into the employee section, she steps into the section for paying guests – the more important section. This woman wants to look at something that she could see far more cheaply in her mirror at home. The men voice their amazement: They have to pinch every penny they secretly spend here hunting women. The hunters peer through the peepholes, and their housekeeping money goes down the drain. Nothing can elude these men when they peer.

All Erika wants to do is watch. Here, in this booth, she becomes nothing. Nothing fits into Erika, but she, she fits exactly into this cell. Erika is a compact tool in human form. Nature seems to have left no apertures in her. Erika feels solid wood in the place where the carpenter made a hole in any genuine female. Erika's wood is spongy, decaying, lonesome wood in the timber forest, and the rot is spreading. Still, Erika struts around like a queen. Inside, she is decaying, but she glares discouragingly at the Turks. The Turks would like to arouse her to life, but they bounce off her haughtiness. Erika, every inch a queen, strides into the Venus grotto. The Turks utter no cordialities, and also no uncordialities. They simply let Erika go in with her briefcase full of scores. She can even pass to the head of the line, and no one protests. She's also wearing gloves. The man at the entrance bravely addresses her as 'Ma'am'. Please come in, he says, welcoming

319

her into his parlour, where the small lamps glow tranquilly over boobs and cunts, chiselling out bushy triangles, for that's the first thing a man looks at, it's the law. A man looks at nothing, he looks at pure lack. After looking at this nothing, he looks at everything else.

Erika is personally assigned a deluxe booth. She doesn't have to wait, she's a lady. The others have to wait longer. She holds her money ready the way her left hand clutches a violin. In the daytime, she sometimes calculates how much peeping she can do for her saved coins. She saves them by eating less at her coffee breaks. Now, a blue spotlight sweeps across flesh. Even the colours are handpicked. Erika lifts up a tissue from the floor; it is encrusted with sperm. She holds it to her nose. She deeply inhales the aroma, the fruits of someone else's hard labour. She breathes and looks, using up a wee bit of her life. There are clubs where you can shoot pictures. Each client selects his model himself, according to his mood and taste. But Erika doesn't want to act, she only wants to look. She simply wants to sit there and look. Look hard. Erika, watching but not touching. Erika feels nothing, and has no chance to caress herself. Her mother sleeps next to her and guards Erika's hands. These hands are supposed to practise, not scoot under the blanket like ants and scurry over to the jam jar. Even when Erika cuts or pricks herself, she feels almost nothing. But when it comes to her eyes, she has reached an acme of sensitivity.

The booth smells of disinfectant. The cleaning women *are* women, but they don't look like women. They heedlessly dump the splashed sperm of these hunters into a filthy garbage can. And now concrete-hard squooshed tissue is lying there again. As far as Erika is concerned, the cleaning women can take a break and relax their harried bones. They have to bend an infinite number of times. Erika simply sits and peers. She doesn't even remove her gloves, so she won't have to touch anything in this smelly cell. Perhaps she keeps her gloves on so no one can see her handcuffs. Curtain up for Erika, she can be seen in the wings, pulling the wires. The whole show is put on purely for her benefit! No deformed woman is ever hired here. Good looks and a good figure are the basic requirements. Each applicant has to undergo a thorough physical investigation: No proprietor buys a pig without poking her. Erika never made it on the concert stage, and so other women make it in her stead. They are evaluated according to the size of their female curves. Erika keeps watching. A single sidelong glance – and a couple of coins have gone the way of all flesh.

A black-haired woman assumes a creative pose so the onlooker can look into her. She rotates on a sort of potter's wheel. But who is spinning it? First she squeezes her thighs together, you see nothing; but mouths fill with the heavy water of anticipation. Then she slowly spreads her legs as she moves past several peepholes. Sometimes, despite all efforts at equal time, one window sees more than the other because the wheel keeps rotating. The peep slits click nervously. Nothing ventured, nothing gained. Venture once more, and maybe you'll gain something more.

The surrounding crowd zealously rubs and massages, and is simultaneously mixed by a gigantic but invisible dough-kneading machine. Ten little pumps are churning away at top capacity. Outside, some customers are secretly pre-milking a bit, so they can spend less. Each man will have a woman to keep him company.

IDA FARÉ NAPLES AND MILAN

from

A Too-Richly-Flavoured
Neapolitan Sweet

TRANSLATED BY LIZ HERON

Naples, April 198..

Sunday, 10 a.m.

Around two, people go and have lunch in a crowd, in the
trattoria below. These are good-humoured meals, full of
noisy banter and jokes and laughter and journalists' gossip.
Neapolitan wit is age old and doesn't translate from the
language expressing it: there are nuances that invariably give
it layers of meaning beyond the words. It looks a long way
back to a history regarded since time immemorial.

I don't need to say anything, they don't ask me anything.
If I were even to begin giving an account of myself, I would
discover that they know or have already worked it out. This
way they're all my friends and men and women are all one in
the sounds of the wisest tongue in the world.

Sometimes in the afternoon I'll go out to do an interview
or some other assignment. But usually I make editorial work
a priority, non-stop right up until nine at night. Long hours,
too long. But not for me, wanting to *be* the things I do. I
want nothing better than a reassuringly tight outside struc-
ture locking me in and setting conditions on what free time I
have. If some days should happen to gape open to the empty
hours, I construct an internal diary for myself that's just as
tightly scheduled.

But this doesn't happen often. The gang of Neapolitans

keeps me busy and organizes nearly all my free time. In the evenings they take me all over the place for dinners and cultural or social outings, to the most amazing houses I've ever seen: blocks of flats right on the sea or farms hidden among vegetable plots that suddenly loom up on the hillsides in among the concrete. Their company is so all-embracing that I have trouble staying at home to make some space for tiredness or the need to be alone.

On Saturday work finishes early when I'm not on a shift, and on Sundays my new friends take me on more outings around this lovely city of Naples that's unknown to me, and to the islands and the ruins nearby.

And it's odd to think that it has become my city.

And it's only now that I've come to think about it.

Milan, April 198..

                                                              at night

So I'll try to tell you kind of how it is.

The city has altered from disorder to order. Nobody can deny that it has become more beautiful. An airy, spacious city, paying its own bills like a fortunate woman.

Milan blooming again. Shops, bars, restaurants, travel agencies, cultural centres, bookshops – that seem to have left behind that moment of silence and uncertainty, the grey zone which in the years just gone by halted our breathing and made it hard, if not entirely suffocating it.

But does a city breathe? During this time I've become adept at listening to the rhythm of things which aren't visible. The transparent threads which become gradually entwined to form a net that then becomes an atmosphere, like days that imperceptibly lengthen, and you find that it's summer and it gets gradually hotter, until it becomes suffocating. Like the uncertain years of the disorder that turned the city upside down and then slid behind us without anyone being able to measure their progress towards oblivion.

There was a certain point when I became aware of an

acceleration of time, merging the before and after into a single instantaneous point, and it was then that I had a sight of what was going on as a brand new image of the game – a single, efficient, unseeing and static image. If you could see your city now: objects, houses, streets, clothes, people's thoughts, have all got fancier. The bakers' shops have been refurbished in light wood and sell special kinds of bread, the old drapers' shops are remodelled and sell lacy silk underwear, the trattorias, done up and done out in plastic, have been turned into pizzerias, the shops are all awash with bright colours.

Public buildings, be they banks or local services, proclaim how much they have to offer. Even the walls of houses are fastidious about the images they convey; sometimes they greet us with smiles, and perfect faces and perfect figures and soft fabrics. Whenever it's a holiday the streets in the centre are full of flowers, lights and carpeted pavements, and at carnival time public monuments get decorated to look like pageant effigies.

People have become tidy too: in our bars everybody's got cleaned up; scruffy, outlandish clothes are now just for real tramps or the Third World poor. Gentle murmuring sounds rise from the clever new salons where waiters have even made a reappearance. Lectures are polite, there's talk of philosophy and civilized societies. Silence reigns in offices at newspaper desks, in universities and publishing houses, where everyone sits in front of ever more numerous computers. And ever more numerous too are the studios where a new breed of workers come up with words, colours and designs for the population of bodies that will inhabit the city.

Now that I'm a professional listener to breathing, I am more and more insomniac. For it is only now at night like this, that, released from the fiction of festivity, can I be aware of thoughts and feelings coming from the hearts of men, straying through rooms, wafting out through windows, roaming the streets, stopping for a moment in the parks, entering those few places still open, in the outskirts or the city centre. And then encountering other invisible networks, and finally creating a different kind of breath.

324

BARBARA BROOKS

Summer in Sydney

The time. When you're not working, the days stretch and float. Swimming in the mornings, reading in the afternoons, going out to restaurants at night. Getting up late and reading the paper. What day is it, and what do I have to do? People come and go, from London, Tennant Creek, Brisbane. Postcards and letters slide under the door.

Summer heat passes over quickly, wilting the garden but leaving some corners of the house untouched. At the beginning of summer it rained a lot.

The unemployed could go on beach crawls, all summer. But couldn't afford the trimmings. We sit around all morning eating croissants and watermelon in gentrified poverty, and go to Bronte at two in the afternoon. By then the sun has gone. There's a storm, hailstones drop out of a green sky. We put ice down each other's backs and shelter under the eaves of the dressing shed. The water is a kind of oily grey with a strip of sunlight along the horizon. All summer long the water is cold; the currents flow in from out in the Pacific, where the French exploded their bomb.

In Europe, it's the new ice age, not to be confused with the new cold war. In Scotland, a man is found with his lips frozen to his car; he was blowing into the doorlocks to thaw them. Peter's plane froze to the ground in Manchester for three days at 27 below. Here in the southern hemisphere this doesn't make sense, but we have already agreed that staying sane fifty per cent of the time is a good average. Down at Bronte on Friday afternoon, we take his jetlag for an airing; it floats in green water, along with a faint slick of suntan oil and the soft touch of well being, or is it cold water? We eat pies and hot dogs and the sun turns us pink and happy.

A postcard from Italy: We're in smog-clouded Venice, but Marian thinks it's Vienna (we must go to the opera). This is the rapid transit method of seeing Europe, concerned with: railway timetables, hot showers, art galleries, cheap restaurants, what day of the week is it and where do we go to keep warm? Culture comes by osmosis; we drift across Europe as the clouds gather – smog, snow, fear? A limited nuclear war for America, he said as we sat at the dinner table, could mean total devastation for Europe. Another glass of wine? What's the rage in Paris and London? Cocaine, herpes, the economic malaise; two million in anti-nuclear marches.
In the supermarket of Europe
what exotica they buy,
the travellers, like the Cruise missiles,
flying high.

We make love, joined at mouth, breast, genitals. I like to think of a circle, bodies looped and joined, continuity I guess. It comes in waves, like water. Afterwards our bodies are at rest, solid, still, still joined together, while our minds drift on the silver cord that ties them to us, and everything is quiet. Then somebody knocks on the door, and we get up and go downstairs.

We swim at Camp Cove on Saturday evening. There's a man on the beach with a metal detector, picking up the debris of affluence – ringpulls from cans, mostly, and the odd gold watch. I bought it for the kids, he says, they never use it but it's paid for itself. The lighthouse is flashing on South Head, and the fishermen are out with the mosquitoes; down below green water turns white around the rocks. We look across to Manly highrise, and back to the city. It's so quiet here, but the city is full of friction. I can close my eyes any night and see a dirt road lined with gum trees, any one of the roads I have driven or been driven along. When you came in through the heads for the first time, what did you think? Back in your past, you talk about the badlands: gold and uranium in the bluffs and buttes, Indian villages on top of them. MX missiles in the tunnels underground. There's a cannon on the cliffs along here, aimed at a paling fence. We grew up in a temporary lull, a period of relative calm and affluence.

Coming back to this country, coming back to your past, the first thing you notice is the size of the sky. Huge, open, clear as a bell, full of a hard metallic light. The country unrolls under the wing of the plane for hours and the travellers shift in their seats, preparing to arrive. Emptied out onto the tarmac in the heat, they waver, then head for the terminal. The duty-free whisky falls out of the SIA bag and breaks on the terminal floor. Watching faces separate out; coming home. Hanging on the fringes of things, backs to the mountains, everyone lives near the sea, waiting to make a getaway when the tide, or history, turns. That empty beach we took with us as our emotional refuge has gone; L. J. Hooker or the Japanese? On the east coast it's sunrise over the water through the palm trees, on the west coast it's sunset; and this summer, the blacks come to Canberra to argue their land claims. Red rocks, heat and dust, uranium mines and tailings dams; white perspex domes sending messages back to . . . Do you want to be the centre of attention? Pine Gap puts us on the map.

The tourists lie on beaches in the Deep North; nothing has entered their dreams except the smell of coconut oil and the taste of warm salt water. The B52s touch down in Darwin and fly over North Queensland on their training runs. Brown bodies roll over all the way down the east coast and the sound of planes is drowned out by hundreds of transistors playing rock music. The DJ says, it's the Clash! the B52s.

The moon is a fish that swims underwater in the daytime. A highly intelligent silver jewfish, swimming from one side of the sky to the other. What is the moon? Something that goes down, in the dark, and is forgotten. In the morning there will be blue hills round the rim.

We are just mooning around this summer, swimming through the weather like fish.

In Brisbane, it's 35 degrees in the shade, and we're flat on our backs. We lie around all day, and get up for the action at five in the afternoon. We sit on the verandah and make desultory conversation. Muggy, isn't it? Feels like a storm. We watch the storm pass, listen to rain on the iron roof, try to tell the difference between the sound of toads and frogs. Do you know that smell that comes from the backyard after rain? This is the edge of the storm, somewhere there are high winds, and as usual the power goes off. We sit on the verandah while it gets dark. The electricity workers have a rolling strike against anti-union legislation. Should have gone to the drive-in, Lloyd says, and goes out to the fridge for a beer. We eat fish and chips, drink beer, light mosquito coils, turn the radio on and off. Lloyd goes inside to read the paper by kerosene lamp. We crack nuts by torchlight, sitting on the back steps, and boil the kettle on the Primus. The lights are back on in the morning and so is the heat. The grass is two inches longer. At five in the afternoon it's cool enough to start the mower. Dozens of little grasshoppers decamp from long wet grass.

*

'The last I heard of Julie she was in an ashram, I thought she looked OK. I can't talk to her about it; it's one of those circular things where everything is explained by a belief that can't be explained. She says it's not the way for everyone, but it is for her.' There are posters at the Oxford Street bus stops saying 'He sees God', and the graffiti underneath says, but only when he's drunk, or, and he smokes Marlboro. 'I will consider anything – acupuncture, yoga, herbal tea – but it must have a rational basis.' Rationality is only half of it; there is nothing to be counted on as a prop. 'I said, you know there is nothing to believe in that justifies the mind suspending its questions, but even so you are always slipping up.' We came out of the church after the wedding, someone was playing the flute. There were white moths around the cabbages in the market gardens, and flies around our faces. We were thinking about love.

The way change happens, it's more like a slow sliding than anything you can put your finger on.

Peter is driving through the hot flat country of western New South Wales in an old Holden with a blanket over the seat and uncertain brakes. Heading for Adelaide, Washington, London and the political life again. We were sitting in the pub looking at brochures on Tahiti. What's happening in Australia? It's hard to find out in summer, seasonal adjustment. The other night, when the heat got worse than the mosquitoes, we went out to sit in the garden; and a voice from the dark on the other side of the table said, summer is a good time for a coup, no one would come back from the beach for anything. The first day of the trip your mind keeps racing, but after that the thoughts begin to untangle.

On the wall of the Casablanca Furniture Factory, over the road from the pub, someone has written: The workers united will never be defeated, and some intellectual has changed it to 'would'. The TAA posters along Moore Park Road have a woman in a bikini on a beach with the caption: Worker's compensation. Ripped off all year, and fucked on holiday. Everyone is reading a novel called *History*.

'I have this feeling that everything is irrelevant, and I'm falling apart at the seams. Don't now if it's objective historical circumstance, some life crisis, lack of sleep or the weather. I wish it would pass, it's disturbingly convincing to experience.' It does, and you're off to the bush with friends, kids, bottles of white wine, to lie on air mattresses in the dam and wait for the cool change. You could always go bush and you might find out you were right; summer is a good time of year. Later, surrounded by books and papers, empty coffee cups: 'It's beginning to make sense.'

There are the floating mornings, and the times at the end of the day when the light changes and the cicadas start, and someone has a radio on, very quietly, so that the sound fades in and out; outside of this sometimes things fail to connect. Sometimes it helps if you stop reading the papers, but even that is a kind of addiction, and it depends what you do for a living. Five days on Stradbroke and you find yourself after the morning swim waiting for the *Courier Mail*; after a few weeks I guess you'd stop worrying, a mind full of salt and blue glaze.

Jane is in the kitchen, insulting us the way only an astrologer can, tracing the planets over our heads. She's written a song about the economic cycle and sings us the chorus: it goes boom depression boom depression boom boom BOOM.

It's the middle of the night in Annandale, dogs barking, someone trying to start a car. We are lying in bed in a weatherboard house, like frozen moments in the yellow room. You are talking about conspiracy theories (What really happened in 1975?) and while I listen I can hear beyond you what the body and the heart say, the old harmony, mystery, short-circuiting logic; there are these moments when you put out your hand and nothing is said but everything is there. In the morning the room seems familiar, there are noises like a tin roof creaking in the heat. You wake up and ask, did you have any dreams? Then you go downstairs and bring the papers, oranges, cups of tea. I am standing at the window, but nothing outside has any significance; I am still interior, and the shape of the room protects me. Did you know this window has a flaw in it, like water?

Do you remember, when you were a child, watching dust moving in the bits of sun that came into a dark room? I used to think about atoms and electrons, stars and moons, other worlds. There always seems to be another door opening. Often, it seems, we go through it alone.

At the State Emergency Service, they have pamphlets: what to do in case of nuclear attack. Don goes to classes at the SES, but all he can tell me is that when it's about to happen we should head for the hills. We are standing in Woolworths at the time, I notice philodendrons, parlour palms, weeping figs, ferns, a spider plant in a teapot on special. I can hear a rumbling, but it's only the trains underneath us in Town Hall Station.

Apart from the new ice age, and the new cold war, there's the New Age. Down the road in Darlinghurst there's the Satprakash Meditation Centre, where they say, don't just do something, sit there. When the mind stops its questions, this is Nirvana. Is this worth serious consideration? This was the summer the orange people moved in, or out; the bagwash is orange, terracotta and red, and the colours are all down Oxford Street, the vegetarian restaurant, the boutique, the orange vegetable trucks, the building teams. Bhagwan is in trouble again, the Rolls is bogged in the Oregon mud. This was the summer Billy Graham asked us to forgive Richard Nixon because he didn't know what he was doing, and several people renounced Christianity in its more obvious forms. There's the Natural Healing and Personal Development Centre and a galaxy of delights for mind and body, colour therapy, yoga, massage with exotic oils, psychotherapy for the mind subject to pressure. It's possible that even here there will be therapy sessions where you can articulate your fears about nuclear war and 'come to terms' with them. Meanwhile you might be cut off the dole. You can buy tapes of dolphins and whales, pay to change your posture, major in Zen, donate money to save the rainforests. Over the road there are books that will change your life. Is this part of the process of evolutionary change, or just a momentary confusion? This is the street of Middle Class Fantasies. It's just near the bus stop, and St Vincent de Paul is over the road. It's the street of All Australian boys, party drugs, gay bars and coffee houses. There isn't a decent supermarket for miles. Something is wrong but you're not quite sure what. Sometimes it occurs to us, like a kind of bad dream, that we live in the shadow of war and can't do anything about it. 'So you think you can tell/Heaven from hell/Blue skies from pain . . .' Are we being conned again?

Tomorrow will be full of possibilities. You can ring up work and say you're sick, drink cafe latte at the Roma, cut off your jeans, take the kids to the park.

Down in George Street, the story is the sound of cash registers, the relatively innocent rustling of paper and money, as the crowds come and go, looking for something to justify the occasion. Money leaps out of your purse like a fish every time you open it, this time of year. Christmas is the silly season; office parties, flights home, cases of mangoes, hams and turkeys. It's late night shopping, the Thursday before Christmas week, Myers' windows full of animated fairy tales, just like the newspapers; somewhere above all this the moon slides through a sky the colour of deep water.

*

And so you say, this is the political life, faint light at the end of the tunnel, and what can I say I have accomplished? There are moments when I think how happy I am, in a car going down the hill to the beach, then the muffler falls off and everything changes. 'We don't live in isolation; the relationships between people can be just or unjust, on the smallest scale or the largest.'

While we are down at the beach that afternoon, in Brisbane it's several degrees hotter, he's working in the sun all day, and when he comes in something happens; something stops functioning for a moment and an inconsistency spreads through the veins and the muscles. Something shifts; it happens quickly and is out of control. Does it make any sense? It's been a hard life, someone without money has to make his body and his strength his capital, working from early in the morning till late at night, seven days a week at times. Some people act on the world, with others you can see they could be crushed. But the heart goes on. What do we know about the heart? When we were twenty we thought the answer was to love someone and make them happy; stuck with love and rebellion for several years we wondered why it didn't work the way we expected. One, we were women, trying to change. Two, we were gullible. Three, we had no context that made any sense – not that you can ask for one.

Inside the train, there are small sleeping compartments. The nightlights are faintly blue, and the sheets on the bunks are starched and ironed. The train goes into a mountain and comes out on the other side and we have crossed a border; we wouldn't have known, that feeling of being stretched tight between different things comes and goes, at random it seems. The landscape passes: still water, rain, paddocks with cows, and houses with lighted windows, empty platforms on country stations, then factories and railway yards. Coming into the city late at night, we've lost the moon, it was somewhere over to the left just before.

At Palm Beach at six in the evening there are people playing football, flying kites, rolling around on the sand in an inner tube. We wonder if they're Christians; very few people hang around in large groups looking lively these days. They don't come from Darlinghurst. But we're tourists ourselves. The water is warm, and there's very little undertow, but there's a slight drift north. Half an hour ago when we went into the water the swimmers were south of us, now they're right in front. In another hour or so they might all disappear behind Barrenjoey into the mouth of Broken Bay, shouting and laughing, while we have moved over to the Pittwater side of the peninsula, and are eating chips and drinking beer, watching the windsurfers and the sun going down behind West Head. This is the life.

This was the summer of early rain, when the roof leaked in two places after the storm. The paper dropped on the doorstep every morning and it all went on, Poland, Ronald Reagan, the nuclear buildup, the blackouts. Everywhere we went someone was listening to the cricket. So what's the story? What's the deal? There were stories, political thrillers with speculative endings, love stories with whatever is a happy ending now – they decided to live together, or separately, he left, she became a feminist, they agreed who would have the kids. There was a revolution, a coup, a large amount of US aid, a 'free election'. This is just what happened; the plots are all different now. Forget the moon; those little lights in the sky were Air America, shuttling money between here and Hong Kong.

Some of this is already in the head. There were times when the mind drifted, weightless, in certain moments, the slanting light in the afternoons, the long blue evenings. We had a good time, mostly, then we packed it in and went back to work. The pages fill with names and 'facts' and the pile of newsprint grows in the corner; there is no one thing that will tell you, but we wait for something still under the surface that meets in between the words. When we touch each other we imagine that we are part of something, but still whole on our own. Do you feel my history, and its tricks, when you run your hand over my skin? Sometimes we don't understand, sometimes we do but it's not quite possible to speak or act directly out of it. 'It may not be as clear as you wanted, but it's there.' Say it: this is what we are, this is what is going on.

THE NINETIES
AFTERWORD

C HANGE HAS been happening so fast and so dramatically in Europe and beyond since 1989 that literature can only lag behind, prompting fictions of personal crisis as national dramas continue their uncertain course. With the Cold War's end new cracks have appeared in once smooth geographies, while a terrible conflict has riven what was Yugoslavia. Whether the cities of Eastern Europe will rise to a new prominence remains to be seen. Perhaps the metropolis will have less importance and the cities of the regions and the new small states assume more; like Bratislava, Lubjiana, Seville, Glasgow . . .

Cities eternally change; the crisis-ridden city may renew itself, but this requires a purposeful civic sense, a belief in democratically shared public space, backed up by resources – for transport, housing, safety. Women bear the brunt of urban blight and neglect, not only because all the most economically and socially vulnerable groups do, but because of what, in a recent essay, 'Penthesilea Perhaps',[1] the novelist Alison Fell calls: 'The free play of male territoriality.'

The stubborn supposition that urban space belongs to men can easily crowd women out, quite literally. There is the way men's bodies spread on public transport, legs splayed, jutting elbows covering the armrests on tube trains, obliging women to tidy themselves away, knees together and elbows pinned to their sides. Or the caution women have to exercise when walking alone, the subtle strategies they employ to draw their boundaries around themselves and avoid provoking too much male notice. It is London Fell is speaking of: 'To live in the city is to live with the decay of the city, with unemployment, overcrowding, homelessness, a run-down public transport system: an embattled zone in which degraded attitudes like sexism, racism and machismo flourish.'

In nineties London, its once brash consumerism now bedraggled, the commercial imperative still rules the streets; Fell notes tellingly that bus shelters are only lit up at night if they carry advertising. In answer to this spatial politics of marginalisation, she invokes the figure of Penthesilia, the Amazon queen, perhaps gently and firmly claiming the ample space that men have narrowed for women, defying male terrors of women as whole and equal and therefore having always to be diminished. Penthesilia returns the male gaze that contains these fears – 'Men look at women: but is it entirely up to us to force them to see us instead?'

Fell envisions a carnivalesque city that abolishes existing hierarchies of opposition: master/slave, white/black, masculine/feminine. This is the narrative drive of Sarah Schulman's *People in Trouble* (1990), a latter-day Greenwich Village fairytale that calls up the dampened spirit of solidarity once again, through a group of AIDS activists. *People in Trouble* is also a lesbian love story, one that's funny and reflective about city life: '. . . Our city is so stratified that people can occupy the same physical space and never confront one another . . .' This, even in the Village with its permissive heterogeneity, its cheek-by-jowl chic and squalor. It is only when one of the lovers, Kate, finds herself walking at night and without her husband that she begins to notice. A bag lady asks her for money and she inwardly responds: *'Do they say the same thing to each person, thirty*

times an hour, twelve times a day? Why aren't they rioting?
Why are they standing so politely on street corners?

'Kate passed graffiti on a wall that said Arm the Homeless.'

New York fictions have long testified to human isolation, yet this novel's combative warmth would not be so out of the ordinary but for the current media-sensationalised emphasis on the brat-packer exponents of post-modern urban nihilism as representative of literary New York. In *The Male-Cross-Dresser Support Group* (1992), Tama Janowitz combines the nihilism with a satirical neo-feminism which derives from the predicaments of a central character upon whom the promiscuous mess and consumer junk of the city tends to collapse. Pamela Trowell is a classic figure of farce in that she is isolated yet boundaryless, permeable to all the city's hallucinatory overflow, be it human or waste.

The Male-Cross-Dresser Support Group is all about surfaces, but doesn't think it worth the trouble of asking what's under them, suggesting that this is all there is, which is what nihilists always say. In *The Colorist* Susan Daitch had already ventured into similar territory, but she probed and explored the crazy surface panorama of New York and the signs and simulacra that govern it, digging beneath. Post-modern, a label subject to confusions, can easily describe fictions which function as critique, rather than as the abeyance of politics or mere struggling resignation. The latter, however, are the versions so often implicit in how the term is used, as is a kind of highbrow philistinism that also takes a surface view of the post-modern world we live in, as if *fin-de-siècle* were synonymous with the ending of culture and history, their flattening out into endless television.

Yet we experience public reality, nowadays hugely mediatised, at many different levels of perception, and of time within ourselves (through personal chronology and all the complex cultural scaffolding this has). Our experience of the world is not simply reducible to mediatised appearances, even though these may be felt as intensely powerful realities.

If this were so we would all be trapped inside those representations, unable to resist or refuse them. It can only be said that the stages of modernity bringing us to our present self-definition as post-modern, have engendered an ever more heightened sense of ambivalence and fragmentation.

> *. . . la forme d'une ville*
> *Change plus vite, hélas! que le coeur d'un mortel*

(Alas! A city changes faster than the hearts of mortal beings.)

Baudelaire's words, written in 1859, still apply. Cities eternally change. But this means that the city gets written and rewritten over and over again, and women's new and rewritten versions of the city multiply; fictions, and genres bordering on fiction, like the city as autobiographical war memoir in Jean Said Makdisi's *Beirut Fragments* (1990), or the imaginative essayistic writing of Danièle Sallenave, the *flâneuse* as savant and melancholic observer, in Rome and Amsterdam, in Bucharest and Prague.[2]

Since change is the very life of the city, then old ways of writing about it need continual metamorphosis. The proliferation of feminist city detective fiction so far yields very little of the city itself, perhaps because in its plotting of character rather than of space it too closely follows the formulae of male detective fiction, where the streets are merely there, in all their abrasive contrasts, but taken for granted. Crucially it is the car that removes these detectives from ground-level contact with the city, and the car is otherwise seldom an aspect of women's city fictions; women's relation to the urban universe being more directly physical, feet eagerly touching the pavement. In any case, fewer women than men have cars, though that is only a partial explanation. Women cannot yet take the city for granted, which is why its spaces have to be explored at close quarters.

I would hesitate to define women's conception of the city as different from men's in any essential way. Woolf, Wolf and Richardson all demonstrate a kind of feminine empathy with the city. But abundant fictional evidence also shows women writers in quite different relation to the city, inventing various ways to be within it, to be women and to be human.

The life of cities is in part the life they have in literature, for this is where the idea of the city crystallises, and where the 'what-if' city grows: the city re-fashioned as a utopia of the here and now. The city is where women cross the threshold of domesticity, declining to stay put in the separate, 'natural' sphere allotted them; instead entering and shaping culture, in all its transformative possibilities, to be in possession of themselves.

NOTES

1. In *Whose Cities?*, Mark Fisher and Ursula Owen (eds), Penguin 1991.
2. Sallenave's most recent book is *Passages de L'Est*, Gallimard 1992, a diary-structured exploration of Eastern European capitals and byways. It belongs very much in that developing genre of European literary-cultural writing whose best-known exponents are Hans Magnus Enzensberger and Claudio Magris. Perhaps because of its de-emphasising of borders and power centres, its connecting of place to cultural archaeologies, this is a genre women seem at home in.

NOTES ON THE AUTHORS

Ingeborg Bachmann (1926–73) is one of the twentieth century's foremost German-language writers. She studied law and philosophy at Innsbruck, Graz, and Vienna universities. Her work includes radio plays and opera libretti (in collaboration with Hans Werner Heuze), several volumes of poetry and short stories, and one novel, *Malina*. She was born in Klagenfurt, Austria, and died in Rome, where she had lived for some years.

Djuna Barnes (1892–1982) was born into an artists' colony north of New York. She was a journalist, short story writer, poet and artist, and became a legendary figure among the expatriot literary community of Left Bank Paris. She is most famous for her cult novel *Nightwood* (1936).

Barbara Brooks lives in Sydney, Australia, where she teaches writing in universities and adult education. She has published one collection of short prose, *Leaving Queensland* (1983).

Angela Carter (1940–92) was a major and influential figure on the literary scene in Britain, although her originality meant that recognition was slow in coming. Her first novel, *Shadow Dance*, was published in 1965, followed by seven others and three collections of short stories, the last, *American Ghosts & Old World Wonders*, being published posthumously. She was a prolific critic and essayist, and some of this work appeared in *Nothing Sacred* (1982) and *Expletives Deleted* (1992).

Susan Daitch was born in New Haven, Connecticut. She is the author of two novels, *L.C.* (1986) and *The Colorist* (1989). Her short fiction has appeared in a number of magazines. She lives in New York City.

Alba de Céspedes (1911–) was born in Rome of a Cuban father. Her first two novels, *Nessuno torna indietro* (1938) and *La Fuga* (1940) were banned by the fascist censors. In 1943 she joined the partisans and broadcast from a partisan radio station. Her postwar fiction investigates women's status within the family and the wider society and features protagonists struggling against the narrow roles assigned them. Several of her novels, including *The Best of Husbands* (1949) and *The Secret* (1952) have been translated into English. A volume of poetry *Chansons des filles de mai* (1969) was inspired by the events of May '68 in Paris, which de Céspedes witnessed.

Carolina María de Jesús (1913–) was born in Sacramento, Minas Gerais, Brazil. In common with many of the country's rural population, she migrated to the city in the hope of finding the means of survival. Forced to bring up her children in the *favelas*, the shantytowns of São Paulo, she began writing her diaries. Her discovery by a journalist who edited and helped her publish the diaries in 1960 brought her overnight fame and the financial rewards of bestsellerdom.

Tove Ditlevsen (1918–76) was born in Copenhagen, where her father worked as a fireman. She published her first book *Pigesind* (*A Girl's Mind*) in 1939, and this was followed by several novels and collected novellas, as well as eight volumes of poetry. In 1973 she published the autobiographical *Vil-*

helms Vaeselse (*Wilhelm's Room*) about a destructive marriage.

Maureen Duffy, born in Sussex, is a poet and playwright, and the author of several novels, of which the first, *That's How It Was*, was published in 1962; her most recent is *Illuminations* (1991). Her other books include biography and literary studies and an animal rights handbook. She lives in London, which has been the setting and subject for much of her fiction.

Claire Etcherelli (1934–) was born in Bordeaux, which she left for Paris in 1956. There she worked on a car assembly line for two years, then in a ballbearings factory, before the publication of her first novel, *Elise ou la vraie vie* (1967), which won the Prix Femina. Later she combined writing with a job as editorial secretary on *Les Temps Modernes*. Her books include *A Propos de Clémence* (1971), *Un arbre voyageur* (1978) and a series of poetic texts, *La Délirante* (1982).

Ida Faré (1944–) lives in Milan, where she works as a journalist and teacher in higher education. Her books include (with Franca Spirito) *Mara e le altre, le donne e la lotta armata* (1979), *La mia signora* (1987) and *Malamore* (1988).

Hayashi Fumiko (1903–51) spent several years struggling in poverty before publication and recognition. She eventually achieved enormous success and became a highly prolific, best-selling writer.

Lidia Ginzburg (1902–1990) was born in Odessa and in 1922 moved to Leningrad, where she studied at the State Institute of Art History. She published many literary historical studies – of Pushkin, Lermontov, Tolstoy and others, as

Notes on the Authors

well as essays, memoirs and a variety of narrative prose. She lived in Leningrad throughout the war and the city's siege.

Shirley Jackson (1919–1965) was born in San Francisco. After her studies at the University of Syracuse she married and had four children, while also maintaining a rigorous schedule as a writer. Her books include several collections of short stories and the novels *The Road Through the Wall* (1948), *The Hangsaman* (1951), and *We Have Always Lived in the Castle* (1962).

Storm Jameson (1891–1986) was born in Whitby, Yorkshire, and published many novels and two volumes of autobiography. In 1939, she became the first woman president of the London Centre of the PEN Club and travelled to Poland and Czechoslovakia as the guest of their governments at the end of the war.

Elfriede Jelinek (1946–) was born in Mürzzuschlag, Austria and grew up in Vienna, where she attended the Music Conservatory. Her novels *Wonderful, Wonderful Times* (1980), *The Piano Teacher* (1983), and *Lust* (1989) have all been translated into English. She is also a playwright, and wrote the screenplay for the film version of Ingeborg Bachmann's novel, *Malina*.

Irmgard Keun (1910–1982) was born in Berlin and later moved to Cologne to train as an actress. She had published two novels by the time the Nazis came to power and these were included in their infamous book-burning. After arrest and interrogation by the Gestapo, she escaped to Belgium, where she joined other writers in exile. In 1940 she returned to Germany with false papers and lived in hiding. Her post-war novels were little noticed, but rediscovery came when she was in her seventies.

346

Carmen Laforet (1921–) was born in Barcelona but grew up in the Canary Islands. After the Civil War she studied law in Barcelona and Madrid. *Nada* (1944) won her the Nadal Prize and instant fame. Among her later novels are *La isla y los demonios* (1952) and *La insolación* (1963). She has also published collections of short fiction.

Olivia Manning (1908–80) was born in Portsmouth and left to live in London in her early twenties, earning a living with a series of jobs while pursuing her writing. The first of her many novels was published in 1937. She is best known for *The Balkan* and *Levant Trilogies* which are based on her own experience of wartime in Bucharest, Athens and Cairo and are distinguished by a vivid sense of place and an intricate exploration of character.

Giuliana Morandini lives in Rome. Her work includes a study of nineteenth-century women writers, *La voce che e in lei* (1980) and another on women in mental institutions, *E allora mi hanno rinchiusa* (1977), as well as books for children and four novels, the most recent being *Sogno a Herrenberg* (1992). Much of her writing reflects an intense interest in German-language culture.

Dea Trier Mørch (1941–) was born in Copenhagen and studied there at the Academy of Fine Arts. Her work as an artist has been exhibited internationally. Two of her novels, *Winter's Child* (1976) and *Evening Star* (1982) have been translated into English.

Toni Morrison was born in Lorain, Ohio and now lives in New York State and Princeton, where she is a Professor at the University. Her first novel was *The Bluest Eye* (1970) followed by five others, including the award-winning *Song of*

Solomon (1978) and *Beloved* (1987), which won a Pulitzer Prize. She is one of North America's foremost writers.

Flora Nwapa (1931–) was born in Obuta, Eastern Nigeria; she worked as a teacher and administrator before becoming a published writer. Her books include the novels *Efuru* (1966) and *Idu* (1967), as well as collections of poetry and short stories. In the 1970s she founded Tana Press.

Anna Maria Ortese (1914–) was born in Rome. Her first book was *Angelici dolori* (1937). She spent several years in Naples before and after World War II, then in Milan, where the city's working class became the subject of two books, *Silenzio a Milano* (1958) and *Poveri e semplici* (1967). Her fiction follows two strands, one realist and socially engaged, connecting with her work as a journalist; the other, like the allegorical *L'Iguana* (1965), involving elements of fantasy. She now lives in Rapallo.

Dorothy Parker (1893–1967) was born Dorothy Rothschild in West End, New Jersey, and grew up in New York. She worked first on *Vogue*, then became drama critic on *Vanity Fair*, soon making her name as a trenchant and witty writer. It is as a wit that she is celebrated, her style in stories, poems and journalism epitomising urbanity and sharp modern humour.

Ann Petry (1908–) was born Ann Lane in Connecticut, USA. She took a degree in pharmacy, then, after her marriage and a move to New York, became a journalist. While working on the *People's Voice* in Harlem she was involved in the American Negro Theatre and published children's plays. Her first short stories appeared in *The Crisis* and *Phylon* and the success of one of these led to a fellowship which enabled her to complete *The Street* (1946), which sold over a million copies. Her later books include *The Narrows* (1955) and *Miss Muriel and Other Stories* (1971).

Jean Rhys (1894–1979) was born Gwendolyn Williams in Dominica and was sent to England at sixteen. After a brief spell at drama school she drifted into jobs as a chorus girl and artist's model, and only began writing when her first marriage broke up in Paris. Her collection of stories, *The Left Bank* (1927) was followed by four novels. After *Good Morning Midnight* (1939) her work went out of print for a long time, but she was subsequently rediscovered, partly through the publication of *Wide Sargasso Sea* (1966).

Dorothy Richardson (1873–1957) was born in Berkshire. A background of impoverished gentility meant that she began earning her living at seventeen, first as a governess, then as a secretary to a Harley Street dentist. Among her friends in London's socialist intellectual milieu was H. G. Wells, who encouraged her to begin writing. *Pilgrimage* was published in a thirteen-volume sequence between 1915 and 1935, while she subsidised its writing with journalism.

Cora Sandel (1880–1974) was born Sara Fabricus in Oslo, where she studied as a painter. She went to Paris in 1905 and stayed for fifteen years. There she began writing and published her first novel, *Alberta and Jacob*, in 1926, followed by two others, completing an autobiographical trilogy. Some of her subsequent novels and short story collections have also been translated into English. She died in Sweden, having lived there for many years.

Albertine Sarrazin (1937–67) was born in Algiers. Abandoned as a baby, she was adopted by a middle-aged couple. As a teenager in France she was placed in an institution because of difficulties with her parents, but she ran away and became involved in prostitution. Because of her part in a hold-up she received a seven-year prison sentence. Her escape and the events that followed are fictionalised in *L'Astragale* (1965), which was written in prison after *La Cavale* (1965). Both these novels were extremely successful, and established

Sarrazin's enduring critical reputation. Her letters, poetry and diaries have also been published.

Alix Kates Shulman (1932–) is a New York-based writer whose fiction and essays often focus on sexual themes. Her novels include *Memoirs of an Ex-Prom Queen* (1972) and *Burning Questions* (1978). She has published two books on Emma Goldman and has taught fiction writing at Yale and New York University.

Agnes Smedley (1892–1950) was born into rural poverty in Missouri and spent her adult life combatting the oppression and disenfranchisement of the poor, both as a journalist and political activist. She was involved in the birth control movement and in struggles for Indian independence. Her writing includes a fictionalised autobiography, *Daughter of Earth* (1928) and several books about China.

Christina Stead (1902–83) was born in Sydney and in 1928 left Australia, where she only returned to live after almost fifty years. She lived in Paris from 1930–35, then settled in the USA where she remained until 1947, continuing to write fiction and working as an MGM scriptwriter; she then returned to Europe and spent some years in England. Her novels and stories (many of these published in the *New Yorker*) draw on the life of the cities and countries she made her home. Although a writer of brilliance and insight, she was little recognised until the late 70s, when her reputation began to grow. She now ranks as one of the century's great writers.

Verena Stefan was born in Switzerland, where she lived until finishing her school studies. She spent seven years in Berlin, becoming involved in the women's movement and beginning to write during this time. *Shedding*, her autobiographical account of a woman's politicization, appeared in 1975 and was an immediate success.

Hirabayashi Taiko (1905–71) was born in Nagano Prefecture and left for Tokyo, determined to become a writer and an active socialist. She became involved in an anarchist group and lived for a time in Korea and Manchuria. In 1927 she joined the proletarian literary movement whose focus was the Tokyo magazine *Bungei Sensen*. In 1937 she and her husband were arrested and several years of hardship followed. After the war she was a recipient of the First Women Writers Award. She published her autobiography in 1957.

Marta Traba (1930–83) was born in Buenos Aires and lived in Bogotá and Montevideo, and in the USA. Although little translated into English, she published over thirty volumes of fiction, poetry, essays and criticism, and won the Casas de las Américas prize in 1966. She was killed in the Madrid air crash, along with a number of other Latin American writers.

Elsa Triolet (1896–1970) was born Elsa Yureyevna Kagan in Moscow. She was the younger sister of Lili Brik, Vladimir Mayakovsky's lover, and with them was involved in the Futurist movement. She left Russia in 1918 to live with her first husband in Tahiti, then made her home in Paris, where she married the Surrealist poet Louis Aragon. The two were important figures in the French Resistance and were involved in Underground publishing during the Occupation. Triolet's many books include novels, stories and studies of Russian art and literature.

Christa Wolf (1929–) was born in Landsberg, Germany and studied at Jena and Leipzig universities. She was a leading literary figure in what became East Germany. Her work has focused on the personal and psychic traumas of life under Nazism and throughout the post-war division of her country. Equally present in her writing is a concern with women's situation, past and present, and an emphasis on the moral questions raised by the nuclear age. Much of her work has been translated into English, including *The Quest for Christa*

T (1968), *A Model Childhood* (1977), *No Place on Earth* (1979), and a collection of essays, *The Writer's Dimension* (1993). She lives in Berlin.

Virginia Woolf (1882–1941) born Virginia Stephen, is recognized internationally as a major twentieth-century writer and a key figure within modernism and feminism. She is associated with a number of writers and painters – including her sister Vanessa Bell and her husband, Leonard Woolf – known as the Bloomsbury Group. Her first novel *The Voyage Out* was published in 1915. Her other novels include *Jacob's Room* (1922), *Orlando* (1928), *The Waves* (1931) and two classics of feminist polemic, *A Room of One's Own* (1929) and *Three Guineas* (1938).

Also by Liz Heron

TRUTH, DARE OR PROMISE
Girls Growing up in the 50s
Edited by Liz Heron

'Again and again, the writing calls up splendidly vivid images, audible voices, places and people that have the special, looming, close-up quality that belongs to childhood experience' – *Lorna Sage*

In this superb collection of autobiographical writing, first published in 1985, twelve women who grew into feminism in the 1970s look back on their childhoods. In feeling, circumstance, class and culture, their experiences were as diverse as they were keenly felt. But the two great landmarks in this post-war Britain of 'you never had it so good' – the Welfare State and the Education Act – were a common feature which gave to many of these girlhoods, so like and yet so unlike those of their mothers, a sense of possibility, of aspiration to a different future. These are intimate, personal memoirs, ordinary and impossible stories that remind us how individual lives are shaped in infinitely complex ways.

Also published by Virago

THE SPHINX IN THE CITY

Urban Life, the Control of Disorder and Women

Elizabeth Wilson

'Stimulating . . . I would recommend it to anyone who wants an introduction to the tensions, texture and contradictions of urban life' – *Times Educational Supplement*

In the pre-industrial West, urban life was seen as civilised, sophisticated and harmonious. The nineteenth-century metropolis offered new excitements and pleasures, but strong fears of urban disintegration emerged – the notion of the industrial city as hell on earth. This urban disorder – represented by the figure of the sphinx – continues to haunt many Western writers and planners.

Elizabeth Wilson's elegant, provocative and scholarly study uses fiction, essays, film and art, as well as history and sociology, to look at some of the world's greatest cities – London, Paris, Moscow, New York, Chicago, Lusaka and São Paulo – and presents a powerful critique of utopian planning, anti-urbanism, postmodernism and traditional architecture. For women the city offers freedom, including sexual freedom, but also new dangers. Planners and reformers have repeatedly attempted to regulate women – and the working class and ethnic minorities – by means of grandiose, utopian plans, nearly destroying the richness of urban culture. City centres have become uninhabited business districts, the countryside suburbanised. There is danger without pleasure, consumerism without choice, safety without stimulation. What is urgently needed is a new vision of city life.

THAT KIND OF WOMAN

Stories from the Left Bank and Beyond

Edited and Introduced by Bronte Adams and Trudi Tate

'This book is a gem . . . the stories are as diverse as the writers themselves' – *City Limits*

This essential collection of short stories brings together for the first time the women at the forefront of modernism, Mary Butts, Djuna Barnes, Colette, H.D., Susan Glaspell, Katherine Mansfield, Anaïs Nin, Dorothy Richardson, Jean Rhys and May Sinclair number amongst its host of accomplished writers. Many were English and American expatriates caught up in the artistic revolt of Paris between 1890 and 1940; others, who ventured forth in imagination only, drew on its innovative spirit. Many refuted traditional concepts of gender and sexuality, all challenged restrictive definitions of femininity.

A woman becomes obsessed by a life-size doll and rescues the memory of its original model from neglect; another keeps an array of Parisian gowns under lock and key rather than join the masquerade of fashion; two housewives use their attention to domestic detail to detect – and shield – a murderer. Here are writers who cast aside conventions. Rebellious, talented, provocative, they parade their tales of those who take life on their own terms – you know that kind of woman.